AN.
Enid Blyton
COLLECTION

The · Adventurous · Four
The · Adventurous · Four · Again
The · Children · of · Willow · Farm

VISCOUNT

CONTENTS

The Children of Willow Farm has been slightly abridged

I

THE BEGINNING OF THE ADVENTURES

Three children ran down a rocky path to the seashore. Tom went first, a small, wiry boy of twelve, his red hair gleaming in the sun. He looked round at the two girls following, and his green eyes twinkled.

"Want any help, you two?"

Mary and Jill laughed in scorn.

"Don't be so silly, Tom," said Mary. "We're as good as you any day when we're running over the rocks."

The girls were twins, and very like each other, with their heads of thick golden hair, tied in plaits, and their deep blue eyes. They often laughed at their brother Tom, and said he should have been called Carrots or Ginger or Marmalade, because of his red hair.

They were all on holiday, staying in a little fishing-village on the north-east coast of Scotland. Their father was in the Air Force, and their mother was with them, knitting hard all day long in the garden of the little white house where they were staying.

The three of them had run wild, and were all burnt as brown as monkeys. Usually they wore nothing but bathing costumes and rubber shoes, and spent as much of their time in the sea as out of it.

At first their mother had been afraid of the big waves that crashed on the shore, for she had thought the three children would surely be thrown on to the sand and hurt, if they tried to bathe in such a rough sea. But they had soon learnt to swim right through the heart of the big breaking waves, and reach the calmer water beyond the shore.

They had one great friend — Andy, the fisher-boy. He was a big, strong lad of fourteen, who had just left school and was helping his father with his fishing. Andy was dark-haired and blue-eyed, and was burnt dark brown by the sun. He knew everything about the sea, boats, and fishing. He could mimic any sea-bird, and could call the wild gulls to him by crying to them.

"Andy's marvellous," said Mary and Jill, a dozen times a day — and Tom agreed. Each day the children went to talk to their friend, and to watch him bring in the catch of fish, clean it, and pack it to be sent away.

Andy was tall and brown. He was dressed in old blue trousers, and a dark-blue jersey. He liked the three children very much, and often took them out in his little boat. He had taught them all to swim like fishes, to row strongly, and to climb the rocky cliffs like cats. It would really have turned their mother's hair quite white if she had seen the things that the three children sometimes tried to do!

Andy sat on the side of his little boat and grinned at the three children running down the rocky path. His white teeth gleamed in his brown face, and his eyes shone as blue as the sea. He was mending a net.

"Let me help you, Andy," said Mary, and she took up the torn net. Her fingers were nimble and she worked with Andy whilst the others lay on their backs on the hot sand.

"Andy, did you ask your father what we wanted you to do?" said Tom.

"Aye, I did," said Andy. "He says, yes — if I work hard all the week."

6

"Andy! How lovely!" said Jill in excitement. "I never thought he'd let you!"

"Do you mean to say your father will really lend you his sailing-ship to take us for a trip to Little Island?" asked Mary, hardly believing her ears. "I never thought he'd say yes."

"I was rather surprised, too," said Andy. "But he

knows I can handle the boat just as well as he can. We'll take plenty of food with us, and we'll sail out to Little Island on Friday. We can spend two days and a night there, my father says—and I'll show you where some queer birds nest—and the cove with yellow stones—and the cliff where about a million birds sit and call."

"Oh, won't it be gorgeous!" said Tom, sitting up and hugging his knees. "All by ourselves. No grown-ups. A little island, far away over there to the east—and no one on it but ourselves! Too good to be true."

In great excitement the children made their plans. "Let's take plenty of food," said Tom, who was always hungry. "I don't know why, but when I'm out on the sea I feel I could eat all the time."

"So do I," said Mary. "It's awful. I've never felt so hungry in my life as I have since we came here."

"Well, we'll get heaps of food," said Tom. "And I'll bring my field-glasses, so that we can see the birds well."

"And you'll bring warm clothes and rugs with you," said Andy.

"Oh, Andy! We shan't need those, surely!" said Jill. "This September is just about the hottest I've ever known."

"It will break soon," said Andy. "And if it happens to turn cold whilst we're in the boat, you'll not like it."

"All right," said Tom. "We'll bring anything, so long as we can go. I say—what about the old gramophone? Music sounds lovely on the water."

Andy was fond of music, so he nodded.

The boat was quite a big one, and even had a little cabin to sit in, with a tiny table and stool, a bench and bunk. Nobody could stand in it, but that didn't matter. The three children had often crowded into it together, whilst Andy sailed the ship around the bay.

They had always longed to visit the island that Andy had told them about — an island of birds, a queer rocky place with a strange cove where most of the stones were yellow. But it was so far from the coast that it had not been possible to visit it in a day.

And now they had permission to go off in the sailing-boat belonging to Andy's father, and spend the night on the island! It would be the greatest adventure of their lives.

On Thursday, the three children tired themselves out taking food, rugs, and other things down to the boat. Andy stared in astonishment at the amount of food.

"Are you wanting to feed an army?" he asked. "Six tins of soup — six tins of fruit — tins of tongue — chocolate — Nestlé's milk — biscuits — cocoa — sugar — and whatever's this?"

"Oh — that's tinned sausages," said Tom, going rather red. "Old Mrs. MacPherson at the village shop said they were awfully good — so I bought some. Think of cooking sausages in a tin on the Little Island, Andy."

"Tom's mad on sausages," said Jill. "He'd like them for breakfast, dinner, and tea. Look — will these rugs be enough, Andy?"

"Yes," said Andy, looking at the odd collection of old rugs that Jill had managed to get together. "Now mind you all wear warm clothes, too — skirts and jerseys, you girls — and shorts and jersey for you, Tom. You haven't got trousers, have you?"

"No," said Tom sadly. "I don't suppose your father would lend me a pair, would he, Andy?"

"He's only got the one pair, and his Sunday ones," said Andy. "And I've only got the ones I'm wearing.

9

Now are you going to bring the gramophone? We can put it safely in the cabin, if you like."

Tom went back to get it, and soon brought it down to the boat, with a packet of records. He also brought a tin of toffee and a camera.

"I'd like to take some pictures of the birds," he said. "We've got a bird-club at our school, and I guess I could take back some photographs that would beat everyone else's. Golly! Aren't we going to have a fine time!"

"What time do we start, Andy?" asked Jill, looking with pride at the sturdy little fishing-boat that was going to take them on their adventure. Its brown sail was now furled – but to-morrow it would fly in the breeze, and drive the boat over the blue-green sea for miles.

"Be down here at half-past six," said Andy. "I reckon we'll be at the island by about three in the afternoon then."

The three children could hardly sleep that night. Mary and Jill kept calling out to Tom, and at last their mother came up to them, very angry.

"Now, if I hear one more shout, I shall forbid you to go to-morrow," she said. "You will have to be up at six o'clock – and it's nearly half-past ten now. Go to sleep."

The children were so afraid that their mother really would forbid them to go that they said not a word more. They turned on their sides and fell asleep.

At six o'clock all three were dressing hurriedly. It was a magnificent day. The eastern sky was glowing red at dawn, and was now pink and gold. The sun was already warm on their faces as they looked out of the little cottage window.

Their mother was awake. The children kissed her

10

good-bye and ran down the rocky path to the beach. Andy was already there—but to the children's surprise he looked rather grave.

"I'm thinking we shouldn't go," he said, as soon as he saw the children.

"Andy! Whatever do you mean?" they cried.

"Maybe you didn't see the sky this morning?" said Andy. "It was as red as the geranium in our window. It was a right queer sky—and I'm thinking a storm will blow up to-day or to-morrow."

"Oh, don't be such a spoil-sport, Andy," said Tom, climbing into the boat. "What does a storm matter? We'll be on the island before it comes—and if one comes to-morrow we can wait another day on the island. We've plenty of food."

"If my father hadn't gone out in my uncle's ship to fish, I think he'd be stopping us from going," said Andy doubtfully. "But maybe the storm will blow off to the east. Get in, then. I'm glad to see you've got your jerseys on. If the wind blows up, we'll be cold tonight."

"I've got my bathing-suit on underneath," said Jill. "So have the others. Come on, Andy—push off. I'm simply longing to go!"

Andy pushed off. The boat grated over the stones, and then rode into the waves. Andy jumped in lightly. He and Tom took the oars. They did not mean to put up the sail till they came out of the bay into the full sea.

It was a marvellous morning. The sea was full of sparkles and twinkles—it was blue and purple at a distance, clear green by the boat. Mary let her hand drag in the cool water. She was very happy. Jill was happy too. She lay on her back in the boat, looking up at the cornflower-blue sky, feeling the boat bobbing up and down

11

on the waves, and thinking she would love to stay like this for ever.

Tom was happy too. He loved to pull at the oars. He enjoyed thinking of his breakfast, and planned what he would have.

Only Andy was not happy. He felt in his bones that he should not have taken the children out that morning. He felt sure this was not going to be the wonderful day they had planned. He wished his father had been there to advise him and he anxiously watched the sky for clouds. But there was not one to be seen.

"Now we're really off on our adventure," said Jill. "Really off!"

But she didn't know what an extraordinary adventure it was going to be!

II

LOST IN THE STORM

As soon as the boat was clear of the bay Andy put up the sail. It was a pretty brown one, like the sails of all the other fishing-boats of the village. It billowed out in the breeze, and the boat sped along. The boys shipped the oars.

"I'll steer," said Tom, and he took the tiller. The sail flapped, and spray flew up from under the bows of the boat. It was lovely.

"We go north-east," said Andy. "Can you steer by the sun, Tom?"

"Of course," said Tom, who had learnt to tell the time almost to the half-hour by looking to see exactly where the sun was. "I'm going right, aren't I, Andy? And I make it about half-past seven by the sun."

"It's twenty-past seven," said Jill, looking at her watch. She whispered something to Mary, who giggled.

"What are you giggling at?" asked Tom.

"Tell you in a minute," said Jill. The boat flew on over the green water, and the spray whipped off the sea, and fell cool and silvery on the children.

"Golly!" said Tom, in half a minute. "I *am* hungry. What time are we going to have breakfast?"

The twins burst into squeals of laughter. "That's what we whispered about just now!" said Jill. "I said to Mary 'I guess the next thing Tom says will be that he's hungry and what about breakfast'. And sure enough you did."

Tom laughed. "Well, I guess you feel the same," he

13

said. "Go on down into the little cabin and see what you can get for our breakfast. Andy and I are busy."

The girls went into the tiny cabin, which was crammed full of their food and other belongings. "What shall we have for breakfast?" said Jill. "What about pineapple chunks—and these hard-boiled eggs Mrs. Andrews did for us yesterday evening—and some Nestlé's milk—and chocolate?"

It was a most peculiar breakfast, but the four children thought it was lovely. They had three loaves of bread with them, and some butter, and they dabbed the butter on to chunks of bread, took the eggs in their hand and bit first at the egg and then at the bread. Jill put a paper of salt down on the deck for them to dip the eggs into.

"Fathead!" said Tom, as the wind promptly blew away paper, salt, and all. "As if the sea isn't salt enough already without adding more salt to it! Is there any more?"

There was some in a tin, and as this didn't blow away the children had plenty. There was fresh water in a barrel, and every one dipped in a cup and had a drink.

"That *was* a fine breakfast," said Tom. "I could do with it all over again."

"I'm going to take off my jersey and skirt," said Jill. "I'm simply cooking!"

"So am I," said Mary. The boys felt hot too, for the sun was now pouring down fiercely. Tom took off his jersey, but Andy didn't remove his. He always kept his on, whatever the weather was.

"This is simply gorgeous," said Jill, lying on a rug on the deck, feeling the spray splash on her hot face and arms every now and again. "How I do love to feel the boat bobbing up and down, up and down all the time! Can I have a turn at the tiller soon, Tom?"

"Everybody can," said Tom. "It's a grand feeling to sit here and guide the flying boat. How the wind is getting up! The sail is billowing out like the wings of a bird."

The sailing-boat simply flew over the water. "We shall be at Little Island before three o'clock if we go on like this," said Andy.

"I'm so hot in the sun," said Jill. She was sheltered where she lay, and felt hardly any wind. "I wish I could be dragged behind the boat on a rope, in the cool water."

The morning slid on. The sun rose higher and higher and at noon it was so hot that every one put on sun-hats. The wind was still strong and whipped the tops from the waves as the boat flew along.

"It's past noon," said Tom. "What about . . ."

"A spot of lunch!" chanted every one, knowing exactly what Tom was going to say.

"I'm more thirsty than hungry," said Jill. "What are you looking worried about, Andy?"

"Queer colour the sky is getting over yonder," said Andy, nodding his head to the west.

They all looked. "It's sort of coppery," said Tom.

"There's a storm blowing up," said Andy, sniffing the air like a dog. "I can smell it."

Andy always said he could smell a storm, and he was always right. The children looked anxiously towards the west. "Shall we get to the island before it comes?" asked Jill. "A storm is all very well to read about in a book—but I don't really want to be in one out on the open sea."

"We'll do our best," said Andy. "The little boat can't go faster than she's going now. As it is the sail is almost splitting with the wind!"

The sea turned a strange colour, a kind of blue-brown. "It's caused by the reflection of that funny sky," said Jill, half nervous. "I say! It's queer being out here on the sea, miles away from land, with the sea and the sky doing odd things like this."

Then an even stranger thing happened. The wind, which had been blowing very strongly indeed, dropped completely. One moment it was blowing the children's hair straight back, as they faced the west—the next there was not a breath of air. The sea fell calm and oily. The little fishing-boat stopped running in front of the wind, and rode silently over the waves, as if she were at anchor.

"I say! That's funny," said Tom. "Not a bit of breeze now! Andy, we'll never get to the island if we don't get some wind. Shall we row?"

"No," said Andy, his face rather pale under its dark brown. "No, Tom. You'll get plenty of wind in a minute —more than we want. We must take in some of the sail. The ship will heel right over if we let her have all this sail when next the wind gets up. There's going to be a gale. I can hear it coming."

There was a queer humming noise in the air that seemed to come from nowhere at all. Then an enormous purple cloud blew up from the west and completely covered the sun. The world went dark, and great spots of rain fell.

"It's coming now," said Andy. "Help me with the sail, Tom. Take the tiller, Jill. Keep her heading the way we've been going. Pull, Tom, pull."

They pulled at the big brown sail—but before they had done what they wanted to the storm broke. A great crash of thunder came from the black cloud, and a flash of lightning split the sky in half.

16

And then the gale came. Tom and the girls had never, never imagined there could be such a wind. They could not hear themselves speak unless they shouted. Andy yelled to the girls:

"Get down into the cabin, quick, and shut the door and stay there."

"Oh, let's be here," cried Jill. But Andy looked so stern and commanding that they did not dare to disobey. They almost fell into the cabin and shut the door. Outside the wind seemed to get a voice—a voice that howled and wailed and lashed the sea into enormous waves that

17

sent the little boat half-over every time. Tins and every-thing else began to fall about. The girls picked them up and put them where they could not fall.

There was a crash as the packet of records fell down. "Blow!" cried Jill. "They'll all be broken!"

So they were—all but one. It was very sad. The girls carefully put the one whole record into a safe place and wondered what the boys would say when they knew. But it couldn't be helped.

Up above, on the deck, the two boys struggled with the wind and the sea. Tom wished he had an extra jersey and he shivered as wave after wave splashed on him, and the wind whipped by.

The deck was wet and slippery. The dark-green waves raced by, and the boat climbed up one steep wave after another, and slid down the other side, only to climb up another enormous wave again.

Up and down, up and down she went, whilst Andy struggled with the sail.

"What are you trying to do?" yelled Tom, who was at the tiller.

"Take in all the sail," shouted back Andy. "We can't go on like this. We'll be over."

But he didn't need to bother—for suddenly the sail ripped itself off the mast, flapped wildly for a second and then sped away into the sky. It was gone! Only a little rag was left, wriggling madly in the wind. The boat slowed down at once, for it no longer had the sail to take it along. But even the little rag of sail that was left was enough to take it at a good speed over the waves.

Andy said nothing. He took the tiller with Tom, and together the boys faced the storm. Thunder rolled around and crashed in the skies. Lightning flickered and lighted up the vast heaving waste of grey-black sea. Stinging rain fell every now and again, and the boys bent their heads to it and shut their eyes. The wind lashed them and the spray whipped them. If this was an adventure, there was a great deal too much of it!

"Do you think we're all right, Andy?" shouted Tom. "Are we near the island?"

"I reckon we've passed it!" yelled back Andy. "At the rate we've been going we'd have been there by now. Goodness knows where we are!"

Tom stared at Andy in silence. Passed the island! A storm behind them! No sail! Whatever were they going to do?

III

SHIPWRECK!

For a long time the boat went on and on, its little rag of sail still flapping. Tom thought that the sail itself must have reached the great dark cloud that still covered the sky, the wind was so strong.

"I should think this wind's almost a hurricane, isn't it?" yelled Tom.

"Pretty near," shouted Andy. "But it's blowing itself out now."

Sure enough it was. Every now and again there was a lull when the wind dropped to a stiff breeze. Then it would blow again furiously. The thunder was no longer overhead, but far off to the east. The lightning shimmered now and again, but did not light up the sea with the fierce brilliance it had two or three hours back.

Then, just as suddenly as it had come, the storm flew off. It was most astonishing. A sheet of bright blue sky appeared in the west, and swiftly grew bigger as the great cloud flew to the east. The world grew light again. The rain stopped. The wind died down to a breeze, and the boat no longer seemed to climb up and down steep hills.

The cabin door opened, and two green faces looked out sadly. "We've been awfully sea-sick down here," said Jill. "It was dreadful."

"What a frightful storm!" said Mary. "Are we nearly at the island?"

"We've passed it, Andy says," said Tom gloomily.

"We don't know where we are."

"Goodness! Look, the sail's gone!" said Mary, shocked. "What *are* we to do for a sail?"

"There's an old one down in the cabin," said Andy. "Fetch it, will you—and I'll see if I can do something with it."

The sun shone down again. It was gloriously hot. Poor Tom, who had been chilled to the bone, loved it. He stripped off his wet bathing-suit, and put on his jersey. Ah, that was better!

Andy did not seem to feel either cold or wet. He took the old sail and had a good look at it. He thought he could rig it, with Tom's help. They must have a sail of some sort to get anywhere.

"I've heard my father say there are some desolate, rocky islands up away to the north of Little Island," said Andy, his wet jersey steaming in the hot sunshine. "We'll make for those. Maybe there might be someone there—or we could signal a ship for help. I don't reckon we're going to get home any too easily now."

At last the old sail was flying in the breeze. Andy headed due north. It was about five o'clock now, and all the children were very hungry.

Jill and Mary had forgotten their sea-sickness and went below to get some food. Soon they were all eating heartily, and felt much better. They drank all the water before Andy knew there was none left.

"We shouldn't have done that," he said. "If we don't strike these islands I'm thinking of, we'll have no water to-morrow. Leave those apples, Mary. We might be glad of the juice in the morning."

Mary had been about to bite into a juicy apple, but she hastily put it down. In silence she and Jill packed the apples away carefully in the cabin. Both the girls felt worried. Whatever would their mother be thinking, when that terrible storm blew up? They wished they were safely back at home.

The boat sailed on to the north. The sun slipped low into the west, and the boat's shadow lay purple on the sea. It was a beautiful evening.

"Look! Gulls!" said Andy, at last. "Maybe we are nearing land. Can't see any, though. We'd better anchor for the night, I should think."

And then the children got a great shock. There was no anchor! Andy stared in horror. How could he possibly have forgotten that his father had warned him to take the old anchor because he was lending Andy's uncle his own? How *could* he have forgotten? Now they couldn't anchor their ship. Now they would have to ride on the sea until they came to land—and in the night they might strike a rock!

Andy stared over the restless sea in dismay. Well—there was nothing for it but to hope for the best. One of them must be at the helm all night long. It would be a moonlight night if only the sky was not clouded. Perhaps they would be lucky and sight land.

Jill and Mary were tired out. Andy ordered them to go below and rest. "You'd better go too, Tom," he said. "You'll have to come up and take your turn on deck tonight, and you'd better get a nap whilst you can."

"But I don't want to," said Tom. "I shall be able to keep awake all right."

"Go below, Tom," said Andy, in the kind of voice that had to be obeyed. Tom went into the little cabin with the girls. They left the door open, for it was warm. The girls lay on the bunk and Tom curled up on the pile

22

of rugs on the floor. In two minutes he was asleep. He did not know how tired he was. The wind, rain and sea had taken all his strength out of him for a time.

Andy stayed alone on deck. The sun had gone down in a blaze of gold. The sky had turned pink and the sea had turned pink too. Now it was evening and the first stars were winking in the darkening sky.

The little boat drove on and on. Andy hoped desperately that land would soon come in sight. He remembered so clearly what his father had said. Right past the Little Island, far to the north, lay other islands, desolate now, but once owned by a few farmers, who tried to get a hard living from the rocky soil. If only they could get help there!

Night fell darkly on the waters. The moon sailed into the sky, but clouds kept hiding her light. First the sea was gleaming silver, then it was black, then it was silver again. Andy wished he could see something besides the sea. But there was nothing.

The boy stayed on deck until midnight. He felt the night wind and wrapped a rug round his shoulders, though he did not feel really cold. After a while he whistled to Tom.

Tom awoke. "Coming," he said sleepily, and went up on deck. He shivered and Andy threw the rug round him. "Keep her heading straight," he said. "Give me a call if you see anything."

It was queer up on deck all alone. The old sail flapped and creaked a little. The water went plash-lash-lash against the sides of the boat. The moon sailed in and out of the clouds as if she were a silver boat in the sky.

Then came a thick mass of clouds and the moon disappeared altogether. Tom couldn't see anything at all.

He strained his eyes to try and pierce through the darkness but except for the gleaming white top of a nearby wave now and then, he could see nothing.

But he could hear something, quite suddenly. It sounded like crashing waves. Tom longed for the moon to come out—and as he wished for it, it came sliding out from a cloud for a second before it disappeared again.

And in that tiny space of time Tom saw something that gave him a shock. The sea was breaking over big rocks just ahead!

"Andy! Andy!" yelled Tom, wrenching the tiller round. "Rocks ahead!"

Andy came tumbling up the steps, wide awake at once. He heard the sound of breaking waves and knew at once there were rocks ahead. He took the tiller.

And then there came a grating noise and a long groan from the ship. She was on the rocks! She had run straight on to them—and there she lay, groaning, half over, slanting so much that the girls in the little cabin were thrown out of the bunk.

"Hold on, Tom," shouted Andy, clutching at Tom, who seemed about to slide overboard. "Hold on! She's settling!"

The ship did settle. She seemed to be wedged between two rocks that were holding her tightly, all on the slant. Waves splashed over one side of her deck.

For a few minutes the children hardly dared to breathe—and then Andy spoke.

"She's fast," he said. "She may have a hole in her bottom, but she won't sink while she's held like this. We must wait till dawn."

So they waited, clinging uncomfortably to the slanting sides of the ship. Dawn was not far off. It silvered the eastern sky as they waited. The light grew stronger, and then a gold edge appeared on the horizon. The sun was about to rise.

And in the golden light of the early sun they saw something not far off that made them shout for joy.

"Land ho!" they yelled, and would have danced in delight if only the deck had not been so slanting. And land ho there certainly was!

A sandy shore stretched to a rocky cliff. Stunted trees grew further inland, touched with gold by the rising sun. It was an island of some sort, desolate, rocky and lonely —but it was at least land! Somewhere where they could light a fire and boil water to make themselves warm. Somewhere where other people might be to give them a helping hand.

"We'll have to swim for it," said Andy. "It's not very far. Once we're clear of these rocks we'll be all right. In fact, now that the tide has gone down a bit we could almost walk over the rocks, to the shallow water that runs up the shore."

Andy held out his hand to Mary. Tom helped Jill. Half-wading, half-swimming, they made their way over and between the reef of rocks, and paddled to shore. The sun had warmth in it now and warmed their cold bodies. How glad they all were that they had taken Andy's advice and had put on warm clothes!

"Well," said Andy, when they had reached the shore, "we'll climb up these cliffs, and see if we can spot anyone's house."

They climbed the rocky cliffs. When they got to the top they looked around. A small stunted wood grew a little way off, on a hillside. Low bushes crouched here and there as if to hide from the strong wind that blew always across the island. Grass crept over the rocky earth, and a few daisies flowered. But there was no sign of any house, or of any human being.

Andy made up his mind quickly.

"If we've got to be stranded here for a time we *must* get out of our ship everything that's in her," he said. "Thank goodness we've got a certain amount of food and some rugs. The tide is at its lowest now—when it is high it will completely cover the deck of our boat—so we must wade back to her and take off everything of value in her. Come on, Tom. You girls can stand halfway to the boat in that shallow water, and we'll carry things to you over the rocks. Then you can take them back to the shore. It will be better than us all scrambling about on the rocks and dropping everything."

And so they began to empty the ship of all it held—food, rugs, gramophone, camera, field-glasses, stool, tables, tools, crockery, kettle, matches, little stove, everything! It took a long time—but before they had finished the tide had risen and the decks were awash. The cabin was full of water!

"We can't do anything more," said Andy. "Let's go and have a rest—and something to eat. I'm simply starving."

IV

ON THE UNKNOWN ISLAND

It was a rather solemn set of children who sat down on the shore to eat breakfast. They had been brave during the storm—but now they all felt very tired and rather scared. It was strange to think they might have to stay for quite a long time on the unknown island until they were rescued—and supposing they were right off the route of the ships and steamers that used those seas?

Andy took charge. He was the oldest and wisest, and the others looked up to him. He was old for his fourteen years. He stared out at their wrecked ship, and wrinkled his forehead.

"Well, we're in a nice fix," he said. "But we'll forget it for a minute and enjoy our breakfast. We'd better finish up all the bread, for it will soon be stale. We'll eat all the food that might go bad—there's that open jar of potted meat, Tom, that we began last night—and the rest of the butter—and those buns that Mrs. Andrews gave us. And what about something hot to drink? I don't feel really cold, but it would do us good to get something hot inside us. Look—I brought the matches with me, wrapped in this oilskin so that they wouldn't get wet. We can't get the stove going till we get the tin of oil out of the locker in the boat—we forgot that—so we'd better make a fire on the beach."

Tom and Jill collected sticks, and soon there was a fine fire going. Andy went off up the cliff to see if he could find a stream to fill the kettle, which they had taken from the boat. He had to go a good way before he found a spring running down the little hill in the distance. He filled the kettle and went back to the cove.

"Good—the fire's going well," he said. "I found a spring, so we needn't worry about water. Where's the tin of cocoa—and we must finish up that Nestlé's milk we opened, or it will go bad."

The kettle soon boiled, and the children made thick cocoa. They added the tinned milk to it and drank with enjoyment. The cocoa was good. The twins, who were cold, felt warmed up at once. Their clothes were still wet, and although the sun now shone down hotly they felt chilly.

Tom yawned. He was not used to keeping awake half the night. The girls were tired out, too, for they had been very sea-sick in the storm.

Andy had laid out the rugs in the sun. He felt them. They were almost dry.

"We'd better get off our wet things and hang them on the bushes to dry," he said. "We'll roll ourselves in these rugs, and lie down in the sheltered corner over there by the cliff, in the sun, and sleep off our bad night."

So in three or four minutes all that could be seen of the children were four tightly-rolled bundles lying peacefully asleep in the sunshine, well out of the wind in a cosy corner of the beach. Their damp clothes were spread out on bushes to dry, and were already steaming in the sun.

Andy awoke first. He knew at once where he was, and remembered all that had happened. He sat up to look at their ship. The tide was going down again now, and the ship looked queer, slanting sideways, caught fast between the two big rocks. Andy wondered what his

28

father would say when he knew what had happened. It was a serious thing to lose a fishing-boat.

The sun was high in the sky. Andy threw off his rug and went to feel his clothes on the bush. They were perfectly dry. He put them on, and then went to the big pile of things they had taken from the ship. He looked among them and found a fishing-line.

He hunted about for a sandworm, baited his hook, and clambered out on the rocks, where deep water swirled around him. He lowered his line into the water. In ten minutes he had caught his first fish, and was baiting the line again.

Tom awoke next. He sat up on the sand, astonished

to hear the sea so close. Then he remembered all that had happened and leapt to his feet. He awoke the girls and they put on their warm clothes. They saw Andy, and waved to him.

"Andy's getting our dinner!" said Jill. "I suppose you're feeling as hungry as usual, Tom?"

"I could eat a whale!" said Tom, and he really felt as if he could.

It was fun cooking the fish over a fire. It smelt delicious. There was no bread left so the children had to eat the fish by itself, but they were so hungry that they didn't mind at all.

"It's about two o'clock in the afternoon," said Andy, looking at the sun. "Now the first thing to do is to find a good place to sleep for the night. Then we'd better explore the island, if we've time. The food we've got with us won't last a great while, but at any rate we can always get fish—and I expect we'll find some berries we can eat, too."

"Look!" said Tom, suddenly pointing to the pile of things not far off. "There's a gull there. Will he peck our tins open—or eat our cocoa!"

Andy clapped his hands and the gull flew off, crying loudly. "We certainly mustn't leave any food out," said Andy. "The gulls would have it at once. Look—there's two or three fishes left we can have for our supper. We'd better make a hole in the sand and bury them under some heavy stones till we want them. The gulls would soon make a meal of them if we left them uncovered!"

They buried the fish. Andy stood up and looked all round the cliff.

"I wonder if there's a cave we could sleep in at night," he said. But there didn't seem to be any cave at all, though the children hunted carefully all along the cliff.

"How will anyone know we are here?" asked Jill. "We shall have to put up some sort of a sign, shan't we, to show any passing ship or steamer that we are here?"

"Yes," said Andy. "I've been thinking about that. I'll take down the ship's sail, and we'll tie it to a tree on the top of the cliff. That will be a fine signal."

"Good idea!" said Tom. "It will flap in the wind and be seen for miles."

"We'll find a sleeping-place for the night before we do that," said Andy. "It looks like rain again now—see that low cloud over there? We don't want to be soaked in our sleep. Come on."

They left the sandy cove and climbed up the steep cliff. It was hard going, but they got to the top at last, and once more looked across the island. They could not see right across it because the hill in the middle stopped their view—so they did not know how big or small it was. All they knew was that, at present, they could not see any sign of anyone else there or of any house or other building.

"How I'd love to see a cow or two!" said Jill.

"Whatever for?" said Mary in surprise. "I didn't know you liked cows so much, Jill."

"I don't," said Jill. "But cows would mean a farmer, silly—and a farmer means a farmhouse—and a farmhouse means lots of people, and help, of course!"

The others laughed. "Well, let's hope we see one or two cows for you, Jill," said Tom. "Which way shall we go, Andy?"

"We'll make our way to the hill," said Andy. "There's bracken there, and heather, and maybe we can find a hill-cave to snuggle in. Bracken and heather make a fine bed, and we've got the rugs for covers."

They ran to the hill. It had a little wood of wind-blown pines and birches, but there was no cave in the hillside they could shelter in. It was covered with thick-growing bracken and heather, with a few stunted gorse bushes — but there was no place that would really give them a safe shelter to sleep.

"Well, we'll have to rig up a tent of some sort," said Andy at last. "I'm not going to be soaked through tonight. I've had enough of that to last me for quite a while."

"A tent, Andy!" said Tom. "Wherever would we get a tent from? Buy it from a shop, I suppose?"

"I'm going to get the old sail off the boat," said Andy. "We can use it for a signal by day and a tent by night. It's big enough to cover us all quite well."

"Andy, you *have* got good ideas!" said Jill. "I should never have thought of that. Well, shall we go back then and help you?"

"No," said Andy. "You stay here with Tom and help him to build a kind of tent-house that we can just drape the sail over. You'll want some stout branches, stuck well into the ground. I'll go and get the sail."

Andy went off down to the shore again, and clambered and waded out to the boat. He was soon taking down the old sail.

The others hunted for good branches. The ones lying on the ground were too brittle and old, they found.

"They'll make good firewood," said Tom. "We'll have to break a few growing branches off the trees."

It was difficult to do this, but they managed it at last. Then they drove the stout sticks into the heathery ground and made a kind of circle with them, big enough to hold them all.

They had just finished when Andy came back, bent double under the heavy sail. He threw it down and panted.

"I thought I'd never get it up the cliff," he said. "I say, you've made a fine set of walls. The sail will go over them nicely."

Eight willing hands helped to arrange the big brown sail over the circle of sticks stuck firmly into the ground. The weight of the sail kept it down, and when the children had finished, they had made a kind of round, brown tent, with no doorway. But as the children could get in anywhere under the tent simply by lifting up the sail, it didn't matter having no doorway.

"We'll gather a nice pile of heather and put it inside the tent to lie on," said Tom. "And with our rugs, too, we shall be as cosy and warm as toast! In fact, we may be much too hot!"

"Well, if we are, we'll just lift up one side of the tent and let the breeze blow in," said Jill. "Oh, I do feel excited! I really feel as if we've got a sort of little home, now we've made this tent!"

"There isn't time to explore the island now," said Andy, looking in surprise at the sinking sun. "We've taken ages over the tent. We'll go all over the island to-morrow."

"That *will* be fun," said Mary. "I do wonder what we'll find!"

V

MAKING THE BEST OF THINGS

The children were all hungry again. Andy thought it would be better to bring everything up from the shore, and put it near their tent.

"We may have to make our tent a sort of home," he said. "We don't want to have to keep climbing up and down that rocky cliff every time we want a cup or a kettle! Besides, we are quite near the spring here, and we can easily get water whenever we want to."

So for the next hour or so the children fetched all their belongings. Some of them were very difficult to get up the cliff. The gramophone was almost impossible till Andy thought of the idea of tying a rope round it and hauling it gently up by that.

"Golly! All the records are broken!" said Tom in dismay, as he picked up the cracked records.

"Yes—they fell and broke when that dreadful storm was on," said Jill. "Leave them behind. They're no use. There's just *one* that's not broken—now, where is it?"

They found it at last and looked at it.

"What a pity! This is a silly record—it *would* be the only one that's left unbroken!" said Mary. "On one side it's a girl singing a kind of lullaby, without even any music—and on the other it's nursery rhymes. The silliest one we've got!"

"Oh well—bring it along," said Tom. "And where's my camera? It doesn't look as if I'll find any good pictures to take—but I may as well have it."

By the time they had got everything to the tent they were really very tired. They cooked the rest of the fish and opened a tin of peaches. They ate an apple each, broke a bar of chocolate into four pieces, and then drank some hot cocoa. It was a good meal and they enjoyed it. The sun was now almost gone and the first star was shining brightly.

"Well, we've had an adventurous day," said Jill, yawning. "I slept all the morning—but I feel awfully sleepy again already."

"We'll turn in early," said Andy. "I'm tired too."

"We can't clean our teeth," said Jill, who was always very particular about nails and teeth and things like that. "I wish I had a tooth-brush."

"Well, here's a brush for you," said Tom, with a grin, handing Jill the brush that was used to sweep bits of fish off the deck. "Brush your teeth with this."

Jill took it and at once brushed Tom's hair with it. Tom was disgusted.

"Don't, you cuckoo!" he said. "I shall smell of fish all night long."

"Come on," said Andy. "We want more heather for our beds. Tom, stamp out the fire. We don't want to set the hill alight, and the heather is very dry."

Tom stamped out the fire. The girls filled the tent with more heather. Andy took the largest rug and spread it all over the springy pile.

"You girls can sleep on this side of the tent, and Tom and I will take the other," he said. "There are plenty of rugs, luckily."

Nobody undressed. For one thing they had no nightclothes, and for another they didn't even think of it. Life seemed quite different on an unknown island.

35

Nobody even thought of going to wash—though Tom's hair smelt so much of old fish that Andy threatened to pour a kettle of water over it.

"I'll wash my head under the spring to-morrow morning," said Tom sleepily. "I really can't go now. I'm simply dropping asleep whilst I talk!"

They rolled themselves up in their rugs and lay flat on the heathery bed. It was beautifully soft and springy, and very comfortable once they had pressed down several sharp bits that stuck into them.

Tom was asleep at once. The girls lay awake for a minute or two. Jill felt very hot, for the tent was airless, and the four of them made quite a crowd in it. The roof was not more than arm's length above their heads.

"Andy," said Jill, in a low voice. "I'm *so* hot. Could we get some air in, do you think?"

"Yes," said Andy. He raised one side of the sail and let the breeze in. It was lovely, for now the girls could see out.

The moonlight lay on the hillside and everything was clear till the clouds sailed across the moon. Mary fell asleep as she watched bracken outside waving in the wind. Then Jill fell asleep. Only Andy lay awake, leaning on his elbow, looking out down the hillside, and listening to the sound of the waves in the distance, under the cliff.

He was old enough to feel that this adventure might not turn out at all well. He wondered what would be the best thing to do for them all.

"We must certainly hang out a signal every day," he thought. "It might be seen by some passing ship. We must find a better place to live in too, for if the weather should break up, this tent won't be any use. And I wonder if it's possible to get the ship off the rocks and patch her up. If we could do that, maybe we might have a shot at sailing home."

As he lay worrying about all these things his eyes closed. He was soon dreaming that he had got the boat off the rocks, but it changed into a large steamer that seemed to have hands and was fishing busily in a pool. There was such a strong smell of fish that Andy opened his sleepy eyes again—only to find that Tom's fishy-smelling head was just under his nose. Andy turned over, grinning. "What a silly sort of dream!" he thought —and then, in half a second, he was dreaming again.

All the children slept soundly that night, and even when the clouds piled up over the moon and a sharp downpour of rain came they didn't wake. The raindrops pattered over the tent, but did not soak through to the sleeping children. Some came through the side where Andy had raised the sail to let in the air, but the children felt nothing.

They awoke when the sun was fairly high—about eight o'clock in the morning. Andy as usual awoke first and rolled out of the tent quietly. But he had waked Tom, and when the boy yawned loudly the girls awoke too.

It was a fine sunny morning with clouds scudding across the sky like big pieces of cotton-wool. The first thing, of course, was breakfast—but it had to be caught!

So Andy and Tom went fishing on the rocks and the girls managed to catch about twenty large prawns in a pool on the sandy shore. They cooked their catch and ate hungrily.

"I do feel dirty," said Jill. "I shall go and wash at the spring. Coming, Mary?"

"Yes," said Mary. "And I vote we all have a bathe today. That will clean us up a bit too."

37

They all felt cleaner after a rinse and splash in the spring. Tom and Andy made the fixing of the signal their next job. They found a good tree—at least, it was a good one for their purpose, for it had been struck by lightning at one time and now stood straight and bare on the top of the cliff.

It took the two boys about an hour to climb the tree and fix the sail-signal. It flapped out well in the breeze and Andy was sure it could be seen from a great distance. They climbed down again and went back to the girls.

"What about exploring the island now?" asked Tom. "I feel just like a good walk!"

"Well, the island may be too small for a good walk!" said Andy. "We'll just see. Ready, you girls?"

They were all ready for their walk. First they climbed the hill and stood on the top, looking to see what they could spy.

From the top of the hill they could see all around their island—and certainly it was not very big—only about a mile and a half long and about a mile wide. They could see the blue water all around it.

But not far off were other islands! They lay in the sea, blue and misty in the distance. But as far as the children could see, there were no houses or buildings of any kind on them. They seemed as desolate and lonely as their own island. The cries of sea-birds came as they stood on the hill, and big white gulls swooped around them—but except for that sound, and the far-off splash of waves, there was no other sound to be heard. No shout —no hoot of a horn—no drone of an aeroplane. They might be lost in the very middle of the ocean for all they could see or hear!

"I don't believe a single soul lives here on these

islands," said Andy, his face rather grave. "Come on —
let's go down to this side of the hill. We may as well find
out all there is to know."

As they went down the hill and came to the level
ground again, Tom stopped in astonishment. "Look!"
he said. "Potato plants!"

The children looked — and sure enough, growing
completely wild around them were plants that looked
exactly like potatoes! Andy pulled one up — and there,
clinging to the roots, were a dozen or more small white
potatoes!

"That's queer!" said Andy, staring round. "At some

time or other there must have been people living here
— and they grew potatoes. Some have seeded themselves and grown wild. But the thing is — if people lived
here — *where* did they live? They must have lived
somewhere!"

"How queer," said Tom, looking all round as if he
expected houses to spring from the ground.

And then Jill gave a shout. "I believe I can see the
chimney of a house! Look! Where the ground dips down
suddenly over there."

The others looked. They saw that the ground did
suddenly dip down into a kind of hollow, well protected
from the wind — just the place where people might
build a house. They tore over the rocky ground to the
dip, expecting they hardly knew what.

And what a surprise they got when at last they reached
the hollow and looked down into it!

VI

A QUEER LITTLE HOME

The four children stood at the top of the steep dip. The hollow ran right down to the sea — and in it was a cluster of small buildings!

But what strange buildings! The roofs were off, the chimneys were gone, all but the one they had seen, the walls were fallen in, and everything looked forlorn and deserted.

"Nothing but ruins!" said Tom, in astonishment. "Whatever happened to make the houses and shed fall to pieces like that?"

"I think I know," said Andy. "A year or two ago there came a great storm to these parts — so great that the people of our village fled inshore for miles, because the sea battered our houses and flooded our streets. The storm must have been even worse on these unprotected islands here — and I should think the sea came into this hollow and battered the farm to bits! Look at that chimney-stack there — all black and broken — that was struck by lightning, I should think."

The four children gazed down at the poor, hollow house and out-buildings. A little farm had once been there — a poor farm maybe, trying to grow a few potatoes in the rocky ground, to keep a few goats or cows, and to take from the sea enough fish to live on.

Now the folk had all gone, unable to battle with the great sea-storms that swept over their farm and destroyed their living.

"This explains the potatoes," said Jill. "That stretch of struggling potato plants must once have been a field."

"Let's go down into the hollow and have a look round," said Andy. So down into the dip they scrambled and wandered round the ruined buildings. Nothing had been left—all the furniture had been taken away, and even the gates and doors removed. Seashore weeds grew up from the floors of the farmhouse.

"A boy must have lived here," said Andy, picking up a broken wooden train from a patch of weeds.

"And here's a broken cup," said Jill, bending over what had once been a rubbish-heap.

They wandered about and at last came to a little wooden shack where perhaps a cow or two had been kept in the winter. For some reason it had escaped being beaten in by the waves, and still stood upright, its one window broken, and its floor covered with a creeping weed.

Andy looked at it carefully. "This wouldn't be a bad place to make into a little house for ourselves," he said. "I was thinking we'd have to try and build one somehow —but this will do if we patch it up a bit. The tent won't be any use at all if the weather breaks up—and also it's going to be a great nuisance to keep taking it down from the signal tree each night for our tent and putting it back again in the mornings."

"Oh yes!" said Tom in delight. "Let's make this our house! That would be fun. Then we could leave the sail flapping for our signal all the time."

They all went into the shack. It was not very large— more like a big bicycle shed, though the roof was higher. A wooden partition divided it into two.

"We'll take that down," said Andy. "It would be better to have one fairly big room than two tiny ones."

42

"Well, we'd better start work at once, hadn't we?" said Tom eagerly. "We shall have to bring all our things here—and make it a bit home-like. And all those weeds will have to be cleared."

"Yes—and we'll spread the floor with clean sand," said Jill. "Listen—you boys clear up the weeds for us —and Mary and I will go to that old potato field and find the biggest potatoes we can, and cook them in their jackets for lunch!"

"Good idea," said Tom, feeling hungry at once. "Come on, Andy—let's start and clean up the place now—we can't do much till that's done."

The two boys set to work. They pulled up the creeping weed by handfuls and piled it outside. They got tufts of stiff heather and, using them as brushes, swept the cobwebs from the walls and rough ceiling. Tom broke the remaining glass of the window, gathered the broken bits carefully together and tucked them into the bottom of the old rubbish-heap so that no one could be cut by a splinter.

Andy made a rough fireplace just outside the shack, with stones from the hearth of the ruined farmhouse.

"We can't have the fire inside because this shack has no chimney," he said, "and we'd be choked with the smoke. Anyway, I've made the fireplace out of the wind and we ought to be able to cook all right on it. Mary, you can bake the potatoes there, once the stones get hot. Tom, get some sticks and start a fire."

Mary and Jill peeped inside the shack. It looked clean and tidy now, though very bare. The two girls had pulled plenty of good potatoes from the old, weedy field, and had washed them in the spring water. They would be fine, baked in their jackets—though it was a pity there was no butter left and no salt.

43

Tom fetched some clean sand from the shore. He had found a very old bucket, which had a hole in the bottom. He put a flat stone over the hole, and then the sand did not trickle out. He carried six pails full of sand to the shack and scattered it over the earth floor. It looked very neat and clean.

"We'll have to get heaps of heather and bracken in for beds again," said Jill, "just as we did for our tent. Won't it be a nice little house! We must bring the little table here, and the stool – and all the cups and things. It will make it seem like home."

The children had quite forgotten how serious their adventure was. It was such fun to work like this and get ready a little house. Mary even began to wonder if there was anything she could use as a curtain for the window!

Their lunch was potatoes and chocolate, with plenty of cold spring water. Tom could have eaten three times as much but he had to be content with five large potatoes and a whole bar of chocolate.

"We'll have fish for tonight," promised Andy. "The water round about this island is just thick with fish. We'll always have plenty to eat so long as we don't get tired of fish! We'll hunt for shell-fish too."

After their dinner the children separated. The girls were to go to the nearest patches of heather and bracken and bring in armfuls for beds. The boys were to make journeys to and from the tent, and bring in all their belongings.

"When the tide's down tonight I'll get the tin of oil out of the locker of the boat," said Andy. "That won't have been spoilt by the sea-water because it's got a tight-fitting lid. We can cook over the stove then, as well as over a fire, if we want to."

The children were very busy that afternoon. Mary and Jill got enough heather and bracken to make two beds, one at each side of the shack. They piled the tough bracken on the floor first, and then the softer heather on top. Then they spread each bed with a rug, and put another rug, neatly folded up, to be used as a blanket at night.

"The beds can be couches to sit on in the daytime," said Mary, quite pleased with the look of them. "We'll have to add more heather day by day, I expect, Jill, because we shall flatten the beds very much with our weight. But we can easily see to that."

The boys brought in the crockery — cups, saucers and plates — thick, common ones used by the fishermen who sailed in Andy's father's boat with him. They were just right for the shack — but where were they to be put?

"We really can't keep them on the floor," said Mary. "They'll get broken. I wish we had a shelf to put things on. It would give us much more room if only we could get these odd things out of the way."

Andy disappeared for a few minutes. When he came back he carried a wooden board. He grinned at the surprised children.

"I remembered seeing an old shelf in what must have been the kitchen of the farmhouse," he said. "So I went in and wrenched it down from the wall. Tom, where did you put the tools and the box of nails?"

"Down there by our bed," said Tom. Andy picked up a hammer and the box of nails. "Where do you want the shelf?" he asked the girls.

"Over there, at the back of the shack, just about shoulder-high," said Mary. "What a lovely shelf that will make, Andy — it will take everything!"

So it did! Once Andy had nailed it up, the girls arranged the crockery there, the kettle, one or two pans, the field-glasses, camera and other things. The gramophone would not go on the shelf so they put it into a corner.

By this time the shack really looked fine! There were the two neat beds at the sides — the table in the middle, with the stool — the neatly-sanded floor — the shelf at the back with its array of goods! The children felt really pleased with it.

Andy filled the oil-stove. "You could *boil* us some potatoes tonight for a change," he said to Mary. "You've got a little saucepan, haven't you?"

"Yes," said Mary. "I'll boil them and mash them for you — but they'll taste a bit odd without butter or salt! And we'll open another tin of fruit."

The boys went off to catch fish. The girls busied themselves with fetching more potatoes, more water, and setting the oil-stove going. They felt very busy and rather important.

They had a most delicious supper and enjoyed every bit of it. They didn't even mind going without salt in the potatoes. They ate their supper sitting outside the open doorway of the shack, looking out to the evening sea. The gulls called high in the air, and the splash of the little white-edged waves came to them every now and again.

"Now we'll turn in!" said Andy with a yawn. "It will be fun to sleep in our little house for the first time! Come on, girls — leave the washing-up till the morning. We are all tired out!"

VII

A STRANGE DISCOVERY

The next day the children went to make sure that their sail-signal was still safely tied to the signal-tree at the top of the cliff. It was. It flapped there steadily, a signal to any passing ship that there were people on the island who needed help.

"Suppose no help comes?" said Tom. "Shall we have to stay here all winter?"

"Yes—unless you like to try and swim dozens of miles back home!" said Andy.

The children looked at one another. Stay there for the winter! It was all very well having an adventure on an island for three or four days—but to stay there all the winter, in the bitter cold and raging storms, was not a pleasant thought.

"Don't look so gloomy," said Andy. "We may be rescued any day. I can't think that no ship ever passes these islands. After all, there were people living here not so long ago—and they must have had supplies from time to time—so the ships must come by here sometimes. And maybe there are people living on one of the other islands. I think perhaps at a very low tide we could cross to the next island by that line of rocks over there—and explore that. We may find dozens of people, for all we know!"

Every one cheered up. Of course! There seemed to be five or six islands near to their own; people would surely be living on one or other of them, especially on the bigger ones. Their own island was so small that it was a wonder anyone had ever bothered to build a house there, and tried to get a living on the rocky soil.

They went to see if their boat was still held fast between the two rocks. Yes—there it was, all on one side, the tide washing right over its decks.

"Perhaps an extra strong tide might lift it off the rocks," said Andy. "If only it would—and we could mend it! I'd try to sail back home again."

"Well, there's nothing left in the boat that could be taken away now," said Tom. "I really think we've got everything movable—ropes, nets, even the oars!"

It was quite true. The boys had brought back with the oil everything in the locker. Ropes might never come in useful—but still, Andy thought they might as well take them. The children thoroughly explored the little island again, but found nothing interesting at all. They could see that the farm-people had used the level stretch of land on the more southerly side of the island for their fields. In one place, Jill found some runner beans growing over a tangle of brambles, and she called out in excitement:

"Beans! We'll eat them for dinner!"

The others came to look. "I expect these seeded themselves too," said Andy. "Maybe there was a bean-field just here. Well—we're not doing too badly, with potatoes and beans and fish!"

There was nothing to do that afternoon, except bathe and fish. The little shack was finished—there was nothing more to add to it. They could do nothing with their wrecked boat. It was of no use going for a ramble for the island was so small. So Tom suggested a bathe first, and fishing afterwards.

It was warm in the sunshiny sea. They swam through the big waves and splashed about lazily. Then they came

out of the sea and lay in the sun to dry. After that, the boys sat on the rocks to fish and the girls went to hunt for prawns, shrimps, and shellfish.

The tide was very low that evening. The wind had completely dropped, and the sea was almost calm—as nearly calm as it ever could be on that rough, rocky coast. The children stood on a rocky ledge, looking to the north where the other islands lay, blue with a summery mist.

"They really look as if they are just floating on the water," said Jill dreamily. "They do look lovely. I wish we could visit them."

"Well, it would be quite easy if we chose low tide,' said Andy, pointing to the line of rocks that were now uncovered, and which seemed to lead in a crooked line to the next island. "I'd like fine to go across those rocks to-morrow morning when the tide is low again. We could take food for the day—and see what was on the next island—and climb back across the rocks at low tide to-morrow night."

"Oh, do let's!" cried the twins, and Tom did a little war-dance on the rocky ledge in excitement. Who knew what they might find on the next island?

That night Jill cooked some potatoes in their skins, and let them go cold to take with them next day.

"We'll cook the sausages that are in the tin, let them go cold, and take those, too," said Jill. "We can catch some fish to-morrow night for our evening meal when we come home."

The next morning they ran to see if the tide had uncovered the rocks again. Yes—there they stretched grey and green, some quite bare, some covered with seaweed. Very deep rock-pools lay between. The sea itself lay pale blue and sparkling, beyond the line of rocks.

"Come on!" said Andy. "We'd better go now, before the tide turns."

They leapt down from the ledge and ran to the sandy shore. They jumped up on to the rocks, and then began to make their way carefully over them. Some were so slippery that once or twice the children nearly fell into the deep pools. These pools looked exciting. Quite big fish swam in them, and Andy said big edible crabs would be sure to be there.

"But we've no time for fishing about here," he said. "We shall be caught by the tide if we don't make haste."

Sure enough, the tide was on the turn—but before it could reach the jagged line of rocks over which the children were climbing, they had come to the end of them, and had waded through a pool to the sandy shore of the next island.

"Now we're on island number two!" said Tom, capering about. "Golly! I *am* hungry!"

So was every one. "Well, if we eat all our food now, we shall have to wait ages for our next meal, unless we can find something on this island," said Andy. But he was hungry, too—so they ate their cold sausages and potatoes, and sucked a toffee each.

Then they set off to explore the second island. They turned to climb the cliffs—and had a big surprise!

"Look! Caves!" said Tom, pointing to big black openings in the cliff. "Look at that! Caves of all kinds and sizes and shapes! Let's have a look at them."

They made their way to the first cave—and just outside it Andy stopped and stared at something in the sand.

"What's up?" asked Tom.

"That!" said Andy, and he pointed to a cigarette-end that lay rolling a little in the breeze.

"A cigarette-end!" said Tom, looking all round, as if he were looking for the one who had smoked it. "Well! Somebody has been here all right—and not very long ago, either. But there's not a single house on *this* island, ruined or whole!"

"Perhaps the people live in these caves," said Jill, looking half-timidly at the first one.

"We'll go in and see," said Andy. He pulled a roll of oilskin from his pocket and out of it took a half-candle and a box of matches. Andy never ran any risk of his matches getting wet—and now the children were glad

51

that he was so careful, for no one really wanted to go into the caves without a light of some sort.

Andy lighted the candle and then, leading the way, he stepped into the first cave. The others followed him. The floor was thick with silvery sand, and the walls of the cave were high and smooth. It ran back a long way, and then narrowed into an archway. Through this the children went into another cave, the tiny light of the candle shining on rocky grey walls, and high, rough roof. The floor of the cave then began to go upwards, and became rocky instead of sandy. The cave narrowed into a passage, whose roof was at times so low that they bumped their heads against it.

And then they came to the Round Cave, which was the name they at once gave the last strange cave. It was almost perfectly round, and as the floor slanted down towards the middle, it felt like being inside a hollow ball!

But it wasn't the roundness of the cave that startled the four children — it was what it held!

Piled high everywhere were boxes, sacks, and big tin chests with strange words on them! Some piles reached to the roof of the cave, others reached half-way.

"Golly! Look at that!" said Tom, in the greatest astonishment. "Whatever's in all those boxes and things — and why are they here?"

The little flame of the candle flickered on the strange array in the cave. Andy set the candle gently down on a flat piece of rock, and pulled the neck of a thick brown sack undone. It was lined with coarse blue paper inside. He undid that — and then gave a low cry of surprise.

"Sugar! Stranger and stranger! I was expecting treasure or something — and it's sugar! I wonder what's in the other sacks and boxes."

Some the children could not force open, but others were already opened, as if some one had taken from them some of the contents. The boxes were full of tins — there were tins of soup, meat, vegetables, fruit, sardines — everything one could think of. There was a chest of flour, a chest of tea, tins of salt, even tins of butter and lard, well-sealed and air-tight.

"Andy — I really don't understand this," said Jill in a puzzled voice. "How did all these come here? And who do you suppose they belong to? As far as we know there isn't a single person on the island."

"I don't know any more than you do, Jill," said Andy. "It's like a dream; but anyway we shan't need to starve whilst there's all this food stored here!"

"But may we take it, if it belongs to anyone else?" said Mary, frightened.

"We can pay the person it belongs to," said Andy. "My father and your mother will gladly pay, to keep us from starving, if we have to spend the winter here!"

"Well, come on then—let's take all we want," said Tom, feeling so hungry that he couldn't wait a minute longer. "We'll keep a careful account of everything we take, and pay the bill and a little more, when we find out who owns this very curious larder."

"You're right, Tom," said Andy, in a puzzled voice. "It is a *very*—curious—larder!"

VIII

ODDER AND ODDER

The children each chose what they thought they would like to take away. Sugar they wanted, and salt. The tinned butter would be splendid, and any tins of meat and fruit. Jill thought she might be able to make some rolls of bread with the flour, or, at any rate, some scones. They took tins of powdered milk too, and each child carried quite a heavy load down the narrow passages that led from the Round Cave to the shore-cave.

When they reached the open air Tom took a deep breath and set down his load. "My goodness, it was stuffy up there," he said.

"What puzzles me is why it wasn't *more* stuffy than it was," said Andy. "Air must get into that Round Cave through some hole we didn't see. Pick up your things, Tom, the tide is coming in. We can't stay on this beach. The sea will reach the cave before long."

"It's all right for about ten minutes," said Tom, pulling a fat little notebook from his pocket. "I just want to jot down a list of all the things we've taken, in case we eat them up and then forget what we had."

"Tom's always so honest," said Jill. "Well, I'll tell you the things, Tom, and you can write them down. Three tins of pineapple. One big bag of sugar. Three tins of tongue. Four tins of —"

"Not so fast, not so fast," said Tom, busy writing. He wrote everything down, shut his notebook with a snap, and pushed it back into his pocket. Then he picked up

55

his load and followed Andy up the steep, rocky path.

Until the tide went out that night the children were prisoners on the second island, for there was no way to get back to their own island except by the line of rocks. This was now completely covered by the tide, and great showers of spray were sent high into the air as the water crashed against the rocks over which they had clambered early that day.

"Anyone got a tin-opener?" asked Tom, his mouth watering at the sight of the labels on the tins.

Andy had. In Andy's pockets there was almost anything that anyone could possibly want, from tin-tacks to toffee.

"You'd better open a tin, I suppose," said Andy, with a grin. "I've watched you sticking your finger into the sugar packet a dozen times already—and there'll be none left to take to our island if you do it much more. Open a tin of tongue and perhaps you won't feel so hungry for sugar!"

They all feasted on the tongue, which was really most delicious. They felt very thirsty afterwards, and as they had not found any spring or stream on the second island they could not think what to do.

"Well, why don't we open a tin of pineapple?" said Tom at last. "The chunks will be lovely and juicy and we can all have a drink of the juice in the tin too."

So a tin of pineapple was opened. Both tins were carefully buried by the children, for even though the island seemed quite lonely and deserted they could not bear to make it ugly by leaving empty tins about. The gulls swooped round them all the time they·ate, screaming loudly.

Andy imitated them and they grew even more excited,

at last landing on the ground behind the children and waiting there almost within touch.

"These gulls know that where there are people, there may be food," said Andy. "But how do they know that? — these islands seem quite bare and empty."

"And how, how, how did all that food come to be in the Round Cave?" said Jill. "Could it have been there for years, do you suppose — and have been forgotten?"

"No," said Andy. "It hasn't been there very long. The sugar was still soft — and sugar goes hard if it is stored for long. That cigarette-end we found too — that had been smoked not less than a week or two ago, or the wind would have blown it into bits."

"Andy, don't you think it would be a good thing to stay on *this* island and live here, instead of going back to our own island?" asked Mary. "We should be near to a good food-supply then!"

"No, I don't," said Andy, at once. "You forget we have left a signal on our island — and if any ship sees it and calls for us, we might be on *this* island, unable to be rescued because the tide was high and we couldn't get back."

"But couldn't we tie the signal up somewhere on *this* island?" said Tom.

"No," said Andy. "No ship could get to us here. This island is almost surrounded by a reef of the worst rocks I've ever seen. Look at them, right out there."

The children looked. Andy was right. A jagged line of rocks ran some way out from the coast. Between the rocks and the coast the sea lay trapped in a kind of big lagoon or lake, calm and smooth.

Tom frowned and looked puzzled. "Well, if no ship can get in to rescue us if we stay on this island," he said, "how in the world did one get in to land all that food in the cave?"

Andy stared at Tom and looked as puzzled as Tom did. "Yes—that's odd," he said. "Well—maybe there is a way through at high tide. But we can't risk it. We must live on the first island, and when we want food we must come here and get it—and maybe we shall run into the folk who so strangely made a larder in the Round Cave."

Mary stood up and tried to see what the next island was like. It looked much bigger than the first two. There was no line of rocks stretching to it, but only an unbroken spread of blue water. To get to the third island they would have to swim, or use a boat.

"Do you think we'd better leave a note in the cave to say that we are on the first island and would like to be rescued?" said Tom. "The people may come back at any time—and we could go away in their boat."

Andy shook his head. "I think we won't leave a note —or anything else to show we've been here," he said. "There's something a bit mysterious about all this, and if there's a secret going on, we'd better keep out of it till we know what it is."

"Oh, Andy! Whatever do you mean?" cried Mary.

"I don't know what I mean," said Andy. "It's just a feeling I have, that's all. Maybe I'm wrong—but one of us will come over here every day at low tide and just see if there's somebody about before we let them know we're here."

"Well, Andy—what about all our footmarks round the cave?" said Tom.

"The tide will wash all those right away," said Andy. "Look over the cliff-edge, Tom—you will see the tide has gone right into the cave now. There is absolutely nothing that will show we have been there."

"Except that some of the food is missing," said Mary. "You've forgotten that, Andy."

"No, I haven't," said Andy. "There's so much in that cave that I don't think anyone will miss the little we've taken. I don't expect it's checked at all. Nobody would think that any strangers would ever visit that cave."

The children wandered over the island and looked for bilberries, which were fruiting there in great numbers. It was a way of quenching their thirst, to pick the small, juicy bilberries. The island was quite deserted. It did not look as if anyone had ever lived there at all.

The tide went down and the line of rocks began to show. The children clambered down to the shore to go back to their own island. They had tied to their backs the food they had taken, and Andy told everyone to be very careful.

"We don't want to lose our food in a deep pool!" he said. "So don't rush along too fast, Tom. You are always in such a hurry!"

The rocks were wet and slippery, but the children were very careful indeed. Once an extra large wave came and splashed right over Jill, and she gave a squeal.

"Oh, has it wet the food?"

"Yes—soaked it!" called Tom. "But never mind—it's all in tins, Jill."

They got back to their little hut at last and all of them were delighted to see it. It really seemed like coming home.

They sat down on their beds, tired out. But Tom was not going to bed without his supper. He wanted hot soup, more tongue, and a tin of peaches. So the stove had to be lighted, and Tom was sent to fill the kettle.

All the children enjoyed the meal, although they were so sleepy they could hardly bother to clear up afterwards. The first stars were in the sky as they flung themselves on their beds.

"It's awfully early to go to bed," murmured Jill sleepily. "But I can't keep awake another minute!"

And she fell asleep at once. So did Mary. Tom blew out the stove and lay down too. Andy sat up for a while, looking out towards the second island and wondering about a lot of things.

Then he too lay down and fell asleep—but not for long!

A strange and curious noise awoke him. It came into his dreams, startled him and roused him so that he sat up, puzzled and alarmed.

"Tom! Wake up!" said Andy. "Listen to this noise. What is it?"

Tom awoke and listened. "It's a motor-bicycle," he said, half asleep.

"Don't be a fathead!" said Andy. "A motor-bicycle on this island! You're dreaming. Come on, wake up—I tell you there's a jolly queer noise."

The noise itself hummed away into silence. The gulls screamed but soon became quiet. Andy sat and listened a little longer and then, as no more noise came, lay down on his bed again.

"Odder and odder," said Andy to himself. "We seem to have come to some most mysterious islands— and I'm going to find out what's happening—or my name isn't Andy!"

IX

THE MYSTERIOUS VISITORS

The next day the children talked about the queer noise that Andy had heard.

"I tell you it sounded exactly like a motor-bicycle," Tom said firmly, and nothing would make him admit that it wasn't.

"If I didn't know there couldn't possibly be any landing-ground on these rocky islands I might have thought the noise was made by an aeroplane," said Andy thoughtfully. "But that's silly. Why would an aeroplane come here? And where would it land?"

"It might be a motor-boat, perhaps!" said Jill suddenly. The others stared at her. For some reason, nobody had thought of motor-boats till then.

"Yes—I believe it was!" said Andy. "It had that throbbing sound that a motor makes. Now what's a motor-boat doing here? But, anyway—it means that we can be rescued!"

"Of course!" said Tom. "Well—let's go and find the motor-boat. What a surprise they'll get when they suddenly see us! They'll wonder wherever we've come from."

"Tom, don't be in so great a hurry," said Andy, pulling the impatient boy down into the heather. "I think there's something funny going on here—and before we show ourselves we'd better find out if we shall be welcome!"

"Oh," said Tom, surprised. The girls looked rather alarmed.

"What do you mean—something funny?" said Jill.

"I don't know, as I said yesterday," said Andy. "But what we'will do is to see where that motor-boat is. It won't have seen our signal because it came in the night —and we know it's not anywhere this side of the island, or we would have seen it this morning. I vote we go to that rocky ledge where we get the best view of the second island and see if by any chance a boat has been able to get through the reef of rocks and sail into the quiet lagoon inside."

The four children made their way to the high rocky ledge.

Andy made them lie down flat and wriggle like Red Indians as they reached it.

"Better not let ourselves be seen, if anyone *is* down there," he whispered. So, as flat as snakes, they wormed their way to the rocky ledge—and when they got there, they had the biggest surprise of their lives!

In the quiet water that lay outside the second island was a large and powerful seaplane!

Yes—a great seaplane, whose wings spread widely over the blue water. No small motor-boat purred there. It was the seaplane's engine that Andy had heard so mysteriously in the middle of the night.

"Whew! Look at that!" whispered Andy, his face going as red as a beetroot with excitement. "I never *thought* of a seaplane! What a very extraordinary thing!"

"Let's get up and shout and wave," begged Jill. "I'm sure they will love to rescue us."

"Haven't you seen the sign on the wings?" asked Tom, in a curiously angry voice. The girls looked. The sign of the crooked cross was painted on each wing— the sign of the enemy, the foe of half the world.

"Golly!" said Mary, and she drew a deep breath.

62

"Enemies! Using these islands! Do they belong to them?"

"Of course not," said Andy. "But they are desolate, and out of the usual ships' course – and they've been noted by the enemy, and he's using them as a kind of base for something – seaplanes perhaps."

"Well – what are we going to do?" asked Tom.

"We shall have to think," said Andy. "One thing is certain. We won't show ourselves till we've found out a little more. We don't want to be taken prisoners."

"That's what that food was for, then – the people who come here," said Jill. "I suppose the seaplanes come over here for food and petrol. It's a good idea. How I wish we could get away and tell my father about it – he'd know what to do. I guess he'd clean up this place, whatever it's used for!"

"I say – hadn't we better take down our signal whilst that seaplane is here?" asked Jill. "If it happens to see it, the enemy will know there are people on this island. And what about the fishing-boat? That might be seen too."

"I don't think so," said Andy. "It's well hidden between those rocks. But the signal had certainly better come down. We won't put it up any more. Come on, Tom – we'll take it down now."

"We'll come with you," said the girls. But Andy shook his head.

"No," he said. "From now on, somebody must keep a watch on that seaplane. We must find out all we can. We will be back with you as soon as possible – but you must stay here and watch."

So the two girls were left behind whilst the boys ran across the island to take down their flapping signal.

"I don't know where in the world we should hide if we were discovered and hunted for," said Andy, rolling up the sail. "There isn't a single place here to hide away in—not a cave or anything."

Tom felt rather uncomfortable. He didn't want to be hunted for on that bare island! "I wish we could see how many men there are in that seaplane," he said, "and what they are doing, and everything."

"Where are your field-glasses?" asked Andy suddenly. "They would be just the thing to use. We could see everything as clearly as could be, then!"

"And my camera, too!" said Tom, jumping for joy. "What about my camera? We could take some photographs of the seaplane—then everyone would *have* to believe us when we get back—if ever we *do* get back!"

"*That's* a fine idea!" said Andy, really pleased. "Golly! If we could take some pictures of that seaplane with the crooked cross showing up clearly, there wouldn't be the least doubt of our story when we got home. Tom, let's go and get your glasses and your camera straight away."

They dumped the sail into a bush and ran to the shack. They took Tom's field-glasses and picked up the camera to see if it needed a new film. No—there was a new one inside.

"Better not use up all the film on the seaplane," said Andy. "There might be other interesting and extra-ordinary things to photograph—you never know!"

"Oh, I've got three or four films," said Tom. "I brought plenty with me, thinking I was going to get some good bird pictures, you know. Come on—let's go back to the girls and see what they have to report.

The girls were very glad indeed to see the boys,

and rushed to meet them. They had such a lot to tell.

"Andy! Tom! As soon as you had gone the men in the seaplane put out a funny little round sort of boat," said Jill in excitement. "And they paddled to shore in it, and went to our cave. What a good thing the sea had washed away all our footprints!"

"It was, indeed," said Andy. "Tom, give me the field-glasses. I want to have a look through them."

Andy stared through the powerful glasses. They were so strong that they seemed to bring the seaplane near enough to touch! The boy saw the great crooked crosses boldly painted on the wings. He saw the little rubber

boat left bobbing in the surf, whilst the men visited the cave—either to take something to it, or to bring something away, Andy did not know which.

"There seems to be someone in the seaplane," said Andy. "And, look—there are some men coming from the cave!"

Andy could see them very clearly through his field-glasses—and the others could see them too, though not so well, of course. To them the men looked like faraway dolls.

"They've gone to get food from the cave," said Andy in excitement. "And I guess there's a store of petrol somewhere else for them to get when they want to. Food—and petrol—just what I thought! Using these islands saves enemy planes from having to go hundreds of miles to their own country's stores. My word—we *have* stumbled on to something queer!"

The men entered their rubber boat and rowed back to the seaplane. Twice more they went to the cave and back. Then they climbed up into the plane and disappeared.

"I'm getting most awfully hungry," said Tom at last. "Can't we go and get something to eat?"

"I'll stay here and keep watch, and you and the girls can go and get your dinner," said Andy. "Don't light a fire, whatever you do—the enemy will see the smoke. Use the stove if you want to cook anything. Bring me something to eat and drink later."

"Right," said Tom, and he and the girls wriggled off the high ledge. They stood upright as soon as they were out of sight of the seaplane and tore to their shack.

They ate a hurried meal, and did not cook anything at all. They made up a dinner-packet for Andy and set

66

off to take it to him. But half-way there they heard a noise. R-r-r-r-r-r-r-r! R-r-r-r-r-r-r-r! R-r-r-r-r-r! They stopped at once and listened.

"It's the seaplane going off!" cried Tom—and then the sound came again, more loudly than ever. R-R-R-R-R-R-R.

"Look—it's there!" cried Jill. "Drop flat to the ground or we'll be seen!"

Jill had seen the seaplane just rising into the air over the cliff. The three children dropped flat to the ground and lay there perfectly still. The seaplane roared over their island, rose higher and higher, and at last was nothing but a speck in the sky.

"What a narrow escape!" said Tom, sitting up and wiping his forehead. "Golly! My heart did go bump! I've spilt the water I was carrying for Andy. I'll have to get some more!"

"It *was* a shock to see that enormous plane coming!" said Jill. "Oh dear—if we have many more shocks, my hair will turn grey!"

X

AND NOW FOR THE THIRD ISLAND!

The children were very glad that the seaplane had gone. "It's a jolly good thing our signal was taken down before it flew over the island," said Andy, eating the food that the others had brought to him. "I couldn't warn you. It started up its engine all of a sudden, taxied over the smooth water there, and then rose into the air."

"Andy, do you think there's anything to be seen over on the *other* islands?" asked Tom.

"There may be," said Andy. "I think we ought to try and find out. That third island looks a peculiar shape to me — very long indeed, but very narrow. On the other side of it might be a fine natural harbour for seaplanes. There may be heaps there."

"Well, we've only heard one so far," said Tom. "It doesn't seem as if they're very busy, if there *are* lots over there."

"No — you're right, Tom," said Andy. "Well, what about going to see what we can find? I don't quite know how we'll get to the third island — have to swim, I think. I don't believe the girls could swim so far, though."

"I don't think *I* could," said Jill, remembering the long stretch of sea between the second and third islands. "You boys would have to go without us. Mary and I will stay behind and be as patient as we can."

"Shall we go to-morrow?" asked Tom eagerly. "We could cross to the second island at low tide in the morning and swim across to the third island. We could carry a little food with us, wrapped up in your oilskin."

"Yes—we'll do that," said Andy. A great feeling of excitement came over the children—a feeling as if some big unknown secret was going to be theirs. Jill shivered a little—it was almost *too* exciting.

"There's one thing I'm worried about," said Andy. "Just suppose we *are* discovered, by any chance—we *must* find some hiding-place."

"Well, there simply isn't any on this island," said Tom. "So we must hope we *won't* be discovered."

Nothing more happened that day. No seaplane came to the calm harbour in the waters of the second island. No sound but the sea-gulls came through the air. It was a lovely day and the children enjoyed themselves bathing and sunning their brown bodies.

Thanks to the store of food they had discovered on the second island they had plenty to eat. Andy caught some nice little fish, and Jill fried them in the tinned butter. They were delicious. Now that they had tinned milk-powder they could make a milk-mixture and use it with their tea or cocoa, and could also sweeten their drinks with the sugar they had brought.

"We are really very well off now!" said Tom, who as usual was thoroughly enjoying his meal. "We'll take another exciting lot of tins away from the Round Cave next time—I saw some baked beans in tomato sauce. I should like those."

The children took turns at keeping watch on the second island from the rocky ledge. But nothing was to be seen at all. They went to bed early because the boys would have rather a hard and long day the next day.

"We shall have to clamber over that line of rocks first," said Andy. "And then we must cross the island and swim to the third one. We shall have to be back on the second island in time to clamber over the rocks at the next low tide. You girls mustn't worry about us. We shall be back all right."

"I do wish we were going too," said Jill. "Don't you think Mary and I could climb over the rocks to the second island and wait for you there? It would be more fun for us to play about there than on this bare island. There are lots of bilberries there we could pick—they are lovely and sweet now."

"All right," said Andy. "But just keep a watch for any seaplane arriving. Lie down flat under a bush or something if you hear one. You mustn't be seen."

"All right," said Mary. "You can trust us to do that."

So the next morning the four children once again climbed over the line of slippery rocks at low tide. The boys had on only their bathing-suits. Andy had tied his oilskin packet safely to his shoulders, and in it was plenty of food for the day. The girls could get what they wanted from the cave.

All four went across the second island, over the heather and bracken to where they could see the third island. It lay in the sea before them, like a long blue and brown snake. Beyond they could see one or two more islands.

"Do you really think you can swim so far, Tom?" asked Mary doubtfully, as she looked at the wide spread of water between the second island and the third.

"Of course," said Tom, who wasn't going to give up this adventure for anything. All the same, the distance was further than he had ever swum before.

"Well—good-bye for the present," said Andy to the girls. "We'll get down to the shore here, wade out as far as we can, and then swim. Have you got Tom's field-glasses, Jill? Good—you can watch us through them all the way to the third island!"

The boys went down to the shore, waded into the water, and then, when they were out of their depth, began to swim. Andy was by far the stronger swimmer —but he kept close to Tom, just in case the younger boy got into difficulties.

On and on they swam, using the breast-stroke because Andy said it was the least tiring. When Tom began to pant a little, half-way across, Andy spoke to him.

"Let's do a spot of floating, Tom. That will rest us a little. It's a long way."

The two boys lay on their backs in the water. It was a little rough and choppy, but quite warm. They floated like logs of wood, spread out flat on the water. It was a fine rest for Tom.

Then once more they swam on—but it began to seem as if Tom would not reach the shore of the third island. His arms felt so tired. His legs seemed to have no push in them. He gasped and panted, and Andy began to feel alarmed.

"Tread water a bit," he called to Tom. "Do you think you'll be able to swim the rest of the way?"

"I don't know," said poor Tom, dreadfully ashamed of himself. But he could *not* seem to make his arms work properly. He was really tired out.

Andy was not in the least tired. He was as strong as a horse, and he trod water beside Tom, wondering what to do.

"Try again, Tom," he said. "It's no use going back! We are more than half-way across."

Tom looked at the cliff of the third island. It seemed a long, long way away still. He tried again, striking out bravely with his tired arms. But after about six strokes he could not swim any more. He turned on his back and floated again.

Andy was really alarmed. "Tom, you can't do any more," he said. "I'll have to help you. I'll swim on my back and you must lie on your front and put your hands on my shoulders. I can drag you along in the water that way, but it will be rather slow."

"Thanks, Andy," said Tom, very angry with his poor swimming, but quite unable to do anything else. He took hold of Andy's shoulders, and Andy, lying on his back with his head towards the third island, began to strike out valiantly with his brown legs.

It was very slow indeed. And now *Andy* began to get tired! Taking two people wasn't nearly so easy as only one, and he began to gasp. *Now* what were they to do? If they both got into difficulties it would be a very serious matter.

It wasn't long before neither Tom nor Andy had any strength left—and goodness knows what would have happened if Andy, striking out desperately with his legs, had not felt something hard beneath him. It was a rock! He felt about with his feet and at last discovered a rock below the water. They had come to a kind of rocky reef rather like the one they had climbed over from their own island to the second one—but this line of rocks was not uncovered by the tide.

"Tom! Tom! Put your feet down and feel where the rocks are!" gasped Andy. "We can stand there—and maybe feel our way along a bit till we come to the sandy bottom."

Tom soon found foothold on the rocks under the water. He felt better at once. He and Andy held hands and together made their way very cautiously over the sunken

72

rocks, bruising their poor feet, but getting gradually
nearer to the shore. And at last they felt the rocks stop,
and there was sand beneath their feet! Good.

"Golly! I didn't enjoy that very much," said Tom.
"Sorry I was so feeble, Andy."

"It's all right," said Andy. "You did your best. We're
all right now."

But in his own mind Andy didn't think they *were*
all right! How in the world was he going to get Tom
over that stretch of water back to the second island
again? He would never, never do it! Andy was very
worried indeed.

But he didn't show it. He grinned at Tom, his blue

eyes shining in his wet brown face. "We're here at last!" he said. "And maybe we shall get a few surprises!"

They lay on the sandy shore in the sun for a while, drying themselves. Tom felt very much better after a meal out of the oilskin packet. He almost felt as if he could swim back home again! It was wonderful what food did to Tom.

"I feel a new man now," he said, leaping to his feet. "Come on, Andy, old chap. Let's go up to the cliff-top and go across to the other side of this island, to see if we can spy anything."

Andy got up too. The two boys climbed up the rough cliff and sat on the top to get back their breath. The island seemed to be about the same as the other two— covered with heather, bracken and grass, and with white gulls soaring over it.

They crossed the narrow width of the island and at last came to the cliff on the other side.

"Wriggle along on the ground now, just in case there's anyone about," said Andy. So both boys wriggled along on their fronts, and came at last to a place where they could see down to the water far below.

And what they saw there filled them with such astonishment and alarm that for at least five minutes neither boy could say a word!

74

XI

THE SECRET OF THE ISLANDS

The sight that the two boys looked down upon was hardly to be believed. There was a very fine natural harbour of extremely deep water on the north-eastern side of the third island—and lying in this water were at least seven or eight submarines!

Submarines! A submarine base in those deserted islands! No wonder so many of our ships had been sent to the bottom in the waters around these islands!

"It's a real nest of submarines," whispered Andy at last. "Enemy submarines! I can't believe it. My word, Tom, we've stumbled on an amazing secret."

The boys lay looking down on the water. Some of the submarines lay like great grey crocodiles, humped out of the water. One or two were moving out of the harbour, their periscopes showing. It was a curiously silent place, considering that so many of these underwater ships were there. There was no noise of shouting—no noise of machinery—just a dull throbbing every now and again.

"They get fuel and food here," whispered Andy. "They are the small submarines—this harbour can easily take a dozen or more. It's a perfect place for submarines. Do you see how they haven't built any jetties or piers—not a thing that anyone could see, if one of our own planes came over? All they would have to do then would be to sink under the water—and then there would be nothing to see. They store everything in the caves—golly, it's amazing."

For a very long time the two boys lay watching the strange sight below. Two submarines slipped silently out of the harbour entrance — a way between two reefs of high rocks. A third submarine came in, and lay peacefully with the others, the men coming out on the deck and looking around.

At first Tom had been so full of surprise and alarm, so swept with excitement, that he could think of nothing but the sight of the queer vessels. Then another thought came into his head and he turned to Andy.

"Andy," he said. "We've *got* to get home and tell what we've seen."

"I know," said Andy. "I'm thinking that too, Tom. And we've got to get the girls off these islands. We are all in danger. If the enemy knew we were spying on them like this I don't know what would happen to us."

"I don't care how much danger we're in," said Tom, and he didn't. "All I know is that we've *got* to go and tell our people at home about this submarine base. It's got to be cleared away. Andy, it's serious."

Andy nodded. Both boys seemed to become men at that moment. They looked gravely into each other's eyes and what they saw there pleased them both. Each boy knew that the other would do his best and even more than his best.

"Do you think we shall be believed if we go home with a story like this?" said Tom. "Grown-ups have some funny ideas sometimes. They might think we had made it all up — or been mistaken."

"We'll get your camera and take a few photographs," said Andy. "Nobody can disbelieve photographs. And another thing we must do is to try to do something with our boat. We *must* get it off the rocks somehow and try

76

to patch it up. It's our only way of getting back home."

They watched the harbour for a little while longer, and then wriggled along the top of the cliff till they came to some bushes. They went down by these and ran along till they came to the end of the harbour. Beyond lay a cove, and in it, drawn up to the sand, were a number of small boats. No one seemed to be about.

The sight of the little boats excited Andy. If only he could get hold of one! Then he and Tom could row round the third island, and get back to the second one safely. Andy knew perfectly well that Tom could not swim back—and he did not mean to leave the boy alone on this submarine island.

"Tom," he said, "see those boats? Well, what about waiting till night-time—and then stealing down to the cove and taking a boat? We could easily row it back to the second island. It would save us having to swim—and we might even fill it with food and water and try our luck at going home. I could fix up the sail somehow."

"Good idea, Andy," said Tom, his face glowing with excitement. "But I say! Won't the girls be awfully worried if we don't swim back before low tide tonight?"

"We'll go to the cliff on the other side of this island and wave to them," said Andy. "They've got the field-glasses and will see us quite clearly. We'll point and wave and nod and try to show them that our plans are altered, but that we're all right."

"Good," said Tom. "Let's go now. I feel so awfully excited that I really must do something!"

The boys went to the other side of the island. After a while the girls appeared and waved to them. Jill put the glasses to her eyes.

"The boys seem frightfully pleased and excited about

something!" she said. "They are waving and pointing and nodding like anything. They seem to want us to understand something."

"Well, it can only be that they have found something exciting and are going to do something about it," said Mary, taking the glasses from Jill and looking through them. "Yes — Tom's like a mad thing. Well, we shall know when they come back tonight. I only hope Tom will be able to swim back all right. I was really afraid he'd drown this morning."

The boys disappeared after a time. They sat down in a little sunny hollow and finished the rest of the food. Andy found a stream of water and the boys drank from it. Then they sat talking quietly, waiting for the night to come.

At last it came. The moon was behind the clouds, and gave only a pale light now and again. The boys slipped quietly to the top of the cliff that overlooked the small cove next to the harbour. They had already planned the easiest way down. Andy went first. He climbed like a cat. Tom followed him, trying not to send any stones clattering down the cliff.

They came to the shore. It was sandy and their feet made no noise. The boys stayed in the shadow of the cliffs for a few minutes, listening. They could hear no noise at all, except the small sound of little waves breaking on the sand. The boats were not far off, upturned in a row. No one was guarding them. Indeed, why should anyone? No one had ever set foot on the islands since the farm-folk had gone — save for the crews of enemy seaplanes and submarines.

The boys crept over the silvery sand. "Take the boat on the left," whispered Andy. "It's just our size."

They came to the boat—and then they heard voices. They seemed to come from the far side of the cliff, and sounded clearly in the night. The boys could not hear any words—but the sound was enough to make them lie down flat beside the boat they had chosen.

Tom was trembling. Suppose they were found out just as they were taking the boat! It would be too bad. The boys listened until the sound of voices died away and then they cautiously lifted their heads.

"When the moon gets into that very thick cloud we'll turn the boat over and run her into the water," whispered Andy. "You take this side and I'll take the other. Be ready."

"Right," whispered back Tom. So when the moon slipped behind the dark clouds the boys rose silently to their feet. They turned over the boat with hardly a sound, though it was awkward and heavy. Then they pulled it over the sand to the water. Tom got in and took the oars. Andy pushed the boat right out and leapt in himself. The moon was still hidden.

Silently the boys rowed away from the shore, hoping that the moon would remain behind the cloud until they had pulled out of sight. No shout was heard. No running feet. They were undiscovered, so far!

They rowed fast. When the moon came out again they were far from the little cove. "Look! Pull round a bit more," said Andy. "We're passing round the end of the island. We've done well to get here so quickly!"

Soon they were right round the narrow end of the third island. They rowed into the broad stretch of water between the second and third islands. Then across to the shore below the cliff where they had left the girls.

Jill and Mary were watching there. They had been

79

very worried when night had come and brought with it no boys. They couldn't imagine what had happened. They were in a great state of alarm and fright.

And then Jill, looking through the glasses when the moon had swum out into a clear piece of sky, had seen a little boat coming into the stretch of water between the two islands. She clutched Mary's arm.

"Look! A boat! Is it the enemy?"

The girls looked and looked, their hearts beating loudly. They could not see who was in the boat. It landed on the beach—and then the call of a seagull floated up the cliff.

"Andy!" cried Jill, nearly falling down the cliff. "It's Andy! I'd know his seagull call anywhere!"

The boys climbed up the cliff and came to the rocky ledge. The girls fell on them and hugged them like bears, they were so relieved to see them.

"The boat! Where did you get the boat?" cried Jill.

"What did you see? What did you find?" cried Mary.

"We'll tell you all about it," said Andy, and the four of them sat close together on the cold, windy ledge, quite forgetful of the chilly breeze, talking and listening eagerly.

The girls could hardly believe the boys' story. It seemed quite impossible.

"And now that we've got a boat, we'll fill it full of food and water, and see if we can get home," said Andy. "It's the only thing we can do—and we must do it."

"But, Andy," said Jill, "just suppose the enemy see their boat is missing—won't they take alarm and search the islands?"

"Yes—they certainly will," said Andy. "And so we must start to-morrow. We will have a good sleep tonight—

take plenty of food from the cave—and see if we can make for home."

"If only we can get away before the enemy finds that boat is missing!" said Tom. "Oh, do you suppose we shall?"

XII

A DARING ADVENTURE

The children did not have a very good night after all, for they were far too excited to sleep. They had all rowed in the stolen boat to their own island, and had landed there, tied up the boat and gone to their shack.

They slept rather late the next morning, for not one of them had gone to sleep before midnight—and they were awakened by the throbbing noise that they had heard two nights before!

"The seaplane again!" said Andy, waking up at once and leaping to his feet. He ran to the open doorway of the hut, and was just in time to see the plane soar overhead. Then it went round in great circles ready to land on the smooth water outside the second island.

"That means we can't get away today," said Tom at once. "We simply *must* get food into the boat—and we can't if that plane is there."

"No—we can't," said Andy. "But I tell you what we might do, Tom. We might row to the third island, tie our boat up in a hidden place, creep to the top of that cliff, and try to take a few photographs of the submarine bay! We meant to take some photos, you know."

"Yes — we could do that," said Tom. "We'll have to be pretty careful, though."

"We will be," said Andy. "Jill, what is there for breakfast?"

There were tinned sausages and baked beans and tomato sauce. Jill proudly produced some little rolls of bread she had made too. They all ate in silence, thinking over everything that had happened.

"That seaplane may not stay long," said Andy. "It didn't last time. I expect it has come to add to the stores — or maybe take away from them. It will be busy that side of the island — so we will row round the *other* side, where we won't be seen, go across to the third one, and tie up there. You girls must stay here."

"Oh, you always have the exciting things to do," sighed Mary. "Can't we really come with you? I don't see why we can't."

"Well, if you promise to do exactly what you're told, you can come," said Andy, after a minute's thought. He didn't really like the idea of leaving the girls all alone again. Perhaps it would be better if they came.

The girls were thrilled. They cleared away the breakfast things and washed up. They prepared a meal to take with them. It was a very good thing they had discovered that store cave — they now had plenty of food of all kinds. They did hope the seaplane wouldn't take everything away!

They all got into the boat. The boys rowed off, and were careful to keep to the side opposite the cave when they came to the second island. They rowed quickly over the space of water separating that island from the third one, and came to the farthest tip of it. Here there was a tiny beach with steep, overhanging cliffs — so overhanging that it almost seemed as if a big piece was about to fall off!

"Just the place," said Andy, pulling into the tiny beach. "Jump out, girls. Take the food with you. Give a hand with the boat, Tom. We'll run it up the beach and put it right under that dangerous piece of cliff. It will be well hidden there."

They put the boat there and looked at it. The end of it jutted out and could be seen. Jill ran to a seaweed-covered rock and pulled off handfuls of the weed.

"Let's make the boat into a rock!" she said, with a laugh. "Cover it with seaweed!"

"Jolly good idea!" said Andy. "I didn't know girls could have such good ideas!"

"You wait and see what fine ideas we have!" said Mary. They all pulled at the seaweed, and soon the boat was nicely draped and looked so exactly like a seaweed-covered rock that no one could possibly guess it wasn't, even if they passed quite near it.

"That's good," said Andy. "Now we'll make our way very carefully across this end of the island till we come to the little cove where we took our boat from. We'll just peep over the cliff and see if there's anyone there looking as though they have missed the boat! Then we'll crawl to the top of the next cliff that overlooks the submarine bay, and Tom shall take a few pictures."

Everything went well. Keeping close to tall bushes of gorse and bramble, the four children crept over the tip of the island and soon came to the cliff below which was the boat-cove. Cautiously Andy parted some bramble sprays and peeped down to the beach below.

There were the rest of the little boats, still upturned. Nobody was about at all. As far as Andy could see, the stolen boat had not been missed. Good!

Andy let the rest of the children look down to the beach. Tom was pleased. "As long as our boat isn't missed we are all right," he said. "I should think the enemy feel they are so safe here that it just doesn't enter their heads that a boat might be taken. I don't believe they'll ever miss it."

"I hope you're right," said Andy. "But it doesn't do to think the enemy is careless or stupid. We must think they are smart and clever, and try to be the same ourselves. Now let's wriggle along to the next bit of cliff—and you girls can see the submarines. That will be a sight for you!"

Going very slowly and cautiously indeed the four of them made their way under bushes and bracken to the top of the next cliff. They all lay on their tummies and peeped between the tall bracken. The girls drew a long breath of surprise.

"Golly!" said Jill. "One—two—three—four—five—six—seven—however many submarines are there? And all of them marked with the crooked cross."

"An enemy submarine base so near our own land!" said Mary. "And nobody knows it!"

"Where's your camera, Tom?" whispered Andy. Tom had it round his shoulder. Carefully he took it out of its waterproof case and set it for taking distant pictures.

"It's got the seaplane on the first two negatives," said the boy in a low tone. "I'll fill up the rest of the film with photos of the submarines. The pictures can easily be made larger when we get home. Then nobody can disbelieve us, or say we made it all up!"

Click! went the camera. "One picture taken," said Tom. "I got in those two big submarines together, just over there."

Click! Click! Click! Click! Tom was as careful as he could be to take good photographs. Soon the whole film was used. "I'll wait till I get back to the hut and then I'll wind off the film in a dark corner," said the boy. "That's a spot of good work done!"

He put the camera back into its case and strapped it up. The four children lay and looked at the nest of submarines in the water below. Another came slipping in as they watched. Two slipped out.

"Gone to sink some more of our ships, I suppose," said Andy angrily. "If only I could stop them! But we will clean up the whole lot once we get the news back

home. I guess we'll have a battleship or two sent out here."

"Where will it be safe to have something to eat?" asked Tom. "I do feel hungry."

"I wish I had five pence for every time I've heard Tom say that," said Jill, with a giggle.

"Well, I only say what the rest of you are thinking!" said Tom. "I bet you're all hungry!"

They were! Andy found a little bracken dell not far from the top of the cliff. Here the bracken was taller than the children, and once they had settled themselves down below the tall fronds nobody could possibly see them either from above or passing by.

They ate a good meal and enjoyed it. They lay on their backs and looked between the fronds at the blue sky. It was marvellous that the weather was still so good. It would have been miserable if it had rained all the time.

"Now we'd better get back," said Andy.

"Oh, why?" asked Jill, lazily. "I was almost asleep."

"I'll tell you why!" said Andy. "Supposing that stolen boat is missed — well, the first place searched would be this island! And we'd be found. No — the best thing for us to do is to get back now, wait till the seaplane has left and then go straight to the store-cave and fill our boat with food. Then we'll start off tonight."

"All right. We'll come along now then," said Jill, getting up. They took one last peep at the submarine bay and another at the boat-cove. Then they made their way very cautiously back to the tiny beach where they had hidden their boat.

It was still there, beautifully draped with seaweed. Nobody had discovered it! The children dragged it down to the waves and jumped into it. Andy pushed it out.

They took turns at rowing. They were half-way round the second island, on the coast opposite to the one where the store-cave was, when a dreadful thing happened.

The seaplane chose that minute to leave the water by the second island and to rise into the air, ready to fly off!

The children had no time to rush their boat into shore and hide. They were out on the sea, clearly to be seen!

"Crouch down flat in the boat, so that the pilot may perhaps think there's nobody in it," ordered Andy. They shipped the oars quickly and crouched down. The seaplane rose up high, and the children hardly dared to breathe. They did so hope it would fly off without noticing them.

But it suddenly altered its course and began to circle round, coming down lower. It flew down low enough to examine the boat, and then, rising high, flew over the third island, and then flew down to the submarine bay.

Andy sat up, his face rather pale under its brown.

"That's done it," he said. "They saw us! Now they'll count their boats—find there's one missing—and come to look for us!"

TOM DISAPPEARS

The children looked at one another in the greatest dismay. To think the seaplane should have flown over just at that very moment! It was too bad.

"Well, we can't sit here looking at one another," said Andy, in a brave voice. "We've got to do something quickly. But what? I can't seem to think!"

Nobody could think what to do. Andy longed desperately for some grown-up who could take command and tell him what would be the best thing to do. But there was no grown-up. This was something he had to decide himself—and he must decide well, because the two girls were in his care.

"We had better row straight round to the store-cave and fill the boat with food whilst we can," he said at last. "Then we'll start out straightaway and hope that the seaplane won't spot us out on the sea. It's the only thing to do."

It was a long row round to the cave, but they got there at last, quite tired out. There was nobody about. They beached the boat and jumped out. It was not long before they were in the Round Cave, carrying out stacks of tins and boxes to the boat.

"Golly! We've got enough food to last for weeks!" said Tom.

"We may need it!" said Andy. "Goodness knows how far it is back home. I've not much idea of the right direction either, but I shall do my best."

Tom staggered out to the boat with heaps of things. Andy looked at the pile of food at the end of the boat and nodded his head.

"That's enough," he said. "We don't want to make the boat too heavy to row! Get in!"

They all got in. They rowed out beyond the reef of rocks where they had found a way in and then towards their own island. Andy wanted to get the rugs, for he was sure they would be bitterly cold at night.

"You girls jump out and go and fetch all the warm things you can find," said Andy. "And bring a cup or two and a knife. I've got a tin-opener."

The girls sped off to the shack in the hollow—and whilst they were gone the boys heard the sound they dreaded to hear—the noise of seaplane engines booming over the water!

"There it comes again!" said Andy angrily. "Always at the wrong moment. Lie down flat, Tom. I hope the girls will have the sense to do the same!"

The seaplane zoomed down low over the island, as if it were hunting for someone. Then it droned over the sea, and flew round in great circles. Andy lifted his head and watched it.

"You know what it's doing?" he said. "It's flying round hunting the sea for our boat—just as a hawk flies over fields hunting for mice! It's a good thing we didn't set out straightaway. I think now we'd better wait for the night to come—and then set out in the darkness. We should be seen as easily as anything if we try to go now."

They waited till the drone of the plane's engines was far away. It was hunting the waters everywhere for the stolen boat. Andy stood up and yelled to the girls, who were lying flat under a bush.

"It's gone for the moment. Help us to take out these goods and hide them. If the boat is discovered here and taken away, and we are made prisoners on this island, we shall at least be sure of stores!"

"If we are able to start out tonight we can easily put back the food," said Tom. They all worked hard, and buried the tins and boxes under some loose sand at the top of the beach. They pulled the boat farther up the beach and then sat down to rest, hot and tired.

And then poor Tom gave a squeal of dismay. The others jumped and looked at him in fright. "Whatever's the matter?" asked Andy.

"My camera!" said Tom, his face a picture of horror. "My camera—with all those pictures I took! I left it in the store-cave."

"Left it in the *store*-cave!" said everyone. "Whatever for?"

"Well, I was afraid I'd bump it against the rocks, carrying it up and down those passages," said Tom. "So I took it off for a minute, meaning to put it on when we went. And I forgot."

"You fathead!" said Jill.

"Don't call me that," said poor Tom, looking almost ready to cry.

"Well, fathead is too good a name," said Mary. "Thinhead would be better. You can't possibly have got any brains if you do a thing like that, so you must be a thinhead with no brains at all."

Tom went very red. He blinked his eyes and swallowed a lump that had suddenly come into his throat. He knew how valuable the pictures were that he had taken. How *could* he have come to forget his camera like that?

"Cheer up, Tom," said Andy. "I know what you feel

like. I felt just like that when I found I'd forgotten to bring the anchor in the ship. It's awful."

Tom was grateful to Andy for not scolding him. But all the same he felt really dreadful. They had gone to such a lot of trouble to get those photographs—and now all because of his carelessness they had been left behind.

"I vote we have something to eat," said Andy, thinking that would cheer Tom up. But it didn't. For once in a way Tom had no appetite at all. He couldn't eat a thing. He sat nearby looking gloomily at the others.

The seaplane did not come back. The children sat and waited for the evening to come, when they might start. Jill yawned. "I must do something for the next two or three hours," she said, "or I shall fall asleep. I think I'll take the kettle and keep filling it with water at the spring, and bring it back to the boat. There's a big water-barrel there, and we could fill it with water."

"Good idea," said Andy. "You and Mary do that. I think I'll just wander up to the bush where we put the sail and see if it's still there. I don't think I've time to rig up some kind of a mast in this little boat so the sail won't be any good. But it might be useful to cover us with if it should happen to pour with rain."

The girls went off. Andy nodded to Tom, who was still looking gloomy, and went across the island to the bush where he had put the sail.

Tom was left alone. "They don't want me with them," thought the boy, quite wrongly. "They think I'm awful. *I* think I'm awful too! Oh, dear—if only I could get my camera."

He thought of the reef of rocks that led to the second island. It wasn't a bit of use trying to climb over them because the tide was getting high now.

But then he thought of the boat! It really wasn't a great distance to row to the cave, from the beach where he was. How pleased the others would be, if he got back his camera!

The boy did not stop to think. He dragged the boat down the beach by himself, though he nearly pulled his arms out, doing it! He pushed ·it into the water and jumped in. He took the oars and began to row quickly round to the second island. He would land on the shore then, run quickly to the cave and get his camera.

"Then I'll be back here with it almost before the others know I'm gone!" he thought.

Nobody would have known what Tom had done if Andy had not happened to look round as he went over the little island to find the old sail. To his enormous astonishment he saw their boat being rowed away!

He could not see that the one in it was Tom, and for a moment he stood still, wondering what had happened. Was it another boat, not their own? He ran quickly to find out.

He soon saw that it was their own boat. He saw where Tom had dragged it down the beach. He could just see the boat rounding the corner of a cliff now.

"That was Tom all right," said Andy to himself. The girls came back at that moment and shouted to Andy.

"What's the matter? Why do you look like that? Where's the boat?"

"Tom's gone off with it," said Andy angrily.

"*Tom!* Whatever do you mean, Andy?" asked Jill in the greatest surprise.

"I suppose he felt upset about leaving his camera behind and he's gone to get it by himself," said Andy.

92

"He really is a fathead. He may be seen and caught.
I'm quite sure someone will be hunting for us soon.
Really, I could shake Tom till his teeth rattled!"

The girls stared at Andy in dismay. They did not at
all like the idea of their brother going off alone in the
boat. Well—they would just have to wait patiently till
Tom came back. It should not really take him a very
long time. The sun was sinking now. He should be back
by the time it was gone. Then they could all start out
again and try to make for home.

Jill set the kettle of water down on the beach. She felt
tired. Mary sat down beside her and looked out over the

water for Tom to come back. Andy walked up and down impatiently. He could understand that Tom longed to get back his camera and put himself right with the others so that they no longer thought him careless and silly—but he did wish he hadn't gone off in their precious boat!

The three children waited and waited. The sun sank lower. It disappeared over the sky-line and the first stars glimmered in the darkening sky.

And still Tom was not back. The girls could no longer see anything on the sea, which was now dark. They could only sit and listen for the plash of oars.

"Tom ought to be back by now," said Andy anxiously. "He's had plenty of time to get a dozen cameras! Whatever is he doing?"

Nobody knew. They sat there on the chilly beach, anxious and worried. If only, only Tom would come back! Nobody would scold him. Nobody would grumble at him. They just wanted him to come.

"I should think he's been caught," said Andy at last. "There can't be any other reason why he's not back. *Now* we're in a pretty fix! No Tom—and no boat!"

XIV

A PRISONER IN THE CAVE

What had happened to Tom? A great many things. He had rowed safely to the beach where the caves lay hidden in the cliff behind. He had dragged the boat up the sand and had gone into the first cave. He stumbled through the rocky archway and into the queer Round Cave, which was so full of food.

He had no torch, so he had to feel around in the dark for his camera. It took him a long time to find it.

"Where *did* I put it?" wondered the boy anxiously. "Oh, if only I had a match!"

But he hadn't. He felt over tins and boxes—and at last his hand fell on the box-like shape of his camera, safe in its waterproof covering!

"Good," Tom thought. "Now I'll just rush down to the boat and row back. I really must be quick or the others will be worried."

But Tom had a dreadful shock as he was about to make his way out of the Round Cave back to the beach. He heard voices!

The boy stood perfectly still, his heart beating fast. Whose voices were these?

They came nearer. Men were on the beach outside! Men had found his boat! Was it the enemy?

Alas for poor Tom—it *was* the enemy! Tom had not heard the boom of the seaplane coming down on the water. He had not seen a rubber boat putting off hurriedly to the cave. But now he could hear the voices of the men.

They had seen the boat on the beach, and had come to examine it. They soon saw that it was the stolen boat, which had now been missed and was being searched for.

The men knew at once where the owner of the boat was—in the cave! And they were going to search for him there.

Tom darted back into the Round Cave and hid behind a big pile of boxes. He felt quite certain he would be found—and as he crouched there, trembling and excited, he made up his mind very, *very* firmly that he would not say how many others had come to the islands with him. He would make the men think that he was the only one —then maybe the other three would not be hunted for.

"I've been a perfect silly to run into danger like this," thought poor Tom. "But, at any rate, I can save the others from being hunted for, perhaps."

The men came into the Round Cave. They had powerful torches which they flashed around—and almost at once they saw Tom's feet sticking out from behind a box.

They dragged him out and stood him up. They seemed most astonished to find only a boy. They had expected a man. They talked quickly among themselves in a language that Tom could not understand.

Then one man, who could talk English, spoke to Tom. "How did you get to this island?"

"I set off in a sailing-boat and a storm blew up and wrecked me," said Tom. "You can see my boat off the coast of the next island, if you look."

"Is there anyone else with you on this island?" asked the man. "Speak the truth."

Tom could reply quite truthfully that there *was* no one else with him on the island!

Thank goodness, the others were on the first island!

"There isn't anyone else here with me," he answered. "Search the cave, and see!"

The men did search the cave again, but found nobody, of course. They did not seem satisfied, however. Tom could see that they felt sure there were others to find.

"How did you find this cave?" asked the man who spoke English.

"By accident," said Tom.

"And I suppose you also found our boat by accident, and saw the submarines by accident?" said the man, in a very nasty voice. "Are you sure there is no one else here with you?"

"Quite sure," said Tom. "Wouldn't you see them in the cave, if there were?"

"We shall not take your word for it," said the man, with a horrid laugh. "We shall search this island and both those next to it—and if we find anyone else, you will be very, very sorry for yourself!"

"You won't find anyone!" said Tom, hoping to goodness that they wouldn't, and wishing he could warn Andy and the girls somehow. "Are you going to keep me prisoner?"

"We certainly are," said the man. "And as you seem so fond of this cave, we'll let you stay here! You've food to eat—and you won't be able to do any spying round if you're here in this cave! We shall put a man on guard at the entrance—so if you try to get out, or anyone else tries to get in, you'll be caught. Our man will be well hidden behind a rock at the entrance—and if any friends of yours try to rescue you, they will get a shock!"

Tom listened, his heart sinking into his shoes. What an idiot he had been! He was to be a prisoner—and if the

97

others tried to find him they would be made prisoners too, for they would never guess a sentry was hidden behind the rocks, watching for them.

Tom sat down on a box. He would not cry. He would not show the men how frightened and worried he was. His face was brave and bold—but inside he felt as if he was crying buckets of tears! If only, only he could get word to Andy!

There was nothing he could do—nothing! He could only sit there in the cave, surrounded by marvellous food that he felt too worried even to look at, and think about the others. Poor Tom! It was a dreadful punishment for being careless enough to forget his camera, and foolish enough to try and fetch it!

The men left a lamp in the cave for Tom. It was getting late and the boy was tired—but he could not sleep. He heard the men go out, and he knew a sentry had been placed by the rocks. He could not hope to escape. But he could try!

So, very quietly, he made his way through the rocky archway, down to the shore-cave below. But his feet set the stones moving here and there, and a voice came out of the darkness.

He could not understand what was said to him, but the voice was so stern that the boy fled back to the Round Cave at once. It wasn't a bit of good trying to escape.

He sat down again and wondered about the others. What were they thinking and doing? Would they guess he had gone to fetch his camera, and come to look for him when the tide uncovered the rocks next day? If so, they would certainly be caught.

Andy and the girls sat up until they could keep awake no longer. They went back to the shack, curled up on their beds, and slept restlessly, worrying about Tom and the lost boat.

In the morning, Andy went out cautiously, wondering if the enemy had already landed a boat on their island to hunt for them. But he could see nothing strange.

He sat talking to the girls as they prepared breakfast. "Tom is certainly caught," he said. "There's no doubt about that, I'm afraid. Well, I know enough of Tom to know that he won't say *we* are here, too. He won't give us away. But they will certainly come and hunt for anyone else who might be here. We have to do two things—hide ourselves so that we can't *possibly* be found—and then think of some way of rescuing Tom."

"Oh dear! It seems quite impossible," said Jill, feeling very worried. Mary began to cry.

"Don't cry, Mary," said Andy, putting his arm round her. "We have to be brave now. We are British children, and so we have plenty of courage and heaps of ideas. We must all think hard and see what we can do to trick the enemy."

"But, Andy, how can we hide on this bare island?" said Mary, drying her eyes and blinking away her tears. "They will beat all through the bracken and heather. There are no good trees to hide in. Not a single cave. Really, there isn't anywhere at all!"

"You're right, Mary," said Andy. "It's going to be very difficult. But we must think of *some*thing. You see, if only we can hide and not be found we can *some*how think of a way to rescue Tom—but if we are found we can't help Tom, and won't be able to escape and tell our secret!"

"Yes—it's very, very important," said Jill thoughtfully. "Let's think of ways of hiding. The bracken is no use at all, is it?"

"Not a bit of use," said Andy. "I did think we might perhaps wade out to the ship and hide down in the cabin —but I know they would look there."

"Could we hide in the shack?" asked Mary. "Pile the the heather over ourselves, or something?"

"No," said Andy. "We should be discovered there at once. And there's no place in any of the other buildings. I wish we knew of a cave or something like that."

"It's a good thing we've got plenty of food hidden in the sand," said Jill. "If we *can* manage to hide ourselves away we need not starve! We've only got to go and dig up that store of food!"

"Yes—that's very lucky," said Andy. "I say, listen! That's the sound of a motor-boat, isn't it?"

Andy crept out to see, keeping well under cover. Yes —there was a motor-boat coming round the corner of the island—a motor-boat with five men in it!

"They're coming!" whispered Andy. "They're in a motor-boat. Quick—where shall we hide!"

"We'd better rush over to the opposite side of the island," said Jill, her face pale. "The first place they'll hunt is this side, where they land. Quick, Mary!"

The three children slipped out of the shack and made their way up the rocky path. They were just out of sight when the motor-boat landed on the beach. They would be able to reach the other side of the island unseen but what could they do there? The shore there was nothing but rocks and sand—they would be found in two minutes!

THE ISLAND IS SEARCHED

Andy and the girls did not take long to reach the opposite shore of the island. They slid down the steep cliff there and reached the beach. It was sandy, but at one side was a mass of seaweed-covered rocks. It was impossible to hide behind them, for a moment's search would at once discover them.

They looked at one another in despair. "Any good wading out to sea and keeping under water?" asked Jill.

"No," said Andy, "we'd have to keep popping our heads up to breathe and we'd be seen at once."

Jill stared at the rocks nearby and then she gave such a squeal that Andy and Mary jumped in fright.

"Sh!" said Andy angrily. "You'll be heard. Whatever's the matter?"

"I've thought of how to hide!" said Jill breathlessly. "It's the same idea I had for hiding that boat. Can't we cover ourselves with sand, and then drape ourselves with seaweed, to look like rocks? We could go and lie down beside those rocks, and if we were well covered with weeds we'd look exactly like them!"

"Golly! That *is* an idea!" said Andy at once. "Quick! I'll cover you girls with sand at once. Come over here."

The three ran to the rocks. The tide was out, and the sand was hard but damp. Andy made the girls lie down together, and then he piled sand high over them, leaving a space over their noses for breathing. He only had his hands to do this, so it was hard work. Then he dragged great handfuls of seaweed from the rocks and threw it over the sandy mound. When he had finished, the girls looked exactly like the seaweed-covered rocks nearby! It was really marvellous.

Andy covered with loose seaweed the untidy places he had made in the sand. Then he began to make a hole for himself, and to cover himself too. He draped himself with piles of seaweed and then poked up his head to look at the girls.

He really didn't know which of the rocks they were! He simply couldn't tell! He looked and looked — but not until one of the rocks moved a little did he see that it was the girls!

"Jill! Mary!" he called in a low voice. "As soon as you hear me screaming like a gull you must lie absolutely still. You look marvellous! I didn't know which rock you were till one of you moved."

"Andy, I'm afraid one of the men might tread on me," said Mary, in a frightened voice.

"Well, let him!" said Andy. "I don't advise you to call out and ask him not to walk on you!"

There was a little giggle from the nearby rock. Although the girls were frightened they could still see a joke. They all lay quietly for a time and then Andy heard voices coming near. He cried like a seagull, and the girls then lay so still that not even the tiniest bit of seaweed above them moved at all.

The men slid down to the sandy shore, calling to one another in loud voices. Andy could not understand anything they said. All the children's hearts beat loudly and Jill wondered if hers could possibly be heard. It seemed to her to be thumping as loudly as a hammer.

The men stood on the beach and looked round. One

shouted something to the others and began to walk over to the rocks. Andy felt most alarmed.

"I do hope we look like real rocks," he thought. "And I hope nobody treads on us—we should be found at once if that happened—to say nothing of being hurt!"

The man came nearer. He stood near Andy and took out a packet of cigarettes. Andy heard him strike a match and knew that he had lighted a cigarette.

The man threw the empty cigarette packet on to the sand, and puffed at his cigarette. A young gull, seeing the man throw the packet away, thought that it might be a piece of bread. It flew down to see, crying "Ee-oo, ee-oo, ee-oo!" very loudly.

The other gulls heard it and soared round in circles, wondering if there was any food to find. The young gull landed on the sand and stood looking at the packet, hardly daring to go nearer to peck it, for it was too close to the man.

The other gulls flew down—and two stood on Andy and one stood on the girls! The children looked so exactly like rocks that the gulls really thought they were!

One gull thought the rock felt unusually soft and warm and he bent down his head and pecked at it. He pecked Andy's knee and the boy nearly gave a yell.

The men joined the one who was smoking a cigarette. They did not even bother to walk over the rocks. One man said that it was plain there could be nobody hiding there for the gulls would not stand about as they were doing if there was anyone hiding. They would know it and be suspicious.

For some time the men stood talking and smoking. Then they turned to go up the cliff again. One walked so near Andy that the boy could feel the thud of his footfall close by. Up the cliff climbed the men and disappeared over the top.

Andy cautiously lifted his head after a while and looked around. There was no one to be seen.

The boy felt that it would be safer if they all stayed where they were for some time longer—but he felt cold and damp, and he was afraid that the girls would catch a dreadful chill.

"Mary! Jill!" he called, in a low voice. "I think the men are gone, but we must still be careful. Slowly and carefully take off the weed and shake yourselves free of the sand. Be ready to lie still at once if I say so."

But there was no need to say so—the men did not come back to the beach. The three children shook off the damp sand, threw the seaweed over the places where they had been lying and ran quickly to the shelter of the cliff, where no one could see them, if they looked over.

The gulls flew off in the greatest surprise and alarm. They could not understand rocks turning into children so suddenly. The young gull made up its mind that it would never land on a rock again—just suppose it changed into a person!

"Golly!" said Andy, as they stood shivering under the cliff. "That was a narrow escape! One man very nearly trod on my hand under the sand!"

"What have you done to your knee, Andy?" asked Jill, pointing to where Andy's knee was bleeding.

"A gull pecked me there," said Andy, mopping his knee. "It's nothing much. I say, wasn't it funny when the gulls thought we were rocks and came and stood on us! They were a great help!"

"One gull stood nearly on my face," said Jill. "I didn't like it very much."

"I do feel cold," said Mary, shivering and shaking. "It was horrid to be covered with damp sand for so long."

She sneezed. Andy looked at her anxiously. It would never do for any of them to be ill just now. He made up his mind quickly.

"The men may be off the island now," he said. "I'll go and see. If they are we'll all tear across to the hut, light the stove inside and dry ourselves. We'll make some hot cocoa and get really warm."

The girls thought that was a splendid idea. Andy set off up the cliff. "Stay here till you hear my seagull cry," he said. "Then come as quickly as you can."

He came to the top of the cliff. Then, keeping to the thick bracken, he made his way to the other side of the island, looking out for any signs of the men. He went right across the island, and came to the hollow where the old buildings were—and he saw the motor-boat putting off from the shore! The men had given up the hunt and were going back to the third island. They had already searched the second one and had found nobody but Tom.

Andy tore back to the girls. He screeched like a gull. The girls at once climbed the cliff and ran across the island, feeling a little warmer as they ran. Andy was in the shack, and the stove was lighted. It gave out a welcome heat.

"Take off your damp things and wrap yourself in the rugs," said Andy, who was already walking about in a rug himself and looked like a Red Indian. "I'm making some cocoa."

In ten minutes' time all the children felt warm and lively. The stove dried their things, and the hot cocoa warmed them well. Nobody sneezed again and Andy began to hope that their long stay under the damp sand wouldn't give anyone a chill after all.

"Andy, what are you going to do now?" asked Jill, sipping her cocoa. "We've got plenty of food, luckily, because we buried it all in the sand at the top of the beach out there—but we can't get away, because our boat's gone and we've lost Tom. Have we got to stay here for the rest of our lives?"

"Don't be silly, Jill," said Andy. "Let's tackle one thing at a time, for goodness' sake. We've done the most important thing so far—hidden ourselves so well that

we weren't found—and now we'll do the next most important thing—we'll rescue Tom! After that we'll think how to escape—but one thing at a time, please, and no worrying about what's going to happen. If we get worried, we'll get frightened, and nobody is any use when they're frightened. We've all got plenty of courage and we'll use it!"

Jill and Mary cheered up at Andy's brave words. "I *would* like to rescue poor Tom," said Jill. "He will be so lonely and upset. Where do you suppose he is?"

"In the cave where he left his camera, I expect," said Andy, pouring himself out another cup of cocoa. "And I'm pretty certain there'll be a guard somewhere at the entrance, for if there were not Tom would soon escape— so we won't run into trouble—we'll see if there isn't some other way of rescuing Tom."

"But how can there be?" asked Jill.

"I don't know yet," said Andy. "But I do know this— we thought it was impossible to hide safely on this bare little island—yet we did it! And so, though it sounds impossible to rescue Tom, there may be a way if we think hard enough. So now—let's all think hard!"

XVI

AN EXCITING DISCOVERY

Nobody could think how to rescue Tom. After all, if there was someone guarding the cave-entrance, how could Andy possibly get in without being seen?

The boy gave it up after a time, and for a change he set the gramophone going. There was only one record that was not broken, and that was the one with the lullaby on one side and the nursery rhymes on the other. The girls listened, rather bored, for they had heard that record scores of times since they had come to the island.

"Turn it off, Andy," said Jill. "If I hear that voice crooning that lullaby any more I shall go to sleep!"

Andy switched off the gramophone and went to the doorway of the shack. He was not afraid of the men coming back again for he was sure they thought there was no one on *this* island, at any rate.

A thought came into Andy's head. He went back to the girls.

"I think it would be a good thing if I crossed to the second island tonight, when it's dark," he said. "I might be able to get into touch with Tom somehow and hear what has happened, even if I can't rescue him."

"Oh, Andy—we shall be left all alone," said Mary in dismay.

"*We* don't mind that, if Andy can help Tom," said Jill. "We'll stay here in the hut, Andy, and try to sleep whilst you go. But do be careful, won't you?"

"I'll be careful," said Andy. "I don't want to be made

109

a prisoner, too—but you needn't be afraid of that! No enemy can catch *me*!"

So that night, when he had only the starlight to guide him, for the moon was not up, Andy crossed the line of rocks to the second island. He went very cautiously, for he did not want a single sound to come to the ears of anyone on the cave-beach.

He waded through the shallow water to the sand at the nearer end of the beach. He stood there, listening— and not very far off, close against the cliff where the cave-entrance was, he heard a cough!

"Oho!" said Andy to himself. "Thanks for that cough, dear sentry! I now know exactly where you are. You are behind the big rock at the cave opening. Well, I shall not go near you!"

The boy stood quite still for a while, listening. The sentry most obligingly cleared his throat and coughed again very loudly. Andy grinned. He made his way carefully round the end of the cliff and then began to climb up, feeling his way cautiously. The cliff there was not very steep, and Andy was soon at the top. He had not made a single sound.

He found a little hollow where heather and gorse grew thickly. He crept under an overhanging piece of bush, piled the heather beneath him, and slept peacefully. He knew he could do nothing till morning came, and he could see where he was.

The sun rose and Andy awoke. He was stiff and he stretched himself and yawned. He was hungry, but there was nothing for him to eat but bilberries.

He wriggled carefully to the edge of the cliff and looked over. Almost below him was the sentry he had heard last night, behind a rock at the cave-entrance. As

Andy looked down he saw a boat coming to the shore, and a man stepped off, and walked up the beach to change places with the sentry. They stood talking for a while and then the first sentry went to the boat, yawning, and the new one settled down to his task of waiting and watching.

Andy sat and thought. He wriggled back to a place where he imagined he must be exactly over the Round Cave. He wondered if Tom could hear him, if he drummed on the ground with his feet. After all, the boy could not be very far below, for the Round Cave was fairly high up in the cliff.

And then a most extraordinary thing happened — so startling that Andy's heart jumped almost out of his body!

A groan came from somewhere under his legs! Andy was lying on the heather, and when the groan came, he shot his legs up beneath him and stared at the place where the groan had come from as if he simply couldn't believe his eyes or ears!

A smaller groan sounded, more like a long yawn. Andy stared at the heather, and wondered if his ears could be right! Heather couldn't yawn or groan! Then what was it?

Very cautiously and gently, the boy turned himself about and began to feel in the heather. He pulled it to one side, and to his enormous astonishment he found a hole below the roots of the heather — a hole that must lead down to the Round Cave for Andy reckoned that he must be exactly over that cave.

Andy felt so excited that he began to tremble. "No wonder that cave didn't smell as musty and stuffy as we expected it to," he thought. "There is an air-hole leading right down to it! Golly! I wonder if there's any chance of rescuing Tom this way."

He pulled up the heather and examined the hole. The earth was dry and sandy. Andy scraped away hard, and found that it was quite easy to make it bigger. Just suppose he could make it big enough to get down—or for Tom to get up!

"I knew there'd be a way if we didn't give up hope!" thought the excited boy. "I just knew it!"

He crawled to the top of the cliff and looked over it. The sentry was there still, and he was busy eating his breakfast. He was all right for some time.

Andy crawled back to the hole. He scraped about a little more, and then lay down with his face in the hole. It seemed to go down and down into the darkness.

Andy spoke in a low voice. "Tom! Are you there?"

And was Tom there? Yes, he was! He had been in the Round Cave, alone and lonely, ever since he had been caught. It had seemed ages to him. The boy had worried dreadfully about the others. He had eaten a little of the food around him, but he had no appetite now. He was miserable and frightened, though he would not show this to any of the sentries who occasionally came up the rocky passage-way to see if he was all right.

The man who could speak English had come to see him the evening before.

"We have searched the first island and this one," he had told Tom. "We have found your shack—and we have found your friends, too!"

Tom's heart sank when he heard this. The man was really telling an untruth, hoping to trap Tom into saying something that would show him there *were* others to be found. But Tom said nothing.

"I tell you we have found your friends," said the man. "They fought hard but they have been captured."

Tom stared at the man in surprise. He knew quite well that the girls would not fight men. What did this man mean? Could he be telling an untruth?

Then Tom suddenly knew that the man was hoping to trap him into saying something about the others. This man did not know that the "others" were only two girls and a boy. He did not even know for certain that there *were* any others!

"Well, two can play at a game of pretend like that!" thought the boy. So he put on a face of great surprise and said:

"Golly! *Are* there others on these islands then? I wish I'd known! I could have asked them for help!"

The man looked surprised. So perhaps this boy had no friends then? Could it be that he was really alone? The man did not know what to think. He said no more but turned and went out of the cave. Tom couldn't help feeling pleased. The man had thought he might trap him—but he felt sure *he* had tricked the man!

It was very lonely in the Round Cave. Tom slept heavily all the night through, but found the day very, very dull.

He sat on a box and groaned deeply. Then he yawned loudly. He was bored. He was lonely.

He sat there, doing nothing; and then he heard a very peculiar noise above his head—a kind of scraping noise. Tom wondered what it could be.

"Perhaps it's a rabbit or something," he thought. "But no—it couldn't be. The roof of the cave is of rock."

The scraping noise went on—and then something happened that made Tom leap up in fright.

A strange hollow voice came into the cave from somewhere! It ran all round the cave and Tom could just make out the words. The funny deep voice said, "Tom! Are you there?"

It was really Andy's voice, of course, coming down the hole to the cave—and the hole had made it sound deep and strange, not a bit like Andy's.

Tom trembled and said nothing. He couldn't understand this queer voice suddenly coming into the cave. So Andy spoke again.

"Tom! It's Andy speaking. Are you there?"

The voice rumbled round the cave—but this time Tom was not so scared. Could it really be Andy, somehow managing to speak to him? He answered as loudly as he dared.

"I'm here! In the Round Cave!"

Tom's voice came up to Andy, all muddled and jumbled, for Tom was not near the opening of the hole. Andy could not make out what he said, but he knew it was Tom speaking.

"Good!" he thought. "Tom's in there all right. I'll speak to him again and see if I can find out what's happened to him."

So once more Andy's voice came rumbling down into the cave. "Tom! I'm speaking down a hole that must somehow lead into your cave. See if you can find it and speak up it. I can't hear you properly. But whatever you do, don't let anyone hear you speaking to me."

Tom felt excited. Good old Andy! He got up and began to hunt around for the hole that led upwards to Andy. He must find it, he simply must!

114

XVII

A MARVELLOUS ESCAPE

Tom picked up the lamp and hunted around the cave. As he was doing this he heard the steps of the sentry coming up the rocky passage to the Round Cave. At once Tom sat down and began to sing loudly the lullaby that was on the unbroken gramophone record.

"Hush! Hush! Hush! You mustn't say a word! It's time for hush-a-bye, My little sleepy bird!"

These were the words of the rather silly lullaby song on the record. But they did very well indeed for a warning to Andy not to say anything for a moment! The sentry heard the boy singing, peeped in at him, said something that Tom didn't in the least understand, and went out again. He seemed surprised that the boy should sing. Tom went on singing the lullaby for a long time till he felt quite sure the sentry was not coming back.

Then he stopped singing and hurriedly began to hunt for the hole again. It didn't seem to be anywhere! The roof of the cave was not very high, and by standing on boxes and tins Tom could examine nearly every inch of it. But he could not find a hole that led upwards.

Andy's voice came booming down again: "Tom! Have you found the hole?"

The voice was so near Tom's ear that the boy nearly fell off the box he was standing on. He held up the lamp to the place where the voice came from. It was at the point where roof and wall met, at the back. The roof was of rock—but the wall just there was only of sand. Tom put his hand up and felt a cold draught blowing down the hole.

"Andy! I've found the hole!" he said, putting his head to it. "I say—tell me what's happened."

In low voices the two boys told one another all that had happened. Tom was very excited when he heard how the others had pretended to be seaweed-covered rocks.

"I _won_dered how you would hide," he said. "I couldn't _think_ what you would do! Oh, Andy, I'm glad you're safe."

"Well, Tom, the next thing to do is to rescue _you_," said Andy. "I'm wondering if we can use this hole. What's it like at your end?"

"Rather small," said Tom. "I couldn't get up it unless I could make it larger. What's it like at your end?"

"I can easily make it as large as I like by scraping at it," said Andy. "Can you make your end large, too, do you think?"

Tom scraped at it with his hands. He could easily scrape the wall away, but not the roof. "I might perhaps be able to," he said. "But I'd want something to do it with—I've nothing but my hands."

"I've nothing but my hands either," said Andy, "and they are bleeding already from scraping at the soil. Listen, Tom—I shall go back to the girls soon, when the rocks are uncovered, but I can't wait till night. I must go now whilst the tide is low. So I want you to call to the sentry and pretend that you want his help in undoing a tin of food or something. See? Then whilst he is in the cave with you, I'll creep over the rocks safely without being seen, and get back."

"All right," said Tom. "What will you do then?"

"I'll collect something for us to work at the soil with,"

116

said Andy. "And I'll bring it back tonight. Then maybe we can make the hole large enough for you to crawl up. I don't think it's more than about six feet long. Now, wait to hear my seagull call, Tom—then yell for the sentry, and I'll make a dash for the rocks as soon as I see him go into the cave."

Everything worked well. When Tom heard Andy's seagull cry he shouted for the sentry, and the man went into the cave to see what was the matter.

He found that Tom had got a large tin of tongue, and seemed to have lost the tin-opener. The sentry hadn't one either, and he spent a very long time trying to open the tin with his pocket-knife. He ended in cutting his thumb very badly, and Tom produced a handkerchief and spent a long time binding up the man's thumb, glad to keep him in the cave so long.

Andy had plenty of time to escape back over the rocks. He knew them well now, and leapt from rock to rock easily. He was back in the shack in no time, it seemed!

The girls were thrilled to see him and he had to sit and tell them all he had done at least four or five times. When they heard about the hole leading down to the Round Cave the girls were tremendously excited.

"So you see," finished Andy, "I plan to get Tom out that way tonight—and I must take back with me something to dig and scrape with."

"Here's an old bit of wood with some jolly big nails in it, all sticking out," said Jill. "Would that do?"

"Yes—that's fine," said Andy. "Is there a bit for Tom?"

They found an old bit that would do. And then Andy said such a funny thing.

"I'll take the gramophone too! And the one record!"

The girls stared at him. "The *gram*ophone!" said Jill

at last. "Whatever for? Are you mad?"

"It does sound rather mad, I know," said Andy. "But I want it for something. I'll tell you afterwards. It won't sound quite so mad then!"

Andy had a very good meal, for he was awfully hungry. Then he settled down to sleep, for, as he said, he would not have much of a night *that* night!

The next night, after midnight, the boy went over the rocks again, carrying the pieces of rough wood with nails in, and the gramophone slung carefully over his shoulder. He reached the shore safely and made his way cautiously up the cliff.

And very soon Tom, half asleep, heard the queer hollow voice rumbling round his cave once more. "Tom! Are you asleep?"

Tom climbed on the chest and put his head to the hole. "Hallo, Andy!" he said. "I'm not asleep. I've been waiting and waiting for you!"

"There's a bit of wood with nails in coming down the hole," said Andy. "Scrape at your end with it and try your best to make the hole larger. I've got one too. I'll scrape my end. Look out that you don't get your eyes full of bits falling down."

The two boys set to work. Both of them scraped and dug for all they were worth. The soil was very dry and sandy, and was easy to move. Heaps of it fell down to Tom's end and he had to dodge it every now and again.

At last Andy's hole was quite big enough to get into. He called softly to Tom, "How are you getting on? My end is big enough for you to get out. I've got a rope I can let down to you if you are ready."

"I'm nearly ready," answered Tom, scraping hard. "Just a minute or two more!"

And then, at last, his end was large enough to climb into! The boy put another chest on the top of the one he was standing on and knelt upon it. His head and shoulders were right in the hole — he stood up and almost disappeared in the long narrow funnel.

"Wait a minute, Tom," said Andy. "I've got something I want to let down on the rope. It's the gramophone."

"The what?" asked Tom, in astonishment, thinking he couldn't have heard aright.

"The gramophone," said Andy. "I'm afraid, Tom, you may make rather a noise climbing down the cliff, and the sentry might think you had escaped — but if I

set the gramophone going, singing that silly lullaby you sang yesterday, he will think it's you still in the cave — and he won't come and see what the matter is. So I'm going to let it down, and you must set it right, and tie a bit of string to it so that I can pull the switch and set the record going when I think it's best to."

"Golly!" said Tom. "You think of everything!" The gramophone came bumping down the hole, on the end of the rope. Tom put it carefully behind a big chest and set the needle ready on the outside edge of the record. He tied a long piece of string to the starting-switch, and then tied the other end to the rope that Andy had let down with the gramophone.

"Pull it up, Andy," he said. "But carefully, please, because the string's on the rope and we don't want to break the needle by jerking the string too hard!"

Andy drew up the rope, untied the string on the end of it, and tied it to a heavy stone for safety. Then he called to Tom. "That's done. Come along up now, Tom. Don't brush against the gramophone string more than you can help. Here's the rope. Tie it round your waist and I'll help you up the hole by pulling — and I say, *don't* forget your camera!"

Tom stood up on the highest chest and began to scramble up the hole. There were plenty of rough ledges each side where he could put his feet. Andy hauled strongly on the rope, and Tom's head suddenly appeared through the hole by Andy's feet!

"Good!" said Andy. "Climb out!"

Tom climbed out. He sniffed the fresh breeze with delight, for it had ben rather stuffy down in the cave. Andy undid the rope from round Tom's waist. "Now you must get down the cliff as best you can without noise," he said. "Wait for me at the edge of the rocks, won't you. I'll give you a hand over those because I know them better than you do now."

Tom went to the cliff and began to climb down. Halfway down he slipped, and kicked out quickly to prevent himself from falling. A whole shower of stones fell down the cliff. The sentry, half-dozing, shouted at once.

Andy knew it was time to pull the string that was tied to the gramophone! He jerked it. The switch slid to one side and the record began to go round on its disc. The needle ran over the record and the lullaby began to sound in the cave. "Hush! Hush! Hush!"

The sentry heard it and thought it was Tom singing. He felt satisfied that his prisoner was still in the cave, as the song went on, and settled himself down again in a comfortable position. It must have been a rabbit that sent stones down the cliff, he thought!

Andy slipped down the cliff after Tom, glad that the sentry had heard the lullaby and had thought it must be Tom. Tom was waiting for him by the line of rocks.

"Didn't I make a row?" he whispered. "But I couldn't help it."

"It's all right! I set the record going and the sentry thinks you are busy in the cave, singing yourself to sleep," said Andy with a low chuckle. "Come on — we've no time to lose!"

XVIII

HEAVE-HO! HEAVE-HO!

Over the line of rocks the boys slipped and climbed, Tom following Andy closely, for Andy now knew the best way very well indeed. Big waves wetted them, but they did not care. All they wanted was to get back to the girls safely.

"The sentry won't look in at me tonight, I'm sure," said Tom, as they at last reached the sandy shore of the beach. "And the one that comes in the morning may not go into the cave to see me at all—he is a surly fellow."

"Well—that gives us a little time to think what to do next," said Andy. "Though I'm blessed if I know what will be best to do!"

They made their way to the shack, which was in darkness, for Andy had forbidden the girls to show a light of any sort in case the enemy saw it. Mary and Jill were lying together on their heather bed in the darkness, fast asleep.

Mary heard the boys come in and she sat upright in bed at once. "Is that you, Andy?"

"Yes—and Tom too!" said Andy. Jill awoke then, and the four of them sat on one bed, hugging one another for joy. Now they were all together again! It was lovely.

"I was an awful idiot to try and get my camera back," said Tom. "I never thought of being caught. Now our boat is gone and it's going to be difficult to know what to do."

"There's only one thing to do," said Andy. "And that

is to get our fishing-boat off the rocks early to-morrow morning somehow—and refloat her. I've noticed she seems to have moved a bit, and it may be that the tides have loosened her. Perhaps the two rocks that held her are not holding her quite so fast now. Anyway, it's our only chance."

"Yes—we'll try and do that," said Jill. "Tom's escape is sure to be discovered sometime to-morrow, and this time such a search will be made that I know we'll all be found."

"Well, let's sleep for an hour or two till dawn," said Andy. "We can't do anything at the moment."

So they all lay down on their beds and slept until Andy awakened them two hours later. Now dawn was in the sky and soon the sun would rise.

The children slipped across the island and came to the beach where they had first landed, after their wreck. They looked at their poor fishing-boat, still jammed between the rocks. Certainly it had moved a little—it was not leaning so much to one side.

They stood and looked at it. The tide was not very high yet, and it was possible to reach the boat without too much difficulty.

It was not long before all the children had reached their boat, and were clambering up the wet and slippery deck. Seaweed lay across it now, thrown there by the waves. The boat looked old and miserable—not at all like the smart little ship in which they had started out so gaily.

The boys went down into the little cabin. It had water lying at the bottom. Andy ripped up the planks and examined the boat underneath the floor of the cabin.

Then he came out and let himself down the side of the

ship, disappearing under the water to feel the bottom of the boat. The girls and Tom watched him anxiously.

"We *must* mend the boat somehow," said Tom. "It's our only chance!"

When Andy joined them on the slanting deck he looked very cheerful.

"Do you know, there's not much wrong!" he said. "I do believe I could patch her up fairly quickly. The waves have shifted her a bit so that I can get at the damaged part—the part where she struck the rocks and damaged a few planks."

"Oh, *good*, Andy!" cried the girls, and Tom slapped the fisher-boy on the shoulder for joy. How marvellous that they could perhaps make the ship seaworthy again! What luck that the waves had shifted her enough to make it possible to examine the damaged part! Tom had no idea at all how Andy meant to patch up the ship, but he meant to help with all his might, to make up for losing the stolen boat.

Tom and Andy went back over the rocks to fetch a rope. Andy felt sure that if they all tugged at the boat at high tide, they could get her off the rocks and float her to the beach, where it would not be difficult to patch her up.

"You see, Tom, she's not jammed very tightly now," said Andy. "And I reckon if we wait till the tide is at its very highest, and big waves are trying to lift the boat up, we could pull her right off the rocks! Then we'll get her into shore somehow, and see what we can do."

"If only we can do it all before the enemy come again," said Tom. "I wonder if they've discovered that I've gone!"

"Don't let's think about that," said Andy.

The boys found all the rope they had and wound it

firmly round their waists. They went back to the shore. The girls were still on the ship, but the tide was rising high and they would soon have to leave, as the sea covered the boat at high tide.

The children fastened strong double strands of rope to the front of the ship. Then, holding firmly to the rope, they clambered over the rocks back to the sandy beach, wet through. The tide came up higher and higher and the children had to stand up to their waists in the water, for the rope would not reach right to the shore.

"Look! There's an enormous wave coming!" shouted Andy. "Pull on the rope, all of you, as soon as the wave strikes the ship! *Heave*-ho!"

They all pulled—and every child felt the ship give a little as the wave lifted her and the rope pulled her. "Now here's another one!" yelled Andy. "*Heave*-ho!"

They all heaved at the rope with all their might. Again they felt the ship move a little. The two big waves ran up the shore and wetted the children to their chins!

"Hang on to the rope, girls," cried Andy. "If we get many waves like that you may be swept off your feet. But as long as you've got hold of the rope you'll be all right."

The waves were smaller after that—and then the wind began to blow stiffly again, and the waves grew bigger. An enormous one reared its green head far out to sea.

"There's a monster coming!" shouted Tom. "Look at it! It will sweep us off our feet!"

"But we'll pull at the boat first!" yelled Andy, who was tremendously excited. He really felt that they could get the boat off the rocks. "Now—*heave*-ho, *heave*-ho!"

The wave struck the boat and the rope dragged at her at the same moment. She shivered and groaned as she

125

tried to escape from the rocks that held her. She slipped a few feet forward.

The giant wave struck the children next, and all of them went down under it, even Andy. They floundered in the foaming waves, and Jill swallowed about a pint of salt water. Mary was very angry because Tom put his foot into her neck, but Tom didn't mean to. The wave struck him so hard that he was flung right off his feet, and had to strike out to get himself upright again.

None of them let go the rope. They all held on for dear life, as Andy had ordered. So it was not long before they were standing up again, gasping and spluttering, salt in their mouths and noses, but all of them determined to heave again as soon as the next big wave came.

"*Look* how the boat has moved!" yelled Andy, in the greatest delight. "She's almost off the rocks! Golly! Isn't this exciting?"

The boat had moved a good deal. Andy was sure that they could pull her in now. He waited patiently for the next big wave to come — and my goodness, it was a monster! The tide was at its height now, and the wind blew very strongly. A green wave put up its head, and the children gave a yell.

"Look at that one!"

"It will knock us all over again," said Mary, afraid. But she didn't let go the rope. Whether she was knocked over or not she meant to do her bit.

The wave grew bigger and higher as it came nearer to the rocks on which the boat lay. It began to curl over a little — and then it struck the rocks, and the boat too.

"HEAVE-HO!" yelled Andy, in a voice as enormous as the wave! And they all heaved. My goodness, what a heave that was!

The great wave blotted the boat from their sight and came raging towards them. Jill gave a shout of fear.

"Hold on!" shouted Andy, half-afraid himself. The wave swept them all off their feet—and alas, swept them all from the rope too, except Andy, who held on with all his might.

The other three children were taken like corks, rolled over and over, and flung roughly on the sand at the edge of the sea. Then the great wave ran back down the beach, gurgling and foaming.

Jill sat up, crying. Mary lay still, quite stunned for the moment. Tom sat up, furiously angry with the wave!

It had bumped and battered him most spitefully, he thought.

As for Andy, he was under water, still clinging to the rope—but as soon as he struggled to his feet he gave a gurgling shout and tried to clear his throat of the salt water there.

"The ship! Look! She's off and floating!"

They all looked—and there was the little fishing-boat, safely off the rocks, bobbing about on the sea that swirled high over the other rocks.

"Come in and help me, quick, before any other big waves come!" yelled Andy. "We can get her into shore now. Quick, Tom!"

The three battered children, dripping wet, ran bravely into the sea again. They caught hold of the rope and pulled hard. *"Heave*-ho, *heave*-ho, *heave*-ho!" chanted Andy, as they all pulled hard.

And the boat came bobbing in to the shore! The children dragged the rope up the beach and the boat followed, scraping its bottom at last on the sand.

"We've got her!" shouted Andy, doing a kind of war-dance on his tired legs. "We've got her! Now we'll just see what we can do!"

XIX

A SHOCK FOR THE CHILDREN

The four children were so excited at getting their boat off the rocks that at first they could do nothing but laugh and chatter and clap their hands. They were all tired out with their long struggle in the sea, but so happy that they forgot all about their aching arms and legs, salty mouths and dripping clothes.

The boat lay on her side in the shallow water. Andy examined her carefully. He was sure that if he could nail planks inside, just where she had been stove-in by the rocks, he could patch her up well enough for her to sail home.

"She will let water in, but you two girls can bail her out all the time," said Andy. "I'll patch her up enough to get her sailing safely. Golly! I never thought we could do this!"

The children had been so busy that no one, not even Tom, had thought of any breakfast. But Andy suddenly felt very hungry, and sent the girls off to fetch breakfast of some sort. "And bring a jug of hot cocoa, too," he said. "We are all wet through, and it would be nice to have something to warm us."

Tom fetched the tools from the shack and the box of nails and screws and bolts. Andy meant to be very busy indeed. Somehow or other that boat had to be finished before Tom's escape was known.

After a hurried breakfast, they all set to work under Andy's orders. Andy stripped some of the wood from the roof of the cabin to use in the patching of the ship. The girls took out the old nails from the strips. Tom waited on Andy and handed him everything he wanted.

The sound of the hammer echoed over the island. "Do you think the enemy will hear?" asked Jill anxiously.

"Can't help it if they do," said Andy. "We can't hammer without noise! Pass me the biggest nails you've got, Tom."

They all worked steadily for the whole of the morning. And at last Andy heaved a sigh of relief.

"Well—I think that's patched up. She won't last long without being bailed out, because I can't patch her really properly—but the girls can easily bail out whilst you and I sail the boat, Tom."

"Is she ready?" asked the girls eagerly.

"As ready as I can make her," said Andy. "Now you girls must go and get all the rugs, and Tom and I will get the food from where we buried it under the sand, at the top of our own beach by the shack. We'll pile in everything we can, push her out into the water and sail off! Golly, I never thought we'd be able to do this!"

The four of them set off to fetch everything. They felt cheerful and excited. It might take them ages to get home—but at last they were going to leave these strange unknown islands safely, and take their secret with them!

The girls gathered up the rugs. The boys tied the tins and boxes together and staggered over the island with their heavy load, back to the boat again.

It was difficult climbing down the cliff so heavily-laden, but they managed it safely. The girls threw down the rugs on the deck, and the boys packed the food into the cabin. Now they could go!

"Wait a bit—we'll take the old sail with us," said

Andy, "I could rig it again, and it would help us."

He set off to get the sail—and then he suddenly stopped and looked down on the beach. There, by his foot, lay something that greatly astonished him.

"What is it, Andy?" called Tom, seeing Andy's puzzled face.

"Look at this," said Andy, picking up a dry, clean match, that had already been struck.

"What about it? It's only a match," said Tom.

"It's a match that hasn't very long been struck," said Andy. "And it is lying on sand that has been covered and uncovered by the tide since we've been working on the boat this morning. Well—has any of *us* struck a match and thrown it down? No—we haven't! Then who has?"

"Oh, Andy—surely you are mistaken," said Jill, looking ready to cry. "Nobody else has been here. We should have seen them."

"I'm wondering if anyone has been here whilst we were fetching the rugs and the food," said Andy, looking all round. "I don't like it—and, oh golly—look at that set of footprints in the sand over there! They are not *our* footprints!"

The four children gazed at the set of large footprints. Whoever made them had been wearing nailed boots—and the children all wore rubber shoes.

The girls were frightened. Yes—someone had been on the beach whilst they had left it to get rugs and food. But who? And where was he?

"Well—let's get the boat launched and hope to get away before we're stopped," said Andy. "Come on—we'll do without the sail."

They ran to the boat and took hold of the rope to drag it down to the sea—but even as they took hold of it,

131

a loud voice shouted to them from round the corner of the cliff.

"Stop! Halt!"

The children stopped hauling the boat and stared round. They saw the enemy—four of them! One of them was the man who spoke English, and it was he who was shouting.

The children stared in fright at the four men, who came quickly over the beach.

They spoke to one another in a foreign language. Then the first man spoke again.

"So! There are four of you—and all children! This is the boy who escaped—ah, you thought you were very clever, didn't you!"

"I did, rather," said Tom boldly. He *felt* frightened—but he wasn't going to show it! No—he was British, and these men shouldn't think they could scare *him*!

"You took your boat off the rocks, and thought you would escape safely, didn't you?" said the man mockingly. "Well, you made a mistake. We shall now take the boat away—and you shall remain prisoners on this island for as long as we want you to! Take out the food and the blankets again. You will need those if you live here for months!"

The children sulkily took out all the food and rugs they had so cheerfully put into the boat. Tom was glad to see that neither Jill nor Mary cried. Good! That would show the enemy how brave British children could be!

"Now we are going," said the man who spoke English. He gave a rapid order to the other men, who ran off round the cliff and then reappeared in a small boat, bobbing on the waves. It was plain that they had landed round the cliff, watched the children, and then come to catch them.

Andy and the others had to watch the men drag their ship down to the sea and launch it. They had tied their little rowing-boat behind it, and now, waving mockingly to the children, they made their way over the water, round the cliff, and out of sight, rowing Andy's boat along swiftly.

The children watched them go, anger and despair in their hearts. All their work for nothing! How they had battled with the sea that morning—how they had slaved to get that boat right! And now they had all been discovered, their boat had been taken, and they were real prisoners.

Andy shook his fist at the disappearing ship, with the small boat bobbing behind it.

"You think you can beat a Scots boy, but you can't," he cried. "I'll beat you yet! You and your submarines!"

Wearily the children gathered up the old rugs and all the food and made their way up the cliff, across the island and back to their shack. They packed the food on the floor in a corner and threw the rugs on the beds.

Then they sat on the beds and looked at one another. Not till then did the girls begin to cry. But cry they did, letting the tears run down their cheeks without trying to wipe them off. They were so tired and so disappointed.

Tears came into Tom's eyes too, when he saw the two miserable girls. But he blinked them back, after one look at Andy's lean brown face. Andy's blue eyes were like stones, and his mouth was stern and straight. Andy was not thinking of crying or grumbling. Andy was angry and fierce, and he sat in silence, looking straight before him, thinking hard.

"Andy—what are you thinking about?" asked Tom at last. "You look so stern. You're not angry with *us*, are you?"

"No," said Andy. "We all did our best—and we've got to do our best again. I tell you, Tom, we've *got* to leave this island! Somehow, we've got to get away and tell our secret. No matter what happens to any of us we must try to get home and tell all we have seen! As long as the enemy remain hidden in these islands, able to come here whenever they need food or fuel, then just so long will our ships be sunk round about these seas."

"Oh, Andy—it's all very well to say things like that —but how *can* we get away now our boat's gone?" said Jill, wiping her eyes.

"I'll think of a way," said Andy. "*Some*how, I'll think of a way. I'm going out by myself now, to puzzle a way out of this fix. Don't come with me. I want to be alone."

The boy slipped out of the shack. He climbed the cliff and sat in the heather by himself, his blue eyes fixed on the sky-line. How could he get home? How could he tell his secret? For two hours he sat there, puzzling and worried, so still that the gulls circled round his head and wondered if he were asleep.

And then Andy straightened himself and got up. He went down to the others, his eyes shining and his head up. "I've thought of a way," he said proudly. "I've thought of a way at last!"

ANDY MAKES A PLAN

Tom, Mary and Jill looked at Andy, excited.

"Do you really know a way of escape, even now that our ship has been taken?" asked Jill. "You *are* clever, Andy."

"Well, it's no use us trying to take one of the enemy's boats again, or to get our own ship back," said Andy. "And it's no use putting up a signal to passing ships, for two reasons—one is that I am perfectly certain no ship ever passes near these islands, or they would have discovered the secret of the submarines before this— and the second reason is that I am jolly sure the enemy wouldn't let us have a signal up anyhow!"

"Go on," said Tom, feeling sure Andy had got a very good idea coming.

"Well, my idea is—we'd better make a raft!" said Andy. "We can't get a boat or make one—but we *could* make a rough kind of raft, and get a mast of some sort to rig a sail on. We've plenty of food to take with us— and you and I, Tom, could set off alone on it to try and make for home. I daren't take the girls—they would be so cold on an open raft, and they would be safer here."

"Not take *us!*" cried Jill indignantly. "Of *course* you'll take us! We won't be left behind—will we, Mary?"

"Listen, Jill—you're only ten years old and not very big," said Andy patiently. "If we take you it will make things much more difficult for Tom and for me. If we get home safely we can have you rescued at once—

if we don't get home you will at least be safe on the island."

The girls cried bitterly at this. They thought it was very unfair. They couldn't know that Andy didn't feel at all certain of ever getting home, and was very much afraid of the girls being washed overboard when big waves came. He and Tom were strong—and besides they were boys— but the girls would never be able to stand tossing about on a raft for days and days.

Andy was quite firm about it, and the girls dried their eyes and listened to his plans. Tom wondered what the raft was to be made of.

"We shall have to pull our wooden hut to pieces and use the planks," said Andy. "Luckily we've got plenty of nails to use."

"But what shall we live in if we pull down the shack?" asked Jill in dismay.

"I've thought of that," said Andy. "You see, if we start pulling down the shack the enemy are bound to notice it and will guess what we are doing. Well—I thought we could make it look as if our hut had fallen down on us, and I could ask the enemy to give us a tent to live in instead. Then we could live in that, and quietly make our raft from the fallen-down shack!"

"That really *is* a good idea," said Tom. "We get the two things we want—somewhere else to live—and wood to make a raft—and the enemy actually help us without knowing it!"

"Yes," said Andy, grinning round at the other three. "We'd better wait a day or two, though, because the enemy are bound to watch us a bit at first, to see if we've any other ideas of escape. We won't do anything suspicious at all for the next few days."

"All right," said the others, and they began to feel excited again. They still felt terribly disappointed when they thought of how their precious boat had been taken from them—but never mind, perhaps their raft would be luckier.

So for the next few days the children just played about, bathing, fishing, paddling, and the enemy, who sent a man over every day at noon, saw nothing to make him think that the children had any plans at all.

"I think there's going to be a storm," said Andy, on the third evening. "That would be a good reason for our shack to fall down, I think! As soon as that man has come and gone today we'll turn the shack into a ruin!"

The man came, looked round the island and went. As soon as he had gone the children set about the hut. Andy removed nails and took out planks. He hammered part of the roof away and made a big hole. He made one side of the hut so weak that it fell in on top of the girls' bed.

"Doesn't it look a ruin now!" said Jill, with a giggle. "We'd better spread the sail over that side of the hut, Andy, or the rain will come in tonight."

"Yes, we'll do that," said Andy. So when they had done all they could to make the hut look as if it was falling to pieces, they draped the sail over the open side for protection, and then grinned at one another.

"And to-morrow we will act a nice little play for the enemy!" said Andy with a chuckle. "We will pretend that in the storm which we can now hear rumbling round, our hut was blown in—and we will bandage up Jill's head as if the hut fell on top of her—and bandage my leg too. And we'll beg for a tent most humbly!"

"I hope I shan't giggle," said Mary.

"If you do you'll deserve a good slapping," began

137

Andy fiercely—but Mary spoke hastily once more.

"I didn't mean it, Andy. I *shan't* giggle. I shall be frightened, really, though I won't show it."

"All right," said Andy, calming down. "Golly! What a loud clap of thunder!"

The storm began properly then. It was not a very bad one, but the children were glad of the protection of the big sail over the open side of the hut. The wind blew fiercely, and Andy and Tom had to weight the sail down to prevent it from being blown away. The thunder rumbled and crashed and the lightning flickered round the islands. In an hour's time, however, the storm was gone, and the wind died down again.

In the morning the children took the sail and hid it safely, for Andy did not want the enemy to know he had an old sail. They made the shack look as if the wind had almost blown it down, and Jill broke a plate and threw the pieces about as if the storm had caused the accident.

"Now I'll tie up Jill's head in my big handkerchief," said Andy, taking out a rather dirty hanky. "And I'll use a rag to tie my leg up with. We'll pretend we got hurt in the night."

When the man came to look at the children and go over the island as usual, he was surprised to find Jill bandaged up, and Andy limping.

Andy hailed him. "Hie! Our shack has fallen down! Come and see!"

The man went to look. He could not speak English, but he understood at once that the shack had fallen down on the children during the storm. Jill sat on the ground, pretending to cry, holding her head in her hand. Mary was trying to comfort her.

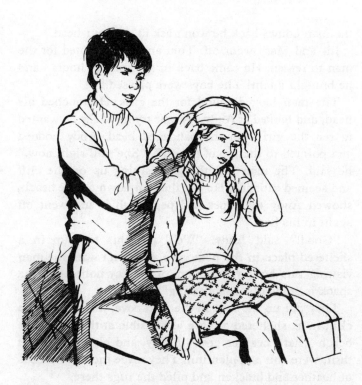

"We want a tent to sleep in," said Andy. The man did not understand. Tom took out his notebook and drew a tent in it. Then the man understood. He nodded his head, said something that sounded like "Yah, yah!" to the children, and set off in his boat.

"Don't cry too much, Jill, or the man will want to see your wound!" said Andy. "I was awfully afraid he would take off the bandage and have a look to see how much your head was hurt."

"Gracious!" said Jill, in alarm. "I didn't think of that!"

"I hope he comes back with a tent," said Tom. "You'd better go up the cliff, Jill, and sit on the top, so that if the man comes back he won't ask to see your head."

Jill and Mary went off. Tom and Andy waited for the man to return. He came back in about three hours—and he brought a tent! The boys were pleased.

The man looked round for the girls. He touched his head, and looked at Andy. He was trying to say he wanted to see the girl with the bandaged head. Andy nodded and pointed to the top of the cliff. "She's all right now," he said. The man saw the girls sitting up on the cliff and seemed satisfied. He put the tent down on the beach, showed Andy the ropes and pegs with it and went off again in his boat.

"Good!" said Andy. "We'll put this tent up in a sheltered place in the next cove. We don't want the man visiting this hollow too often, or he may notice that the shack is gradually disappearing!"

They put up the tent in the next cove, just around the cliff, in as sheltered a place as possible at the end of the beach where heather grew thickly, and big cushions of thrift were soft and plentiful. They made themselves beds of heather and bracken and piled the rugs there.

The man came again next day and Andy showed him where they had put the tent. Andy limped about with the rag still on his leg, which made the others want to smile—but the man did not once guess that it was all pretence. As soon as he had gone Andy walked and ran just as usual!

The weather was not so good now. The sun was not so warm, and clouds sailed over the sky, bringing showers of rain at times. The children often had to sit in the tent, and they longed to begin making the raft.

"I don't want to start it till I'm sure the man has forgotten about the tumble-down shack," said Andy.

"Yesterday he brought his boat in to this beach instead of the next one, and hardly looked over the island at all. If he comes to this cove today, we can begin the raft this afternoon."

The man came at noon as usual. This time he brought a large supply of food, and tried to make the children understand that he would not be back for a few days. He pointed to three fingers and shook his head.

"I think he means he won't be back for three days," said Andy, his heart jumping for joy. He nodded to the man, who, instead of looking over the island as he usually did, got straight back into his boat and rowed off.

"Well, if that isn't a bit of luck!" said Andy joyfully, as soon as he had gone. "I'm sure he won't be back for some days—and he's brought us a marvellous supply of food, that will just do beautifully for the raft! We can safely begin building it this afternoon!"

XXI

THE BUILDING OF THE RAFT

The four children tackled the shack that afternoon and tore out as many planks as they could.

"Pile them up in different sizes," ordered Andy. "Come and help with this long plank, Tom—it's too heavy for me to pull out alone."

By the end of that day the children had sixteen planks of different sizes piled up. Andy was pleased.

"If we can get as many as that to-morrow, we'll be able to make a really fine raft," he said. "Tom, you are saving all those long screws and nails, aren't you? We shall need them soon."

"Yes—they're all safe," said Tom, showing Andy a tin into which he had put all the screws and nails he had taken out of the planks.

"Do you think we'd better hide these planks in case the man *does* come to-morrow, although we feel sure he won't?" asked Jill.

"Well—perhaps we had better," said Andy, who was feeling tired and not at all eager to carry heavy planks about. So he and Tom took the planks one by one and hid them in thick heather. Then they went to have a good meal, which the girls had been getting ready.

"I've never been so hungry in my life!" said Tom.

"You've said that about a thousand times since we've been on this island," said Jill. "Well—see if you can eat *that* plateful!"

Tom took the plate. It was full of cold tongue, baked

bake beans

potatoes, and tinned asparagus tips which the man had brought yesterday. There were also sliced pears, tinned milk to eat with them, and hot cocoa. The pears and tinned milk were so delicious that Tom wanted a second helping.

"Good gracious! At the rate you eat you'll want about a thousand tins on the raft!" said Mary, opening another tin of pears. "Andy, I hope you won't forget to take a tin-opener when you go. It would be so awful to be hungry, and have heaps of tinned food round you—and not be able to eat any of it because you had forgotten an opener!"

Andy grinned. "I shan't forget *that*," he said. "Golly, I *am* tired!"

They were all tired, and they fell asleep in the tent almost as soon as they lay down on their heathery beds. They awoke late the next day and Andy could not make up his mind whether to get on with the raft or not.

"I'm pretty sure that fellow meant he wouldn't come for a few days," Andy said. "But if he *did* happen to come and found us at work on a raft, it would be *too* disappointing for anything."

"Well, one of us could go up to the rocky ledge and keep watch all the time, couldn't we," said Jill eagerly. "We could easily see anyone coming, then, and give warning in time to let you and Tom hide everything."

"Yes—of course," said Andy. "That's a good idea! Take it in turns of about two hours each. You go first, Jill, and Mary next."

So Jill went up to the rocky ledge and sat there. She could see the cave-beach of the next island and had a good view of any boat that might come over the water.

No boat was to be seen—but all that day the islands

143

were very noisy indeed! Seaplanes flew over many times, their engines roaring loudly. Three came down in the calm water opposite the cave-beach. Jill watched them carefully.

Stores were taken to the cave, as she could plainly see. The seaplanes roared away after a time—but all ·that day others flew over the islands, and the children wondered to see so many.

"Well, there's one thing that's lucky," said Andy with a grin. "Those seaplanes make such a noise that no one could possibly hear the sound of any hammering today —so I vote we get on with it and make as much noise as we like now there's a chance!"

So the sound of hammering was heard on the children's island that day, as Andy and Tom nailed twelve big planks crosswise to twelve others below. Then on top of the two crosswise rows Andy nailed yet another row of shorter planks to make the raft really solid and heavy.

The boys added a kind of rim to the raft to prevent things rolling off too easily. Andy was clever at carpentry and he knew all the best tricks of making each plank hold the other fast. It was a very solid-looking affair that began to take shape by the time that night came.

Andy had found a strong post that would do for a mast, but he did not mean to put this up till the raft was almost ready to launch. "We can't very well hide a raft with a mast," he said. "It is easier to hide a flat raft with no mast, if that man pays us a visit too soon."

"How can we hide it, though?" asked Tom, looking at the heavy raft. "We really can't toss it lightly into the heather as we could do with planks!"

Andy grinned. "We'll hide it in a very easy place," he said. "We'll simply rig up the tent above it, and pile heather on the raft, which will then make the floor. I don't think anyone is likely to think that our tent hides a raft!"

In three days the raft was quite complete, and was very sound and solid. Andy had decided to take all the food in the big wooden box in which the man had brought the tins and jars on his last visit.

"We can nail the box to the floor of the raft," said Andy, "and our food will stay there quite safely! If we put it loose on the deck of the raft, everything would get thrown off in a rough sea, even though we've put a kind of rail to the edge of the raft."

There came a warning cry from Jill not long after that. She had seen a boat coming round the cliff on the far side of the cave-beach. Hastily the boys put up the tent over the raft, and Mary strewed the heather and bracken over the deck. She could not hide the box of food in the middle of the raft, however.

"Never mind about that," said Andy. "Put a rug over it, and it will look like a seat or something."

There were two men this time, and one of them was the one who spoke English.

The boat drew up in the cove where the raft was, and one man got out. It was not the man who had seen the fallen-down shack, but the one who spoke English.

Andy went down to meet him. "Please, sir, won't you give us a boat to go home in?" asked Andy, knowing perfectly well that the man would say no.

"No," said the man at once. "You will stay here for as long as we wish. But soon the winter will come, and a tent will be no good to you. Is there any building here that can be mended?"

"No," said Andy, who did not wish the man to examine the buildings, and perhaps ask where the tumbledown shack was. This had almost disappeared by now, for the children had taken all the planks for their raft!

"Let me see your tent," said the man. Andy's heart sank. It would be too bad if the raft was found just as it was finished. He took the man to the tent in silence.

The man looked inside. He saw the box in the middle covered with a rug. "What's that?" he asked.

"It's the box of food the man brought us the other day," said Andy, and he pulled off the rug. The man saw at once that it *was* only a box of food and he nodded. He did not go inside the tent, luckily, or his nailed

146

boot might have gone through the heathery covering and struck against the wooden raft below. Then he would certainly have pulled aside the heather and seen the children's secret.

Jill and Mary watched, very pale and scared. Tom sat nearby and whistled. The man still stood looking into the tent, and all the children felt very anxious indeed — and then a great seaplane roared over the island, making a terrific noise.

"Look! Look!" yelled Tom, jumping up. "Isn't it a big one!"

The man looked up, at Tom's yell, and followed the seaplane with his eyes. "I must go," he said, and he went down the beach to the boat. "I will send men to put you up a rough hut for the winter. Be sensible children and you will be looked after — but if not, you will be very sorry for yourselves."

The children were very thankful indeed when they saw the boat go off over the water. They heaved deep sighs of relief and looked at one another.

"Thank goodness, that seaplane came when it did and Tom let out that yell," said Jill. "It just took the man's attention away! I really thought he was going to go inside the tent and look at everything!"

"Well, I think we're safe to make our escape soon now," said Andy. "I don't expect any men will be sent for a while. We'll drag the raft down to the shore early to-morrow morning, and I'll set up the mast and rig the sail as best I can. Then Tom and I will start off."

The girls said nothing. They did not like being left alone on the island — and yet they knew that Andy was right. Somehow he must get home and tell the people there the secrets they had discovered. The raft would not

147

really take four—and the girls were not strong enough to stand days and nights of tossing about on the sea.

"Well, Andy, it's very important that you should get back and tell the secret of these islands," said Jill at last. "So, for the sake of our country, Mary and I will stay behind here without any fuss and do the best we can, whilst you and Tom set off for home. But do rescue us as soon as possible!"

"Of course we shall," said Andy, glad to see that the girls were going to be brave and not make any fuss. "You are good sports, you two girls—I really do feel proud of you both—don't you, Tom?"

"*Very* proud," said Tom. And the girls went red with pleasure.

"We'll wish you luck to-morrow!" said Jill. "Oh, how I hope you'll soon get back home, Andy! Mary and I will watch every day till you come back."

They all went to bed early that night, for to-morrow was to be an important day! They did not sleep very well, for they were too excited.

And in the morning, early, they took down their tent, dragged off the heather that covered the raft, and tied ropes to it, to pull it down to the beach.

"Now we're off on another adventure!" said Andy, dragging the raft. "Heave-ho! Heave-ho! Down to the sea we go!"

XXII

AWAY ON THE SEA

The raft was dragged right down to the sea. In the middle of it Andy fixed the post that was to be the mast. He rigged up the old sail very cleverly. The box of food was firm below the mast—they had enough to last them for some days. They took a big tin of water with them too, but expected to use the juice of the tins of fruit to quench their thirst after they had drunk all the water.

Andy had made two rough paddles to help the boat along and to guide it. The girls handed the boys the two warmest rugs to wrap themselves in at night, though Andy said they wouldn't be any use—they would get wet with the very first wave that splashed over the raft! But to please the girls he took the rugs.

"Andy, you can dry them in the sun in the daytime," said Jill, "and you *might* be glad of them. Mary and I have got plenty here."

The raft was ready to float off at last. The boys gave the girls a hug and said good-bye.

"Now don't worry," said Andy, jumping on to the raft. "You won't hear for days and days, because we've got to get back home, and then tell our tale and then ships have got to find their way here. So you'll have to wait a long time."

"What shall we say if the enemy want to know where *you* are?" asked Jill anxiously.

"Just say we have disappeared," said Andy. "And if you like to do another bit of pretending and make a fuss—well, do it!"

"All right," said Jill. "Anyway, you may be quite sure we shan't tell them you've gone on a raft."

"No—we don't want their seaplanes hunting the sea for us!" said Andy, letting the sail unfurl. "Now—good-bye, Jill! Good-bye, Mary! See you soon!"

"Good-bye, Andy! Good-bye, Tom!" cried the girls, trying to smile cheerfully, though they felt very miserable and lonely to see the boys setting off together. "Good luck!"

Tom pushed out the raft and jumped up on it. He took a paddle and guided it. Andy let the sail billow out. The wind caught it and the little raft leapt along over the waves like a live thing!

"I say! It *can* get along, can't it!" cried Jill, jumping up and down in excitement. "Look how it bobs over the waves!"

The boys waved wildly to the girls. Little waves splashed over the deck of the raft and wetted the boys' legs. If they ran into a stormy sea they would soon be wet through—but at the moment they cared nothing for what might happen! They were very excited and very anxious to guide their little raft on the right course.

The sail flapped and billowed finely. Andy had rigged it most cleverly, and the wind shot the little craft along swiftly.

"It's going nearly as fast as the ship!" said Tom in delight.

"No—it isn't really," said Andy, shaking his head. "No raft could ever equal a boat for speed—it's so clumsy and heavy. But I must say our raft isn't bad! Look out —there's a fat wave coming!"

The raft sailed into the wave—slap! It drenched Tom, and he laughed and shook himself like a dog. The sun

150

was out and the boy's clothes soon dried.

The boys looked back at the shore of their island, which now seemed far away. They could just make out the two girls, who had now climbed to the top of the cliff and were standing there, watching the raft out of sight.

"I hope Jill and Mary will be all right," said Tom. "Poor kids—it was awful having to leave them alone."

"Yes," said Andy. "But it was the only thing to be done. We've happened on very big things, Tom—and so we've got to be big enough and brave enough to meet them."

"Well—I'm not afraid," said Tom stoutly. "And as for you, Andy, I really don't believe anything in the world would frighten you!"

"Oh yes, it would," said Andy. "But I'd not show I was frightened! Look, Tom—you can see *all* the islands now!"

The boys stood on the raft, holding on to the mast and looked back on the cluster of islands. They lay in the sea together, and looked very small now that the boys were so far off. They could no longer see the girls. And soon even the islands too would disappear—then the boys would be quite alone on the wide sea.

"Do you really know which way to go, Andy?" said Tom.

"More or less," said Andy. "I can guide the raft by the sun in the day-time, and by the stars at night. It's a good thing for us that the wind is just in the right direction. I hope it lasts. It's easy enough now—but if the wind changes, things will be very difficult!"

Now the boys could no longer see any land at all. They were alone on the wide green sea. Below them the

151

water was very, very deep. The sea was not rough, but a little choppy, and the raft bobbed like a cork over the waves. Every now and again a wave hopped over the side and wetted the deck of the raft. The boys got used to this and didn't even move when a wave reared its head to run across the raft.

Tom dragged his hand in the cool water. He liked the movement of the raft running over the sea. The sun shone steadily down and the boys became very hot. Tom took off his jersey and hung it safely over the top of the mast, out of reach of the waves.

"Golly! I'm cooking!" he said. Luckily the boys had got hats with them, and these shaded the sun from their heads or they might have felt sick. The sun blazed down, and at last the boys let themselves drop into the sea, holding on to the edge of the raft all the time. This cooled them a little, and they scrambled back wet and panting.

"It would be an awful thing if one of us let go the raft," said Tom. "It's going at such a pace that it would soon leave us behind in the sea and we'd never be found again."

"Well, for goodness' sake hang on tightly then, next time we cool ourselves," said Andy. "What about something to eat?"

They opened a tin of salmon and a tin of pears, and had a good meal, though Tom longed for some bread with the salmon. It was odd sitting there eating on the bobbing raft, all by themselves in the midst of a wide heaving sea.

The day seemed endless — but at last the sun slid down the sky and the sea turned from green to purple in the twilight. "It's not so warm now," said Tom, taking his jersey down from the mast and putting it on.

"Tom, see if you can have a nap for a while," said Andy. "I don't think we ought both to sleep at once. The wind might change, or a storm might blow up—you sleep now and I'll have a nap later."

Tom wrapped himself in a rug and tried to go to sleep. Andy slipped a rope round his waist and tied him to the box in the middle.

"You might roll off the raft in the middle of the night," he said with a grin. "I shouldn't like to look round and find you gone, Tom!"

Tom lay on his back and looked up at the night sky. It was a clear night, with no moon and the stars shone brightly. Andy pointed out the North Star to Tom.

"That tells me we are still going in the right direction," said Andy. "At this rate we should sight the coast we're heading for in about three or four days."

"Oh—as long as that!" said Tom in great disappointment. "I thought we'd only be a day or two, going at this pace."

"This is a raft, not a sailing-smack," said Andy. "Now go to sleep. I'll wake you if I need you for anything."

Tom slept. He dreamt he was on a swing, going up and down, up and down in the air. It was very pleasant. Then he dreamt he was being scolded by Jill for something and she suddenly threw a pail of cold water right over him! He woke with a jump and sat up.

"Did that wave wake you?" said Andy with a grin. "I thought it would. It popped its head up, saw you asleep and jumped right on you!"

Tom laughed and lay down again. He thought about Andy—what a good sort he was—always doing what he felt was best and wisest—never grumbling—always willing to do the hardest job. It was a good thing Tom and the girls had had Andy to help them.

Andy awoke Tom near dawn and told him to sit up and keep watch. "The wind's still right," he said. "Watch it, Tom. You can see the North Star, can't you? I'm so sleepy I can't keep awake much longer."

Andy tied himself up safely, lay down and was asleep as his head touched the rug that made a pillow for him. Tom sat and watched the dawn coming. It was a wonderful sight. First the sky turned to silver and the sea turned to silver too. Soon a pink flush came into the eastern sky and then it changed to a blaze of gold. The sea sparkled and glinted with gold too.

Tom wished he could wake Andy up and make him see the magnificent sight. There was nothing but sea and sky, all glowing with colour. But Andy was tired and Tom sat and watched it by himself, half afraid of the strange beauty around him.

After a while Tom felt very hungry. He burrowed in the box of food to see what there was. He felt like a meal of tongue or ham. He picked out a tin of tongue and opened it. It smelt delicious.

Andy woke up after a while and shared the meat with Tom. They opened some pineapple and had that too. The juice was very pleasant. They poured water into the tin and made a kind of pineapple drink to have later on in the day.

Andy sniffed the wind, and looked at the sky. "There's a change coming," he said. "I do hope we shan't be blown out of our way. We were getting on so well!"

The sea was rougher. Waves slopped over the deck almost every minute now. Only by sitting up on the box of food could the boys keep dry from the waist up. Once or twice the raft heeled over, and Tom had to clutch the mast to keep from over-balancing.

"Blow!" said Tom. "What does the sea want to get so rough for? It's a good thing we're both good sailors or we'd be very ill."

Andy looked anxiously at the sky. "I'm afraid the wind is changing," he said. "We shall be blown right out of our way if it does. The sea is getting very rough, Tom. I think we'd both better tie ourselves firmly to the mast. It won't do for either of us to be thrown off the raft —and a big wave could easily dash one of us overboard!"

So they tied themselves to the mast, and then watched the scurrying clouds, wondering if they would suddenly slow down—and fly the other way!

XXIII

A WONDERFUL SURPRISE

Alas for Tom and Andy! The wind did change and blew strongly the other way. Andy took down the sail hurriedly. "We don't want to be blown back to our island!" he said. "We must just bob along without a sail now and hope for the best. When the wind changes again we'll put up the sail once more."

"I wonder if the enemy has found out that we've escaped," said Tom. "They might send a seaplane out after us if they've found out we've gone. They'd know we were on a raft."

"Well, the girls wouldn't give us away, that's certain," said Andy. "But the enemy might easily guess we'd made a raft, if they searched the island for us and missed us —and they could send out a seaplane or two to hunt the seas for us. We're a good way from the island now—but a seaplane could easily find us."

"I hope one doesn't," said Tom. "Isn't this wind hateful, Andy? It just won't stop! It's wasting all our time."

The wind blew cold. The sun was behind the clouds. Big waves slapped around the raft and seemed really spiteful. "Almost as if they want to snatch us off," said Tom, tightening the rope that tied him safely to the mast. He shivered. There was no shelter at all on the open raft, and no way of getting warm or dry now that the sun was not to be seen.

"Do a few arm exercises, Tom," said Andy. "That will

get you a bit warmer!" The boys swung their arms and slapped themselves.

The waves raced along and the raft raced along too — but not in the right direction, Tom was sure!

And then, towards afternoon, the wind dropped again, and the sun shone out! What a relief that was! The boys sunned themselves gladly, and were soon warm. Andy rigged the sail again. "We'll get the wind we want this evening," he said. "We'll be ready for it."

Sure enough, as the sun slid down the western sky, the wind got up again — and this time it was blowing from the right quarter! Andy was delighted.

The sail flapped and the little raft raced along nobly. "I think the wind's set in properly now," said Andy, pleased. "If only it holds for another couple of days we may be home — or, at any rate, see a ship we can hail."

The wind became stiffer as the evening drew on. The sun was just about to slip over the sky-line when Andy sat up straight and looked alarmed.

"Can you hear a noise?" he asked Tom.

"Plenty," said Tom. "The wind and the waves and the sail!"

"No — not that sort of noise," said Andy. "A noise like — a seaplane!"

Tom's heart almost stopped beating. Surely their escape hadn't been discovered after all! He sat and listened.

"Yes — there's a seaplane about somewhere," said Andy. "Blow! If it's really hunting for us it will be sure to find us. Just as we've got away so nicely, too — and the wind helping us again, and all!"

Tom went pale, and looked up at the sky anxiously. Both boys could now hear the hum of the engines quite clearly.

And then the seaplane appeared, flying fairly low and quite slowly. It was plain that it was hunting the seas for something.

"Can we do anything, Andy?" said Tom.

"We had better jump into the water, hold on to the raft, and hope maybe the seaplane will think there's no one on it," said Andy. "Only our heads will show beside the raft—they might not notice them. Come on, quick!"

The boys slid into the water over the side of the raft. They hung there with their hands, only their heads showing. They waited anxiously.

The great seaplane came zooming overhead, very close to the water. It had seen the raft and was coming to examine it more closely. How the boys hoped that when the raft was seen to be empty the seaplane would fly off!

The plane flew over the raft. It circled round and came back again, flying once more over the raft. It circled round again and the boys hoped it would now fly off. But once more it flew over the raft—and then, to the boys' great dismay, it skimmed over the water and landed there, not very far off.

"It's no good, Tom. We're discovered," said Andy. "We may as well climb back on to the raft. Look— they're letting down a boat."

The boys climbed back on to the raft, angry and disappointed. And then Tom gave such a tremendous yell that Andy nearly fell overboard with fright.

"Andy! ANDY! Look at the sign on the seaplane! It's British! It's BRITISH!"

Andy looked—and sure enough there was the well-known mark that all British machines wear! And then such a change came over the boys. Instead of sitting there sullen and angry, they went completely mad. They stood

up and danced on that rocking raft! They yelled, they
waved, they stamped! And, as you can imagine, Tom lost
his balance and fell right into the water.

Andy pulled him in, gasping and spluttering. "Oh,
Andy, it's a British seaplane—not the enemy. Golly!
Suppose it had flown off and not come down to examine
the raft!" And then Tom went mad again and shouted
for joy.

The boat from the seaplane came nearer. It had two
men in it, and they hailed the boys.

"Ahoy there! Where are you from?"

"Ahoy there!" yelled back Andy. "Ahoy there!" He was too excited to shout anything else. The boat came alongside the raft and the men pulled the two boys into it.

"Why, it's only a couple of boys," said one man. "We reckoned you might be men from a sunk ship or aeroplane. How did you get here?"

"It's a long tale to tell," said Andy. "I think I'd better tell it to the chief, if you don't mind."

"All right. The commander's in the plane," said the first man. They rowed off to the seaplane, and left the little raft bobbing about on the sea alone. Tom was quite sorry to see it go. He had got fond of it. He was sorry to think of the wasted food, too!

The boat reached the enormous seaplane. The boys were pushed up into it, and a grave-faced man turned to receive them.

And then Andy got a second shock, for Tom once more let out a yell that really scared him!

"DADDY! Oh, DADDY! It's YOU!"

The grave-faced man stared at Tom as if he couldn't believe his eyes. Then he took the boy into his arms and gave him such a bear-like hug that Tom felt as if his bones would break!

"Tom! We've been hunting for you ever since we heard you had gone off in that boat and hadn't come back!" he said. "Where are the girls—quick, tell me!"

"They're safe," said Tom. "We left them on the island. They're quite safe. Oh, Daddy—isn't this too good to be true! Daddy, this is Andy. He's been such a brick. We'd never have escaped if it hadn't been for him."

"What do you mean—*escaped?*" said Tom's father in surprise. "Escaped from what?"

"We've got a big secret to tell you," said Tom. "We've

160

found out something queer. You tell him, Andy."

"Well, sir," said Andy, "we got thrown off up the coast of some desolate islands where nobody lives now. The enemy are using them for their submarines and seaplanes. There are caves stored with food—and there must be stores of fuel somewhere, too."

"What!" shouted Tom's father. He called his men near and they all listened to Andy's tale. The boy told it well.

"And we were just escaping on the raft we had made when we saw you," finished Andy. "We slipped over the side of the raft to hide—but you must have seen us."

"We didn't," said Tom's father. "But we were puzzled about the empty raft and came down to examine it. Little did we think you and Andy were there! This seaplane and two others have been scouring the seas about here looking for the sailing-ship you went off in. We were afraid you might be drifting about in it, half-starving. Your poor mother has been dreadfully upset."

"Oh dear, I was afraid she would be," said Tom. "But, never mind, we're all safe, Daddy—at least, I *hope* the girls are safe!"

"They will be, very soon," said the boy's father in a grim voice. "We shall rescue them—and clean up those submarines and seaplanes in no time! How clever of the enemy to have a base just under our noses—but it won't last long now! You've done a marvellous thing, Tom and Andy!"

"I hope my father won't be very angry with me for losing his boat," said Andy. "Though we might perhaps be able to get it back from the enemy now."

"Your father won't be angry with you for anything once he sees you are safe, and hears the tale you have

161

just told me!" said Tom's father. "Settle down now—we're going up."

"Back to the island to rescue the girls?" asked Tom eagerly. His father shook his head.

"No," he said. "They must wait, I'm afraid, till I get this news through. I'll wireless home that we've got you safe, and have got great news—but that's all. This is too important to be told to anyone but the chief himself."

With a great noise of engines, the seaplane skimmed over the water, and then rose gracefully in the air. She shot away southwards, and the boys looked out over the sea, which was now far below.

"Well, what luck to be rescued like this!" said Andy. "And oh, Tom—what a shock the enemy are going to get!"

XXIV

WHAT HAPPENED TO THE GIRLS

The two girls felt very lost and lonely when the boys went off on the raft. They climbed the cliff quickly so that they might watch the boys till they were out of sight.

They waved until the raft was a tiny speck on the sea. Then they lost sight of it. It was gone.

"I do hope Tom and Andy reach home all right," said Jill, as they made their way down the cliff to the shore again. "It would be awful if they got lost on the sea."

"Don't say things like that!" said Mary. "Let's think of something cheerful! Let's have something to eat."

But neither of them really wanted anything. They kept thinking of the two brave boys on their little raft.

"I do hope nobody comes to the island today," said Mary. "I don't feel as if I shall be able to act very well."

Nobody did come that day. The girls were left quite alone. They bathed in the sea and dried themselves in the sun. Then they bathed all over again. There really wasn't much else to do!

They missed the two boys very much, and when night came they even felt a little frightened.

"Cheer up!" said Jill, seeing Mary's long face. "We shall be all right cuddled up in the tent together! The enemy don't know the boys are gone—that's the main thing. I should think the boys are pretty safe by now—there has been a good wind blowing all day and they must have gone a long way already."

The girls lighted their little stove and put it just at

163

the tent-opening when night came. They liked to see the small light it gave. They boiled a kettle of water on it and sat inside the tent, drinking hot cocoa, whilst the stars came out in the sky.

As they were about to curl up and go to sleep they heard the sound of a seaplane droning overhead. It came over the island twice, and then went away.

And then, about an hour later, the girls heard the noise of the motor-boat! It grounded on the sand of the cove and the girls heard men's voices.

"Good gracious!" said Jill, sitting up in alarm. "What are they coming here at this time of night for? They will soon see the boys aren't here! Quick, Mary, get up. We'll slip out of the tent and go into the bracken. Maybe we can pretend we've been roaming over the island, and they'll think the boys are somewhere about too."

The girls left the tent and ran into the heather and bracken in the middle of the small island. The men left their boat on the beach and two of them came up to the tent.

They lifted the flap of the tent and flashed a torch inside. There was no one there, of course! One of the men called out loudly.

"Now, you children! Where are you?"

"Here!" answered Jill. She nudged Mary. "You shout too," she whispered. "Then I'll shout again, and they'll think we are all here."

"We're here!" yelled Mary valiantly, though her heart was beating hard.

"In the bracken!" shouted Jill.

"Come along down here," commanded the man. He was the one who could speak English.

"We shall have to go," said Jill. "Now don't you give

the boys away, Mary. Pretend they are about somewhere."

The girls made their way to the men, who flashed a light on them.

"Where are the boys?" demanded the man.

"Haven't you seen them?" asked Jill. "They must be about somewhere. Maybe they are in the tent. Have you looked?"

"Yes," said the man. "Now look here – what do you mean by lighting this stove out here? Are you trying to signal to anyone?"

"Good gracious! Of course not!" said Jill. "We only made some hot cocoa, that's all. Look – there are our dirty cups."

She wished she had not said this when the man looked for the cups – for he saw at once that there were only two! He looked at Jill suspiciously.

"Why did the boys not have the cocoa?" he asked.

"They weren't here when we made it," said Jill. "Why don't you go and look for them?"

The man turned out the stove, and the light flickered and went out. "Now don't you dare to show a light at nights," he said. "If I think you are signalling to anyone you will be very sorry!"

"Who could we signal to?" asked Jill. "We don't even know where we are!"

The man took no notice of her. He stood and shouted into the night. "Boys! Come here at once!"

There was no answer, of course – there couldn't be, for the boys were miles away on the sea.

"To-morrow I will come to tell those boys that when I call, they must answer," said the man in an angry voice. "I am going now – but to-morrow I come again. You will tell the boys they must be here, by the tent."

Jill and Mary said nothing. They could not tell the boys—and they wondered what would happen when the men found that they were not on the island.

The men went off in their boat again. "What a pity we lighted that stove!" said Jill. "I suppose that seaplane saw it and reported it—and they thought we were signalling to someone. How clever they must think us! I only wish we *could* signal to someone!"

Neither of the girls could imagine what the men would do when they came to find the boys the next day, and saw that they were gone. They cuddled up together and tried to go to sleep. They awoke early and got themselves some breakfast. Then they sat waiting for the men.

There was nothing else to do—it was of no use trying to hide. They must just pretend that they did not know where the boys were.

The motor-boat did not arrive until mid-day. Then two men came up to the tent, and the one who could speak English looked at the two girls.

"What about those boys?" he said. "Why are they not here?"

"I don't know," said Jill, trying to speak bravely.

"Where are they?" asked the man angrily.

"I don't know," said Jill again, quite truthfully.

"You don't know! You don't know!" said the man in disgust. "It is time you did know. Are they on this island?"

"Why don't you look and see?" said Jill. "I am sure you will not believe what I say—so you had better look."

The men glared at the plucky little girl and then went to hunt over the island. They found no one, of course, and returned looking worried.

They spoke to one another in a language that the girls could not understand. Then they went to the ruined buildings and looked around carefully. It did not take them long to see that the boys had pulled the old shack to pieces.

"So!" said the first man. "The boys tried to make a boat!"

Jill and Mary shook their heads. They were really feeling very much alarmed.

"It is a raft they made then?" asked the man. "What! You will not tell me, you naughty little girls! Then I shall order out my seaplanes and they will find those bad boys, and bring them back again. And you will all be made prisoners on another island till we take you far away to our country where you will stay for a long time."

The girls began to cry—not because they were afraid for themselves but because they did not want the seaplanes to hunt for Andy and Tom.

The men spoke quickly to one another. It was plain that they wanted to get back to the third island and tell their chief what had happened.

"We shall come back for you to-morrow," said the first man. "And maybe by that time we shall have caught the two bad boys. They will be punished, you may be sure!"

They left in their motor-boat, leaving two miserable girls behind them. "Oh, I do hope they won't catch poor Andy and Tom," wept Mary. "It's too bad! Now they will hunt all over the sea till they find them. And they'll catch us to-morrow too, and take us all away."

"Well, they just won't take *me* away!" said Jill, drying her eyes fiercely. "I shall give them a good old hunt

167

for me! I shall go to the second island and make them hunt all over the first one and not find me! That will give them a shock! I shall hide in the food-cave!"

"So will I!" said Mary, dabbing her eyes fiercely too. "We'll wait till the tide goes down and then we'll clamber over the rocks!"

So when the tide was low that day the two girls clambered hurriedly over the line of rocks that led from one island to the next, and came to the sandy beach. Not far off was the entrance to the cave that led up to the Round Cave.

"Nobody has seen us," said Mary, as they ran up to the cave. "We'll hide here and make the enemy think *we've* escaped from the island too! Perhaps they will be so busy looking for us that they will forget about the boys."

"I don't think they'll forget Andy and Tom," said Jill, making her way up the passage to the Round Cave. "I am sure that seaplanes are out looking for them already. I have heard three or four leaving the third island. Look, Mary—this chest is almost empty. Let's take out the tins and things that are left and get inside. We can shut the lid down on us if we hear anyone coming."

The girls got the chest ready, and then amused themselves by trying to find the funnel opening that led from the cave to the surface of the cliff above. But they could not find it.

"I wonder if it's night yet," said Mary, for it was impossible to tell in the dark cave. The girls had Andy's torch, for no daylight came into the cave at all. They crept to the shore-cave to see. Yes—it was twilight outside. Night would soon fall.

"I vote we make a nice soft bed in the sandy floor,"

said Jill. "We can cover ourselves with those empty sacks. And in the morning we'll peep out and see if we can see anything!"

So they made sandy beds and threw the sacks over themselves. They fell fast asleep and did not wake till morning.

And then, when they went to peep out of the shore-cave, they had a great surprise! Coming gracefully down to the smooth water was an enormous seaplane, droning like a great bumble-bee.

"It's coming to get us!" squealed Mary in fright, and the two girls scuttled back into the Round Cave!

XXV

RETURN TO THE ISLANDS

If only the girls had stopped to look carefully at that seaplane, they would have noticed that it bore the signs of their *own* country! It was the very same seaplane that had rescued Tom and Andy! It had flown to headquarters, had made its report, and had handed Tom's camera in.

As soon as the pictures had been developed, and the seaplane and submarine photographs had come out clearly, there was great excitement.

Tom and Andy had been questioned closely. They told their story clearly and well, and the men who listened to them were amazed at the adventures the four children had been through.

"Well, you have stumbled on an astonishing secret," said one man who had been listening. "We are proud of you! Now we shall be able to spring a real surprise on our enemy, and clean up all the submarines and seaplanes that have been worrying our shipping for some time. We did not know they had a base so near us. No wonder they have been able to do such damage!"

"Please, sir, what about my sisters?" asked Tom anxiously. "Will you get them away before you do anything?"

The men laughed heartily. "Of course!" said one. "That will be our first job. You don't really suppose we should forget those two plucky little girls, do you? Oh no—we shall send your father's seaplane to rescue them—and after that—oho! A big surprise will come to those islands!"

The boys grinned. "May we see the surprise, sir?" asked Andy.

"No," said the man. "It will be a bit too noisy." He turned to Tom's father and gave him a few quick orders.

"Come along," said the boy's father. "You and Andy must come with me to the islands so that you may tell me quickly where the girls are. We have to get them off before we attack the enemy—and I'd like to do it as quickly as possible before anyone knows we've discovered their secret!"

The boys were thrilled! To go off in that wonderful seaplane again—to the islands! And to rescue the two girls under the very noses of the enemy! What fun!

They all went aboard the great seaplane. They rowed out to it in a little boat and climbed up the ladder over the side, and into the plane. A few quick orders, and the great engines were started up.

R-r-r-r-r! R-r-r-r-r-r-r! R-r-r-r-r-r-r-r-r! The seaplane skimmed over the water for a little while and then rose from the surface as gracefully as a gull. It soared up and round, and then flew in a straight line towards the far-off islands.

The boys were trembling with excitement and joy. They had had many adventures, but this last one, the rescue of the girls, was the finest of the lot! They looked out over the sea, watching for the first sign of the islands they now knew so well.

"As soon as we sight the islands, we are going cautiously," said Tom's father. "We don't want to warn the enemy if we can help it! You say there is a good landing-place off the shore of the second island, Andy.

Well, you must guide us there when the islands come in sight, and we'll land on the water. Then you and Tom and a couple of men can get to the first island and take off the girls. Then off we'll go again and give the signal for the warships to go and surprise the enemy!"

"Warships!" cried the boys. "I say! What a shock for the enemy!"

"It's a shock they deserve," said Tom's father grimly. "We are sending three warships and some aeroplanes to deal with the submarines and seaplanes. So, you see, we want to get the girls off as quickly as possible."

"Oh, golly, wouldn't I like to join the fight!" groaned Andy. "Oh, couldn't I, sir?"

"No," said Tom's father. But he smiled at the eager boy and clapped him on the shoulder. "You're a good lad, Andy," he said, "and I'm glad that my three children had your help in their amazing adventures!"

Andy went red with pleasure. He thought Tom's father was a fine man, dressed in his grand uniform. He wondered what his own father would say when he heard all their adventures—and in his secret mind he felt a little uncomfortable because his father would have to hear the news that his fishing-boat had been lost.

The boys kept a watch for the islands—and as soon as they caught sight of them, lying flat in the sea, they both shouted loudly:

"There they are!"

"The islands, the islands!"

"Which is the one the girls are on?" asked Tom's father eagerly. Tom showed him.

"The first one," he said. "And the next one is where the food-cave is, and the third one is where the submarines are. I don't know anything about the other islands further off. We didn't have time to explore those."

"Well, *we* shall," said the boy's father, in a grim tone. "Now, Tom, we are almost on the coast of the second island. Is that the smooth bit of water we can land on, just down there?"

"Yes!" cried both boys, as they saw the flat stretch of water that lay between the reef of rocks and the cave-beach. The seaplane circled round and flew down gracefully. She skimmed the water a little, like a swallow, and then came to rest, bobbing up and down as she lay there.

"The tide is a bit too deep over the rocks that lead to the first island," said Tom in disappointment. "We can't climb over them to rescue the girls yet."

"We'll take a boat, then," said his father. "Are those the caves you hid in, Tom?"

"Yes—that one just there is the one that leads to the food-cave," said Tom. "Like to see it, Daddy? You might find something of importance there, perhaps."

"Yes—we might as well have a look," said the boy's father. So a boat shot off from the seaplane carrying the two boys, Tom's father, and two men. They landed on the beach and went towards the cave.

The girls were hiding inside the chest when they heard footsteps coming up the passage-way that led from the shore-cave to the Round Cave. They lay there trembling, wondering when they were going to be discovered.

Tom led his father into the cave. "Look!" he said, "do you see all these boxes and chests, Daddy? They are absolutely *full* of food of all sorts. I can tell you it came in handy when we were so hungry. At first I kept a list of the things we took, thinking that we would pay for them when we discovered the owner, but——"

Tom stopped. A queer noise was coming from a big chest near by. He stared in surprise.

"What's that noise?" said Tom's father at once.

"I don't know," said Tom. "Listen!"

It was the girls inside the chest, of course! They had heard Tom's voice, and they were quite mad with joy and excitement—but they couldn't lift up the lid of the chest which they had carefully shut down over themselves! It had got so tightly fastened that they could not push it up, and the two girls were shouting and banging on the lid to make themselves heard.

"There's something in that chest," said Tom in a trembling voice. "Is it the enemy playing a trick?"

"We'll soon see," said his father, in a fierce voice. He rapped out an order to the two men with him, and they went over to the chest. They ripped off the lid—and everyone stood ready to fight the enemy.

But it was two small, excited, and most untidy little girls who rose up from the chest, shouting loudly:

"Tom! Andy! It's us! We hid here because we thought you were the enemy!"

Their father picked them out of the chest and hugged them. They were as surprised as he was! They simply couldn't believe their eyes!

"Daddy! It's you! However did you get here? Oh, Tom! Andy! You've come to rescue us just in time. Oh, what a good thing you came to the cave!"

"Why are you here?" asked the boys.

Jill and Mary told their tale, their words tumbling over one another. When their father heard that the enemy guessed that the boys had left on a raft, he hustled them all out of the cave very quickly.

174

"We'll get back to our plane," he said. "We shall get into a spot of trouble if the enemy see us here. If they really think the boys have gone to tell their secret they will be watching for us—though not expecting us quite so soon. Come along!"

They all rowed off to the seaplane. The girls were thrilled to get inside it, and even more excited when it rose into the air and left the sea far below.

"Good-bye, little islands," said Jill, watching them get smaller and smaller as the plane left them behind. "We've had lots of adventures on you—but I'm very glad to leave you, all the same!"

The boys were looking down as the plane flew swiftly along. Suddenly Tom gave a shout.

"Warships! Look! Steaming below us at top speed! Are they going to the islands?"

"They are," said his father. "There will be quite a lot of noise round about your islands very soon! And, look—here are aeroplanes, too, to help the warships."

A flight of aeroplanes flew near the seaplane. The children felt tremendously excited. What a pity they had left before the fun began!

"And now, home we go to your mother," said the children's father, "and to Andy's father. Both will be so very glad to have you back again."

"But what will my father say about his lost fishing-boat?" wondered poor Andy. "Whatever *will* he say?"

THE END OF THE ADVENTURES

The seaplane flew over the water, and at last came to the shores of the little fishing-village where Andy lived, and the other three children had been staying. It glided down to the water, and rested there, its great wings spread out beside it.

The little beach was soon crowded with people — fishermen and their wives, children, visitors — all shouting and cheering. The news had gone round that the four missing children had been found!

A boat set off to fetch the children from the plane. It was rowed by Andy's father! How Andy shouted to see him!

"Dad! We're back again!"

The bearded man in the boat smiled and waved. He had been terribly worried about Andy and the children — but now his heart was glad. They were safe!

The children tumbled into the boat, all talking at once. Andy's father patted his boy on the shoulder and smiled at him out of eyes as blue as Andy's. Neither of them said very much, but their hands pressed one another joyfully. Tom's father came with them. He had two days' leave and was going to spend it with his wife and children.

The people on the beach cheered and shouted. The little boat grounded and was pulled up the shore by willing hands. Everyone wanted to shake hands and say how glad they were to see the children back. And then the children saw their mother! They rushed to her and hugged her like bears, shouting and laughing.

"Now, now, give me a look in," said their father, smiling, and the whole family went up the beach together. Andy went off with his father. He had no mother, so he thought twice as much of his father.

What a talking and chattering there was that evening! The children's mother made them all strip off their dirty clothes and have a good bath before they did anything.

"I don't know you when you look so dreadfully dirty!" she said. "Put on clean clothes, for goodness' sake!"

Soon they were all clean and dressed in other clothes. It felt nice to be tidy and fresh again. They hung round their mother and tried to tell her all their adventures at once.

"Andy was marvellous," said Tom. "We could never have done what we did if it hadn't been for him. The girls were pretty brave too—I was proud of them."

"And old Tom didn't do so badly—except that he left his precious camera behind and got us all into a fix!" said Jill. "He was as brave as could be."

"Well, I'm proud of you all," said their mother, hugging them. "But oh, I was so awfully worried when you didn't come back. I sent a message to your father and he came in his seaplane and hunted for you for days. He wouldn't give up hunting—and it's a good thing he didn't, for he found you just in time! You and Andy would never, never have got home on that little raft, you know, Tom."

"Wouldn't we?" said Tom, surprised. "I thought we really might."

"I don't think Andy thought there was much hope," said the children's father, "but he knew it was your only chance—and he knew, besides, that it was his duty to tell someone the great secret you had discovered. It means a lot to our country to know the secret of those desolate little islands."

There was a dull booming sound as the children's father finished speaking. Tom looked at his father.

"Is that guns?" he asked.

"Yes. It will be the end of those hateful submarines," said his father gravely. "There will be no more of our ships sunk without warning by *that* nest of submarines! And I rather think that our aeroplanes will drive off any seaplanes round about those islands—those that are not destroyed will fly to their own country in fear! They are no match for our pilots!"

The children were silent as they listened to the guns booming far away again. They were all imagining the islands echoing to the terrific sound of gun-fire. Mary began to cry.

Her father put his arm round her. "Yes, Mary," he said, "it is something to cry about, to think that we have to fight so much evil and wickedness. It is right against wrong and we have to be strong and courageous when we fight such a powerful and evil enemy as ours. But dry your eyes—you are on the right side and that is something to be proud of!"

Andy came tearing up to the cottage. "I say!" he yelled. "Do you hear the guns? I guess they are waking up the islands! What a shock for the enemy!"

"Andy, was your father angry about his fishing-boat being lost?" asked Tom, who knew how much Andy was dreading what his father might say about that.

"He hasn't said a word about it," said Andy. "Not a word. He's been fine about it. We're going to fish with my uncle, now that we've lost our own boat. Maybe one day we'll save enough money to get a boat again."

"I wouldn't worry about that, if I were you," said Tom's father unexpectedly. "I rather think there is a surprise coming for you to-morrow!"

"Oh, what?" cried all the children, and Andy stared at Tom's father in surprise.

"Wait and see," was the answer. So they had to wait —and the next day the surprise arrived!

Andy saw it first. He was on the beach, mending nets, and the other children were helping him. Andy happened to look up—and he saw a fishing-boat rounding the corner of the cliff

"Hallo!" said Andy. "Whose boat is that? I haven't seen it before! My word, what a smart one! Look at its red sail!"

The children stood up and watched the little fishing-boat drawing in to shore. It was a real beauty, fresh with new paint, and with its red sail billowing out in the breeze.

It came in to the beach and a man jumped out. He saw the children and hailed them. "Hie, give a hand here!"

They ran to help. "Whose boat is this?" asked Tom.

"I've got to find the owner," said the man. "It's for the boy whose name has been given to the boat."

The children looked at the name on the boat. There, painted boldly, was Andy's own name—ANDY!

"*Andy!* The boat is called *Andy!*" squealed Jill. "Oh, Andy, does that mean it's for you?"

Andy stared at the boatman in astonishment and joy. "It *can't* be for me!" he said.

"Well, if you're Andy, it's yours," said the boatman. "I understand that it's a little reward from the Government of our country for good services; wasn't it you who discovered the secret of those islands, and lost your own boat in doing so?"

"Golly!" said Andy, and could say no more. He stood and stared at the lovely boat in delight and pride. It was the finest in the bay. It was beautiful all over. Never, never could Andy ever have saved enough money to buy a boat like this!

The other three children were full of joy. They had been so sorry for Andy when his boat had been lost, for they knew that he and his father got their living from fishing. And now Andy had a much better boat—they couldn't keep back their joy. They danced and shouted and clapped Andy on the back till the boy almost fell over.

"You shall share the boat with me," said Andy, suddenly finding his tongue again. "It shall belong to all of us!"

"Well, we have to go back to school again soon," said Tom, rather sadly. "But we're to come here for holidays always, Andy—so we can share it then. Can't we go out in it now?"

Many people had come down to the beach to look at the fine new fishing-boat. Andy's father and uncle came running down—and when they heard the news they could not believe their ears!

"It's called *Andy*," said Tom proudly. "Isn't it a fine boat? It's because Andy was so brave and helped his country such a lot. And he's going to share it with us when we come here for our holidays."

Andy's father got into the boat and looked at it carefully. His blue eyes gleamed with joy. "Ah, Andy lad," he said, "this is a wonderful boat. We'll go out on the tide this evening, and do a wee bit of fishing together! And you must write to the Government to thank them for their bonny present! It's most generous of them!"

Andy was not a good writer, so Tom wrote the letter for him and posted it. And then Andy, his father, and the three children all got into the fishing-boat that evening to make the first trip together.

The red sail billowed out against the sky, as the evening breeze filled it. Like a sea-bird the little boat bobbed gracefully on the water—and then raced away on the tide. The *Andy* was away on her first trip!

"Now don't get lost on any more adventures!" shouted the children's father, who had come down to the beach to watch. "Just go fishing now—and bring me back something for breakfast! I don't want submarines and seaplanes this time!"

Everyone laughed. The sail flapped happily, and the boat sped on like a live thing towards the fishing-grounds.

"She feels a good boat, bonny and brave!" said Andy's father.

"The *Andy* is like her master then!" cried Tom. "For he's just the same. Good luck to the *Andy*, so bonny and brave—and good luck to you too, Andy!"

And there we will leave them all, scudding along in the *Andy*—and we'll say the same—good luck to you, Andy, and your red-sailed boat! Good luck!

The Adventurous Four Again

CHAPTER I

BACK WITH ANDY AGAIN

THREE very excited children bumped along a rough country lane in a farmer's cart. The Scottish carter sat in front, saying nothing, but listening with a little smile to the children's happy voices.

"We shall see Andy again soon! We haven't seen him since our exciting adventures last summer!" said Tom, a red-haired boy of twelve.

"It was bad luck getting measles in the Christmas hols. so that we couldn't come up here and stay in our little cottage," said Jill. She and her sister Mary were twins, and were very like each other. They each had long golden plaits and blue eyes, and were younger than Tom.

Tom spoke to the carter.

"Jock! Did you hear about our adventures last year?" he asked.

Jock nodded his head. He hardly ever said a word.

The children, with their friend Andy, had indeed had some thrilling adventures. They had gone out in Andy's father's fishing-boat one day, and had been caught by a storm. They had been swept miles out of their course on to a lonely island—and had found a nest of enemy submarines in the waters there, hiding to pounce on any ships that came within their reach.

"And poor Andy lost his father's boat," said Jill, remembering how afraid Andy had been of what his father might say about the lost boat.

"But it didn't matter—because Andy was given a much, much better boat!" said Mary. "And it was called *Andy* —do you remember, it had his name painted on it? Wasn't Andy pleased?"

185

The fisher-boy had been more than pleased. He had been filled with the greatest delight. The new fishing boat was a magnificent one, with a lovely red sail. Andy's father had been overjoyed too, for a fishing-boat meant his livelihood to him. Catching fish and selling them was his work and Andy's — and now they had one of the finest boats on the coast.

The farm-cart jolted along, and soon the children came in sight of the sea. The coast there was rocky and dangerous, but the sea was a lovely blue, and the children shouted in joy to see it.

"The sea! There it is! And look — there are the fishing-boats out on it!"

"I bet I can see Andy's," shouted Tom. "Look — that one with the bright red sail! Isn't that Andy's, Jock?"

Jock nodded, and the three children fixed their eyes on the red-sailed boat.

Andy's boat! Andy was out there on the restless sea — and soon they would go out with him. What fun they would have!

Their mother was already waiting for them in the cottage she had bought in the fishing village. She had gone there two days ahead of the children to get things ready for them, when they broke up from school. It was the Easter holiday, and everywhere the trees were leafing, the hedges were greening, and the banks were starred with primroses, violets and celandines.

"A whole month's holiday by the sea — with Andy and his boat!" said Tom. "I simply can't think of anything lovelier. I don't expect we'll have any adventures *this* time — but that won't matter."

"We had enough last summer to last us for years," said Jill. "I was frightened sometimes — but it all ended happily."

"Except for those hidden enemy submarines!" said

186

Tom. "They didn't have a very happy ending! Look—
there's Mother!"

Sure enough, it was their mother, standing at the next
corner, waving. The children tumbled out of the cart and
flung themselves on her.

"Mother! It's lovely to see you. Is everything all right?"

"Is the cottage ready? Have you seen Andy?"

"I'm awfully hungry, Mother. Is there anything nice
to eat?" That was Tom, of course. He was always
hungry. His mother laughed.

"Welcome back to our little village, children! Yes,

there's plenty to eat, Tom. And yes, I've seen Andy. He was sorry he couldn't meet you, but there's a good shoal of fish in, and he had to go out to help his father in the boat."

"Does the boat go well?" asked Tom eagerly. "It was marvellous last summer. I've often thought of Andy whilst we were at school, and envied him. There he was, sailing out in all weathers, having a wonderful time — and I was writing Latin exercises at school, and being ticked off because I threw a rubber at someone."

"Oh Tom — don't tell me your report is a bad one!" said his mother, as they all walked down a slope to the little fishing village below. Jock came behind carrying large trunks as easily as if they were empty boxes!

"When will Andy be back?" asked Jill. "Has he changed, Mother? Is he still the same old Andy?"

"Of course," said her mother. "He's grown a bit taller — and a bit broader — but he's almost fifteen now, you know. You're nearly thirteen, Tom! You've grown too. So have the girls. You'll see Andy later in the evening, when the fishing-boats come back. He promised to come straight up and see you."

"We'll go down to the shore and wait for his boat to come in," said Tom. "After we've had something to eat, I mean. What is there, Mother?"

"Ham, eggs, three kinds of scones, two kinds of jam, and a fish-pie," said his mother. "Will that do for you?"

"I should think so," said Tom, who felt as if he could eat the whole lot at once. "Golly, it's good to be back again, Mother — and to think of all the sailing we'll have!"

"Well — don't find enemy submarines this time," said his mother, as she swung open a little white gate that led through a tiny garden to the cottage. "I really couldn't bear it if you got lost on a lonely island again."

They all ran up the path to the wooden door. It stood

open. A bright fire burned in the living-room, and the table was set with so many dishes of food that Tom gave a whoop of delight.

"Golly! Must I wash my hands? Can't we begin now?"

"No. Wash first," said his mother firmly. "You all look like sweeps. Would you like boiled eggs to begin with, or fish-pie?"

"Both!" shouted Tom, and ran to wash in the little sink that was the only place where water ran from a tap.

They all made an enormous meal. "I can see I shall have my work cut out to satisfy your appetites these holidays!" said their mother. "No—you needn't help to clear away and wash up, twins. I've got Mrs. MacIntyre coming in to help. You can put on your jerseys and shorts and go down to meet Andy. I expect the boats will be putting in soon, if they've made a good catch."

The children hurriedly pulled off their school-clothes, and scrambled to find their jerseys and shorts. The weather was fine and sunny, almost like summer. If only it would stay like that all the holidays!

They raced down to the shore. Fine, soft sand lay between the rocks that jutted up all over the beach. A little stone jetty ran a short distance into the water. To this jetty the fishing-boats came with their hauls.

Andy's boat was clearly to be seen, a good way out. But now they were all coming in—the *Sea-Gull*, the *Mary-Ann*, the *Jessie*, the *Andy*, the *Starfish* and the rest. The breeze filled the sails, and they billowed out prettily.

"It's a fine sight, a fishing-fleet coming home!" said Tom, running up the jetty and down, so excited that he couldn't stand still. "I wish I had a boat of my own! Hi, Andy, Andy! Come in first, show us what your boat can do!"

Almost as if Andy had heard, the red-sailed boat surged forward in front of the others. The wind swept down on her, and she glided along like a red-winged bird on the water.

"There's Andy! There's his father too!" shouted Jill. "Andy, we're here! Have you made a good catch?"

"Ahoy there!" came Andy's voice. "Ahoy!"

Then the beautiful boat came deftly to the stone jetty, and Andy leapt off. He and Tom shook hands, both grinning widely in delight. The twins flung themselves on the fisher-boy and hugged him, squealing in delight.

"Andy, you've grown! Andy, you're browner than ever! Oh, Andy, we're all back again, isn't it lovely?"

"Grand," said Andy, as pleased as they were. He repeated the word and rolled the *r* in it even more. "Gr-r-r-r-rand!"

Then his father jumped out to make the boat fast. He smiled at the three children, and shook hands gravely with them all. He never had much to say, and the children knew he was strict with Andy, and made him work hard. But they liked him and trusted him.

"You'll help with the fish, Andy," he said, and the boy turned at once to bring in the great catch they had made. The children helped too.

"I do think the beginning bit of a holiday is lovely," said Mary. "I think I like it best of all."

"Yes. The middle and end parts slip away so quickly," said Jill. "But you sort of feel the beginning bit will last for ever!"

"Can we go sailing with you soon?" asked Tom. "This evening, Andy?"

"No—not today," said Andy, knowing that his father would not let his boat out again. "Tomorrow perhaps, if we're allowed. Dad may not want the boat tomorrow. We've had such a good catch today."

"Is it nice to see your own name painted on your boat?" said Mary. "*A-N-D-Y*—doesn't it look lovely?"

"It's your boat as well," said Andy. "I always told you you could share it when you were here. It ought to be called the *Andy-Tom-Jill-and-Mary!*"

All the other boats came in. The children greeted the fishermen. They knew them all, and they knew the fine little fishing-boats that bobbed gently up and down beside the jetty. But they felt that Andy's boat—their own boat—was the very best of all!

"It's getting dark," said Tom, with a sigh. "We'd better go home. We promised Mother we'd be in before dark—and golly, I do feel tired. We've had a jolly long journey today, and we'll feel better tomorrow. I just feel now I want one thing—to fall into bed and sleep!"

"What—don't you want any supper!" said Jill. "You *must* be tired, Tom!"

Andy laughed. He was happy to see the twins again and to have his friend Tom. Four whole weeks together! They would have some fun.

"See you tomorrow," said Andy, as the three said good-bye and turned away from the shore. "I'll be along."

Back they went to the cottage, all feeling suddenly tired. They could hardly eat any supper—and then they undressed quickly, washed, and fell into their beds, half-asleep before their heads touched the pillow.

"Tomorrow—lots of tomorrows!" said Jill, but Mary didn't answer. She was asleep and dreaming of all the exciting tomorrows.

CHAPTER II

OFF ON A SAILING TRIP

THE next few days were lovely. Andy took them sailing in his boat, which he insisted belonged to them all — a quarter each.

"I'll have the red sail for *my* quarter," said Jill. "I do love it so! Andy, can't we go out with the rest of the boats, when they go fishing?"

"Oh yes," said Andy, and out they went the next time the little fleet went out. Andy taught the children how to let down the nets. They watched with excitement the jumping, slithering, silvery fish caught in the meshes of the great net.

The fisher-boy taught them how to set lobster-pots, too, in the right places. They took home enough fish and lobsters, scallops and crabs to keep them in food for a week!

The sun shone. They grew brown. They climbed the rocky cliffs all about, and had a wonderful time. Then Tom grew restless and wanted to go off on a much longer trip.

"Let's go somewhere exciting," he said. "Can't we take the *Andy* and go on a trip somewhere? Don't you know anywhere thrilling, Andy, you could take us to?"

"Well," said Andy, "I promised your mother I wouldn't take you right out to sea any more, to visit any of our islands — in case a storm came up, like last year, and wrecked us. So it would have to be somewhere along the coast."

"Do think of somewhere," begged the twins. "Somewhere that nobody goes to."

"There's the Cliff of Birds," said Andy suddenly. The others stared at him.

192

"The Cliff of Birds," said Jill. "What a funny name!"

"It's a good name," said Andy. "There are thousands of birds there—I couldn't tell you how many—all kinds! Gulls, shags, cormorants, puffins—they nest there and all round and about—on the cliffs, in the cliffs, over the cliffs —everywhere. They say you can't walk a step this season of the year without treading on a nesting-bird. They're a sight to see."

All the three children were fond of birds. Their eyes shone.

"Let's go there!" said Tom. "What a sight it would be! I'll take my camera. We're having a snap-shot

193

competition at my school next term, and I could enter some bird pictures for it."

"Yes, do let's go," said Jill. "It sounds exciting. I wonder you never told us about the Cliff of Birds before, Andy!"

"Well, last time you were here, it was full summer," said Andy. "The birds have left their nesting-places on the cliffs by then, and are out on the open sea. There's not much to see. But at nesting-time it's different. They're all there."

"Well, we'll go," said Tom. "How far is it? Can we get there and back in a day?"

"We'll have to," said Jill. "Mother won't let us go off for a night, I'm sure!"

"If we start early in the morning we'd be back before dark," said Andy. "It's a long way — and it's a lonely part of the coast too. We'll have to be careful, because there are rocks all about. But there's a passage between them that my father knows. I'll get him to tell me. I've been twice with him."

"When shall we go?" asked Jill, beginning to feel excited. "Tomorrow?"

"No. I'm wanted on the boat with my father," said Andy. "But maybe the next day. You'll have to do without me tomorrow. You get out your book on birds and read it well, then you'll know the birds on the cliff when you see them."

So, all the next day, the children pored over their books on birds, looking up each sea-bird, studying it, and learning its name. Tom got out his camera and put a new roll of films into it. They told their mother where they were going.

"It certainly sounds exciting," she said. "I hope Andy knows the way down the coast well. It's rather dangerous round here."

"Oh, Mother, Andy could sail a boat anywhere!" said

194

Tom. "He's been twice before, anyway. Won't it be exciting to go somewhere that nobody ever goes to?"

"The Cliff of Birds," said Mary. "Thousands of them, Mother. You'll see them if Tom gets some good snaps. I suppose we shall climb the cliff."

"I'd better have a word with Andy about that," said her mother, and she did. But Andy assured her that he would not let anyone do anything they couldn't do safely and easily.

Two days later the children awoke with a jump, as the alarm clock went off. It had been set for dawn – how early it was! Tom slipped into the girls' room to make sure they were awake, and not going off to sleep again.

"The sky's just turning silvery in the east," he said. "Hurry up. We've got to be at the jetty in a few minutes. I bet Andy's already there."

Their mother appeared in her dressing-gown, looking sleepy. "I thought I would just see you off," she said. "Now, you do promise to be careful, don't you? Andy's got life-belts on board, hasn't he?"

"Oh, Mother, you know we can all swim like fish!" said Jill.

"Yes – in calm or slightly rough water," said her mother. "But if you fell overboard in stormy waters you'd find things much more difficult. You've packed the food on board, haven't you?"

"Oh *yes*," said Tom, who could always be trusted to look after the food side. "We put it on board yesterday evening – everything you gave us, Mother. It will last us nicely for a day."

"It would last most families for a week!" said his mother. "Now – are you ready? Take woollen coats with you, because it isn't summer, you know. Tom, where's your mack?"

Soon they were off. The sky was much lighter now. The

children could see golden fingers coming up from the east. The sun was just below the rim of the world there. They raced down to the jetty, feeling the wind quite cold on their faces and their bare legs.

Andy was there, of course, waiting for them patiently. He grinned when he saw their excited faces. "Get on board," he said. "Everything's ready. I'll cast off."

The children tumbled on board the fishing-boat they loved. It was roomy, but not too big for them to handle. It had a small, cosy cabin below. All three children were good at helping Andy now, and could be trusted with anything.

The boat slid away from the jetty. The breeze billowed out the red sails. Then, quite suddenly it seemed, the sun appeared above the sky-line, a dazzling rounded edge, and at once the water flashed with golden lines and twinkled brilliantly as the boat plunged forward.

"The sun's rising," said Jill, and caught her breath at the sudden beauty of it all. "The world's all new again. Look at the sun—it seems to be climbing out of the sea itself!"

Soon the children could no longer look at the sun, it was so big and bright. The boat went slipping along in waves that seemed made of golden light and blue shadows. It was worth coming out so early just to see the enchanting beauty of the rising sun.

"Heaps of people have never seen the sun rise," said Jill, as she leaned over the side of the boat to look at the gold-flecked waves. "Hardly any of the girls at my school have. They've missed something! I think there ought to be a law that says everyone must watch a sunrise, and everyone must see a bluebell wood, and a buttercup field, and..."

"Look out for the sail!" yelled Andy, as the big red sail swung across. Jill ducked, and forgot what she was

196

saying. Andy was at the tiller, looking browner than ever. His dark hair blew straight upright in the wind, and his eyes shone as blue as the sea.

"I say," began Tom, "isn't it about time to . . ."

Everyone interrupted him. "To . . . have something to eat!" they all chanted, knowing Tom's ways very well indeed.

"I wasn't going to say that," said Tom, aggrieved. "I was going to say—oughtn't we to keep closer to the shore now? We're heading right out to sea."

"Got to," said Andy, keeping a firm hold on the tiller, as the boat swept into a strong current. "There are rocks farther in. Can't risk them in this boat. We must keep out

a fair bit, then, when I see the spot my father told me of, I'll swing inland a bit."

Andy had a rough chart with him. He pushed it across to Tom, holding on to it till the boy had it safely, because of the rushing wind.

"Look at that," he said. "Those dots are rocks. See how the sea nearer in is peppered with them. Sly rocks they are — just below the surface. They'll scratch a hole in the bottom of a boat in the twinkling of an eye. It takes us longer to go out to sea, and then turn in, but it's safer. We've got to look out for three tall pine-trees on a cliff, before we turn in. They're marked on the map."

Everyone studied the map with interest. What a long way down the coast the Cliff of Birds was! No wonder Andy said they must start early.

"What time shall we be there?" said Mary.

"We should be there about eleven, with luck," said Andy. "Maybe before. We'll have our dinner then. We'll be hungry!"

Tom looked really alarmed. "What! Are we to wait till then? We'll be starved!"

"Oh, we'll have breakfast first," said Andy. "We'll have it at seven, or half-past. Maybe a few biscuits now would be nice. What do you say, girls?"

Everyone thought it was a very good idea. "Biscuits *and* chocolate!" said Jill. "They go so well together. I'll get them."

She disappeared into the little cabin below, and came back again with four rations of biscuits and chocolate. Everyone was soon munching, Andy still at the tiller. He said he was not going to let anyone else steer the boat that day, it was too dangerous!

The sun was much higher in the sky now. It was warmer, though the strong sea-breeze was cold. Everyone was glad of woollen jerseys, cardigans and macks on top.

"Now—here's where we head inland," said Andy suddenly. "See those three pine-trees on the cliff, far away over there?"

"You've got eyes like a hawk, Andy," said Tom, screwing his up to try to see the pine-trees on the distant coast. He could just make them out. But neither of the girls could see them clearly.

Andy swung the boat round a little. The sail flapped hard. The boat now ran even more quickly, and the children felt thrilled with the speed, and the up-and-down swing of the fine little boat.

"Breakfast-time!" said Andy. "We're doing very well— we deserve a jolly good breakfast!"

"We *do*!" said Tom, and scurried to get the food.

CHAPTER III

THE CLIFF OF BIRDS

BREAKFAST was a very welcome meal. There were hard-boiled eggs, scones and butter and a tin of peaches. Jill heated some milk down in the little cabin and made cocoa, which they all enjoyed.

Now the boat was heading shore-wards, and the rocky cliffs could be clearly seen. It was about eight o'clock. The sun was higher in the sky, and its warmth was very welcome.

"My word—what a lonely, desolate coast!" said Tom, watching it as the boat sped along. "And look at those wicked rocks, Andy, nearer the shore."

"Yes—there are some out here too, so we've got to keep a look-out," said Andy. "The worst are marked on that chart. I know them all. In about an hour's time we have to slip between an opening in a rocky ridge we'll come to, and skim along in a kind of channel between two rows of rocks. We're all right if we get into the channel. It's like a sea pathway, and so long as we keep in the middle of it, we're all right."

At about nine-o'clock the children saw ahead of them a very turbulent stretch of water. The waves frothed and surged and sent spray high into the air.

"Look out!" said Tom, pointing ahead. "There must be rocks there."

"Yes—just about here is the opening I told you of," said Andy. "We've got to slip through it as soon as we come to it. I think it lies beyond that big surge of water."

He cleverly skirted the bubbling, frothing patch, where the waves were torn into shreds on rocks that hardly showed above the surface. Then the children gave a shout.

"Here's the entrance — look — a nice, calm little bit!"

Andy steered the boat deftly through the little passage, the opening through the outer ridge of rocks. The boat careered along, its sails full of wind, and slid into a channel between the outer and inner rows of rocks. Fairly calm water ran there.

"There are horrid rocks on each side of us," said Jill. "But here we're safe! How far does this queer calm channel go, Andy?"

"It flows to Smuggler's Rock," said Andy, "but we swing landwards before we get there, to the Cliff of Birds."

"Smuggler's Rock! What an exciting name!" said Tom, and he looked at the map. "Oh yes — your father's put it in — at least, I suppose this dot, with S.R. beside it, means Smuggler's Rock?"

"That's right," said Andy. "We've a good way to go still. My, aren't these lonely waters? We haven't sighted a ship on the sea or seen a soul on land since we left our village behind!"

"It's a wild bit of the coast," said Tom. "I wonder why Smuggler's Rock was given that name, Andy? Were there smugglers there in the old days?"

"I don't know," said Andy. "I've only seen the Rock from the distance. It's like a small steep island made entirely of rock. Nothing grows there, I should think — except seaweed round the foot. Maybe there are caves there that smugglers hid things in. I don't know anything about it. Nobody goes there now — and maybe they never did! Maybe it's just a name."

"It's half-past ten," said Tom, after a time. "Shall we soon be there, Andy — at the Cliff of Birds?"

"Why, are you getting hungry again?" asked Andy, with a grin.

"Well — I am," said Tom, "but I wasn't thinking of that. I was thinking of the time, and how long we'd have there.

201

We'll have to allow a good many hours for getting back."

"We'll have a couple of hours at the Cliffs and no more," said Andy. "But it will be enough. You'll be able to climb up the cliff and explore it a bit, and have some dinner, and maybe take some photographs. Then we'll have to go back."

"Is that Smuggler's Rock, look, right over there!" suddenly shouted Jill, pointing westwards. The others looked, and saw a small, rocky island rising above the waves a fair distance away. Almost at the same moment Andy swung the boat to the left, and headed for the shore.

"Yes — that's Smuggler's Rock," he said. "And did you notice that the channel we were in went on towards it? But I've swung away now, because we're coming to the Cliff of Birds. See the birds on the water now, and flying above it!"

As they sailed nearer to the Cliff of Birds the children shouted in amazement at the amount of birds to be seen everywhere. Gulls called, and the sound of their laughing voices, which Jill said reminded her of the mewing of cats, echoed all round them. Birds bobbed up and down on the water, skimmed the waves, soared high and low in the the air.

"Now, when we round this rocky point, you'll see we come into a kind of shallow bay, and the cliffs behind are the ones I've brought you to see," said Andy. "They are covered with the kind of little narrow ledges that sea-birds love for their nests. They must have used the cliff for hundreds of years."

The *Andy* rounded the point, and then swept into a shallow bay. The children gazed at the towering cliffs behind, too astonished to speak.

There were birds there by the thousand! They lined every ledge, they called from every point. They launched themselves from the steep cliffs into the air, and soared

and glided on the currents of air, crying and calling at the tops of their wild voices.

The sight of the red-sailed ship startled them. A hundred or so flew up from the cliffs, and their flight startled hundreds more, so that the rushing of wings sounded like a mighty wind. Tom gave a cry.

"What's that falling down the cliff—look, it's like a rain of white drops tumbling down!"

"Eggs!" said Andy. "These sea-birds lay their eggs on the bare ledges of rock, you know—and they are jolly careless with them. When they fly off suddenly they often make their precious eggs roll off—then down they fall and smash on the rocks below."

"What a waste," said Jill. "I wish we hadn't frightened them. But what a sight, Andy! I've never, never, in all my life seen or heard so many birds together before!"

"Andy, look—there's a river rushing out at the bottom of the cliff," said Tom, excited. "*Is* it a river? It seems to be coming out of a cave! Right out of the depths of the cliff."

"Yes, it's a river," said Andy, bringing the boat in gently. "It must flow right through the cliff. And look— do you see that waterfall splashing half-way down the cliff? That comes out of a hole somewhere up there. I suppose it couldn't find a way to seep down through the rock, so it has forced itself out up there, and made a waterfall."

"It's a very exciting place," said Jill. "I wish the birds wouldn't make quite so much noise, though. I can hardly hear myself speak!"

"Where are we going to put the boat?" asked Mary. "There's no jetty—and no sand to drag her on to. What shall we do?"

"I'll guide her into the deep pool under that overhanging cliff," said Andy. "And let down the anchor. She'll be all right there. We can jump across to the rocks nearby."

"Let's have dinner first," said Jill.

"Well—only just a snack now," said Tom, to everyone's surprise. "I'm longing to explore that bird-cliff. It's marvellous, really marvellous. We don't want to waste too much time eating. If we had a snack now, we could make a good meal on the way back."

"Right," said Andy. So they hurriedly made some sandwiches of bread and butter and potted meat. They ate them, had a drink, and then, with the *Andy* lying quietly at anchor, looked to see which rock would be the best to jump to.

"There's a rock just under water here," said Jill, peering

over the side of the boat. "We'll tread on that, and then we can easily get to that big rock there, and so to the rocky ledge at the bottom of the cliff."

They took off their shoes and tied them around their necks. Then they made their way across the rocks to the foot of the cliff. Not far off, the river that came out of a cavern in the cliff surged into the sea, frothing and seething where its current met the waves of the sea. The waters there boiled and surged and made a great noise. Altogether it was a very deafening place, for the sea-birds never once stopped their loud clamouring and calling.

"I'll find the easiest path up the cliff," said Andy, who was as good as a goat on hill or cliff. "You follow me carefully. It's a steep cliff, but not dangerous to anyone like us that's used to climbing about. Look out for any slippery bit. You go last, Tom, in case one of the girls should slip."

With the clamour of the birds round them, and a ceaseless swish of wings, the four children began their steep climb.

There were plenty of good footholds and handholds, but their parents would certainly not have liked to watch them going slowly upwards, higher and higher. Soon they looked like specks against the towering cliffs.

They had their rubber shoes on again now, and Tom carried his camera slung over his shoulder. Soon they came to the nesting-places, high up beyond the reach of any stormy waves. The frightened, angry birds flew off their eggs. There were no nests at all. Jill was grieved to see yet more eggs roll into the sea.

"Some of them don't fall off," she called. "They just roll round and round. Look what a funny shape they are — awfully pointed at one end."

"Eggs shaped like that don't roll away so easily," said Andy. "They are meant to roll round and round in exactly the same spot."

Soon they came to a narrow ledge that seemed almost like a pathway round the cliff-side. It was about halfway up. Jill suddenly gave a cry.

"Andy! I've just looked down! And oh, I don't like it a bit! I might fall, it makes me giddy."

"Don't be silly," said Andy, who didn't mind heights at all. "You've never minded before. Follow me, and I'll take you round the cliff a bit, where there's a wider place you can rest in. You're tired!"

Trembling, poor Jill followed Andy closely, not daring to look down at the far-away sea again. Neither Tom nor Mary minded a bit. They thought it was funny of Jill to feel afraid.

The ledge was a favourite nesting-place for the birds, and the children had to be careful not to tread on the eggs. Jill was glad when the rocky pathway widened out, and became a fine resting-place. At the back of this resting-place was a shallow cave. The children crawled into it, and lay there, panting, warm with their climb.

"I'll just go out and see if I can take a few snaps," said Tom, at last. But just as he was about to go, he stopped. He heard a noise that sounded most peculiar in that deserted, sea-bird-haunted place—the sound of somebody whistling a well-known tune! How very strange!

CHAPTER IV

A REAL PUZZLE

THE whistling sounded loud and clear. The children listened in the utmost astonishment. Somebody on the Cliff of Birds! Who in the wide world could it be?

A wild clamouring of sea-birds began again and the whistling was drowned in the noise. The children looked at one another.

"Did you hear that?" said Tom. "It was someone whistling!"

"We'll see who it was," said Andy, and he half-started up. Jill pulled him back.

"He might be cross if he knew we were here. He might be a bird-watcher or photographer or something—and if he thought we had disturbed the birds, he'd be angry."

"Well—it's our cliff as much as his," said Andy, shaking his shoulder free from Jill's hold. The whistling sounded again, very clear indeed, and a scraping sound told the children that the whistler must be coming near.

"He's just above us!" said Jill, in a startled whisper. "Oh—look!"

Above the cave they were resting in was a narrow ledge. On this ledge the whistler had sat himself down, for, dangling over the top edge of the cave suddenly appeared a pair of bare legs.

The children stared at these legs in silence. They didn't like them a bit. They were enormous legs, and on the end of them were enormous feet, very dirty indeed. The legs were covered with thick black hairs, almost like the fur of an animal.

Somehow the children felt that the owner of these legs would be as horrid as his dangling feet! They didn't say a

207

word. Jill's heart beat rather fast. She stared at the swinging feet, and wished they would go away.

The whistling went on and on. Then, dropped deliberately down to the rocky ledge that lay in front of the cave, came some sea-birds' eggs. They were flung down to make a splash as they smashed. The children felt indignant. How horrid of anyone to break birds' eggs on purpose like that!

But no one said a word. There was something about those great legs that made them feel rather afraid. Whoever was up there didn't know there was anyone about but himself—and he would be the kind of fellow who wouldn't welcome children at all! Whatever could he be? Not a fisherman, surely.

And how could he have come to the Cliff of Birds? The children had seen no boat in the bay below. They hoped that the man wouldn't spot their boat, either. At the moment they felt sure it couldn't be seen from where the man sat.

"Let's wriggle right to the back of the cave," whispered Tom. "In case that fellow comes down a bit lower and sees us."

They wriggled back. They could still see the dangling legs, with their big ugly feet and toes. Then they saw something else. The man was swinging a pair of field-glasses by their strap, and the children could see them going to and fro by the man's feet.

The whistling stopped. "Twelve o'clock. Noon," said a growling voice. The glasses were swung up again, and the children wondered if the man was using them. What was he looking for? Something out to sea?

There was a low exclamation. Clearly the man had seen what he was looking for. The children strained their eyes into the distance, trying to see if any ship was on the horizon—but they could see nothing at all.

After a while the man got up. His horrid legs were drawn up one by one and disappeared. Thank goodness! The children imagined that a man with such enormous legs must be almost a giant!

There came a scrambling noise and a few bits and pieces fell from the ledge above the cave as the man walked off. The whistling sounded again, but stopped after a little. Then there was silence.

Andy crawled out of the shallow cave and listened cautiously. Nothing to be heard. He went out on to the wide ledge and peered up. He came back to the children.

"Not a thing to be seen," he said. "I say, you know, it's a bit of a puzzle — how did that man get here?"

"He must have come overland if he hasn't got a boat," said Tom. Andy shook his head.

"No. There's no way overland at all. Never has been. Sometimes bird-men have come to this cliff to study the sea-birds, but they always had to come by boat. The cliff is unclimbable the other side, and very dangerous."

"Well, but Andy — he must have come by boat then!" said Tom.

"Then where has he hidden his boat?" said Andy. "We couldn't help seeing it down there in the water, if it had been there, could we? It's impossible to hide a boat in this shallow bay."

"Where's he gone now?" asked Jill. "Up the cliff-path?"

"He must have," said Andy. "But I always thought the path stopped not far above where we are. Perhaps there's a cave where he's living. I've a good mind to go and see!"

"No, don't," said Jill. "I didn't like the look of his legs at all. I'm sure he is a huge, ugly, hairy kind of man — like a big gorilla, or something!"

"Silly!" said Tom. "He may be quite nice. Though I must say I don't feel as if he is, somehow! Nasty growly sort of voice he had too."

"Well — I'm going to see if I can find out where he's gone," said Andy, getting up. "After all, even if he sees me, what does it matter? Anyone can come here and watch the birds."

"I'll come too," said Tom. "I've had enough of resting. You two girls stay here. We won't be long."

The girls wanted a little more rest after their long climb, and were quite content to be left. They lay back, and listened to the sound of the boys climbing up to the ledge above the cave entrance.

"The ledge makes a kind of narrow path here again," they heard Tom say. "Come on — this is the way that man must have gone!"

210

The boys climbed up the rocky path. They were glad the girls hadn't come, for in places it was very narrow — nothing but a goat-path, Andy said. There were no goats though, in that part of the country, for there was not enough for even a goat to eat! Very little grew on that rocky cliff, except for a hardy cushion of sea-pinks here and there.

As they rounded a corner of the cliff, they heard a rushing sound. "The waterfall," said Andy. "It must come out of the cliff just near here. As far as I remember it quite bars the way."

They saw the waterfall the next moment. It was a magnificent sight, though the waterfall was not a very big one. But the sight of the torrent of water suddenly flinging itself out of the cliff, making a slight arch in the air and then falling headlong down the steep rocky cliff, gleaming and glittering as it went, made the two boys stop in wonder.

"I wish the girls could see this," said Tom. "Let's go back and get them."

"There's not time," said Andy. "Tom, it's queer we haven't spotted that man yet, isn't it? There's been no place he could hide in at all on our way here. Not even a place where a rabbit could hide. Where's he gone?"

"Beyond the waterfall, of course!" said Tom.

"He couldn't go beyond," said Andy. "Can't you see how the water completely bars the way? Who could get through that terrific gush? He'd be swept down the cliff with the torrent!"

The boys were now beside the waterfall. It fell down the cliff with a clamour as loud as the gulls made. It almost deafened them, and they had to raise their voices to speak to one another.

Tom gazed at the water gushing out from the hole in the cliff. He imagined it rushing through the dark, silent heart of that towering cliff, hidden away in narrow channels and tunnels—to come out suddenly into the sunshine, and leap downwards in joy, to join the sparkling sea below.

He felt puzzled. Certainly it was very strange to think that the man whose legs they had seen was nowhere about! Had he fallen off the cliff? Horrid thought!

"Do you think he's fallen off?" said Tom. Andy shook his head.

"No. He must be used to these cliffs, or he wouldn't be on them. He's somewhere here."

"Well, *where?*" demanded Tom, feeling quite exasperated. "We haven't overtaken him—and you say no one could get across this waterfall without being jerked down the cliff with it—and you don't think he's fallen down the cliff! Then where is he!"

"I don't know," said Andy, frowning. He looked to see if there was a way above the waterfall, but the rocky cliff there was smooth and steep. No one could climb over the waterfall that way. He bent down and looked under the water, that formed an arch as it jerked itself from the cliff.

"No. It would be too dangerous to try and creep under that," he said. "And anyway there doesn't seem to be any ledge the other side. Golly, it's a puzzle!"

They turned to go back, quite baffled. As they made their way along the ledge the noise of the waterfall suddenly seemed to lessen. The boys looked back.

"The torrent isn't so strong," said Tom. "There's less water coming out, look."

"I expect it varies," said Andy. "Sometimes I suppose it's a great gush of water, other times it slackens, and there wouldn't be much waterfall to see."

"Yes. I bet after a heavy rainfall the waterfall gets enormous," said Andy. "And in a very dry spell in summer there would hardly be any water coming out at all. It just depends on how much rain we've had."

"It's funny—the waterfall has almost stopped now," said Tom. "Just a trickle coming out! I wonder why."

"Come on," said Andy, getting impatient. "The girls will be wondering what's become of us."

They rounded a corner, and made their way back to the girls, who were now waiting impatiently for them.

"Not a sign of that man," said Tom, to their great astonishment. "He's simply vanished into thin air! Queer, isn't it?"

"Yes," said the twins in surprise, and demanded to know everything about the waterfall, and what it was like.

"We'll tell you when we get back to the boat," said Andy. "It's getting a bit late, and we ought to be starting. Also I'm hungry for my dinner. We only had a snack, you know."

They all started down—and when they had gone just a little way, they heard a sound that once more gave them a surprise.

"That whistle again!" said Andy. "Well, the man *is* somewhere about then! Where in the world does he hide? How I'd like to know!"

CHAPTER V

A GOOD TRIP BACK

IT was certainly astonishing to hear the man whistling again, when they felt certain that he wasn't anywhere near!

Andy stopped and looked back, but he could see nothing. "We can't go back and have another look," he said. "We haven't time. Golly, *where* could the man have been, Tom, when we went all the way to the waterfall?"

"It beats me," said Tom. "But never mind—we'll give it up! I want my dinner much more than I want to go and find out where that man hid!"

So down they went and down. It was much easier to go down than up. Jill was sensible and did not look at the sea at all this time, in case she felt giddy again. After a time they all stood safely on the rock at the bottom of the cliff. Not far off was the underground river, sliding turbulently out of the cavern at the foot of the cliff.

Soon they were in their boat again. It was bobbing gently on the pool where they had anchored it. They clambered aboard, and the girls went down into the cabin to bring up some food. Cold ham. Hard-boiled eggs again. Rolls. And a big tin of sliced peaches. What a lovely meal when you were terribly hungry.

"Chocolate to follow if anyone's hungry still," said Jill. "Mother seems to have put in dozens of bars! There's some with fruit and nuts in too. It looks gorgeous."

"Have we time to eat our dinner before we go, or had we better set sail straight away?" asked Tom, who felt that he would like to have his meal then and there. Andy looked at the sun in the sky.

"The sun's a good way past noon," he said. "I think we'd better set off now, and eat our dinner as we go. The wind won't help us so much going back, though it's shifted a bit. I'll take the tiller again."

The two boys rowed the boat out of the pool and into the open sea. Soon they were speeding along again, though not so fast as they had come. It was very pleasant on deck in the warm afternoon sunshine. The four children ploughed their way hungrily through the ham, bread, eggs and peaches. Only Tom could manage the chocolate at the end, and even he ate it lazily, as though he didn't really want it!

"We'll be back just before dark, I think," said Andy. "Look, here's the channel between the rocks — and that's where it goes off to Smuggler's Rock. See?"

The children looked at the water that lay smoothly in the channel between the two ridges of rock, and screwed up their eyes to have another look at the queer, steep rocky island called Smuggler's Rock. Yes, there it was in the distance, a desolate, lonely rock, where nobody ever went to nowadays. It might be rather fun to explore it though!

"Shall we go there one day, Andy?" asked Tom. "It might be rather fun. We could hunt for the old caves the smugglers used."

"All right," said Andy. "If you like. It's a nice sailing trip all the way here. Doesn't the boat go like a bird?"

She did. She was light and sweet to handle and seemed like a live thing to the children. They loved the flapping of her sail and the creaking noise she made. They liked the lapping of the water against her hull, and the white wake that spread behind them like a feathery tail.

"I think all children ought to have a boat of their own," said Tom. "I wish I had a boat, and a horse and a dog, and . . ."

He stopped suddenly, and looked so upset that the two girls felt alarmed.

"What's the matter?" said Jill.

"Do you know what I've done?" said Tom. "I've left my camera behind! I'm always doing that! My best camera, the one Daddy gave me at Christmas. It cost an awful lot of money and I promised faithfully to be much more careful with it than I was with my old one. And now I've gone and left it behind, on the Cliff of Birds!"

"Idiot!" said Mary. "You're jolly careless. Mother will be awfully cross."

"Well, one of you might have been clever enough to notice I'd left it behind," said Tom crossly. "Haven't got eyes, I suppose! Dash! Andy, can we turn back?"

"What! Turn back, and climb all the way up that cliff again!" said Andy. "Don't be stupid. We haven't got time, you know that. I'm not steering this boat home in the dark through these dangerous waters."

"I didn't take any snaps, and now I've left my camera," lamented Tom. "It's such a beauty too. I must have left it at the back of that shallow cave where we lay and rested. Golly—I hope that whistling man doesn't find it and take it!"

This was a really alarming thought. Everybody looked solemn at once. A camera as fine as Tom's was very valuable, and a treasured possession. Tom couldn't think how he had come to forget it. But Tom did do very foolish things at times. How cross his parents would be!

Tom looked so woebegone that Andy was sorry for him. "Cheer up," he said. "We'll go back for it one day this week. If I can get my father to spare the boat, we'll sail to the Cliff of Birds again—and maybe visit Smuggler's Rock!"

Everyone cheered up. That would be lovely! They would start off even earlier—or would Mother let them spend the night on board the boat? Then they could have a whole day on Smuggler's Rock! They began to talk about it, their eyes shining.

"Don't be too hopeful," said Andy, steering the boat deftly between the two dangerous ridges of rock. "You know what happened last time your mother gave you permission to spend a night or two on a sailing trip—we got wrecked and lived on an island for ages, and found ourselves in a nest of enemy submarines and seaplanes!"

"Well, nothing like that could happen *here*," said Tom, looking at the desolate, lonely coast they were passing. "Why, there isn't a ship or a 'plane to be seen."

"Then I wonder what that man was looking for, with his glasses," said Jill. That made everyone remember the whistling man.

They began to talk again about the puzzle of how he could have disappeared between the place where the chidren sat and the waterfall.

"I tell you, there wasn't a hole big enough on the way to hide even a rabbit," said Tom. "He ought to have been somewhere along there—and he wasn't. He had vanished into thin air! I almost thought I'd dreamt him!"

"Well, he came back again from thin air all right!" said Mary, with a laugh. "We heard his whistle just as we were leaving. His hiding-place can't be far away."

The puzzle of the man's hiding-place kept them interested for a long time. It was Jill who made the first sensible suggestion.

"I know!" she said, sitting upright on the deck. "I know where he went!"

"You don't!" said Tom.

"I bet he waited till the waterfall lessened its torrent a bit—like you said it did, you remember—and then he shot into the opening the water pours from, and made his way into the cliff from there!" said Jill triumphantly. But the others hardly took in what she said, it seemed so queer.

"What—do you mean you think the man got into the cliff through the waterfall opening?" said Tom at last.

"What an idea! He'd never hide there. He'd be wet through."

"Well — where *did* he hide, then?" said Jill. "*You* can't think of anywhere better, I'm sure. I dare say there's a way into the heart of the cliff just there. I'm sure there is!"

Jill was very pleased with her idea. She went on talking about it, and gradually she got the others excited. "Jill may be right," said Andy, his eyes fixed on the blue waters ahead of him. "It's true that it might be possible to get in at the waterfall hole, once the water had lessened and become a trickle — as it did when we were walking away from it."

"Let's go and see when we go back for Tom's camera!" said Mary. "We must! I simply can't bear an unsolved mystery. I can't bear not to know where that whistling man went to — and what he is doing there, too!"

"What horrid legs he had!" said Jill. "I'd like to find out his hiding-place and who he is — but I don't want to have anything to do with him at all!"

"We'll keep out of his way all right," said Andy. "Here, Tom, would you like to take the tiller for a little while? It's easy going for a bit."

Tom took the tiller eagerly. The girls, suddenly feeling sleepy, lay down on rugs on the deck. It was lovely to feel the hot sun. The boat careered on joyously. She always seemed to enjoy her trips so much.

"She's a happy boat," said Jill drowsily. "She likes us coming out in her. This is a day off for her. Golly, I do feel sleepy. Wake me up at tea-time, somebody!"

They had tea at five o'clock, when the sun was sliding down the western sky. The wind whipped the sea into little waves and the *Andy* dipped up and down joyfully. The children were all very good sailors, and it didn't even occur to them to feel seasick. The sun went behind clouds and an evening chill crept over the sea. Everyone put on

an extra coat and then a mackintosh. After all, it was only
April!

"We'll be home before it's dark," said Tom, looking at
the sinking sun. "We've had a lovely day on the sea. It
was fun climbing up that cliff too, and seeing all those
birds."

"And it will be fun to go back and see if there really is
a hiding-place behind that waterfall," said Jill. "And I
shall *love* going to Smuggler's Rock. When can we go,
Andy?"

"I think the weather's changing a bit," said Andy, looking at the sky. "There'll be rain and squalls tomorrow

and maybe for the rest of the week. We must choose a fine day to go off again. It would be a most uncomfortable trip in bad weather."

They got in before dark, with big clouds sweeping overhead and heavy drops of rain falling. Their mother was most relieved to see them. But she was very upset when she heard that Tom had left his camera behind.

"You will have to go and get it," she said. "It's much too good a one to leave lying about. How careless you are, Tom! It's not a bit of good giving you anything nice!"

"I'm most awfully sorry, Mother," said Tom. "I promise you we'll go and get it the very first fine day we have. Andy says the weather's broken for a while—but as soon as it's fine again, we'll go off and get my camera."

"And find that hiding-place and see Smuggler's Rock," said Jill under her breath. "Mary, don't you hope Mother lets us stay away for a night? Then we can explore Smuggler's Rock properly!"

CHAPTER VI

SAILING AWAY AGAIN

THE next few days, as Andy had foretold, were wet and squally. But fishing was good, and the children, in macks, rubber boots and sou'westers, had a lovely time helping with the fish. Andy worked hard. The hauls were excellent and his father was pleased.

"Maybe he'll give me two or three days off," said Andy. "When the fine weather comes back we'll take the *Andy* and go off again. I like that better than anything."

Andy's father came to supper one night. The children's mother liked the silent, stern-faced man, and gave him a very fine supper. The children shared in it, and chattered like magpies.

"They must make your head ache!" their mother said to Andy's silent father.

"Och, their chatter is no more than the calling of the gulls!" said the fisherman, with a twinkle.

"But we're much more useful than the gulls!" said Mary. "We've helped you a lot this week. You said we had!"

"So you have," said the fisherman. "Andy's taught you a bonny lot of things! You're right good children. You don't mess about and get into mischief like most silly little scallywags."

This was a long and handsome speech from Andy's father. The children were delighted. Jill made the most of his good temper.

"Will you be able to let Andy off for a day or two soon?" she asked. "We do so want to go out in the *Andy* again all by ourselves."

"I'll give him a two-days' holiday," said the fisherman,

drawing out his pipe. "May I smoke, ma'am? Thank you."

"Thanks, Dad," said Andy.

"We'll go to Smuggler's Rock then!" said Tom. "Hurrah!"

"Where's that?" asked his mother quickly.

"Oh, it's a place we saw the other day when we went to the Cliff of Birds," said Tom airily. "Mother, as Andy will have two days off, could we spend the whole time on the boat? I'd like to go to the Cliff of Birds and have time to take some proper snaps—if only I can find my camera again—and we do want to sail to Smuggler's Rock. It looks exciting."

"Not a *night* away!" began his mother. "You know I don't like that."

"But Andy will be with us. He'll look after us, won't he?" said Tom, turning to Andy's father, who was now puffing out big clouds of thick smoke. "Andy's often out all night with you, isn't he?"

"Oh, Andy's used to being on the boat for nights on end!" said the fisherman, in a very good temper after his fine supper. "You'll not come to any harm with Andy there. You can trust my boy, ma'am."

"Oh, I know I can," said the children's mother. "It's only that—well—after their adventure last year I just don't feel I want them to go travelling on their own again."

"Why, ma'am—you don't suppose two adventures like that could happen, do you?" said Andy's father. "Theirs was an adventure that only happens once in a lifetime, if that! You let them go—they'll be all right with Andy. He can anchor the boat somewhere quiet, and they can sleep on her in comfort if they take plenty of rugs."

It all seemed to be settled without any argument or difficulty at all.

How lovely! The children glowed with pleasure and felt very grateful to Andy's father for making things easy

222

for them. He seemed to have conquered their mother's fears completely!

The next evening Andy came up to the cottage. "Weather's changing," he said. "See that sky? We'll set off tomorrow, shall we? Get what food you can and I'll bring some too. Knowing young Tom's appetite I reckon we'd better lay in a good stock for two days and a night!"

Their mother always kept a fine stock of tinned food handy, and she told the children to take what they wanted. They took her at her word and soon the *Andy* was well stocked with all kinds of things, from sardines to tins of pineapple. Andy brought a few offerings too, and stared in surprise at the store already in the cabin cupboards.

"We shan't want all that!" he said. "Well—never mind—we won't bother to take it back again now. Got some rugs? We'll want plenty to sleep on. The girls can sleep down in the cabin tomorrow night—and we boys will sleep up on deck. I can rig up a tarpaulin round us to keep the wind off."

Soon there were piles of rugs on board the *Andy* too, and some of the old cushions from the cottage. It was almost dark before the children had finished stocking the little boat. They felt as if they were going on a long, long trip—a night away from home made all the difference!

They set off at eight o'clock in the morning, and their mother came down to the jetty to wave good-bye. "Have a lovely trip, and take some fine pictures, and find plenty of smugglers on Smuggler's Rock!" she said. "Tom and Andy, be sure you look after the twins well."

"Of course!" said the boys. Andy took the tiller, and the little boat glided away with the morning sun on her. Tiny white-topped waves curled against her smooth sides, and she bobbed a little.

"She's happy again!" said Jill. "And so are we! Good-bye, Mother! See you tomorrow evening!"

Soon the boat rounded the corner of the rocky bay, and was out of sight. The children settled down comfortably to enjoy the trip. They all loved the sea, and were at home on it. They watched the sea-gulls soaring in the wind. They saw them floating on the water, bobbing over the curling waves. Now for a lovely trip!

The wind was strong and the *Andy* galloped along. Mary, who had lain awake from excitement the night before, fell asleep. Spray splashed over her, but she did not wake. The others talked, and Jill once more aired her views about the hiding-place which she felt sure must be behind the waterfall.

"What I really want to know," said Tom, "is where I left my camera. I'm pretty certain I put it down in that shallow cave where we rested. I hope to goodness it's there."

Now they were running along the channel between the ridges of rocks. Later they would sight Smuggler's Rock in the distance. But they would not go there today. They would go tomorrow!

They turned into the shallow bay they had anchored in before, and at once there came to their ears the terrific clamour of the thousands of nesting sea-birds. "I shan't look at the cliff and see their eggs falling this time," said Jill. "Careless birds! I wonder how they know their own eggs—and what do they think when they fly back and see that they are gone?"

"Just lay some more, I suppose," said Tom. "Mary, wake up! We're there! You've been asleep for ages."

"We'll anchor in that deep pool again," said Andy, and very soon the anchor was going down with a splash.

There was no one about. The place seemed as deserted as before, except for the noisy sea-birds. But perhaps the whistling man was in hiding somewhere? Or maybe he had gone.

"Let's take some food with us and go up to that place we rested in before," said Andy. "We could have a picnic there. It's a marvellous view, right over the sea. Maybe we shall find your camera, Tom, and you can take some photographs."

Everyone thought this was a good idea, and they collected what food they wanted, and put it into kit-bags which the two boys slung over their shoulders.

"Now, don't look down at all this time, Jill," said Andy. "That's always a mistake when you're climbing. Look upwards all the time. Ready, everyone?"

Yes, they were ready. They began their steep climb up,

225

following the cat-like Andy, who seemed to know all the best handholds and footholds. Jill didn't look down once and was quite all right. Soon they were all panting and puffing, for the day was warm.

They were glad when they reached the place where they had rested before. Jill threw herself down, tired. Tom gave a delighted exclamation and picked up his camera, which lay at the back of the shallow cave, where he had put it a few days before.

"Look! It's here! What a bit of luck. I should think that whistling man's gone, or he'd have seen it and taken it. Golly, I *am* pleased I've got it again."

They had a large and leisurely meal on the wide ledge, marvelling at the great expanse of slowly moving blue sea below them. Gulls moved like white specks, and their mewing voices came on the wind all the time.

"You could easily take some photographs of the birds on their eggs," said Jill. "They come back to them very quickly."

"I'm glad we haven't got those horrid hairy legs to look at this time!" said Mary, lying down flat. "Golly, I'm sleepy again!"

"Well, don't go to sleep, because we want to go and have a look at that waterfall rushing out of the cliff," said Jill, giving her some little digs.

"Yes, come on," said Andy, getting up. "And be careful along this next path, because it's jolly narrow in places. You come just behind me, Jill, in case you get giddy."

They all went along the ledge that led round the rocky cliff to the left of their resting-place. They looked out for the waterfall. It was there all right — but the torrent was not nearly so powerful as before. It was a mere trickle compared with what it had been the other day.

"Funny!" said Andy. "I should have thought that with all the rain we've had the waterfall would be pretty big.

Come along. We don't need to be afraid of being thrown off the cliff by *that* bit of water! It's no more than a gushing spring at the moment!"

They made their way to the waterfall. Beyond it the cliff-ledge along which they were walking came to a sudden end. There was no way the other side at all. The water ran out of a hole in the cliff, and fell headlong down. Andy made his way cautiously there and looked into the opening.

He gave a shout. "Anyone could get in here now! Anyone! I bet that's where the man went. He waited till the torrent lessened, then hopped up. That was his hiding-place."

"But what's he hiding for?" said Jill, puzzled. "There's nothing and no one to hide from here!"

"Can we get in?" asked Tom excitedly. "Yes, I bet we can."

"No, you're not to," said Andy. "Suppose the water came out again in a sudden great rush? You'd be sent right off the cliff, you idiot! I can't allow anything like that."

Tom looked sulky. "All right," he said, and turned back. "Well, that puzzle's solved. That's where the man went. But if you're not going to let us explore any farther, we shan't know what kind of a hidey-hole he's got or anything about him. You're a spoil-sport!"

"Can't help it," said Andy, giving him a cross little shove. "I'm in charge. Go and take some pictures of the birds while the sun is so bright!"

Tom said nothing more. But he made up his mind that as soon as the others were not looking, he would go back to the waterfall and find out a bit more for himself. He'd climb right in if he wanted to! He'd show Andy he would have his own way!

CHAPTER VII

TOM IS DISOBEDIENT

"I'D like to climb down the cliff again and explore the rocks at the bottom," said Jill, as they all turned back from the waterfall. "I'd like to go to where that underground river comes rushing out of the cliff too. It looks exciting down there."

"Yes, let's do that," said Mary. "It will be nice to get out of the wind a bit too. It's rather cold up here today."

"Right. Let's go down again then," said Andy. "Coming, Tom?"

But Tom had other ideas. He called back. "No — I don't think I'll come. I'll try and get some pictures of the birds now I'm up here and have found my camera again. I'll join you later. I'd rather try to take snapshots alone — the birds may not settle quietly with us all about."

"Well — don't be too long!" called back Jill, beginning to go down the cliff-ledge with Andy just in front of her. "And for goodness' sake don't forget your camera *this* time, Tom!"

Tom sat down and looked at the gulls and other sea-birds soaring and gliding in the current of air that blew straight up the cliff. They were magnificent, and Tom wished he too could spread great white wings and go gliding and circling on the strong breeze. It must be a wonderful feeling, he thought.

He could hear the voices of the others coming up to him on the wind, as they climbed slowly down. Then the gulls began suddenly clamouring all together, as they had a habit of doing, and he could hear nothing else.

"I'd better take a few pictures first, before I try any exploring up that waterfall hole," thought Tom. So he crept round the ledge, and waited till the sea-birds he had disturbed had come back again to their eggs there, and were sitting on them.

He took a few pictures that he thought should be very good. Then he put his camera down at the back of the shallow cave where they had had their meal, and made his way round the cliff to where the waterfall was.

His heart beat fast. He knew that Andy would be cross if he found out that he was going to disobey orders. "But after all, I'm thirteen, and quite able to look after myself!" thought Tom. "I'm surprised Andy hadn't the spunk to go into that waterfall hole himself! Golly, won't the others stare when they find I've been into the hole and found out where that whistling man hid the other day!"

He came to the waterfall. It was still not much more than a gushing spring now. There didn't seem any danger of a great torrent of water pouring out, as there had been the other day.

Tom peered cautiously into the opening out of which the water poured. It flowed out of a rocky bed, and had made quite a channel for itself there. Beyond, as far as Tom could see, was a ledge above the water. Anyone getting up there should be safe and dry.

He felt in his pocket. Yes, he had his torch there. It was wrapped in a few layers of thin oilskin, so that spray or splashes of sea-water would not wet it. He would need it once he got into that waterfall hole!

He climbed into the rocky hole. It was high but narrow. The water wetted him as he went in, but he didn't mind that. He dragged himself through the water and up on to the rocky ledge that lay above it.

Now he was safe from the water — unless, of course, the torrent suddenly grew bigger for some reason, and swept out of the hole, filling the opening completely, as it had done when the children had first seen it. Tom shivered a little as he thought of that. It wouldn't be pleasant for him if that happened! He had better get a bit farther inside, then he would feel safer!

He switched on his torch, and looked up the dark tunnel down which the water came. It flowed in the rocky channel it had hollowed out for itself during the long years, and beside it was the narrow rocky ledge, a continuation of the one that Tom lay on at the moment.

"I'll just explore a little way," thought the boy, feeling excited. "Just to see if I can find that man's hiding-place! I might find something there that would tell me what he is — it seems so funny for a man to be living in this desolate place. Perhaps he is hiding from the police!"

He began to wriggle along the narrow ledge. The roof of the queer little tunnel was low, and it wasn't very comfortable to wriggle along like that. Tom put his torch in his teeth so that he might have both hands to grasp the rock with and pull himself along.

The ledge ran for a few yards, and then dipped a little, so that the water ran over it! Bother! Couldn't he get any farther?

Tom took his torch out of his mouth and flashed it beyond him. He saw that not far in front the narrow rocky tunnel seemed to open out — into a cave perhaps? He really *must* go and see, even if it meant a wetting!

This time he had to wriggle through the water on the ledge, and he got the front of himself very wet indeed. But he was very excited now, and didn't even feel the icy cold. He wriggled along, and found that, quite suddenly, the narrow tunnel stopped, and beyond was a very large cave, in the very heart of the cliff itself! How extraordinary!

Along the floor of the cave, almost level with the rocky floor, flowed the stream that entered the rocky tunnel, and became the waterfall! It was a strange sight to see the silent water flowing in the darkness, coming from goodness knew where.

Tom flashed his torch round the cave. This would make a fine hiding-place! This must surely be where that man had gone to. But there didn't seem to be a sign of anyone at all.

It was silent there in the heart of the towering cliff. No sound of calling sea-birds came in through the long narrow entrance. No rush of wind disturbed the still air. It was like being in a curious dream.

"I wish the others were here," thought Tom. "I'd like them to share this with me. I'll go and get them! But first I'll just flash my torch all round the cave to see if I can find even a small trace of that whistling man—a cigarette end perhaps—or a match."

He flashed his torch about. The cave had a high rocky roof, an uneven rocky floor, and gleaming walls. The water that flowed silently through it came from what looked like the entrance to a smaller cave at the back— but somehow Tom didn't want to go any deeper into the black darkness!

Something gleamed on the floor near the water. Tom's torch shone on it, and he wondered what it was. He went to pick it up.

It was a small pearl button, the kind that is sewn on to men's shirts! But it was red, not white. Tom looked at it eagerly. Ah—that was a sure sign that somebody used the waterfall hole and had come into this cave. But it was plain that they didn't live here, for there was no sign of any food-stores, or bed. Whoever came here or made it his hiding-place must have gone farther into the cliff. Perhaps the whole cliff was honeycombed with caves and tunnels! Tom remembered the underground river that flowed out so turbulently at the foot. That must come down winding channels of its own from somewhere!

He wished very much that Andy was with him. He couldn't make up his mind whether to go farther in or not. He was afraid of being caught by the whistling man —or anyone else! The whistling man might not be the only person in the cliff. There might be someone else too.

"I don't know—I think I'll go back to the others after all," said Tom to himself. "It's a bit frightening being here in this cliff all by myself—and if I go farther in I might get lost. I'll go back."

He flashed his torch round the cave once more—and then suddenly noticed that the stream flowing in its channel across the floor of the cave, had quietly risen higher! It was now flowing over the rocky floor, almost reaching to where Tom stood.

"Look at that!" said Tom in surprise, and he stood watching the water. "Why has it risen like that? Golly, it's flooding all the floor of this cave!"

So it was. The water rose higher and swept over the floor. It began to make a noise. Tom felt alarmed.

"Gracious! I know what's happening! The torrent of water farther in must have suddenly been increased for some reason—and it's pushing its way out here—and will make that waterfall simply enormous again! If I don't go now I'll be swept out with the torrent and go down the cliff in the waterfall!"

This was not at all a pleasant thought. Tom ran over the flooding cave-floor back to the narrow tunnel into which the water flowed on its way to the open air. But already the narrow little tunnel was filling with water! The rocky ledge he had wriggled along could hardly be seen, for the water had risen high above it. In a few minutes the whole of the narrow opening would be blocked by the suddenly increased torrent of water!

"I daren't go along it now," thought Tom. "I simply daren't. I'd either be drowned or swept out and down the waterfall."

The water had now flooded the whole of the floor of the cave. It was up to Tom's knees. He felt frightened. Had he better go to the inner cave, the one his torch had shown him when he had flashed it on the water at the farther side of his cave? Perhaps he had. It wasn't safe in his cave now! Goodness knew how high the water would rise there, and there was no place he could climb up to and sit until the water went down again.

"I wish I hadn't explored in here," he thought in dismay. "Now I may be kept a prisoner for hours. The others will get worried about me. What an idiot I am!"

He made his way to the farther side of the cave he was in. Through a fairly high tunnel there the water came from an inner cave. Tom stepped into the water. It was up to his waist already. He would have to wade along until he came to the inner cave.

It was not very far in—only a matter of a few yards. Water flooded over the floor of this cave too—but to Tom's surprise and delight, he saw rough steps cut in the wall, going upwards, at the back of this inner cave. He flashed his torch there. Yes, those steps led to an opening in the cave-roof. If he got up there he would be quite safe from the rising water. Good!

"Wonder if the steps lead into another cave!" thought the boy. "This is all very weird. Who would have guessed there were these caves leading one out of the other like this, in the heart of that enormous cliff!"

He went up the rough rocky steps. There was a hole in the roof, and iron footholds had been driven into the rock there, to act as a help in the climb. Tom put his torch between his teeth again, and hauled himself up. He came out into a dark and silent tunnel, that twisted in front of him, leading to he knew not where!

"Well—I suppose I'd better go along," thought Tom, trying to sound much braver than he felt. "It must lead *some*where!"

CHAPTER VIII

THE HIDDEN CAVE

TOM went down the winding passage. It smelt funny, and he didn't like it. He hoped his torch wouldn't suddenly run out. He was glad that it had a new battery in! It would be horrid to wander about in the dark, inside the cliff all by himself!

The tunnel twisted downwards. It was narrow most of the time, and sometimes the roof went low so that Tom had to bend his head or he would have bumped it. Sometimes the roof became so high that Tom's torch showed him nothing but darkness. It was all very queer.

"I'd be enjoying this more if only the others were here!" thought Tom, still trying to feel brave. "I do so hope this tunnel *leads* somewhere! I almost wish I could meet that whistling man. I'd at least have someone to talk to!"

But he met nobody. The tunnel went on and on, always downwards. And then, stealing up it, came a curious, familiar smell!

Tom sniffed. "Tobacco smoke!" he thought. "Gracious! Somebody must be near then—somebody smoking a cigarette or pipe. I'd better go carefully."

He trod as quietly as he could, shading the light of his torch with his hand. Then suddenly he switched it out. He could see a light in the distance! The tunnel must come out into a cave again, he thought—and there was a light in that cave, which meant that people must be there!

He crept nearer. He could hear voices now—men's voices. One of them was the growly voice of the man with the hairy legs. Tom didn't know what he was like

236

to look at of course, because he had only seen his legs. But he knew that growly voice again, although he had only heard the man say a few words up on the cliff.

The boy's heart began to thump. He was very glad indeed to think that people were near—but somehow he felt that they wouldn't welcome him at all! Could they be smugglers?

He tiptoed to the end of the tunnel, and peeped cautiously into the cave. Two men were there—one of them plainly the hairy-legged man, for his legs were bare, and Tom could see his enormous feet. The boy gazed at the men, wondering if they would be angry at his sudden appearance or not.

He somehow thought they would not welcome him at all. The hairy-legged man was not the giant the children had imagined him to be—he was a curious-looking fellow, with a strong, stumpy body, hairy bare arms, a big head with hardly any neck, and a flaming red beard.

The other man looked like an ordinary fisherman, but wore something that fishermen rarely wore—a pair of spectacles! They looked odd on his extremely brown face.

The men sat on boxes, talking. Tom could not hear what they were saying. He stared round the cave, astonished, for the sides of it were piled with wooden boxes and crates. Tom couldn't imagine what was in them. This was clearly a store-house of some kind. But why? And where did all the boxes come from?

There was a rough mattress in one corner of the cave. One or both men slept there, then. What a curious place to live in! Tom was completely puzzled by it all. But he did feel certain of one thing—that these men would not welcome his presence there at all! Whatever they were doing was something secret and private, something they wanted to be kept hidden.

"I daren't go in and ask them for help," thought the

boy desperately. "I simply daren't. I hate the look of that man with the hairy legs. He looks as if he'd think as little of hurling me down the cliff, as of dropping and smashing those birds' eggs!"

He strained his ears to hear what they were saying. But he couldn't make out a word. Perhaps they were talking in some foreign language. Certainly the man in the fisherman's clothes, the one wearing glasses, looked like a foreigner. It was all most extraordinary.

Tom wondered if he could possibly be in some sort of very real dream. Then he got another whiff of tobacco smoke and knew he wasn't. Things never smelt as strong as that in dreams!

One of the men looked at his watch. He got up and jerked his head at the other. They made their way to a hole in the ground that Tom could not see clearly from where he stood, and seemed to drop right down. At any rate, they completely disappeared!

Tom waited a few moments and then cautiously crossed the floor of the cave and looked down the hole. There was nothing to be seen. The men had gone. Tom didn't feel at all inclined to follow them. For one thing he couldn't see how to get down the hole! There were no steps or footholds of any sort that he could see!

He looked round the cave. He could hardly see its walls, they were stacked so high with boxes of all sizes. What could be inside them?

The men had left a lantern burning on a box in the middle of the cave. Did that mean they were soon coming back? Perhaps it did. Tom felt that it would be a good thing if he were not there when they returned.

But where could he go? He stood still in the cave, thinking — and as he stood there, he heard a muffled sound. It seemed to come from somewhere to the left of the big cave.

"It's a kind of rushing watery sound," thought Tom. "Whatever can it be?"

There was a big stack of boxes on the left of the cave. Tom went to them, and saw the wall of the cave behind them. There was a hole in the wall, almost round, just about as high as Tom's waist. The rushing noise came from there.

Tom poked his head through the hole. He switched his torch on—and saw a strange sight. An underground river flowed there, swift and rushing!

"Why—that must be the river that comes out at the foot of the cliff," thought Tom. "Golly—if I could follow it, I'd soon be out of here!"

He stood and gazed at the swiftly-flowing river by the light of his torch. The dark, strong torrent moved quickly. Tom wondered how far from the foot of the cliff it was. After all, the winding, twisting tunnel he had followed had come down and down and down—maybe he was almost level with the base of the cliff now, and this river would take him very quickly to the shallow bay outside, and the sunshine.

He went back into the lamp-lit cave and looked round. He hoped that he might see another torch that he could take with him. He felt sure his own would not last much longer! He didn't want to face another long journey without being sure he had plenty of light for it!

Before he could see anything in the shape of a torch, something startling happened. There came the sound of someone scrambling up the hole in the cave floor, down which the men had gone—and, before Tom's alarmed eyes, the big, bearded face of the man with the hairy legs popped up out of the hole!

Tom stared at him, petrified—and he stared back at Tom as if he really couldn't believe his eyes. A boy! A boy in his cave! Could he be dreaming?

Tom swallowed hard, and tried to say something, but he couldn't think what to say. The bearded face just above the hole opened its eyes wide, and then the mouth opened too, and a bellow came out.

"What you doing here?"

Tom couldn't move. His feet seemed to be growing into the ground. He watched the stumpy, short-necked man heave himself out of the hole and come towards him. He was frightened, and backed away, suddenly finding himself able to move.

240

He backed straight into the box on which the lamp was set. The box went over and the lamp with it. It smashed at once, flared up, and then went out. The cave was instantly in black darkness.

The bearded man began to mutter something and to feel about as if he were looking for another lamp or a candle. Tom knew that this was his only chance of escape. He ran softly behind the pile of boxes to the hole in the wall that looked out on to the underground river.

He was through the hole in a trice. He had hoped there would be a ledge there, or a rock of some kind he could hold on to, whilst he flashed his torch round to see what kind of a way of escape he had chosen. But there was no rock and no ledge — only the cold, rushing river!

Tom landed in the water with a splash. He caught his breath with the coldness of it. Then he began to strike out with all his might, fearing that the bearded man might come after him.

The current of the swiftly-flowing river bore him away rapidly. Tom let himself be taken along, keeping himself afloat quite easily, but shivering with the cold. He thought of his torch gloomily. It was in his pocket, but not wrapped up in the oilskin. It would be of no use at all now. If this underground river landed him somewhere inside the cliff again, he would be in complete darkness.

"Lost for ever!" said Tom dolefully. "Oh why did I disobey Andy? I'll never get out of this mess, never! Golly, how cold the water is!"

The river bore him along, gurgling in a deep voice as it went. It apparently ran in a deep channel of rock. Tom could not see if they were passing through caves or not, nor could he see if there were any banks of rock or sand to the river. He just had to go on with it, trying to keep his balance and not be rolled over and over like a log of wood. Once his foot struck against a jutting rock, and it was badly bruised. But there was no one to hear his cry. He bit his lip with the pain, and after that was very much afraid of being bumped against a rock again.

He grew very tired and cold. And then, just as he felt he really could not go on one moment longer, he saw a bright light in front of him, a big wide, dazzling patch of light that filled him with joy.

"Sunshine!" said Tom. "That's sunshine! I must be getting near the place where the river rushes out of the cliff. I've escaped!"

Yes—it *was* sunshine! Hurrah! Tom suddenly felt so weak with relief that he couldn't seem to keep his balance any more, and the current took him and rolled him over and over. He gasped and spluttered, striking out as best he could to hold his face and shoulders out of the swift-running water.

He was taken to where sea and river met. A big wave ran up and caught him as the river took him there. Luckily for him he was thrown sideways on to a rock, and managed to pull himself up out of reach of the water.

He couldn't move. He lay there on his back, gasping for breath, shivering and trembling, whilst just below him river and sea fought their eternal battle, as one met the other, sending up spray and foam that fell pattering down on poor tired-out Tom.

CHAPTER IX

WHEREVER IS TOM?

MEANWHILE, what were Andy, Jill and Mary doing? They had been having quite a good time, though not so exciting a time as poor Tom.

They climbed steadily down the cliff, to the great alarm of all the sea-birds whose nests they passed. Once more dozens of eggs fell into the sea, knocked in by the excited uprush of the sitting birds. Jill almost made up her mind she would never climb the cliff again! She really couldn't bear to see so many eggs wasted.

They came at last to the foot of the cliff. There were some glorious rock-pools there, full of the finest sea anemones that the children had ever seen.

"Look—here's a red anemone whose feelers are as big as a peony's petals!" said Jill. "I should think he feeds on prawns and crabs—nothing so small as a shrimp would do for *him*!"

The three explored the pools thoroughly, and disturbed some enormous crabs.

"Look out!" said Andy. "A nip from a big fellow like that won't be very pleasant!"

It was warm down there at the foot of the cliff. The wind was not strong there as it was up on the cliff, and the sun felt hot. Mary glanced up at the steep, towering cliff above.

"I bet Tom's beginning to feel hungry again!" she said. "I'm hungry myself—but I suppose we'd better wait till Tom comes down. He'll come as soon as he feels hungry!"

"It shouldn't take him very long to take a few snapshots," said Andy. "I'm surprised he isn't here by now.

243

Maybe he's watching the birds. They're as good as a show sometimes!"

"Let's go and sit near that river," said Mary. "We'll take some food there, and wait for Tom. It would be rather a nice place to have a picnic. Look how the spray flies in the air where river and sea meet on the rocks."

"Yes. Let's go and get some food and eat it there," said Jill. "I really do feel very hungry. We can give Tom a call when we see him come down the cliff."

They went to where they had anchored the boat in the deep pool. In the cabin were the plentiful stores of food they had brought with them. They rummaged about, finding it hard to choose what to take.

"Sardines, bread and butter, potted meat, hard-boiled eggs — and tinned plums," said Jill.

"No — tinned pears," said Mary. "Those are nicest of all. Here's a big tin. And where's the ginger-beer? Mother gave us plenty this time. Oh, here it is."

They took everything to a high rock overlooking the spot where river and sea met.

Spray was sometimes flung as high as their rock, but they didn't mind that — it was all part of the fun to dodge it when it came!

They set out the meal, and then looked up at the side of the cliff to see if there was any sign of Tom coming down. But there wasn't.

"What *can* he be doing?" said Jill impatiently. "He's been ages!"

"Well — we'll wait five minutes more, and then begin without him," said Mary. "And if there's nothing left he'll jolly well have to go and get something else himself!"

They waited for five minutes, but still there was no Tom. Andy looked a little worried, but he said nothing. They opened the sardines, spread butter on their bread, and began a delicious meal. By the end of it there was not much left—and still no Tom!

"Andy—you don't think Tom's in any difficulty up there, do you?" said Jill suddenly. "It's so unlike him not to turn up long before a meal-time."

"Well—I've been wondering about that myself," said Andy. "I think I'd better go up the cliff again and fetch him down. He may have gone to sleep."

"What a nuisance he is!" said Mary. "Poor Andy—having all that climb again!"

"Oh, I don't mind," said Andy. "Now you girls stay here till we come. It's nice and sunny, and you're not much bothered with the wind. I'll be as quick as I can."

Off he went. Soon the girls could see him, small and far off, up the cliff-side, climbing steadily, the sea-birds flying wildly round his head.

"I bet he gives Tom a scolding!" said Jill, lying down on her back, enjoying the feel of the sun-warmed rock behind her. "Won't Tom be famished when he comes back!"

Andy climbed steadily, and at last came to the resting-place where they had had their dinner. There was no one there, of course—but what was this at the back? Tom's camera again! So he was *not* photographing the birds after all! Well, what was he doing then—and where was he? Andy began to feel frightened.

He left the camera where it was, and went on round the cliff, on the narrow ledge that led to the waterfall. It was now no longer a trickle, but was pouring out in a great cataract!

Andy went right up to it. An awful thought came to him. Could Tom have been foolish enough to try and get into the cliff through the waterfall hole? Surely, surely not!

"I forbade him to, anyway," said Andy, but he couldn't

245

help feeling that Tom would have disobeyed him easily if he had wanted to badly enough. Had he gone inside? And had the water suddenly grown in volume, and closed his way out again?

Andy stood looking at the waterfall, knowing there was nothing to do for Tom, if he really had gone inside. Either the boy would have to wait till the waterfall lessened in volume again—or find some other way out. And what way was there? None, so far as Andy could see!

The boy sat there for some time. Then, thinking that he must not leave the girls alone any longer, he got up to go. But he did not feel at all happy.

As he moved away from the waterfall its noise grew less. The boy turned round and saw that once again it had lessened, until now it was no more than a gushing spring. What a queer thing it was! He turned to go on again, and then stopped, his eyes almost falling out of his head!

Out from the waterfall exit came an enormous hairy leg! Then another! Andy knew perfectly well they were the same legs he and the others had seen before. For some reason or other they filled the boy with fright. He climbed hurriedly round the edge of the cliff, to be out of sight of the man when he emerged from the hole.

He climbed down steadily. He passed the place where Tom's camera was, without thinking about it. He was just below this place, clinging to a rather difficult bit of the cliff, when he heard the growling voice not far above him. Then something hurtled past him, something with a long brown strap. It flew downwards, but the sea-birds and wind were making such a noise that Andy did not hear crash or thud as the thing struck the rocks below.

He clung to the cliff-side, wondering if the man would come after him, or had seen him. But apparently he had not, for no one came down the cliff-path, and all was quiet except for the sounds of wind, sea and birds.

246

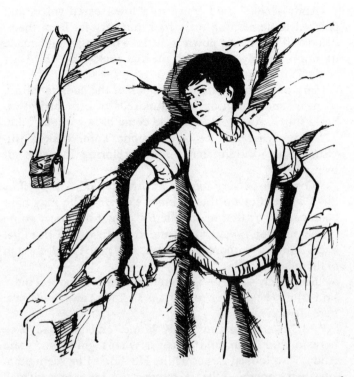

Andy, his mind in a turmoil, climbed down the rest of the cliff as fast as he could. He knew the girls could see him, and would be watching anxiously to see if Tom were following. What *had* happened to Tom? It was terribly worrying.

He reached the girls, and found them sitting upright on their rock, looking pale and frightened.

"Couldn't find Tom," said Andy. "I think the silly little idiot's got inside the waterfall hole—and goodness knows what's happened to him. You were right, Jill, when you said that hairy-legged man made that place his hidey-hole. He came out of there when I was quite near!"

247

"Andy—look!" said Mary in a low, scared voice, and pointed to something on a rock not very far from them. "Look! That came down a little while ago, and made us jump terribly. It crashed on that rock—and oh, Andy —it's Tom's camera!"

Mary burst into tears. The shock of the camera falling so near, and smashing into hundreds of bits, had given her a shock. And now Andy had come back without Tom.

"Andy, what *are* we to do about Tom?" asked Jill. "Surely he wouldn't have gone exploring like that all by himself?"

"Tom can be very foolish at times," said Andy. "*Why* did I leave him up there alone? I'm afraid he may have been caught by that man. There's something queer going on here. I don't want to be mixed up in it. I want to get back home. No more adventures for me! I had enough of them last year."

"But, Andy—*Andy*—we can't go home without Tom!" said Mary, beginning to cry again. "We can't leave him here all alone."

"I'd better take you safely home, and get Dad back here to find Tom, and discover what's going on," said Andy, who looked rather white. He didn't like seeing that smashed camera. What a temper the hairy-legged man must have to fling a beautiful camera down the cliff and smash it like that! Andy remembered how the man had smashed the birds' eggs too, and he didn't at all like the thought of coming into contact with him, when he had two small girls to look after!

He stood up. "Collect the things and come back to the boat," he ordered. "We must go."

"No," said Mary. "I'm not going. I'm not going to desert Tom, if you are!"

"Don't be silly," said Andy. "We're not deserting him. We're going to get Dad and come back and find Tom.

248

Come along. Don't argue. I'm the skipper here."

Jill began to gather up the things, but Mary was still obstinate. Andy hauled her to her feet and gave her a rough shake. "Do as you're told! Can't you see I'm worried stiff? It's Tom's disobedience that has led to this — I'm not going to have any *more* trouble! You'll come along with Jill and me straight away!"

Mary, with tears streaming down her cheeks, began to help Jill to collect the things left over from their tea. Jill, almost in tears herself, gave a last glance down at the underground river, which flowed so swiftly from the foot of the cliff. Then she stood still, her eyes wide and her mouth opened to give a cry. But none came.

She reached out her arm and pointed downwards. The others looked. Rolling over and over on the river, swept from side to side like a log, came a strange dark object.

"Andy! It's Tom—poor, poor Tom!" said Jill, in a choking voice. "It's too late to save him. The river's got him."

Very white under his brown, Andy looked down at the tumbling body. He saw it swept to one side, on to the rocks, where sea and river met. It tumbled out and lay there. Then he saw how the tired arms heaved up the exhausted body to a place of safety.

"He's all right!" yelled Andy, almost startling the girls out of their skins. "He's all right. Hi, Tom, Tom, you scamp, where have you been? How did you get here?"

All three rushed down the rocks to the one where Tom lay, slipping and sliding as they went. He looked up at them and grinned feebly.

"Hello!" he said. "Nice to see you all again! I'm sorry to say that we've plunged into the middle of a most exciting adventure! You wait till I've told you everything. Anybody got anything to eat? I'm most *frightfully* hungry!"

249

CHAPTER X

WHAT HAPPENED ON THE WAY BACK

ANDY, Jill and Mary were so relieved to see Tom alive and hungry that for a moment they could only stare at him in joy, and say nothing at all. Then Jill rushed to get something for him to eat. Andy called after her. "Bring a couple of rugs. Tom's wet through and shivering."

Soon Tom was sitting in a sheltered corner, munching bread and potted meat, his wet clothes drying in the wind, and a couple of warm rugs tucked round him.

Andy wouldn't let the girls ask him any questions till he had got some food inside him and had stopped shivering. They could hardly wait to know what had happened to him. How extraordinary it had been to see Tom come rolling over and over in the restless waters of the underground river!

"Now—tell us everything!" said Jill, when Tom had finished his meal. Tom glanced at Andy, and looked rather embarrassed. He didn't like to own up to his disobedience, which had nearly brought disaster on him.

Andy saw the look. "I suppose you played the fool, and got in through the waterfall opening?" he said, not unkindly, but sternly. Tom went red and nodded.

"Yes—I did," he said. "I'm sorry, Andy. I know you're the skipper here. I just felt I *had* to. But I wished and wished I hadn't been such an idiot, once I'd got through."

"I'm very glad you're safe," said Andy. "But you listen to me, young Tom—any more disobedience from you and you don't come out in my boat any more. See? I'm in charge, and if you can't be loyal to your skipper, you're no use."

"I know, Andy. I know," said Tom humbly. "I won't

250

play the fool again. I've had my lesson. You wait till you hear!"

"*Do* tell us!" begged Jill. "Don't scold him any more, Andy. Let him tell us his story."

So Tom told them how he had wriggled through the waterfall opening, found himself in the cave, which became flooded, so that he had to make his way farther in. He told them about the rough steps leading out from the inner cave, and the long, winding, downhill passages through the heart of the cliff.

When he described finding the cave down below, used apparently as some kind of store-house, and the two men sitting there, talking, the others sat listening intently, holding their breath so as not to miss a word!

"Golly!" said Andy. "This is amazing. There's something queer going on. But what can it be? You were lucky to escape, Tom. But you must have had a shock when you fell into that swirling, underground river."

"I did," said Tom. "And wasn't it a bit of luck that it took me right out here, almost to your feet? I shouldn't have liked it much if the current had thrown me into that foaming surging bit over there, dashing over the rocks. I'd have been knocked to bits!"

"It's a pity those men know somebody is here," said Andy. "I simply can't imagine what they're up to. Can they be smugglers? But what are they doing inside this cliff? There's no road overland to take smuggled goods. It's a real puzzle."

"Do you think the men will come after us?" said Jill, looking rather scared.

"Well—they only know about Tom—and maybe they think he's fallen over the cliff now," said Andy. "It's plain they thought he had gone back up the winding passage to the waterfall opening. They must have gone up there themselves, thinking they were chasing him—and all they

251

found was his camera on the cliff-ledge. They must have thrown it down in rage. What a shame! It's smashed to bits."

Tom was feeling much better now. In fact, he was feeling quite a hero! True, he had disobeyed Andy – but things had come out all right, and he had made some queer discoveries. He began to look a little cocky. But Andy soon put a stop to that.

"I think we ought to get back home as soon as we can," he said. "Tom's sure to get a chill after this. That river water is icy-cold. It's a pity to bring our trip to such a sudden end, but I don't want Tom down with pneumonia!"

Tom's face fell. "Oh, Andy – don't be such an idiot! I'm perfectly all right, you know I am."

"Anyway, Andy – isn't it too late to start back?" asked Jill, looking at the sun, which was now well down in the west.

Andy looked at it too and made some calculations. "The wind's in our favour – and we can get past the worst rocks whilst it's still daylight. I think we ought to go. Also, those two men will be on the look-out for our boat, I expect, and may try to surprise us in the night."

"Blow!" said Tom. "Why did I go and upset things like this? Spoiling our lovely trip. And we haven't been to Smuggler's Rock either!"

Once Andy had made up his mind to do something, he didn't take long to set about it. "Come on," he said, getting up. "Those men are sure to start prying around soon. We'd better go now."

They all went back to the *Andy* with sad faces. What a sudden end to what had promised to be a really exciting trip! They clambered on board and put up the red sail. The evening sun shone softly down, and the sail glowed as they pulled it up, throwing a brilliant shadow on the pale blue water.

The wind was very strong now. Andy deftly steered his boat out of the bay, her sail filling with the wind. Soon she was scudding along fast.

Nobody said anything. They were all disappointed. It was horrid to leave an unsolved mystery behind too. How they would have loved to find out why those men were in the cave, what they were doing there, and who they were! Probably they never would find out, because neither Andy's father nor the children's mother might take much notice of their excited tale.

The sun seemed to go down very quickly. Just as it was about to disappear over the western edge of the world, Tom gave a yell and pointed ahead.

"What's that?" he cried. "Look, over there, by those tall rocks."

Andy's sharp eyes made out what it was at once — a motor-boat! It was lying still, not moving. Could it be waiting for them?

There was nothing to do but go on. The *Andy* swept along, her red sail glowing. When she came near the waiting boat, they heard her motor being started up, and the boat swung out into the centre of the channel down which the *Andy* was flying.

Andy saw that he could not get past in safety. The channel between the two ridges of rock was narrow there. He would go on the rocks if he tried to swing past!

They came up to the motor-boat. A tall, foreign-looking man leaned over the side.

"Who are you? What are you doing here?" he shouted.

"That's none of your business!" shouted back Andy. "Get out of our way!"

"Anchor your boat and come on board here," ordered the tall man most surprisingly. "If you don't, we'll capture you, boat and all!"

"Who are *you*?" bellowed back Andy angrily. "Clear

253

out of our way! We're children out on a sailing trip."

"Andy! Turn back! Let's go back to the Cliff of Birds," begged Jill, frightened. Andy looked scornful, then seemed to alter his mind. He looked anxiously at the sky, which was now dark and overcast with the coming night and with heaped-up clouds. In a short time it would be almost dark.

The man, joined by another man, began to yell at Andy again to come on board. He could not really see if Andy's crew were children or not, for there was a little distance between the boats. Then something happened.

A great wave surged up, and took hold of the motor-boat, swinging her round violently. She must have struck a rock just below the surface, as the wave receded suddenly, for there was a grinding noise and the motor-boat shivered from top to bottom.

The two shouting men were almost thrown overboard. They disappeared at once to see what the damage was.

"Now's our chance!" said Andy. "We'll turn and go back—but not to the Cliff of Birds, which is where they will expect to find us, I've no doubt—but to Smuggler's Rock! You remember where this channel forks off to it? We'll take that course—and we must hope it won't be too dark for me to see it!"

So, whilst the men were trying to find out what damage had been done to their boat, the Andy turned round and stole off, tacking a little to get the help of the breeze. Andy did not think that the motor-boat would dare to come after them in the gathering dark, so, as soon as he could, he pulled down the sail, and took the oars, with Tom.

"Look out for the place where the channel forks," he said. "It's a good long row, but never mind!"

Fortunately the current helped them, and it was not so hard as Andy had expected. They found where the channel forked off for Smuggler's Rock, and then, to their joy, saw that the moon was sliding out from behind the thinning clouds.

"That will help a lot," said Andy. "Look—you can see the faint shape of Smuggler's Rock over there!"

They slid along the channel, which was wider here, and came nearer to the tall, steep rock. They could not see it very clearly, for it was full of shadows. They took the boat into a small cove. Andy thought they had better drop anchor there and hope for the best. He didn't think anyone would come looking for them at Smuggler's Rock. Perhaps next day they could escape out to sea.

They let down the anchor. "Are we going on to the little island?" asked Jill.

"No," said Andy. "We shouldn't be able to find our way properly, with the moon slipping in and out of clouds like this. We'll sleep on the boat—as we planned to do!"

"Can we all sleep on deck?" asked Jill.

"No—you and Mary must sleep down in the cabin," said Andy. "Have a rug each—that should keep you warm enough down there. We'll have the rest of the rugs and cushions because it will be chilly up on deck."

"I feel a bit scared now," said Mary. "I didn't like those two men yelling at us."

"You needn't be afraid," said Andy. "You will be quite safe down in the cabin—and Tom and I will take it in turns to keep guard up here in case anybody *should* come. But no one will."

Puzzled, tired, and still a bit frightened the twins went down into the cabin. They passed up rugs and cushions to the boys. Then they settled down to sleep.

Andy said he would take the first watch, and wake Tom up in three hours. Tom, tired out with all his adventures, was asleep at once, Andy sat beside him, covered in rugs, on guard. What a curious adventure this was! Andy couldn't make head or tail of it!

CHAPTER XI

A NIGHT ON THE BOAT

IT was a lovely night, with scudding clouds going across the moon. In the quiet cove there was very little movement of the water, and the boat hardly stirred. Andy heard the tiny lapping sounds against her sides as he kept his watch.

He puzzled over everything that had happened. Tom had said that the big cave inside the cliff, at the foot, where the underground river rushed by, was stored with boxes and crates. Where had they come from?

"And how did the men get them there?" wondered Andy. "Surely they couldn't have taken them up that steep cliff, through the waterfall opening, and down the winding passages that Tom described? That's quite impossible. Could a motor-boat get up that rushing underground river? No—the current is much too strong—and by Tom's description of it I should think the roof is too low in parts."

No—it was too much of a puzzle and Andy soon gave up trying to solve it. "All I'm certain of is that there's something queer going on, something unlawful—and the sooner we get back now and tell the grown-ups, the better," thought Andy. "We can't possibly tackle this ourselves. And there are the girls to think of—I daren't let them run into any more danger than I can help."

When his three hours were up he woke Tom. He was soon sitting up straight, the rugs well wrapped round him, looking out on the moonlit cove.

"Three hours, Tom—then wake me again," said Andy, snuggling down in the rugs as close to Tom as he could, for warmth. It was a chilly night.

Tom felt terribly sleepy. He found that his head was

256

nodding and his eyes were closing. That would never do! To go to sleep when guarding the others would be a real crime—he couldn't possibly do that. Andy would never, never trust him again.

"I'd better walk about a bit," said Tom to himself. He cautiously wriggled out of his rugs so as not to wake Andy, and paced the deck. He thought he heard a movement down below, and he opened the cabin-hatch softly.

"Are you all right down there?" he said in a whisper.

Mary's voice answered him. "I can't go to sleep, Tom, I've tried and tried. I simply can't. Let me come up on

257

deck with you a bit and keep watch. I'm sure Andy wouldn't mind. I'll bring up some chocolate."

Chocolate sounded pretty good to Tom. He called back softly. "Well, don't wake Jill. Come on up and bring your rug. Just for a little while."

Mary came up into the moonlight, dragging her rug with her. She looked round.

"Oh – isn't it lovely up here with the moonlight making the sea all silvery. What black shadows there are in Smuggler's Rock! I wonder if we'll have time to explore it tomorrow. Here's your chocolate, Tom."

They sat down together, cuddling into the thick rugs. They munched the chocolate, which tasted delicious, eaten in the middle of the night like that! Tom felt quite wide awake by now. He and Mary began to discuss the day's happenings in low tones, so as not to wake Andy.

"Did you get your torch wet?" asked Mary. "You know – when you fell into the underground river?"

"Yes, I did," said Tom, and felt in his pocket for it. "I expect it's quite spoilt. I'll try it."

He pressed the little button that usually set the torch alight – but nothing happened. It was quite spoilt. Tom put it back into his pocket again. As he did so he felt something else there – a tiny round thing. What was it?

He took it out. It was the little red pearl button he had found on the floor of one of the caves. He showed it to Mary."

"Look," he said. "I forgot about this. I found it on the floor of the cave behind the waterfall. That's what made me feel certain the hairy-legged man must hide somewhere in the cliff. After all, a button means a shirt or a vest, doesn't it?"

"Did he wear a red shirt when you saw him in the hidden cave far below?" asked Mary, turning the red button over in her hand.

258

"No. I don't think so," said Tom, trying to remember. "I don't think the other fellow did, either. He was dressed like a fisherman. I didn't much like the look of either of them."

He put the button back into his pocket, and the two fell silent, enjoying the soft motion of the little boat and the wisha-wisha noise that the water made against her. Mary thought it was such a lovely sound. She bent over the side and dabbled her hand in the water.

"Awfully cold," she said, and yawned. "Have you finished your chocolate? I think I'll go back now. I feel sleepy. I don't think anything will happen tonight, Tom. We're quite safe here."

She went below, taking her rug with her. Tom had no fear of falling asleep now. He felt wide awake. He looked at Smuggler's Rock. What a tall, steep, rocky place it was! He felt sure that there would be heaps of sea-birds nesting there too. He hoped Andy wouldn't rush them all away in the morning, without letting them land on the island and have a look at it.

The moon went behind a cloud. At once Smuggler's Rock became dark and black. Tom glanced idly at the top of it—and then he straightened himself up suddenly, and looked very sharply at something.

"There's a light of some sort up there!" he said under his breath. "Yes—there it is again—flash, flash, flash! Somebody's signalling from there. Gracious, are there people here too?"

The light went on flashing. Tom woke Andy by shaking him roughly. The fisher-boy awoke at once and sat up in alarm, expecting he knew not what.

"Look, Andy, look—there's a light flashing at the very top of Smuggler's Rock!" said Tom. "Up there, see. Can you see it? It's a signal of some sort, I should think."

Andy looked. He soon spotted the light. He watched it

intently. It went on for some time and then stopped.

"What do you make of that?" said Tom.

"I don't know," said Andy. "One more puzzle added to the other puzzles! Anyway, I'm determined to get away home as soon as possible tomorrow. We ought to report all these queer doings – and we'd better not be mixed up in them more than we can help. I don't like this kind of puzzle!"

The light did not flash any more. Andy looked at his watch, and then curled himself up. "I've got another hour of sleep," he said. "Keep a sharp look-out, Tom, and wake me if you see anything else going on."

But nothing else happened in the rest of Tom's watch, much to his disappointment. He woke Andy up at the right time, and then curled up again in the rugs himself. "I don't feel a bit sleepy," he said. "I could sit up all night now."

But he was asleep almost before Andy had walked across the deck and back. Below, in the cabin, Jill and Mary were asleep too. It was all very peaceful.

At dawn Andy woke them all. "You girls get a quick breakfast going," he ordered. "Take these rugs down, Tom. We'll start off as soon as we can."

"Which way are we going back?" asked Tom, dragging the rugs to the hatch, to drop them down to the girls.

"I'm not sure," said Andy. "If I were certain that that motor-boat had gone, I'd risk the way we know. I've no idea if we can get out to sea from here – or what is the best course to take, if we can. I wish I dared climb up to a high bit of Smuggler's Rock, and have a look-see. I can't see anything from here."

"Well, why shouldn't you climb up Smuggler's Rock, and have a look round the sea?" said Tom. "You might spot the motor-boat. You might see clearly how we could best make our way home from here."

"Have you forgotten those lights we saw flashing last night?" said Andy. "There's somebody on the island. We don't want to get caught by them. It seems as if there is a perfect network of people in this desolate part of the coast!"

"But it's so early in the morning," said Tom. "No one will be about now. Let's all have a quick breakfast, Andy, and then hop across to Smuggler's Rock quickly, climb up to that high point up there — see where I mean — and have a look-out from there. We could see for miles. I bet you'd spot the motor-boat if it was lying in wait for us anywhere about here."

"Well — perhaps, I'd better try and spy out the way," said Andy. "Maybe no one will be about yet, as you say. We won't talk or laugh as we go. We'll be absolutely quiet."

They sat down on the deck to have a good breakfast. This time it was hot soup out of tins, with bread, and plenty of biscuits spread with marmalade. There was hot cocoa to drink too, sweetened with condensed milk. Everybody enjoyed their queer breakfast very much indeed.

"Hot soup was a jolly good idea," said Andy to Jill, who looked pleased at his praise. "It's so jolly cold this morning. But then, it's very early — the sun is only just coming up. Look!"

They finished their breakfast watching the blue water in the cove turn to dancing gold as the sun came up. Everything looked clean and beautiful and washed, Mary said. So it did! Even the rocks gleamed in the early sun as if somebody had been along and given them a good cleaning!

Andy glanced up the steep rocks of the island nearby. "I think that high point that Tom thought would be a good one is about the best to choose," he said. "I don't quite like you girls coming, but I'd rather we were all together. We'll be as quick as we can."

They left all the breakfast things as they were, and leapt across to a nearby rock. Soon they were clambering over the shining rocks, going up as fast as they could. There were no steep cliffs as there were in the bay they had anchored in before—just masses of rocks, covered with seaweed as far as the spray reached, but dry and black beyond.

They went right up to the high point that Tom had chosen. Certainly there was a wonderful view from there. They looked all round the sea as far as they could. It was rough that morning, and white horses galloped everywhere.

There was no sign of the motor-boat to be seen. Andy looked everywhere, his hawk-like eyes ranging for miles! He had the fine sight of the fisherman, and could often see things out to sea that neither Tom nor the girls could see.

"Nothing to be seen," said Andy, pleased. "Good thing too, because I can't for the life of me see how we would escape any other way than the one we know. I'd be afraid to sail out to sea, with all those rocks about."

"Well—let's get back home as quick as we can," said Jill, and began to leap from rock to rock downwards. Andy yelled a warning—but he was too late.

Jill slipped and fell. She tried to get up and couldn't. Andy hurried to her in great alarm. Whatever had she done?

CHAPTER XII

A HORRID SHOCK

JILL was sitting on a rock, looking very white indeed. She nursed one of her ankles and moaned a little. Tears ran down her cheeks.

"What's up? Have you hurt your ankle?" asked Andy, kneeling down beside her. "Oh, Jill—how foolish to skip down those steep rocks like that!"

"I know. Oh, Andy, my ankle does hurt so. Oh, what shall I do?" wailed poor Jill. "I'm a baby to cry, but I can't help it."

Mary was almost crying too as she bent down by her twin. She took off Jill's rubber shoe. The ankle was already swollen.

Andy felt it tenderly. "I don't think it's a real sprain," he said. "You've just given it an awful twist. It will be all right soon. Don't walk on it just yet."

"Pull her near this pool," said Tom, seeing a big, clear pool of rain-water in the hollow of a rock. "She can put her foot into it. That will be as good as bathing it, I should think."

Jill's foot did feel better in the cold water. Soon the colour came back to her face and she rubbed away the tears.

The foot was still very swollen. Andy thought she had better wait a while before trying to walk on it. So they sat by the pool and talked, Andy keeping a sharp look-out in case anyone came. He told the girls about the lights he and Tom had seen the night before.

After a while Jill thought she could try to walk. Andy helped her up, but as soon as she put her hurt foot to the ground, she gave a cry and crumpled up again. "I don't think I can—not just yet, anyway," she said.

"Well, rest a bit longer," said Andy, trying not to look worried. He did so badly want to get back home quickly. He looked down the steep stretch of rocks below, leading to the cove where the boat was. He could not see the boat, but it was quite a distance below. It wouldn't be much good trying to help Jill down the steep rocks at the moment. She would probably slip and fall again, dragging them with her. They must all wait in patience.

They looked round them. Smuggler's Rock was truly a lonely, desolate-looking place. The sea-birds did not nest there in such thousands as they did on the Cliff of Birds, but there were plenty of them about, circling in the breeze and calling loudly. The island rose to a steep pinnacle. Anyone at the very top would have a perfectly marvellous view for miles out to sea.

"I wish I could go right to the top and have a look what it's like there," said Tom longingly.

"You won't do anything of the sort!" said Andy sharply. "You got into a nice mess yesterday, and I'm not having you get into any more trouble today! Besides, you know perfectly well that that was where those lights showed last night. If anyone is on this island now, they would most likely be up there."

"All right, Andy, all right," said Tom. "I only just said I'd *like* to go up there. I'm not going."

It seemed a long time till Jill was able to put her foot to the ground again without too much pain. It was still swollen, but not quite so much. It wasn't a sprain, but she certainly had twisted it very badly.

"It's about half-past ten," said Andy. "If you feel you can possibly limp down now, Jill, with Tom and me helping you, we'd better go."

Jill tried her foot. Yes—if she didn't put her whole weight on to it, but held on to Tom and Andy, she thought she could manage.

They started down. It was a slow little procession that went down the rocks, taking the very easiest way so that Jill would not have to do any jumping. Twice she had to sit down and rest. Andy was gentle and patient, but inside he felt anxious and worried. Suppose anyone on the island saw them and stopped them? He was longing to get back to the boat and sail away.

They got down to the cove at last. There lay the boat, rocking gently where they had left her. But immediately they saw her the children saw that something was lacking. What was it?

"Where's the sail?" said Tom. "We left it folded on the deck at the end there. Where is it?"

Andy said nothing. His keen eyes swept the boat from end to end, and his heart went cold. Had someone taken the sail?

He left Jill to Tom and Mary, and went jumping down to the cove, landing like a sure-footed goat on the rock, beside the *Andy*. He leapt on board.

He made a hurried search, whilst the others came slowly nearer, Tom and Mary helping Jill along. He turned to them with a grim face as they came aboard.

"Do you know what's happened? Somebody's been here and taken, not only our sail, but our *oars* too!"

The three stared at him in horror. The sail gone — and the oars as well? How could they get home then?

"But, Andy — we can't go home now," said Jill, looking very pale with shock and pain.

"I'm afraid not," said Andy, and he helped Jill to a comfortable place on the deck. He looked all round searchingly, but he could see nobody at all. Who had taken the sail and the oars?

"Someone came along whilst we were up on that high point," he said. "Someone who meant to keep us here. And the easiest way to keep us was to do something that would make it impossible for us to take the boat home. So he removed the sail and the oars. If I could just get hold of him!"

Jill began to cry again. Her ankle was hurting her once more, and she was longing to get back home and be comforted by her mother. She sobbed bitterly. Andy put his arm round her.

"Poor old Jill. Never mind, we'll manage somehow — even if we have to swim home!"

But Jill couldn't smile. "You see," she sobbed, "if I hadn't been such an idiot as to jump down the rocks like that, and twist my ankle, we'd have had plenty of time to get away. It's all my fault — and my ankle hurts again — and I feel simply awful."

"You go down into the cabin and lie down," said Andy. "Mary will put a wet, cold bandage on. Tom and I will talk over things, and see what we think is best to do."

Jill managed to get down into the cabin. She was glad to lie down on the little bunk there and put her foot up. Mary wrung a bandage out in cold sea-water, and wrapped it carefully round the swollen ankle.

The boys sat up on deck and talked gravely together. Andy felt that things were serious now.

"We've stumbled on to something that those men wanted to keep secret," said Andy. "They chose this lonely, forgotten bit of coast for whatever it is they wanted to do — smuggle, I suppose. And now we've butted in and spoilt their little game."

"They'll be very angry," said Tom.

"You bet they will!" said Andy. "It's quite clear they don't mean us to get home and talk about it. They'll keep us prisoner here till they've finished their job, whatever it is. Something to do with all those crates and boxes, I suppose."

"I wonder what's in them," said Tom.

266

"Forbidden goods of some kind," said Andy. "It's very worrying. Your mother and my father will be very anxious when we don't turn up."

"Well, they know where we've gone," said Tom, brightening up. "They'll come and look for us. Your father will get your uncle's boat and come and see what's happened. He's sure to come to Smuggler's Rock if he doesn't find us at the Cliff of Birds."

"Yes. He will," said Andy. "But I bet our captors, whoever they are, have thought of that. They'll deal with that when the time comes."

"How?" asked Tom. "What do you mean?"

"Well, I mean that if they see Dad's boat coasting along, they'll take steps to see we're not about!" said Andy, grimly.

Tom looked scared. "What about our boat?" he said. "They can't hide that."

Andy said nothing to that. He was silent so long that Tom looked up at him. To his enormous alarm he saw what looked like one bright tear in the corner of the fisherboy's eye. He was so alarmed that he caught hold of Andy's hand.

"*Andy!* Whatever's the matter? Why do you look like that?"

Andy swallowed, and blinked back the unexpected tear. "Well, idiot," he said, trying to speak naturally, "they'll probably scuttle my boat, that's all! That's the best way to hide a boat you don't want found. I think they're pretty desperate fellows, and they won't stick at sinking a boat if it suits them."

Sink the *Andy!* Scuttle their beautiful swift-running boat? Tom stared at Andy in horror. They all loved the boat, but Andy loved her most of all, because he had used her for a long time now, and knew all her little ways. All the fishermen loved their boats, of course, but this was

267

Andy's first boat, and a beauty.

"Oh, Andy," said Tom, and couldn't think of anything else to say at all. "Oh, *Andy*."

They said nothing for a few minutes. Then they heard Mary coming up to soak Jill's bandage again. "Don't tell the girls what we're afraid will happen," said Andy in a low voice. "No good scaring them before it happens."

"Right," said Tom. He managed to give Mary a grin as she came up. "How's Jill?"

"She says her ankle feels better now her foot is up," said Mary. "We've been talking about the oars and the sail, Tom. Couldn't we go and look for them? We might find them hidden somewhere."

"Not very likely," said Andy. "It was pretty smart work on the part of the person who came along and saw our boat. He went off with them at once."

"I do feel hungry," said Tom. "Gracious, Andy, I've just thought of something. We've brought quite a bit of food with us, luckily—but not enough for more than two or three days. I hope we shan't starve!"

"We'll be rescued long before that," said Andy, seeing Mary's alarmed face. "Anyway, we'll have something to eat now. It's about twelve-o'clock. Look at the sun!"

They had a good meal, and Andy and Tom kept a look-out all the time in case they saw anyone stealing about. But they saw no one.

"We must make up our minds to stay here for a while," said Andy. "And I think we'll remove all the food and rugs and things from the boat, Tom. We'll find a good little home somewhere on Smuggler's Rock—in a cave or somewhere—and make ourselves as comfortable as possible."

"Almost as if we'd been wrecked!" said Mary, feeling suddenly cheerful. "That sort of thing is fun, even if we *are* in trouble! Come on—let's find a good place."

CHAPTER XIII

A GOOD LITTLE HOME

THEY left Jill on deck, because her ankle was still painful, though very much better. She could hobble about now, and felt more cheerful. She was very disappointed not to be able to go with them and find a good sleeping-place for that night.

"But why can't we sleep on the boat?" she asked, surprised. "Like we did last night."

The boys did not like to tell her that at any moment they thought somebody might come along and scuttle the boat—sink her down to the bottom of the pool; so that it was necessary to remove everything to some good place, in order not to lose the things on the boat.

"We'd be more comfortable, I expect, if we found a sandy cove, sheltered from the wind," said Andy. "We'll keep the boat in sight, Jill, as we go, so you needn't be afraid by yourself. We'll be able to see you all the time, and you'll be able to see us."

The three of them set off. They went over the rugged rocks, keeping the *Andy* in sight all the time. The boys did not think anyone would go to the boat just then, but Andy was not going to risk leaving Jill completely alone. If they kept the boat in sight they could see what was happening at any moment.

"It's no good going the way we went this morning, up to that high point," said Andy. "For one thing the boat is out of sight from there, and for another I didn't see a single place where we could get comfort and shelter. Did you?"

"No," said Tom. "It all looked jolly hard and windswept and uncomfortable, I thought. Let's go the other way — look, is that green grass, over there? No, it's cushions of some kind of sea-shore plant. We might find a good spot over there, but higher up. I reckon that if a storm came the sea would sweep right over these rocks we're on now."

"Yes, it would," said Andy. "You can see bits of seaweed here and there — clinging on in the hope of sea-water, I should think. I hope a storm *doesn't* come! That would about finish the *Andy,* lying there among those rocks. She'd be torn from her anchor, and smashed to bits."

"Well — it doesn't look as if a storm is near," said Tom, not liking this conversation at all. "It's fine today, though it's cold. Look, Andy — let's climb up here to that broad ledge. It looks pretty sheltered there. Is that a cave behind the ledge?"

They climbed up to the broad ledge of rock, keeping the *Andy* well in sight all the time. "We don't want to go too far from the boat," said Andy. "It would be such a fag carrying everything. If there's a cave there it would be very convenient!"

There *was* a cave — rather an awkward one with a very low roof at the front, so that the children had to crawl in almost flat. But inside it opened out into a fairly roomy cave, with a higher roof. It smelt clean and fresh, and had a sandy floor, which Andy was surprised to see.

"This will do," he said, switching on his torch and looking round. "We can make the opening bigger by pulling away some of those overhanging tufts of roots, and burrowing down in the sand below. It will be rather fun lying in the cave and squinting out through that narrow opening at the sea."

"We've got a very fine view," said Mary, and she lay down to peep out. "I can see the *Andy* from here. Jill's still sitting on deck. And look, you can see the Cliff of Birds too — over there in the distance — and make out the

channel between the two ridges of rocks."

"We could see anyone coming to rescue us!" said Tom. "Couldn't we, Andy? We could easily see your father's boat from here. We could signal!"

There was a rocky ledge at one side of the cave. Mary patted it. "This will do to put our stores on," she said. "And we'll put our cushions and rugs on the sandy floor. We shall be very snug here. It would be great fun—if only Mother wouldn't be worried about us!"

"This cave will do fine," said Andy. "We'll go back and get our stores. Come on, Tom—squeeze out."

They all squeezed out. Andy looked up at the top edge of the entrance. He began to pull away some of the earth and roots that hung down from above. Soon he had made the entrance a little bigger.

"That will let more air in," he said. "It might be stuffy at night with four of us in. But it will certainly be warm! No wind can get in here to make us shiver and shake!"

They went back to the boat, pleased that they had found somewhere fairly near. They told Jill all about it. She showed them her ankle.

"It's *much* better!" she said. "It feels almost all right now. I could help to carry the things up."

"No, you can't," said Andy. "You rest it as much as you can. We'll take the things up, and leave you in charge of the boat whilst we go to and fro."

They went down into the cabin. They collected all the food—and there was quite a lot! What a good thing they had stocked the *Andy* so well!

They staggered off with the food. Jill got the little oil-stove ready for them to take too. They would need to boil water for tea or cocoa. She put the kettle ready to be taken.

It was very tiring work carrying the things over the rocks up to the cave. There were so many things to take. Andy did not mean to let anything be lost, if the boat were sunk. He meant to save all he could.

Rugs, cushions, fishing-tackle, the cabin lamp, mugs, plates, everything was stripped from the fishing-boat. The girls, not knowing that the boys were afraid that the boat might be scuttled, were astonished to see everything being taken. Mary thought it was most unnecessary work.

"Why do we take so much?" she grumbled. "I'm tired now! Andy, it's silly to take *every*thing!"

"Do as your skipper tells you!" said Tom.

"You're a good one to talk!" snapped Mary. "It was

272

you who disobeyed Andy and got into a mess."

"You're tired, Mary," said Andy. "Stop carrying the things and let me finish them. Go back to Jill and see if you can help her part of the way up. Her foot is so much better that I believe she can manage with just your help."

By tea-time the cave was well stocked. Mary arranged the food on the rocky ledge there. "That's our larder," she told the boys. "And this bit is the dresser, with the plates and mugs and things. At the back here is the kitchen, because that's where we've put the stove and the kettle and saucepan. The other part is a bed-sitting-room, because we shall have to live there and sleep there too!"

When Jill came up to the cave, helped by Mary, she was delighted. She thought it all looked most exciting. The only thing was that it was rather dark there, and Andy did not want to use their torches too much, because of wearing out the batteries.

"We could light the cabin lamp," said Jill.

"There's not a great deal of oil," said Andy. "We'll only light that when it's really dark—at night. We can just manage to see inside the cave, if nobody stops up the entrance with his body! Tom, get out of the way. You're blocking our daylight!"

"I was just having a look-see," said Tom. "We've got the *Andy* under our eye all right here. If anyone tries any little tricks, we can see them."

"I suppose your father will rescue us tomorrow," said Jill. "We shall only have a night here. It's a pity really, because it's such fun to sleep in a cave, and keep having picnics."

"Do you suppose the people on this island—the ones who took our sail and oars, and flash those lights at the top—do you suppose they know we've come to this cave?" said Mary.

"I expect so," said Andy. "I've no doubt they've got

273

look-outs posted, who see any ship, and can watch any-one's actions. They must have seen us there early this morning, down in the cove, and been very surprised. They couldn't have seen us coming last night — it was too dark."

"How annoyed they must have been, to see our boat there," said Tom. "We've butted in at just the wrong time for them. I guess they were jolly glad when they saw we were only children."

Jill and Mary were now getting tea. They wondered what to do for water to boil.

"Easy!" said Tom. "There is plenty of rain-water in the hollows of the rocks up here — left from last week's rain-storms, I should think. I'll fill your kettle for you, from one of the pools."

"Right," said Mary, and handed over the kettle. Tom squeezed out of the cave, found a good pool of rain-water quite nearby, and filled the kettle. Soon it was boiling on the oil-stove, making a nice gurgling sound. Jill cut some bread and butter, and put out a jar of plum jam.

"We'd better not have tins of meat or sardines, had we?" she said to Andy. "Just in case we aren't rescued tomorrow, and have to go on living here. We'll want the sardines and meat for dinner then."

"Yes," said Andy. "We must go slow on the food till we see what's going to happen. Anyway, this is a very nice tea. I like plum jam. I expect poor old Tom could eat a whole loaf, but he'll have to be content with a few slices! Have you got tinned milk for tea, Jill, or did we finish it all?"

"No. I've got plenty," said Jill. "As a matter of fact, we like spreading it on bread and butter like jam, so I brought quite a lot of tins. We shall be all right for tea and cocoa. Pass your mug, Andy. I'll fill it."

Even Andy, worried as he was about what might happen

to his beloved boat, couldn't help enjoying his tea up there in the cave. But soon the cave felt very hot, because the oil-stove warmed it, and the children went and sat out on the ledge in the sunshine. It was a very beautiful view spreading before them.

"Rocks—and sea—and more rocks—and more sea—and sky and clouds and birds making a pattern in the air," said Jill, munching her slice of bread and jam. "I like looking at things like that when I'm having a picnic. It makes my bread and jam taste nicer!"

"Things always taste better when you eat them out of doors," said Mary. "I've often noticed that."

"Look!" said Andy suddenly. "Is that someone coming round the left-hand side of the cove down there? See—where that big rock sticks up. Yes—he's going to the *Andy*. Let's get back into the cave and watch. If he doesn't know where we are, we've no need to show ourselves!"

With beating hearts the children squeezed into the cave. They lay flat on their tummies and peered down to the cove below. They could see a man—he looked like a fisherman, and had big sea-boots on.

"He's going to the *Andy*," whispered Tom. "What's he going to do?"

CHAPTER XIV

THE HUNT FOR THE CHILDREN

HARDLY breathing, the four children watched the man walking over the rocks towards the *Andy*. He was a tall, burly man, very dark, and with a black beard.

"Do you know him, Andy?" whispered Tom. Andy shook his head.

"No. He doesn't come from our district. Look—he's getting into the boat."

A faint shout came up to the children. "He's shouting to us to come out!" said Mary. "He thinks we're still there!"

The man stood on the deck, waiting. But when no one answered him, or came up from below, he went to the cabin hatch and opened it. He looked down and saw no one there. He also saw that the boat looked remarkably empty of goods as well as of crew!

"He's found out that we've removed all our things from the boat!" said Andy.

The man went down into the cabin. Then he came up again, stood on the deck, and looked all about, as if he expected to be able to see the children somewhere.

"Look—there's another man now," whispered Tom. "See—coming round the cove where the first one came. What a funny little man!"

He was. He was bandy-legged, and walked as though he sat on a horse. He had on sea-boots and a sou'wester, and a black oil-skin that flapped in the wind. He was short and squat, and he yelled to the other man as he came. His voice came faintly on the wind to the children.

"Now they're talking together about our disappearance," said Tom, quite enjoying himself. "Do you think

they'll come to find us, Andy? We're well hidden here."

The men talked together. The little bandy-legged one had a look round the boat and peered down into the cabin. It made Andy go red with rage to see strangers on his boat. He longed to go down and turn them off!

But if he did that he would give away the hiding-place. So he lay still, red to his ears, and Jill put her arm over his shoulder to comfort him. She knew what he was feeling. Andy was so proud of his boat, and loved her so much.

The men separated and went off in different directions. It was plain that they were hunting for the hidden children. They peeped about down in the cove, and occasionally shouted, though the children couldn't hear the words.

"Shouting to us to come out, I suppose," said Tom. "As if we would! I bet they don't find us!"

The men came up a bit higher, and looked all about the rocks. There were one or two places where the children might have hidden.

Now they could hear what the men shouted to one another. "Where are those brats?" yelled the bandy-legged man. "Wait till I find them! Wasting my time like this!"

The children lay quite quiet. They didn't like the look of the bandy-legged man at all as he came nearer. He had bushy eyebrows that almost hid his eyes, and a scar went all the way down one cheek. The dark man was good-looking, and spoke with a foreign accent. He looked stern as he went about the hunt.

"We'd better wriggle back right into the cave," said Andy. "If they come any higher they might just catch sight of us."

So they wriggled back. Soon they were crouching right at the very back, catching a glimpse of the distant sea through the narrow entrance. They kept very quiet, for they heard the sound of the men's climbing feet coming near.

"There's a cave somewhere about here!" they heard the bandy-legged man call. "I remember my dog going into it once. Maybe they've gone there."

"We will look," said the dark man, and his steps came nearer. The children saw his feet walking past the entrance! Their hearts almost stopped beating with fright. But the feet went right past and out of sight. Good!

Then they saw the bandy legs of the other man going by too. But just as he was passing, the legs stopped.

"I'm sure that cave was here," said his rather hoarse voice. "Wait—what's this!" His foot kicked into the entrance of the cave. Then he bent down and looked inside, finding it very awkward indeed. But he could see nothing, of course, for it was pitch-black inside the cave.

"They cannot be in there," said the nearby voice of the dark man. "No one surely could creep in there! Look, there is a cave higher up. Maybe they are in that."

To the children's enormous relief the bandy-legged man moved on. They breathed more easily, but did not dare to move. They heard more shouting and calling and then there was silence.

"Is it safe to peep out?" said Tom, who was longing to know what was happening.

"No," said Andy. "They may be sitting quietly somewhere waiting for us to show ourselves. Keep still, Tom."

They all kept very still and quiet, only moving when their arms or legs felt cramped. Then they heard the voices again. The dark man sounded thoroughly impatient and exasperated.

"I tell you, Bandy, it is important that we find these children. If anyone comes to look for them they will signal to them—and they know too much! We must find them. It is impossible that they should have hidden themselves away so well."

"You can see for yourself they aren't here," said the other, sounding sulky. "They've taken all their things and maybe gone to the other side."

"I hope not!" said the other man. "They will fall into trouble there! No—they have not gone far, Bandy. They could not carry so many things very far."

The men were standing near the cave again now. The children heard the dark man suddenly give an exclamation.

"Look!" he said. "What's this? Spots of oil! Who could

have spilt oil here but those children? They took the lamp out of the cabin—and the little cooking-stove, for it wasn't there. So maybe it was oil from one of those."

"Blow!" said Andy, between his teeth. He remembered how he had tipped the stove a little, bringing it to the cave over a rather difficult rock nearby.

"It looks as if they must be in that cave then, after all!" said the bandy man. "Yes, that's oil all right. Little pests, to give us so much trouble. I'll strike a match and look in the cave."

"He'll see us now," whispered Andy. "Now you leave everything to me, you others. I'll manage this."

Soon the bandy legs were to be seen outside the cave entrance once more. Then the man knelt down and looked with difficulty into the low, ground-level entrance. He struck a match, and held its flame inside the entrance. He gave a loud cry.

"Hey! Here they are, the whole lot of them, lying as quiet as mice in a nest! Come on out, all of you!"

The children said nothing. The match went out. The man lit another and this time the dark man knelt down and looked into the entrance, his head almost on the ground. He saw the children too. He spoke to them with authority.

"Now, come out! We shan't hurt you, but we want to see you out of here. Come along."

"We're not coming," said Andy.

There was a silence. Then the bandy man began to lose his temper. He began to yell. "Look here, you, you . . ."

"That's enough, Bandy," said the dark man. He called into the cave.

"How many of you are there?"

"Four," said Andy. "And let me warn you that the first man who wriggles in here will get a blow on the head with the stove!"

280

"That's no way to talk," said the dark man after a moment's pause. "We're not going to hurt you. We want to take you somewhere much more comfortable."

"We couldn't be more comfortable than we are, thanks," said Andy politely.

"Are you coming or have I got to come in and get you!" yelled Bandy suddenly.

"Come in, if you like," said Andy. "If you come in feet first we'll send you out double-quick, with a good shove. And if you come in head first, we're sorry for you. We've got the oil-stove waiting!"

"Leave them, Bandy," said the dark man, standing up. "Little idiots! It will be the worse for them when they do come out. We can always get them out when we want to."

"How?" asked Bandy.

"Easy enough. You'll see!" said the other. The children wondered what he meant.

"Well, we'll want them out as soon as we sight anything," said Bandy, standing up too. "Better give me your orders, chief!"

"We can leave them for tonight," said the dark man, and began to walk away. "We have other things we can do!"

Soon there was silence again. It was getting darker in the cave now, for the sun had gone, and twilight was coming. The children lay quite quiet for some time, but could hear nothing. Finally Andy crawled to the entrance and peered out.

"Can't see down into the cove," he said. "Too dark. Can't see any sign of those men, either. Beasts! How do they suppose we're going to be got out of here?"

"You wouldn't really drop the oil-stove on that man's head, would you?" asked Jill, very horrified at the thought.

"No," said Andy. "But I thought the threat might keep

281

them out of here till tomorrow, when I hope my Dad will come with Uncle Ned and his boat. Then we'll creep out and yell for all we're worth!"

"That's what those men were afraid we'll do," said Tom. He yawned. "I feel sleepy. One of us will have to be on guard during the night, Andy. We don't want anyone creeping in to surprise us."

"Jill and I will take our turns tonight," said Mary. "You two boys hadn't much sleep last night. Can't we rig up a pile of tins at the entrance, so that anyone trying to creep in would knock them over, and warn the one on guard?"

"Jolly good idea, Mary," said Andy. "We'll do that at once. I feel as sleepy as Tom does. You can have the first watch, me the next, Jill the next, and Tom the next. Where are the tins? I can't see in this darkness!"

Mary lighted the lamp, and the cave at once glowed into warm yellow light. It seemed cosy and snug in there. The children wrapped their rugs round them and put cushions at their heads. Mary sat bolt upright, proud to have the first watch. She had built up a pile of tins at the entrance to the cave. Now no one could get in without being heard at once.

Andy blew out the lamp. Darkness settled on the cave once more. Jill put out her hand and took Mary's. "I'll hold your hand just to keep you company whilst you're watching," she whispered. "Good night!"

Soon there was silence in the cave except for the peaceful breathing of three sleeping children. Mary sat tense, holding her breath at every sound. She did hope that nobody would come whilst she was keeping watch!

282

CHAPTER XV

PLENTY OF THINGS HAPPEN!

MARY watched and listened until it was time to wake Andy. She felt quite worn out by the time she had been on guard for two hours. They were each keeping guard for the same time—two hours. But it seemed a very long time, when everything was dark and still.

Andy had nothing to report when he woke Jill. Jill kept watch for two hours, feeling rather sleepy at times but keeping herself awake by reciting softly all the poetry she had ever learnt.

Tom's turn came next. He was very difficult to wake, as usual. Jill thought she never would wake him! But at last she had him sitting up, rubbing his eyes.

"You're to wake Andy in two hours' time, and he'll take the dawn watch," she said. "He says he doesn't mind, he'll have had plenty of sleep by then."

Tom couldn't keep his eyes open! He nearly yawned his head off. Then he felt hungry and wondered where the girls had put the chocolate. He felt about for Andy's torch and found it. He switched it on and flashed the light on to the little ledge where the food was stored.

Andy was awake immediately the torch flashed on. He sat upright with a jerk, blinking.

"What's up?" he said.

"Nothing!" whispered Tom. "I only wanted some chocolate. I'll never keep awake unless I have something to eat. Lie down. I'll wake you when it's your turn again."

He saw the chocolate piled at the end of the ledge. He took a bar, snapped off the torch, and began to tear the paper off the chocolate. Andy lay down with a grunt and was soon sleeping soundly again.

283

Nothing happened in Tom's watch. He woke Andy just before dawn. The boy sat up, and saw the first grey light filtering in through the low cave-entrance. He wriggled there and looked out. He could see nothing at all.

When the sun rose the others awoke. Jill sat up, stretching. She knew where she was at once, but Mary couldn't imagine.

"Where am I?" she said, sitting up, half-frightened.

"Only in the cave, silly," said Jill. "It's daylight again. Golly, I feel stiff. I'm a bit cold too. I vote we get the stove going and boil some water for cocoa."

Tom was wriggling to the cave entrance to have a breath of fresh air. He sniffed eagerly, and looked down to the cove below. He gave such a loud cry that everyone jumped, and Mary dropped the match she was about to strike.

"What's up? What's the matter?" they cried.

"Our boat—it's gone. It isn't there!" cried Tom. "Look! The cove's quite empty. No boat there at all!"

All four looked down to the cove below. It was just as Tom had said. The boat was gone. The *Andy* was no longer there.

Andy looked very miserable. He didn't say anything at all. Tom knew how he was feeling.

"Oh, Andy, you don't think those men have sunk her, do you?" he said in a hushed voice. "Surely nobody could do such a wicked thing to a beautiful boat like that!"

Andy still said nothing. He left the others and went to the back of the cave, where he busied himself lighting the stove and putting the kettle on to boil. He couldn't bear to think that his lovely boat might be lying far down at the bottom of the water.

"Poor Andy!" whispered Jill, with tears in her eyes. "Isn't it awful? Tom, why should those men sink our boat?"

"I suppose so that no one should see it and guess we

were here, if they came to look for us," said Tom, feeling that the girls ought to know how serious things were. "You see, we have stumbled on some kind of secret, and those men don't want us to tell anyone. But they know someone will be sure to come hunting for us, so they've sunk our boat, and mean to hide us away somewhere, so that we can't be found—then we shan't be able to tell what little we know!"

The girls looked scared. Then Jill cheered up. "But they *haven't* taken us anywhere, and when we see Andy's father's boat coming, we'll all climb up on to the high rocks above the cave and signal. I'll take off my vest and wave it!"

"Kettle's boiling," came Andy's voice from the back. "Going to make the cocoa, Jill?"

Jill scrambled back. Her foot was practically all right again. But she blamed herself very much for her accident, for if she had not twisted her ankle, they might all by now have been safely back at home. So she was eager to please Andy in every way and show him how sorry she was.

Andy looked very miserable. Jill didn't say anything to him, but she gave his arm a quick squeeze. She too felt very gloomy when she thought of the beautiful boat lying on the bottom of the sea—but she knew that to Andy his boat meant much more than a lovely plaything. That was all it really was to the three visitors, but to Andy the boat was a friend and a comrade.

"Dad ought to be along soon," said Andy, as they ate their breakfast. "When we didn't come home last night, as we should have done, everyone would get the wind up and be worried. Dad would start out for the Cliff of Birds early this morning. If he didn't find us there he'd come along here. We must keep a look-out."

They finished breakfast. Andy peered out of the cave. "I must just slip down to the cove and have a look to see

285

if the poor old *Andy* is at the bottom there," he said. "I won't be long. And I won't be caught, so don't be afraid. But I've just *got* to go and have a look. Keep a watch out, Tom."

The boy wriggled out of the cave, and the others saw him running and skipping like a goat, down the steep rocks that sloped to the cove. They saw him standing where the *Andy* had been anchored, peering down into the water here and there.

"Poor old Andy. This has upset him," said Jill. "It's awful to lose his boat like that. I feel it's all my fault too."

"Look—there's that bandy man again!" said Tom, suddenly. "And two others with him! They've seen Andy— but he's seen them too. Look at him leaping up the rocks! Oh, Andy, hurry, hurry!"

Andy was not afraid of being caught by the three men. He was far swifter than they were. They yelled at him and ran, but they were no match at all for the boy. He leapt up the rocks, and came panting to the cave. He wriggled in with plenty of time to spare.

"I don't know if they've come for us," he panted. "But they won't make us come out! I don't see how they can unless they like to risk wriggling in on their tummies— and they are at our mercy then!"

"Andy, did you see the boat?" asked Jill anxiously. Andy shook his head.

"No—they haven't sunk her just there. I think they must have taken her out to sea a bit and scuttled her in really deep water. There's no sign of her down there."

"I suppose they thought your father might spot her, lying in the cove at the bottom," said Tom. "They must have taken her out in the night. And not one of us heard a thing!"

"Well, the cove is a good way off," said Andy, getting

286

back his breath. "Now look out—here come the men."

There was the dark man with the beard; the bandy-legged man—and one that Tom recognized at once.

"Look—see the fisherman with the glasses on his nose? Well, that's one of the men I saw in the cave at the Cliff of Birds! How did he get here? Did the motor-boat call for him and take him off?"

"He's not the one with hairy legs, is he—the man whose legs we saw when he sat above us on the Cliff of Birds?" asked Jill.

"No. He's not here," said Tom. "Nasty-looking collection, aren't they?"

Andy felt desperate. He was angered by the disappearance of his boat, and quite ready to push any of the men down the rocks, if only he could! He was anxious, too, for the girls. Their mother had put them into his charge — and here they were in the midst of danger. Andy was quite determined to fight with any weapon he could, if the men tried to wriggle into the cave.

The three came to the cave. The dark man called out to them. "Well, children, are you more sensible this morning? Are you coming out? I advise you to."

No one said anything. The man called again, impatiently. "Come along now! No one will hurt you! You'll be sorry if you don't come out of your own free will. We don't want to *make* you come!"

Still no reply. There was a short silence, and the dark man gave a rapid order.

"Set it going, Bandy."

Bandy set something down by the cave, just within the entrance. It looked like some sort of can. The children couldn't quite make out what it was. They watched in silence.

Bandy struck a match and held it to something in the can. It flared up. Bandy seemed to damp it down and, instead of flames, smoke came out.

The wind was blowing in their direction and it blew the thick, billowing smoke into the cave. Tom got a smell of it first and he coughed.

"The beasts!" said Andy suddenly. "They're trying to smoke us out of the cave — like hunters smoke out wild animals."

The smoke poured in. The children coughed. The smoke was thick and smelt horrid. It was quite harmless, but the children didn't know that. They felt frightened.

"We'll have to go out," spluttered Andy. "It's no good. We'll have to go. Keep close to me when we're out, girls, and do exactly what I say. Don't be afraid. I don't think for a minute we'll come to any harm."

Before he went out, Andy felt along the ledges for the packet of salt he knew was there. The others didn't see him and would have been surprised if they had. Andy tore open the packet, and slipped the salt into his pocket. He had a little plan for that salt!

Then, panting and coughing, he crawled out of the cave. The girls came next, and then Tom. The men stared at them.

"Why, they're only kids — except for this fisher-boy," said Bandy. "Interfering little varmints."

"Look! Look, Andy! There's your father's boat!" suddenly cried Tom, and they all swung round. Sure enough, away in the distance was a big fishing-boat, the one used by Andy's uncle and his father when they wanted a bigger boat than Andy's.

"Hurrah!" yelled Tom. "We're all right. You'll have to let us go now! There's Andy's father."

"Come on. Take them away," said the dark man. "There's no time to be lost. Blindfold them!"

To the children's great dismay they were each blind-folded with big red handkerchiefs. Where were they going? And why were their eyes bandaged? Were they going to some secret hide-out that no one must know the way to?

The men pushed them forward roughly, and they stumbled over a rocky path, not seeing where they went.

"Oh," wept Mary, "let us wait! Let us wait for Andy's father! We'll go home then. Let us go, please let us go!"

But the men pushed them on, and when Andy's father sailed into the cove, there was no one to be seen!

CHAPTER XVI

PRISONERS!

THE four children were pushed along by the men. They were afraid of falling, but the men guided them over the rough places. It seemed to them all as if they were going upwards, not on the level. How they hoped that Andy's father would spot them, if only he had his field-glasses!

Andy was doing his best to try and memorize the way, as they went along. "Up all the time—to the left first and then fairly straight—then a steep bit up, where they had to help us—then to the left again, keeping inwards. I suppose we are behind big rocks now, so that no one can see us from the sea."

Andy was doing something else too, that he hoped his captors were not noticing! He was dropping little pinches of salt here and there as he went! He had made a hole in his pocket, and he let out a bit of the salt every now and again.

He wanted to be able to find his way to the smugglers hiding-place, if ever he got free and had the chance to! He hoped that he might be able to follow the little trail of salt he was leaving!

"If only it doesn't rain!" thought the boy. "If it rains, the salt will melt and there won't be any sign of it. Well, I must hope for the best."

After about ten minutes' rough stumbling, the men told the children to halt. There was a pause. Andy strained his eyes, and then tried to pull off his bandage. But he got a hard clip on the ear at once.

He heard a grating noise that puzzled him. Then the children were pushed roughly forward again, and it seemed darker, through their bandages.

"Going into the island itself—a cave of some sort, or a passage," thought Andy, as the men pushed the children along again. They went upwards again, and Andy cautiously put his hands out to the side of him. He felt rocky walls each side. Yes, they were in a passage inside the island!

At last they all came to a stop. "You'll be safe here for a bit!" said the jeering voice of the bandy-legged man, and he stripped off the red handkerchiefs that bound their eyes.

They blinked. They were standing in a high-roofed place, looking at a big door. Andy felt something bright at the back of him and swung round. He gave a gasp.

They were in a cave, very high up, that opened on to the sunlit sea. It lay very far below, moving slowly. There was an absolutely sheer drop down from the cave to the sea—a very frightening drop!

There was a bang, as the heavy wooden door behind them shut. The children heard bolts being shot into place. They were prisoners—but what a strange prison!

"It's a big cave, with a door at the back—and a terribly steep drop down outside," said Jill, peeping out and drawing back very quickly. "Goodness—I shan't look out again like that. It makes me feel awfully giddy. We couldn't possibly get out that way."

"Can we see Andy's father's boat?" asked Tom, almost dazzled by the brightness outside, after having his eyes bandaged for so long.

They all gazed out earnestly. But there was nothing to be seen at all except a dangerous, treacherous, rock-strewn shore, where waves battered themselves into foam and spray.

"It's said that no one can get beyond a certain point in a boat, if they want to sail round the island," said Andy. "I don't believe anyone ever *has* sailed right round it. You can't get near the other side — it's too dangerous. We must be almost on the other side now, I should think. I doubt if my father could get round as far as this."

"I bet those men knew that then," said Tom gloomily. "They knew that we couldn't possibly signal from here, because we wouldn't see your father's boat. Beasts!"

"I hope they're not going to keep us here long," said Andy. "I don't fancy being shut up like this, without any food or rugs or anything."

"This is as bad as last year's adventure," said Jill. "Well — almost as bad!"

The four children sat down in the cave. Andy got up after a while and went to the door. He tried it, but, of course, it was fast shut.

"I knew it would be. But I thought I'd just try," said Andy. "I do wonder how long they'll keep us here — till my father's gone home again, I suppose! And I do wonder too where they sank the poor old *Andy*. I hate to think of her at the bottom of the sea."

"With fish swimming in the cabins, and crabs getting into the bunks," said Jill. "Horrid!"

For about three hours nothing happened. The children gazed out to sea, hoping against hope to see a boat or a ship they could signal to. But not one came into sight. Only the gulls circled and glided nearby, calling to one another in their loud voices. The children watched them, for they had nothing else to do.

Then there came the sound of the door being unbolted. They all sat up at once. Who was it?

It was Bandy. He came in, carrying a big jug of water and a plate of bread and meat. Nothing else at all.

"You don't deserve a thing!" he said in his rather hoarse voice. "Interfering, tiresome nuisances you are! Eat this, and be glad of it!"

"Bandy! How long are we to be kept here?" asked

Andy. "And what have you done with my boat? Sunk her?"

"Why? Are you thinking of trying to sail away in her?" asked Bandy, with a nasty smile. "You can give up all hope of that! She's sunk all right!"

Andy turned away, sick at heart. He had hoped against hope that his lovely boat wasn't really sunk.

"Can't you let us out now?" asked Tom. "I suppose you shut us up because Andy's father came. Cowards!"

"Do you want a clip on the ear?" said Bandy, coming into the cave and glaring at Tom.

"Shut up, Tom, now," said Andy. "It's no good provoking him. It's pretty boring here, Bandy. Can't we have something to do? And the rock is very hard to sit on."

"Serves you right. Children that come sticking their noses into what isn't their business deserve all they get," said Bandy, who seemed to enjoy being nasty. "Maybe you'll be here for weeks! Ha ha—how do you like the thought of that?"

"I think, Bandy, if you do a thing like that, you'll be very sorry for yourself later on, when all this is known," said Andy in a quiet voice. "You'll be severely punished."

"Bah!" said Bandy rudely, and went out and shut the door, bolting it noisily. "Bah!" they heard him say again outside.

The food made them feel a little better, though the bread was very stale and hard, and the meat tasted a bit musty. But they did not feel very cheerful as they gazed out through the opening at the sea and the sky, thinking that they might be there for weeks.

Jill and Mary looked so upset that Andy tried to cheer them up. "He was only being beastly," he told them. "Just trying to scare us all. He'll let us out as soon as my father's boat has gone away. Don't you worry, girls!"

They saw no sign of Andy's father that day. They did not know how he and Andy's uncle sailed up and down, and round about, looking for the missing boat and the children. They did not see them sailing to the Cliff of Birds and anchoring there to climb the cliff. Nor did they see them come back again and again to Smuggler's Rock, hunting for a cove where they might see the *Andy*.

Towards five o'clock, when they were all feeling very hungry indeed, they heard the bolts of the door being pulled back. This time it was the dark man who came in. He spoke to them in his deep voice, and they heard again his slightly foreign accent and knew that he was not English.

"You can go now. The ship that has been hunting for you has given you up, and has gone. But I warn you that if it is sighted again, you will once more have to come here to this cave, where you will be imprisoned until the boat has once again gone."

"We shall have to be set free of the island some time," said Andy. "Why all this mystery and fuss? What are you doing that you want to hide?"

"Children shouldn't ask dangerous questions!" said the man, and his eyes gleamed angrily. "When we have finished here, you shall go, but not till then. You will now be blindfolded once again and taken down to the rocks you know."

So, once again, the red handkerchiefs were tied tightly round the children's eyes, and Bandy and the dark man took them out of the cave. Downwards they went, and then came out into the open air. They were taken some way farther over the rocks, and then the bandages were stripped off their eyes.

They blinked. "We're near the cove!" said Tom. "Good. Let's go up to our cave and get a meal. I'm jolly hungry."

Andy watched to see which way the men went. They rounded a corner of steep rocks and were soon out of sight. "If only I knew where they went and what they do!" he said, in a low voice. "What *is* going on here? Well — I'll find the way into the heart of the island, and discover what's going on before I'm much older!"

"But how can you?" said Tom. "We were blindfolded. We'd never find the way."

"I'm going to look for it," said Andy, "but not till we've had something to eat. I want those men to get well out of the way first!"

295

They went to their cave. It seemed almost like coming home, to squeeze in at the narrow entrance! Jill and Mary were full of delight to be there again. They looked at their larder hungrily.

"What shall we have? I think we'll go a splash, and have something good," said Jill. "What about a tin of tongue — and shall we hot up a tin of peas to go with it? We've got just one. And have a tin of pineapple chunks afterwards?"

"With condensed milk," said Mary. "And we'll make cocoa too — lots of it."

"Well, for goodness' sake hurry up about it," said Tom. "I'm hungrier than ever when I hear you talk like that!"

They had a most delicious meal, and ate every single thing they had prepared for it, and drank the last drop from the cocoa jug. As Mary put back the mugs, she missed the packet of salt.

"Where's the salt gone?" she said in surprise.

"I took it!" said Andy. "And I'll tell you why! I made a hole in my pocket, and as we went blindfolded on our way this morning, I kept dropping out pinches of salt — so, you see, I ought to be able to find the way into the depths of the island, by following my trail of salt!"

"Oh, Andy — what a *marvellous* idea!" said Tom. "Let's go now and see if we can find the trail. Come on, do let's! I do think that was a clever thing to do! We'll go and spy on those men this very evening!"

CHAPTER XVII

A TRAIL TO FOLLOW

TOM, Jill and Mary thought it was very exciting to have a salt trail to follow.

"Now we'll be able to get inside the island, and see what the men are doing," said Mary, squeezing out of the cave entrance. "Come on. Let's all go now. My goodness, we'd better hurry! Look at those black clouds."

Andy looked at them in alarm. They were rain-clouds. "Blow, blow, blow!" he said.

"Are you talking to the wind, or just being annoyed?" asked Jill.

"I'm being annoyed," said Andy, as he felt the first drop of rain on his cheek. "The rain will melt all my trail of salt! Isn't that enough to make anyone annoyed?"

"Well, let's buck up then, before it begins to pour!" said Tom, and they scuttled down the rocks. They found a pinch of salt on a rock, and exclaimed at it.

"Here's one! We passed by here. And there's another! Come on, we can easily spot the white grains!"

They followed the salt trail for a little way up the rocks, and round to the left. Then the rain came down properly, and in a trice the salt had disappeared! Andy looked very gloomy.

"Just my luck! Why didn't I follow the trail straightaway, without stopping to have a meal? And why didn't I think of something more sensible than salt? But I was in such a hurry, and it was the only thing that came into my mind. Blow!"

"Never mind, Andy," said Jill. "It was an awfully good idea. I'd never have thought of it at all!"

"Well—couldn't we do it again, if those men take us

off to the high-up cave another time?" asked Tom. "I bet your father won't give up hunting for us yet, Andy. I bet he'll be along again tomorrow. If so, those men will shut us up again. Bandy said they would."

"Yes. There's a chance Dad might sail this way again tomorrow," said Andy. "He might even bring out some of his friends, in their boats, to search all round. We could try out my idea again."

"But not with salt," said Jill. "That's too easy to melt— or it might be blown away if it falls in a wind-swept place. Let's think of something else."

"It must be something the men don't notice," said Mary. "What can it be?"

Nobody could think of anything for some time. Then Tom had a brain-wave. "I know! Do you remember seeing those little pink shells down in the cove? Well, what about gathering up those, filling our pockets with them? No one would notice shells here and there—they're so usual by the sea. We could all drop one now and again as we go, and there would be a lovely trail to follow!"

"Yes—and one that wouldn't melt away if it rained!"

"Good idea, young Tom," said Andy. "We'll do that. We could collect them now—then we'd have them ready in case the men took us off to that cave again tomorrow."

So they all hunted for the little pink shells in the cove, and found dozens of them. They put them into their pockets. It wouldn't matter in the least if the men searched their pockets and found the shells—because children always did collect them. Tom felt very pleased with his idea.

It grew dark. "Better go back to our cave," said Andy. "We'll light the lamp and have a cosy evening. It's rather cold now too. We got a bit wet in that squall of rain, though it didn't last long. It will be nice to be warm and dry—and we'll make some tea and have biscuits for

supper—if Tom hasn't eaten them all yet!"

"Of course I haven't!" said Tom indignantly. "I've had just the same number as you!"

They went up to their cave and squeezed in. Andy lighted the lamp, and the stove too, so that they could boil the kettle. He had filled it with rain-water, which most conveniently lay in a nearby hollow, not far from the cave.

The cave certainly looked very cosy, and was soon warm and stuffy. But the children didn't mind that, for they were cold and wet.

"This is nice," said Jill, pulling a rug round her. "I

know horrid things have happened, and I hate to think of people being worried about us—but I can't help enjoying being in this cosy cave, and feeling warm and dry, and having ginger biscuits to nibble."

Everyone felt the same, though Andy looked rather stern and thoughtful. Jill knew he was always thinking of his lost boat. He seemed to have lost his ready smiles and jokes now. She gave him an extra biscuit because she felt sorry for him.

They slept well that night in the cave, and no one kept watch, because there didn't seem to be any need to. They didn't feel that the men would really harm them, and they all wanted a good night's sleep.

So they slept soundly, and nothing disturbed them. They woke when the sun was quite high, and Andy was surprised. "We're late this morning!" he said. "I'm going to rinse my face and hands in that pool over there—I feel messy."

They all did the same. Jill produced a comb and they made their hair tidy. They had begun to look like little savages, Mary said!

They had a rather poor breakfast of stale bread and butter and jam. But they did not like to open any more of their precious tins, in case the men were mean with food. They hadn't much liked the bread and meat they had had the day before.

"Andy! The men are coming again!" said Tom. He was sitting outside on the ledge. "And oh golly, look over there! One—two, three—four—*five* fishing-boats! My word, your father's got half the fleet out to look for us!"

"Let's signal, quick!" cried Andy. But the boats were too far away to see them, and at the same moment the men came up to the cave. They were the same three as before, with red handkerchiefs dangling ready in their hands to blindfold the children.

"Remember the shells," said Andy in a low voice.

"Come out, all of you," said the dark man's voice. Tom had scrambled back, so they were all in the cave now.

"We'll go out without making a fuss," said Andy to the others. "We don't want to be smoked out again. That was horrid. I coughed all day and so did the rest of you."

They squeezed out of the cave and stood up. The men blindfolded them quickly. Then once more they were pushed along the rocks, and made their staggering, stumbling way as before. Again they went to the left, and upwards, and again they came to a standstill, and heard the curious grating sound.

Then they were pushed into a darker place and knew they were inside the rocky hill. Before long they were in the same cave as before, looking out to sea from a great height, and heard the wooden door being bolted behind them.

"I dropped my . . ." began Jill in an eager voice, and broke off with a groan as Tom and Andy gave her sharp digs with their fingers. "Don't! What did you do that for?"

Andy nodded his head towards the door. "You don't know if any of them are behind, listening to what we may say," he whispered. "Don't say a thing till I nod my head at you."

They all stayed silent for a while. Then, when Andy was certain their captors had gone, he nodded his head. "But speak low, all the same," he said.

"I dropped my shells all the way," whispered Jill. "I haven't a single one left! They just gave out when we got here!"

"I've dropped all mine too," said Mary. "I was so afraid the men would notice. Did you drop yours, Tom?"

"Of course," said Tom. "I kept *hearing* mine drop too, and thinking the men would notice."

"You've got very sharp ears," said Andy. "Nobody else

301

would hear those tiny shells dropping! I've got about four left. I was afraid I'd drop them all before I came to the place, and that would be sickening!"

"Well, we seem to have done all right between us," said Tom. "We ought to be able to track down the trail here easily enough. We could get inside the hill then and snoop round and find out a lot!"

"I think we'll have to do it at night," said Andy. "The men will be about in the daytime — but at night I imagine they sleep — except the man who flashes that light at the top of the hill."

"Oooh — at night?" said Jill, rather scared. "I wouldn't like that!"

"Well, only Tom and I will go," said Andy. "We will leave you cosily asleep in the cave, and get back to you before dawn. We'll take your torches too — then we shall have plenty of light."

"I wonder if those fishing-boats are sailing all round and about, looking for signs of us everywhere," said Tom. "I wish we had left something about, so that if they landed on the island, they would see it, and know we were here."

"I'd thought of that," said Andy. "But you may be sure the men would remove every single thing that might tell we were here. Dad won't find anything. He'll have to go back again today, with all the others, and report that there's nothing to be found. I wish we could send some message to your mother. She'll be so anxious."

"Yes, she will," said Jill. "She'll never, never let us go out alone with you in a boat again, Andy! Last year we got wrecked in a storm, and had a tremendous adventure for weeks — and this year we've got caught by smugglers — if they *are* smugglers!"

"Well, we couldn't help it," said Andy. "How were we to know that there was all this going on in the Cliff of Birds and Smuggler's Rock?"

Once more dry bread and meat were presented to the children by Bandy. This time it was ham, which tasted a lot nicer. Then, sooner than the day before, they were set free. But they were blindfolded just the same, and led, stumbling and unsteady to the rocks above the cove.

"I think your friends will now give up the search for you!" said the dark man in rather a nasty voice. "So you will be free to roam on the island. But you will find that steep, sheer rocks make it impossible for you to get round to the other side, so do not try. You may fall and be hurt —and if so, we shall not help you."

"What kind people you are!" remarked Andy. Bandy looked as if he would like to box his ears, but he didn't. The men went off and left them alone.

Jill ran a little way up the rocks as soon as they were out of sight. She came back, her face pink with excitement.

"Our trail of shells is there, quite easy to see! You'll be able to follow them well, Tom and Andy. They stretch up over the rocks," said Jill. "I can make out the trail for quite a long way!"

"Well, I hope the men don't spot it then," said Andy. "We'll do a bit of tracking tonight, Tom. It will be most exciting!"

CHAPTER XVIII

A QUEER MIDNIGHT JOURNEY

THE boys thought they would not start following the trail till about midnight. Then they could be fairly certain that the men would be asleep. They decided to try and go to sleep themselves for a few hours first, so that they would not be too tired.

"I'll keep awake for you, and wake you at midnight, if you like," said Jill. "I've got a watch. If I have the lamp on, I know I shall keep awake."

"No. It's all right. I shall wake at midnight," said Andy. "We can all go to sleep."

So they cuddled up in their rugs, put their heads down on the cushions they had brought from the boats, and were soon asleep and dreaming.

At midnight, just as he had said he would, Andy awoke. He sat up and switched on his torch. Almost twelve o'clock! He shook Tom hard and woke him.

"Oooh!" said Tom and woke with a jump.

"Sh! Don't wake the girls!" whispered Andy.

"Give me Jill's torch," whispered Tom. "You know mine's no use. I must have a torch."

Andy handed him one. Then the boys squeezed out of the cave and stood on the windy hill. It was cold and dark. Clouds covered the night sky.

"Now to pick up the trail!" said Andy, and shone his torch cautiously down, shading it with his fingers so as not to show too much light.

They soon picked up the trail of pink shells which gleamed brightly in the torch-light. The boys made their way over the rocks, following the shells easily. There was one bit where the trail broke, and they went wrong, but

304

they soon came back to the trail, and found the right way.

"We must all have stopped dropping shells at the same moment!" said Tom, thinking it was queer to find such a gap. "But it wasn't much of a gap. Come on."

They went on and on, round to the left and upwards. Then the trail of shells suddenly stopped.

"This is where we must have gone inside," said Andy and he shone his torch on the rocks that towered beside him just there. But there was no way in at all. The wall of rock stood there, unbroken. There was no entrance into the hill.

"Funny!" said Andy. "Perhaps the trail goes on after all. Perhaps we've come to a gap again, where none of us threw down shells! I'll go on and see. You stay here and shine your torch out now and again, so that I shall know where to come back to, if I can't find any more shells."

He soon came back. "There's no more to be seen," he said. "This *must* be where we went in. But how in the world can anyone walk through solid rock!"

He shone his torch on the rocky wall again. He discovered a crack of about an inch wide, that seemed to go inside the hill.

"Funny!" said Andy, and shone his torch up and down the crack. "Look, Tom—this crack seems the only way into the hill—but how could anyone squeeze through a crack like that? We certainly didn't!"

The boys tried to find some other place to get in, but there was none. They were forced to come back to the same place once more. Andy remembered something.

"Do you remember the funny noise we heard?" he asked Tom. "Sort of grating noise. I wonder if by any chance this rock moves—you know, like the stone moved in the Open Sesame cave in *Ali Baba and the Forty Thieves*."

"But how could we move a heavy, rocky wall like that?" said Tom.

Andy went to the crack again. He shone his torch down it. Then he shone his torch above and below – and he found something on a ledge below that made him almost shout.

"Look, Tom – an iron bar! Put there to use as a lever, I shouldn't wonder! Well, I'll try!"

He picked up the strong iron bar, and slipped it into the crack. He and Tom pressed hard – and lo and behold, part of the rock slipped aside with a curious grating noise! It was evidently balanced so finely on its base that it could be moved almost at a touch. When it was open, the boys saw the dark entrance into the hill. Andy shone his torch in. It looked rather frightening.

"Well – who would have thought of a way in like that!" said Andy in a whisper. "Don't let's try and shut the rock behind us, in case we can't open it from the inside. We don't want to make ourselves prisoners."

They left the rock as it was, put down the iron bar and went inside the hill. A long tunnel yawned in front of them. After they had followed it for some way it split in two. One tunnel then went upwards and the other downwards. Which should they follow?

"Up, I think," said Andy. "The upgoing one may lead us to the light at the top of the island and we could have a good look at it."

The boys crept on up the tunnel, using their torches, but switching them off at once if they thought they heard anything. But the inside of the rocky hill was dark and silent. It was weird to be there in the middle of the night, not knowing what they might see or hear!

The tunnel split into two again. One tunnel ran on the level and the other still went up. Andy and Tom went along the level one to see what they could find. They came to a strong wooden door, with bolts and a lock.

"I bet this is the door of the cave those men shut us in

today and yesterday," said Andy. "We'll see, shall we?"

Cautiously they opened the door. Yes—it was the very same cave. They retraced their steps and joined the tunnel that went on upwards.

They suddenly saw a light shining somewhere in front of them. "Quiet!" hissed Andy. "Stand still and listen."

But there was nothing at all to be heard. So they went cautiously on towards the light. They came into an enormous cave, lighted by a great ship's lantern that swung from an iron hook in the rocky roof. This cave was

furnished most comfortably, with two or three mattresses, a table, chairs, and cupboards in which stores were evidently kept. A stove was burning, with a kettle boiling away on top.

On the table was set a meal—a very good meal too, which made Tom feel very hungry indeed. The pink slices of ham lay on a dish, and a jar of tongue had been opened nearby. A rich dark plum-cake stood on a plate, and a tin of peaches had been opened.

"Look at that!" said Tom, his mouth watering, "I really *must* have a slice of that ham!"

"Be careful! The meal is set for someone and the kettle is boiling, so that the man it's meant for can't be far away!" whispered Andy. "He'll be back soon. We don't want to be caught."

"Can't we just nip in and get some of the ham?" begged Tom. "There's time!"

"Well, quick then!" said Andy. He nipped in with Tom. The boys snatched four slices of the ham, and a half loaf of bread. Andy cut an enormous slice of the cake. They stuffed everything into their pockets. They were just about to run out of the cave into the tunnel when they heard someone coming!

The Someone sang as he came, a sea-shanty. It was Bandy's hoarse voice.

"Quick! Hide!" said Andy, looking round. "Into that chest, quick!"

They lifted the lid of an enormous chest and got inside it, putting the lid down quietly just as Bandy came into the lighted cave. He came in singing lustily, and took the kettle off the stove.

He made himself some tea, and then sat down to the table. He stared at the ham.

"Look at that! Where's half the ham gone? And where's my bread? If that greedy pig of a Stumpy has come in here and taken my supper again I'll knock him down!"

Bandy growled and muttered. Then he saw that someone had cut a huge slice of the plum-cake and he rose to his feet in anger.

"My cake too! I'll teach him! I'll box his ears till he can't tell if he's standing up or sitting down. I'll — I'll . . ."

He disappeared out of the cave, taking the tunnel that led downwards. Andy and Tom badly wanted to laugh. Poor Stumpy! He would deny till he was black in the face that he had taken Bandy's supper, but Bandy wouldn't believe him.

"Let's get out of here whilst we've got the chance," said Andy, walking out. "We'd better go on upwards, or we shall run into Bandy. Come on, Tom."

Tom stopped to snatch a few more bits of ham, and another piece of cake. Then he ran after Andy into the tunnel again. Upwards they went, wondering where they would come to.

They had to use their torches again. Presently there were rough steps cut in a steep upward passage. It seemed as if they were never coming to an end. Tom gave a huge pant and sat down.

"Andy, I *must* have a rest! Those steps are so steep."

Andy sat down beside him, panting too. He switched off his torch. He smiled in the darkness to think of Bandy going off to accuse Stumpy, whoever he might be, of taking his supper. The ham, bread and cake were now safely disposed of, and both boys felt very satisfied.

They got up after a rest and continued on their way. Suddenly the steps stopped, and they came out on to a kind of platform. The wind swept suddenly and viciously on them.

"We're on the top of Smuggler's Rock, the very top — where that light was flashed from!" cried Andy. "My, isn't the wind fierce!"

309

"Look—here's the enormous lamp that must have flashed those signals!" said Tom, and he flashed his torch on to a great lamp, which was, of course, not now lighted. "See, Andy—the beams from this would flash a long way —to ships far out, waiting to come in with smuggled goods!"

"My word!" said Andy. "That's just about right! We're very high up here. Ships many miles away could catch these signals."

Suddenly he clutched Tom's arm. "Listen—aren't those footsteps—and whistling again? Perhaps Bandy is coming up to signal. Hop under the platform that the lamp's on. We may not be seen at all!"

They crept under the wooden platform on which the great lamp stood. Then Bandy came, and began to do something to the lamp. In a minute or two brilliant flashes lit up the night. The lamp was signalling to someone.

Bandy signalled for ten minutes. Then he turned out the light in some way and went down the steps again. The boys didn't dare to follow. They went down a few steps, found a rough, hidden corner in the rocky wall, and lay down there. In a few moments they were asleep!

They awoke at dawn, stiff and shivering, cross at having been to sleep. Andy went on to the windy platform and looked all round—what a perfectly marvellous view. Why, he could see all round the rocky island!

He looked down on the side he had never seen before, —and gave a low cry. "Look, Tom—look down there. Whatever do you make of that!"

CHAPTER XIX

MORE DISCOVERIES

THE two boys gazed down, far, far down, to where the sea gleamed in the early sunlight. They saw a blue harbour, an almost round cove, protected on all sides by steep, rugged rocks. At first it seemed as if there was no outlet to the sea itself at all—the harbour looked more like an inland lake.

It was full of motor-boats, some large, some small! They lay at rest, all but one, which was just making its way cautiously into the cove, through so narrow an opening that the boys could scarcely make it out from where they were.

"Look at that!" said Andy. "Whoever would dream there was this cove, this natural harbour the other side of the island! No one can see it from the other side—and I imagine that unless you know your way among those far-flung rocks stretching out there for miles, you'd never find your way in here. Well, well—I must say it's a nice little smugglers' haunt!"

The motor-boats looked like toys from where the boys stood. They were very high up indeed. The strong wind almost blew their heads off their shoulders. They could see for miles and miles round the island, on every side.

"No wonder the smugglers knew when my father was coming!" said Andy. "They could sight his boat miles away! I wonder if they sighted ours, when we went to the Cliff of Birds."

"They did the second time," said Tom. "That's why they sent out that motor-boat to stop us!"

"You're right," said Andy. "My word—what a huge smuggling business this must be—all those motor-boats! I suppose they send them out to ships lying at anchor some miles away—ships that have seen this signal—and take off their goods to bring them here in safety. This is a wonderful hiding-place."

"Where do they smuggle the goods to?" said Tom. "And why do they smuggle them? To save paying duty on them, I suppose. They get them into the country this way. But how do they get them away from here! There's no road overland even from the Cliff of Birds."

"It's a puzzle," said Andy. "If only we could escape and report all this."

"Do you remember I told you about all those boxes and crates in that cave in the Cliff of Birds?" said Tom. "How do you suppose they get them there from here?"

Andy couldn't answer him. The two boys stood looking out of the magnificent view for some time, watching the motor-boats at rest, and seeing men unload the motor-boat that had just come slipping through the narrow opening.

"I bet that boat went out last night to whatever ship Bandy was signalling to with his lamp," said Andy. "I just bet that motor-boat was loaded up miles out to sea, and slipped back here whilst it was still not dawn. She just got in in time."

"They must have men who know these rocks like a book," said Tom. "I wouldn't care to chug through them!"

"I think we'd better get back to the girls," said Andy. "They'll be longing to know all we've seen. If only we could get back home!"

They turned to go down the steps. It was dark down there. But they did not like to switch on their torches now, in case Bandy was about and spotted them. So they made their way down cautiously, feeling for the steps with their feet, and taking rather a long time to get down.

"Be careful! We're getting near to that big cave-room where we took the ham and cake from," whispered Andy.

They came to the big cave. It was still lighted by the big ship's lantern, swinging from the roof. Quietly Andy slid his head in to see if Bandy was there.

He could hear him as well as see him! The little bandy-legged man was lying on one of the mattresses, flat on his back, fast asleep. His mouth was open and he was snoring loudly.

"There's no one else there," said Tom, looking round quickly. "But he hasn't finished that tongue or the peaches, Andy. Let's get them."

"No—he might wake up," said Andy, pulling Tom back.

"He won't. He's snoring hard," said Tom. "Come on, let's get the stuff. We haven't had any breakfast!"

He and Andy stole quickly into the huge cave. They snatched up the dish of peaches and the dish of tongue. As they turned to go, Bandy gave such an enormous snore that he made Tom jump. The boy tripped over an uneven piece of rocky floor and fell headlong. The glass dish he was carrying smashed to pieces, and both Tom and Andy were covered with juice.

"Fathead!" hissed Andy, and dragged him up. They tore to the passage. But Bandy was wide awake now, and sitting up. He yelled loudly:

"What, you come back again to steal my food, Stumpy! After the lamming I gave you last night too! You greedy fellow, you pig, you. . . ."

"Run! He thought we were the fellow that he went and lammed last night!" gasped Andy. "Run! We'll hide somewhere before he catches us."

Bandy was really on the warpath this time!

The boys fled down and down. They passed the forking tunnel that led to the cave where they had twice been bolted in. They tore on down, hoping soon to get to the place where the tunnel split in two, one part going down,

313

and the other going back to the place where they had entered the hill by way of the moving rock.

"Once we get to that forking of the tunnel we'll be all right!" panted Andy. "We can slip out of the entrance there and make our way back to the girls!"

They came to it at last and ran along it to get out into the sunshine. But when they got to the end of that passage, the big rock had been slid back into place again! There was no way out.

"Blow! How do we move it from this side to open?" wondered Andy. He pushed and pulled and shoved, but the rock would not move. There seemed to be nothing at all that the boys could find to use as a lever this time, either. The rock was fast shut.

"Somebody's been along here, found the rock entrance open and shut it," said Andy at last. "It's no good. We can't open it."

"Well, we can't go back up the tunnel to Bandy's room," said Tom. "He'd be sure to catch us sooner or later."

"Let's go to where the tunnel forks, and take the downward path this time," said Andy. "We'll see where it leads to. It might perhaps take us out another way. It's no good us staying here to be caught like rats in a trap."

So back they went once more, listening cautiously for Bandy. They took the downward way at the forking of the tunnel, and made their way along dark, musty passages, winding here and there.

"These passages must be right in the heart of the hill like the tunnel in the Cliff of Birds," said Tom. "Listen —what's that?"

It was the sound of a quarrel. The boys crept nearer to the shouts. "It's Bandy going for Stumpy again!" said Andy. "Poor Stumpy! We do seem to be getting him into trouble!"

Out of the tunnel another cave opened, rather like the

one above, which was apparently Bandy's. This one, however, was smaller and not so well furnished. In it Bandy and Stumpy were quarrelling. The cave was not very well lighted, and the boys felt certain they could not be seen, as they stopped in the dark passage to peep in for a moment.

"Why—Stumpy is the hairy-legged man!" whispered Tom. "See his bare, hairy legs and enormous feet! He's the one that swung his legs above us that day—and I saw him again in the cave down at the foot of the Cliff of Birds, with the other man too."

There was a fine old fight going on in Stumpy's cave. Roaring and shouting and yelling, chasing round and dodging! The boys wished they could stop and watch, for the sight was comical. But they thought the chance of slipping by unnoticed was too good not to be taken, and they dodged quickly past the entrance of the cave. Neither of the men saw them.

And now the tunnel dipped very steeply indeed, and went downwards for a long way. "Into the very depths of the earth," said Tom in a hollow voice that quite startled Andy.

The walls of the rocky tunnel suddenly began to gleam in a queer way. "Phosphorescence," said Andy. "Isn't it curious, Tom? Most unearthly!"

"Let's go back," said Tom suddenly. "I don't like this at all. And I don't like that funny noise right over our heads, either."

Andy had noticed a queer noise too—boom, boom, boom! Boooooooom!

"What can it be?" he wondered. "No, Tom, we can't go back now after coming all this way. We'll come out somewhere soon. We must! If only this tunnel would go upwards again. It's gone down so deep."

They went on again, between the wide gleaming walls.

315

There was plenty of room in this passage—room for three men to walk abreast, if need be—and the roof was well above their heads.

They walked on, using their torches, and feeling very tired of the long, dark way. Andy was puzzled. Smuggler's Rock was not a big island. They could have walked right through it by now! Where were they going?

He suddenly stopped and clutched Tom's arm. Tom jumped violently. "Don't do that!" he said. "What's up?"

"Tom—I know where we are—and I know what that noise is!" said Andy, in an excited voice.

"What is it?" said Tom, looking at him, startled.

"It's the sea we can hear—above our heads!" said Andy.

"Above our heads?" said Tom, looking up as if he expected to see waves breaking over him. "What do you mean?"

"We're under the rocky floor of the sea!" said Andy, in a loud voice. "We're in an underground tunnel, right under the sea itself—and I bet I know where it leads to! It goes to the Cliff of Birds."

Tom gaped. He was so astonished that he couldn't say a word. He stared at Andy, and listened to the dull, muffled boom above him. Yes—it must be waves pounding away up there, far above their heads. Tom hoped the floor of the sea was good and strong! It wasn't nice to think of all that water away up there.

"That's why that tunnel sloped so steeply," said Andy. "It goes right under the sea. We must be a good way under by now—but I don't know how far we are from the Cliff of Birds. I suppose we'll get there sooner or later. Now we know how the smugglers take their goods there—and store them in that cave you saw there! They carry them here, under the sea itself!"

"Come on," said Tom in excitement. "Come on—let's see where this leads to—quick!"

316

CHAPTER XX

AN UNEXPECTED FIND

THE two boys went eagerly forward along the strange tunnel. It was so wide that it could have taken two train-tracks. No wonder the smugglers could so easily carry goods from Smuggler's Rock to the Cliff of Birds!

Boom, boom, boooooom! The restless sea went on pounding away overhead. "I hope," said Tom, "that there isn't a leak in any of the rocks in the roof of this queer under-sea tunnel! It would be awful to think of of the sea pouring in."

"Don't be silly! This tunnel must have existed for years," said Andy. "There's no reason why it should suddenly spring a leak! We're all right."

"I suppose we are, really," said Tom. "Blow! My torch is giving out!"

"Well, I've got two — mine, which I'm using, and Jill's," said Andy. "I gave you Mary's. We'll make do with just mine now, because we may need Jill's torch later on if mine gives out. Walk close to me. My word, don't these walls and roof gleam! It's a weird tunnel. It must have been used in the olden days quite a lot."

"I wonder who first found it and went along it," said Tom, stumbling over an uneven piece. "Here, shine your torch more downwards, Andy. I can't see where I'm going."

They went on for a long while. Andy tried to reckon out how long a tunnel would be that stretched between the Cliff of Birds and Smuggler's Rock. Surely they must be nearing the end of it now.

"Listen — that booming noise isn't nearly so loud," said Tom, suddenly stopping. "Andy, listen."

"You're right," said Andy. "Well, that can only mean

one thing — we're out from under the sea now — maybe under the Cliff of Birds."

"You know, Andy — *I* think we shall probably come up into that cave where I saw all those boxes and crates stored," said Tom, thinking hard. "When I was there, I saw Stumpy and the fisherman with glasses disappear down a hole in the floor of the cave — and I bet that hole led down into this tunnel."

"I should think you're right," said Andy. "Come on, we'll soon see. It's nice not to hear the sea booming overhead any more. It wasn't a very pleasant sound. It made me feel a bit queer."

"Me too," said Tom. "I felt as if I was walking along some kind of unpleasant dream!"

On they went again. The passage was still very wide indeed, and grew even wider as they stumbled forward. Then Andy's torch flashed on more stores!

The tunnel had now widened into what looked like a big underground hall. It was lined with hurriedly piled cases of all kinds. Andy went over to them curiously, and shone his torch on them.

"Maybe they're brandy," he said. "I know that's smuggled in sometimes. Each case has got some sort of scribbled letter or numbers on. Look at all those green ones, too."

"Here's one half broken," said Tom. "Bring the torch over. We might be able to see what's inside."

Soon the torch was flashing on to the half-broken case. The boys pulled out handfuls of straw, packing and padding material.

Then Andy gave a long low whistle, and stood staring in astonishment. Tom looked at him impatiently.

"What is it? Do you know what's inside?"

"Yes — look here — see that shining barrel? There are guns here — and revolvers too, I expect. And ammunition

318

in those green boxes over there! I bet I'm right. My word — this is more than smuggling."

"What is it then?" said Tom in a whisper. "I don't understand."

"Nor do I yet," said Andy. "I only know that those men are bringing in thousands of guns — and ammunition — and sending them from here somewhere else — either to sell to countries who are not allowed to have these things, or to use against our own country in some way. It's a plot of some sort — a dangerous plot too, which might mean peril to our land and people in some way. My goodness me — no wonder those men sank our boat, kept us prisoner, and did all they could to prevent my father from finding us!"

Tom felt scared. "They won't hurt the two girls, will they?" he said, thinking of Jill and Mary left alone in the cave.

"I don't think so," said Andy. "What *are* we to do? What *can* we do? We ought somehow to get back and report this strange find — and we ought to get back to Jill and Mary and look after them! But how are we to do either!"

Tom sat down on a box. Things were happening a bit too fast. He looked fearfully round the great underground store-house. Guns! Guns by the thousand! Gunpowder too, perhaps. Ammunition waiting to be used in wicked ways by wicked people. He shivered.

Andy sat down beside him to think. The fisher-boy looked worried. He wished he was grown-up. Grown-ups always seemed to know the right thing to do and they could do it. But he didn't know what *was* the right or best thing, and even if he did, how could he do it?

"The thing is," he said out loud, "is it best to go back and try and get out on Smuggler's Rock, and find the girls — or is it best to go on, and make our way into the Cliff of Birds? Perhaps that would be best, because we could go up the tunnel there that leads to the waterfall, Tom, and maybe climb out of the opening there, into the daylight, and wait to see if my father comes hunting for us again. Then we could signal."

"Yes — that's a jolly good idea," said Tom. "The men couldn't possibly guess we have found the under-sea tunnel and come to the Cliff of Birds. Why, they may not even know we are not with the girls, if they don't go snooping round our cave. We could wait our chance and signal from the Cliff of Birds."

"It sounds all right," said Andy rather gloomily. "But

I doubt if my father will come again today — he's been two days running and found nothing. Maybe they'll all be off searching other places now."

"Still, it really is the only thing we can do," said Tom, getting up. "Come on, we'll go right on now, shall we? We'd better be careful, though, because we might run up against one of the men in the Cliff of Birds."

So they left the underground hall behind them and made their way cautiously onwards again. The tunnel narrowed after a little while and became more as it had been before — a wide rocky passage, with a high roof.

It ran upwards suddenly. "I bet it's leading to that cave," whispered Tom. "Don't make a row, and shade your torch with your hand, Andy."

Moving very quietly now, the two boys went on. The passage suddenly came to a very abrupt end. A rocky wall barred their way!

"A blind end!" said Andy, feeling up and down it with his hands. "Blow! What does this mean?"

It didn't seem to mean anything except that the passage had ended. They could go no farther at all. Andy gave a huge sigh. He was exhausted now with his long stumbling walk, and it seemed the last straw that they should not be able to find a way out.

He sat down suddenly, and Tom fell beside him, his legs shaking with tiredness. "It's no good," said Andy. "I can't go back. I'm tired out. We're beaten!"

Tom felt the same. But after a short rest Andy felt more cheerful. He flashed his torch round again, and then suddenly turned it upwards, shining it above his head. He gave a cry and clutched Tom's arm.

"Look — what idiots we are! There's the way out — above our heads! A big hole in the roof, of course!"

Tom gazed up and saw a big round hole in the roof of the suddenly-ended tunnel. He gave a gasp.

"Of course, Andy! Didn't I tell you those two men disappeared down a hole in the floor of their cave? Well—that's the hole, I bet! It's got to lead somewhere, and it led down to this passage. Why didn't we flash our torch upwards before?"

Both boys immediately felt better. So much better, in fact, that they both leapt up and were prepared to go on for miles again, if need be! Andy tried to see how to climb up. But there was no sign of steps or footholds of any kind.

"What's that—twisted round something there?" whispered Tom suddenly. Andy shone his torch. He saw a rope caught round an iron staple driven into the rock. The rope was as dark as the rock, and neither of the boys had noticed it before. They had been looking for steps cut out, or for iron footholds.

"That's it—that's the way to get up and down!" whispered Andy. "We'll go up right away! I don't imagine there's anybody in the cave above, or we should see a light of some sort. I'll go first, Tom. Hold the torch for me."

Tom took the torch. His hand was trembling with excitement and relief, so the light was rather shaky! Andy untwisted the rope and took hold of it. It was firm and strong. The fisher-boy went up it like a monkey. He was used to ropes!

He found himself in the darkness. He had no idea where he was, once he had climbed up out of the hole. He looked down and saw Tom's anxious face in the light of the torch.

"Throw up the torch!" he said. "Careful, now. That's it. Now, I'll shine it down for you. Catch hold of the rope. Come on!"

Tom climbed up the rope too, and Andy gave him a helping hand at the top. They stood up and looked round by the light of their torch.

"Yes—this is the cave I told you about—the one with

the stores—where the underground river rushes nearby," said Tom. "Good thing there's no one here!"

Andy flashed his torch at the piles of boxes. "Those are food-stores," he said. "See? There's a box half-unpacked, look—full of tinned food to feed all the men who help in this unlawful work. My word, whoever planned this planned it very thoroughly! I suppose this food goes to feed all the crews of those motor-boats."

"I'll show you where the underground river flows," said Tom, and dragged him behind the pile of boxes at one side of the cave. He showed him the hole beyond which the dark river rushed in its narrow tunnel. "That's where I jumped in!" said Tom.

"Well—we won't go that way," said Andy. "It's a bit too dangerous for my liking! We'll go up, not down, Tom —up that twisting tunnel you found, that leads to the water-fall opening—and we'll hope the torrent of water will be small enough today for us to creep out of the opening."

"And then we'll wait on the cliff and signal!" said Tom. "We'll soon be rescued! Come on, Andy—into the tunnel we go!"

CHAPTER XXI

ANDY GETS A REAL SURPRISE

ANDY and Tom left the store-cave behind, and went into the tunnel that led upwards. Tom was sure he knew the way. He remembered how he had first found his way into it—he had squeezed through the waterfall entrance, found himself in a big cave, gone into the next cave and found steps leading upwards . . . and from there had found his way down the twisting tunnel to the store-cave they had just left.

Yes, he knew the way all right. There was no chance of making a mistake, anyway, because as far as he remembered, there had only been the one tunnel to follow. It hadn't kept forking into two, as the tunnel had in Smuggler's Rock.

So flashing their torches in front of them, the boys began the long, tiring pull upwards. It seemed much longer to Tom than it had been before.

"Well, it's because it goes *up* this time, not down!" said Andy, who was panting too. "It must be much easier going down it than up. My, what a climb!"

After a time, Tom stopped in surprise. He shone his torch in front of him and stared, puzzled.

"Why, Andy, look—the passage splits into two here, after all—and I felt sure it didn't. I felt sure there was only the one way to follow! Blow! I can't have noticed it, when I came down!"

Andy examined the fork of the tunnel. "No—you wouldn't notice it," he said. "You'd come round that dark corner—see—and wouldn't see there was another way leading off here, because of that jutting-out rock—and you'd just go on down without noticing it. Come on."

"But, Andy, wait—I'm not at all sure which passage I came down in!" said Tom. "I might have come by either, and not noticed the other one. Oh, which one did I take?"

"Well, really—I should have thought you would have known that!" said Andy rather unfairly, for the two tunnels looked exactly alike in the darkness. Tom didn't know. He stood and stared at them both, wondering which was the right one.

"Well, it doesn't really matter," said Andy at last. "We'll take the right-hand one and hope for the best. If it doesn't lead out on the cliff, we can easily go back and take the other one."

"Yes, we could," said Tom, relieved. "Come on, then, let's take this one. It may be the right one. I have a feeling it is."

But his feeling was wrong. It was most decidedly the wrong one! It twisted and turned much more than the right one had, and Tom soon was quite certain they were wrong.

"Better go back," he said. "I'm sure this isn't right."

"Well, I wonder where it leads to then," said Andy, puzzled. "It's going upwards. Do you think it leads to the top of the Cliff—or goes to the other side of the shallow bay where we once anchored the *Andy*? It must come to an end soon, I should think. We might as well just see what happens!"

So they went on, and were soon rewarded by seeing what they thought must be daylight shining far ahead. And sure enough it was!

The passage suddenly came out from a deep cleft in the high cliff, and there, below them, was the sea, crashing over the rocks that studded that coast for miles on end.

They sniffed the fresh air in delight. After the mustiness of the tunnel, it was delicious. It was lovely, too, to feel the clean, cool wind on their faces.

They sat down on the ledge, scaring away half a dozen

indignant nesting-birds. The disturbed eggs rolled round and round in a circle, but fortunately did not drop off the ledge.

"Now if we just had something to *eat*," said Tom. He put his hand into his pocket, and to his great delight found a piece of ham and a half-piece of cake. The boys shared his find together hungrily, wishing there was more.

"We are higher up than we were before, when we were on the waterfall ledge," said Andy. "I wonder where we are exactly? We're not right at the top of the Cliff. I think we've gone beyond the Cliff of Birds, and are now on a ledge the other side. Let's lean over the ledge and see if the cove we anchored in is down below us, or not. I don't think it is."

"Well, you look down," said Tom. "It's a bit too high up even for me! I shall feel giddy if I lean over the ledge at this height."

"Hold my legs and I'll go to the edge and put my head over," said Andy. He lay down flat on his tummy and worked himself to the edge of the sharp ledge. Tom laid hold of his legs and held them firmly.

Andy looked down. Miles below, as it seemed, the sea moved silently and slowly towards the cliff. The boys were too high up to hear any sound of the sea at all. It was queer to look down and see so far below.

Andy's eyes swept the coast-line just there. It was as he had thought—they were no longer above the cove where they had once anchored the *Andy*. They must be farther round the coast.

The boy's eyes examined the shore below closely—and then he saw something that made him stare so hard that his eyes blurred and he couldn't see.

"Hold me fast, Tom, hold me," he cried. "I'm going to wriggle a bit farther forward—I must see what's exactly below us, miles down. Hold me tight!"

326

Tom tightened his grip of Andy's sturdy legs, as the boy hung himself a bit farther over the ledge, the better to see what was below. He stared. He stared in silence for so long that Tom got impatient.

"What is it?" he said. "I'm tired of hanging on to you. What can you see?"

Andy couldn't believe what he saw. He shut his eyes, and then opened them again. Yes, it was still there. How very extraordinary — and how very, very marvellous!

He slid back on his tummy, and sat up, his face happy

and glowing. His eyes shone so brightly that Tom was startled.

"Andy — what's up?" he said.

"Tom! Do you know what's down there — hidden in a little channel of water, in a fold of the cliff itself?" said Andy, in a voice that shook with excitement. "You'll never guess, never!"

"What?" cried Tom.

"Our boat!" yelled Andy, and beat on the rocky ledge with his hands. "OUR BOAT — the *Andy*!"

"But she's sunk," said Tom, thinking that Andy must be mad. "You know she is."

"I know she *isn't*!" said Andy. "Wouldn't I know my own boat, that I've sailed in scores of times? Those men were telling lies to us. They haven't sunk the *Andy*! They've got her down there, hidden in a fold of the rocks — oh, a very, very clever hiding-place indeed! I don't believe anyone could possibly spot her from the sea. She could only be spotted from just up here!"

"But, Andy — oh, Andy, it can't be!" said Tom, a ridiculous tear spurting out from the corner of one eye. "I was sure she was sunk! What a mercy we took the wrong passage and got up here! We wouldn't have known about her if we hadn't, would we? How simply, absolutely marvellous!"

"Want to see her?" said Andy. "Want to have a peep at our dear old boat? She hasn't got her sail up, but I knew it was her! I nearly fell over when I first spotted her. Good thing you were holding my legs, Tom!"

"Well — you hold mine jolly tightly," said Tom, and laid himself down on his tummy. Soon he was peeping over the edge of the cliff, and saw, far down below, a tiny boat tucked away in a small channel of water, hidden by a fold in the rocks.

"Is it really the *Andy*?" he said. "I wouldn't be able to

328

tell. She looks all deck to me. But there's a red spot on her which must mean her sail is folded up there. They've put it back again."

"It's the *Andy* all right," said Andy joyfully. "I'd know her out of a million boats. What a bit of luck! She hasn't been sunk! We know where she's hidden. Now we've only got to get her, and we can sail away home!"

"Yes—but how are we going to get her?" said Tom, wriggling back. "*That* won't be easy!"

The two boys leaned against the rock at their backs and discussed what would be the best thing to do now. Plainly they must try to get down to the *Andy*. The whole difficult problem of escape would be solved if only they got her.

"We can't possibly climb down the cliff here, and get to her," said Andy. "We should fall and be dashed to pieces. It seems to me that absolutely the only thing to do is to get down to our own cove somehow—the one the underground river flows into—and climb round the rocks at the base of the cliff till we reach the *Andy*. It will take ages!"

"Oh goodness—and we've got no food," said Tom dolefully. "That doesn't seem a very good idea to me."

"Well—think of a better idea then, and we'll follow it," said Andy. But of course Tom could think of nothing else at all.

"You're right," he said at last with a sigh. "It's the only thing to do. But, Andy, let's get back to that store-cave, where the boxes of food are kept. We could open some of those tins and at least have something to eat. We can't go on too long without food. At least, I can't."

"All right," said Andy. "Anyway, Tom, I think it would be better to keep in hiding till the evening, in case anyone sees us clambering about the rocks to get to the *Andy*. Come on, we'll get down to the store-cave now and get what food we want. Then we'll take it up to the ledge by the waterfall—if we can get through the waterfall entrance

—and wait there till we think it's safe to climb down and get round the rocks to find the *Andy*."

It was easier to get down to the store-cave than it had been to climb from it up to the Cliff! There was no one there. The boys hunted about and found two or three tin-openers. Good! They each put one in their pockets and then chose a few tins to take with them.

"Tongue," said Tom. "And spam. And pears and apricots and plums. That's *my* selection!"

They hunted about for sacks to put them in and found some old bags. Each boy put his selection of tins into a bag, threw it over his shoulder, and set out again to the cliff—but this time they took the other tunnel, when they came to the fork. Andy was amazed to see the caves where the torrent of water ran through, on its way to the waterfall.

"There's hardly any water pouring out today, thank goodness!" said Tom. "Come on, Andy—it'll be difficult wriggling along that narrow ledge to the entrance with our tins."

It was—but they managed it. And there they were at last, out on the ledge of the Cliff of Birds, and sitting down at the back of the shallow cave where Tom had left his ill-fated camera!

"Now for a meal!" said the ever-hungry Tom. "And then—a good long doze in the sun! After that—all set to find the good old *Andy*!"

CHAPTER XXII

DOWN TO THE *ANDY* —
AND WHAT HAPPENED THERE

THE boys had a very good meal up on the ledge in the sun.
They talked about the girls and wondered how they were
getting on, and if they were all right.

"At any rate, they've got food," said Tom. "I wish they
could share this spam and peaches with me. It's an
awfully good mixture."

"How you can cut yourself a bit of spam and then spear
a peach and eat it beats me!" said Andy. "I don't like
mixing up things like that. Isn't this sun delicious, Tom?
The wind has dropped a bit. I say — what shall we do when
we get the *Andy*? Go and rescue the girls first — or run
straight for home and report what we know?"

"I don't see how we *can* rescue the girls," said Tom,
spearing a bit of spam and a peach together on the end of
his knife. "We should only be seen by the men looking out
for your father's boat, and they'd capture us again. We'd
better run for home. The wind will be behind us, won't it?
So we could get back fairly quickly."

"Yes. I feel worried about the girls, though," said Andy,
lying down on his back, unable to eat any more. "I'm
afraid those men will be very angry when they find we've
escaped — if they do find it out — and they'll make things
unpleasant for Jill and Mary, perhaps."

This was a horrid thought. Andy was very fond of the
two girls, and Tom loved his twin sisters dearly. But if
they went back to Smuggler's Rock to get the girls, they
might get captured themselves again, and what would be
the use of that?

Andy fell asleep before he had time to worry any more

331

about it. Tom drank the last drop of sweet juice from his tin, then lay back in the sunshine too, and shut his eyes. Both boys were really exhausted with their exertions.

They did not wake until the sun was well down in the west. Andy sat up and shook Tom.

"Tom! Wake up! It's time we climbed down and made a search for the *Andy*. We'll get down to the foot of the cliffs, and then try to make our way westwards, round the place where those rocks jut right out. We ought to come across the fold in the cliff where the *Andy* is hidden, sooner or later. The tide is going out, so the rocks will be fairly well uncovered."

Tom yawned as he sat up. He felt stiff. He did not like the thought of the long climb downwards. But it had to be faced. Andy began to climb down first, and Tom followed.

When they were at the foot of the cliff at last, Andy turned westwards, and began to clamber over the rugged rocks uncovered by the tide. They were slippery with seaweed, but both boys were very sure-footed and hardly slipped at all.

They made their way round the point and came in sight of another stretch of wild, rocky coast. Somewhere hidden along there was the *Andy*! But where? There was no sign of her from where they stood. She was in a very clever hiding-place indeed.

"See—that's the way they brought her in," said Andy, pointing to a narrow little sea-path free of rocks. "The men must know these coasts like the palm of their hands! There are some jolly clever sailors among them."

Slowly they made their way along the rocks that skirted the cliff, looking out for some bend that would mean the sudden fold that hid the *Andy*.

Then they found it! They rounded a steep rock, as tall as a church—and saw a narrow deep-blue runway of water running into a fold of the cliff.

"This is it!" said Andy in delight. "See? Quite hidden except from above, way up the cliff there—or here where we stand looking right in. What a blessing we spotted the boat from above. We'd never have found her any other way."

They went up the little runway of water that lay quietly in a hollowed-out channel of rock. It twisted right into the fold of the cliff—and there, at the end of it, lying quietly at anchor was the *Andy*! The boys stood still and stared at her in proud delight. What a darling of a boat she was!

"And not sunk after all!" said Tom. "Poor old Andy— you were awfully miserable about that, weren't you?"

"Yes—more than I'd ever been in my life before," said Andy. "Anyway—there she is, waiting for us. Is anyone about, do you think?"

There didn't seem to be anyone at all. Not a sound was to be heard except the usual wind and sea and bird noises. No one whistled, no one shouted. It seemed quite safe to go and explore the *Andy*.

She hadn't got her sail up, but it was there on the deck. Andy saw that the oars had been put back too. Good!

The boys made their way towards the boat. She was stripped of everything, of course, for the children had taken the things from her themselves, and put them in their cave in Smuggler's Rock. Still, what did that matter? The boat herself was there, safe and sound!

They were soon on board her. Andy examined her lovingly from top to toe. Yes, she was all right. No harm had come to her at all.

It was getting rather dark. Andy looked up at the sky. "I think it wouldn't be a bad idea if we set off now," he said. "It will be dark long before we get home—but we must chance the journey, and hope we shan't strike a rock. I know the way pretty well now."

The boys thought they would row the *Andy* carefully out

of the narrow little creek, and put up the sail as soon as they got out to sea. They began to make ready to pull up the anchor.

They were just about to haul it up when Andy's sharp ears caught an unusual sound. He stopped and put his hand on Tom's arm. "Listen," he said. "Can you hear anything?"

Tom listened, trying to make out something besides the wind and the sea. At first he could hear nothing. Then he did hear something.

"Yes. I can hear the sound of some regular noise," he said, "chug, chug, chug, chug. Oh, Andy, is it one of their motor-boats somewhere near?"

"Yes," said Andy. "That's just about what it is! Oh, I hope it's not coming in here! Just as we were getting off too. The noise is louder, Tom. We'd better hide in case the motor-boat *is* coming in here!"

The boys climbed over the side of their boat and looked about for a hiding-place. There were plenty there! Rocks stuck up all over the place.

"Let's climb up a bit, just over there," said Andy, pointing. "See where I mean? There's a good rock there we can hide behind, and see everything from. Hear everything too! Come on! The engine of that motor-boat is going more slowly. I believe it's nosing its way in here this very minute."

The boys climbed quickly up to the big rock, about six feet above the *Andy*. They crouched down there, waiting. Andy suddenly clutched Tom and pointed.

"There it is!" he whispered. "See, coming in down the little creek, up to the *Andy*. Pity it's so dark now. I can hardly see who's on the motor-boat."

The motor-boat nosed its way up and came to rest beside the *Andy*. A man jumped out and called to someone else.

"It's Bandy," whispered Tom. "I think the other man is Stumpy, isn't he? The man with the hairy legs. What are they going to do?"

A lamp was lighted on the motor-boat, and another one was placed on the fishing-boat nearby. Then Bandy and Stumpy got very busy. What they were doing the boys could hardly make out, in the deepening twilight.

"They seem to be carrying things from one boat to the other," whispered Andy. "What *are* they doing? It's a puzzle, isn't it!"

To and fro went the men, carrying all kinds of things. Andy suddenly recognized something and he gave a low exclamation that quite startled Tom.

"Look! That's our little cooking stove, isn't it?" whispered Andy. "You can just see it in the light of that lamp. They are putting it into the cabin of the *Andy*."

Then both boys were silent, for the same thought had come to them both. The stove had been in their snug cave up on the rocks of Smuggler's Rock. Were all the things being put into the *Andy*, the things that had been taken from that cave? And if so, what was happening to the girls? The men must have climbed up to the cave, discovered that the boys were gone and that only the girls were there — and then what had happened? Where could the girls be? They must have been turned out of the cave if all the things were taken away.

Now the two boys were really worried. They couldn't bear to think of Jill and Mary, frightened and alone, in the hands of those grim smugglers.

Everything seemed puzzling again. Why bring the things back to the *Andy*? What was the sense of it? Why not leave them where they were — and the girls too? And above all, *where* were the girls?

The two men worked hard for some time, and then, apparently, had transferred all the things they meant to, for they put out the light on the *Andy*. Both of them went back to the motor-boat, sat down and lighted cigarettes.

"Are they going to stay here all night?" whispered Tom in dismay. "We'll never get away if they do!"

"Well, we can't get off till they go, because they are blocking the way out for the *Andy* now," said Andy in a gloomy whisper. "Pity we didn't get off a few minutes sooner."

"They'd have seen us and given chase," said Tom. "It's just as well we didn't. I wish they'd go. It would be so nice to get back home with the *Andy,* everything complete in her again! If only we knew about the girls."

When they had smoked their cigarettes, the two men got up. They had had very little to say to one another, and then only commonplace remarks. Andy wondered if Bandy was still angry with Stumpy for apparently stealing his food.

"We'll go and have a word with the Chief," said Bandy, throwing his glowing cigarette end into the water. "We'll see if anyone has found those dratted boys. Good thing we've got the girls to bargain with—nice little hostages they are!"

The men climbed on to a ledge, and made their way up the creek. Andy and Tom could not see where they went, because it was now almost dark.

"Must be some entrance into the Cliff of Birds up that way," muttered Andy in Tom's ear. "I wonder who the Chief is! Perhaps that fellow with the glasses you once saw in the store-cave with Bandy, Tom. Wonder how long they're going to be? I've a good mind to take their motor-boat and chance the run home in it! I know how to drive one!"

Tom was cold with the evening wind, and with suspense. He shivered now with excitement.

"What! Take their boat, Andy?" he said. "Would you really dare?"

CHAPTER XXIII

WHO IS IN THE CABIN?

IT was quite dark now. The sky was perfectly clear, and the stars shone out, giving so little light that in that shut-in creek there was none to see by. Only the lamp on the motor-boat gleamed out, showing the deck there.

Andy listened for the men's voices. No — there was no sound of them. They had gone — but for how long? What had to be done must be done now if they were to get away quickly.

The boys got down from their hiding-place and crept softly over the rocks to the waiting motor-boat. It was quite still on the narrow waters of the calm little creek. They climbed over the sides, and examined it.

It was whilst they were looking at it to see how to start it up that they were startled by a noise in the cabin of the boat. It was a curious noise — a kind of long-drawn-out groan! The boys stood absolutely still, almost startled out of their wits, for they had been so certain they were alone. They listened. The groan came again.

"There's someone here — in that cabin!" whispered Andy in Tom's ear. "We'd better get out, quick! We don't want to be discovered here. Come on. Quiet now!"

The boys climbed out as quietly as they could. They made for their hiding-place again, puzzled.

"Who's in there?" whispered Tom. "He sounded as if he was ill, or hurt. Who is it?"

"Goodness knows!" said Andy. "All I know is he's a frightful nuisance, whoever he is — he's prevented us from taking the boat."

"What shall we do now?" whispered Tom. "We can't stay up here all the night!"

338

"Oh, those men will come back soon," said Andy. "Then maybe they'll push off, and we can get going in the *Andy*. We must wait and see."

The boys sat themselves down and prepared to wait with what patience they could. Tom shivered again. He and Andy sat as close together as possible, for warmth.

"Can you hear any more groans?" asked Tom. Andy shook his head. "No. They seem to have stopped."

But they began again a little later. Then other noises began. Someone hammered on the door of the motor-boat's cabin. Someone shook the door violently and kicked it hard! The boys listened, more startled than ever.

Then a voice they knew very well indeed came up to them, a voice muffled by the door of the cabin, but quite unmistakable!

"Let me out! Where am I? You let me out or I'll kick the place down!"

The boys felt their hearts jump, and they stared down at the motor-boat in amazement.

"It's Jill! It's Jill's voice!" said Andy, forgetting to whisper in his enormous astonishment. "But what's Jill doing there? Quick, let's go to her!"

The boys leapt down again, not caring if they fell or not, they were so eager to reach the little girl. She was going quite mad with fury in the locked cabin. She was now hitting the door with something — crash, crash, crash. Andy couldn't help smiling. He had seldom seen Jill in a temper, but he knew she had one. He wondered if Mary was there too. If so, she was very quiet.

Andy landed on the motor-boat first and ran to the cabin-door. Jill was now raining heavy blows on it, and shouting so loudly that she could not hear Andy's voice calling to her.

"Jill! Jill! Stop all that hammering so that I can unlock the door and get in! You'll hit me if you don't stop it!"

But the furious little girl went on and on, quite beside herself. Crash, smash, crash! What in the world had she got in her hand?

There was a pause at last, and Jill, plainly quite tired out, began to sob bitterly. Andy hammered on the door with his fist.

"Jill! It's me, Andy! We're going to unlock the door and come in. Don't smash at it any more!"

There was a dead silence inside the cabin. Jill evidently couldn't believe her ears! Then there was a wild cry of joy.

"Andy! Oh, Andy, darling Andy, unlock the door quick!"

Andy unlocked and unbolted the door. Jill flung herself on him and Tom, weeping for joy.

"I thought you were lost for ever!" she sobbed. "We didn't know what to make of it when you didn't come back. The men said you never would. We thought you must be drowned. Oh Andy, oh Tom, let's go home!"

"Where's Mary?" asked Tom.

"In the cabin – on that bunk there – she won't wake up," said Jill. Andy took the lamp from the deck of the motor-boat and flashed the light on to where Mary was lying in a bunk.

"What's wrong with her?" he asked, hearing her breathing very loudly indeed.

"I don't know," said Jill. "I think it must have been something those men gave us to drink that sent us off to sleep like that. I didn't drink so much as Mary did – I didn't like the taste of mine – but Mary drank all hers. And then we fell fast asleep, and didn't know what was happening. I woke up just now and felt awfully sick, and I groaned and groaned."

"Yes – we heard you," said Andy. "Poor old Jill. I expect Mary will wake up soon. My word, Jill, you nearly broke that door down! What did you hit it with?"

340

"That stool," said Jill. "I felt so angry when I knew those men had put us somewhere and left us. I don't know where we are, you see. We fell asleep in that cave high up in Smuggler's Rock—where the men put us all before, when Andy's father came to look for us."

"You've got a lot to tell us," said Andy, "and we've got some pretty peculiar things to tell you too. But we can't stop now to exchange news, because those men may come back at any time. We don't want all to be captured again."

"No—this is a jolly good chance to escape, the whole

lot of us," said Tom. "But, Andy—we must tell them *one* thing!"

Andy knew what that was, of course! "Oh yes," he said. "Jill—the *Andy* wasn't sunk! She's close by this very boat, sails and oars and everything! The man must have taken her and hidden her there. She's safe and sound. Tom and I were just about to run home in her, if we could, when Bandy and Stumpy brought this motor-boat up the creek and we had to hide."

"*Oh!*" said Jill in joy. "Andy, I'm so awfully glad. I was miserable about her, of course, but I knew you must be ten times more miserable!"

"We were almost at the top of the cliff when Andy saw her," said Tom. "He'd have fallen over with joy if I hadn't had hold of his ankles!"

Andy suddenly remembered that Bandy and Stumpy might come back at any moment. "Look here—we mustn't chatter like this," he said. "We must make up our minds what we are going to do. Tom and I were thinking of running for home in this motor-boat, as we can't get at the *Andy*. This boat is blocking up the way, and we can't get the *Andy* out."

"Well, let's go, then!" said Jill eagerly. "It's awfully dark, though. I don't know how you'll see your way, Andy."

A deep groan from the cabin bunk made them jump. It was Mary, waking up after her long sleep, feeling sick. Jill went to her.

"It's all right, Mary. You'll soon feel all right."

Mary, half-asleep still, and feeling very sick, groaned again.

"Let's get her up into the open air," said Andy. "She'll feel better then. She's awfully pale."

The two boys helped the poor little girl out of her bunk. Still feeling very sick she went on deck, and was glad to feel the cool wind on her face. She soon stopped groaning.

"I feel a bit better," she said feebly. "Tom, Andy—how is it you're here? Where are we?"

"Tell you all about it soon," said Andy. "No time now. We'll start up this motor-boat and get going as soon as we can. Jill and Tom can tell you everything as we go."

He went to start up the engine. But no matter how he tried, the engine wouldn't start up. It made a humming noise, but nothing more happened. Andy could have cried!

"What's up? Can't you get her going?" said Tom. "Here —let *me* have a try!"

But although they all had a try, nobody could start up the motor of the boat. Why, they didn't know. It was most aggravating—especially as they couldn't possibly go on the *Andy*, because the motor-boat was in the way!

"Look out—there's someone coming," said Tom, suddenly. "See the light of their cigarettes up there?"

The four children stared up the narrow creek. Yes, there was certainly someone coming—two people, for there was the glow from the ends of two cigarettes. It must be Bandy and Stumpy coming back. Blow!

"Skip out of the boat quickly!" whispered Andy, giving Jill a helping hand. "Shut the cabin-door, Tom, and lock it. The men may slip off without looking in and seeing that the girls aren't there. If they do go, we can all get away in the *Andy*. Hurry!"

Tom locked and bolted the door of the cabin. Then he joined the others on the ledge and they all crept behind a rock, wishing their hearts were not beating so loudly.

Bandy and Stumpy came along, smoking. They clambered on board their boat. The children hardly dared to breathe.

Would they be able to start up the engine, and go? How they hoped and prayed that they would hear the roar of the engine, and know that it would soon take the boat

343

safely away from them. Then into the *Andy* they would climb, and away they would go!

Stumpy's voice came to them. "Those girls all right, do you think, Bandy? They ought to have waked up by now. That sleeping-draught you gave them wasn't too strong, was it? Funny they haven't come round from it yet."

"Aw—let them alone," came Bandy's hoarse voice. "What does it matter if I gave it to them strong? Keep them quiet! We'll have to carry them from the cabin to their boat, if they're not awake, that's all. We'll dump them down into their boat's cabin, and lock them in safely. No one will ever know where they are—and if those two boys ever get back home and split on us, well, we'll have those two girls as hostages—our safety against theirs! A nice bit of work."

"Well, I'll get one of the girls now," said Stumpy, and he unlocked the cabin-door. "Here, hand me the lamp." There was a moment's silence as he took the lamp and swung its light into the cabin. Then he suddenly gave a loud cry.

"What's this! There's nobody here! Those two girls have *gone*!"

CHAPTER XXIV

ANDY HAS A FINE IDEA

BANDY and Stumpy were filled with the utmost amazement to find their two prisoners gone. The children heard their astonished remarks as they searched the little cabin.

"But the door was still locked and bolted! How *could* they have gone?"

"Kids can't walk through locked doors — and there's no window they could open."

"We left them fast asleep here. I looked in at them before we went — *and* locked and bolted the door afterwards!"

"I know. I saw you. I'll swear to that."

"Then what's happened to them? Here's the cabin, just as it was when we left it — locked *and* bolted — and we come back to find it still locked *and* bolted — and the kids gone, I don't like it."

"Look here — do you suppose anyone came along and let them out — and locked and bolted the door again?" suddenly said Bandy's hoarse voice. There was a pause before Stumpy answered.

"It's possible — but who's about here in the middle of the night — here, in this lonely place? Nobody! It's a queer thing! Shall we go and tell the Chief?"

"Not me!" said Bandy at once. "What do you think he'd say to us if he knew his two precious prisoners were gone — his only means of bargaining, if this little game gets reported! No, Stumpy — we've got to find those girls somehow. They can't be far away. Now can they?"

"No. You're right there," said Stumpy. "Their own fishing-boat is still here — and they're not likely to swim down this creek, or to climb the cliff here either, unless

345

they want to break their necks. They must be hereabouts."

"Search the motor-boat first," said Bandy. "And then the fishing-boat yonder. It's a pity we didn't carry them there, as we were told to do, dump them down in the cabin and bolt the hatch over them."

"Well, if they could get out of a locked and bolted door here, they could have got out of a bolted cabin in their own boat," said Stumpy. "Come on—they're not on our boat. Let's take our torches and look around all these rocks."

The children began to tremble. Bandy and Stumpy were two fierce men, and angry ones now too. It would not be pleasant to be found by them.

Andy frowned. What could he do to distract the men from hunting round the rocks?

An idea came to him. He bent down and groped about for a stone or piece of rock. He found one and stood up again. He tried to make out where the *Andy* was, and then, taking aim, he flung the rock as hard as he could in her direction. It fell on the deck of the fishing-boat with a loud crash, that echoed up and down the little creek.

Tom, Jill and Mary jumped violently. They had not known what Andy was going to do. But Bandy and Stumpy jumped even more violently!

"Gosh—did you hear that?" said Bandy's voice. "What was it? It sounded as if it came from the fishing-boat yonder. That's where they are! Come on, quick. We'll get them, the tiresome little brats!"

Forgetting all about searching the rocks, the two men hurried to where the *Andy* floated. They climbed on deck —and after them climbed Andy, as soft-footed as a cat. A wild plan was in his head. He didn't know if he could carry it out or not—but it was worth trying!

The men flashed their torches about the boat and lifted up the folded sail. Nobody there, of course.

"They'll be down in the cabin!" said Bandy. "Come on

—we'll see. And won't I shake the little varmints when I get hold of them!''

He opened the hatch and leapt down into the little cabin. Stumpy stood above it, looking down. And suddenly something happened to him that gave him the shock of his life!

Something hurled itself at his back and sent him right off his balance! He gave a shout of terror, and then fell headlong down the open hatch into the little cabin below. He fell right on top of the equally startled Bandy, knocking him over, so that he fell and struck his head hard against the wooden table.

His torch flew from his hand and crashed, its light going out. The little cabin was in darkness. Bandy, quite sure that some unexpected enemy had fallen upon him to kill him, began to fight like a madman.

He struck out at the horrified Stumpy, who tried in vain to stop him. Bandy was quite beside himself with anger and panic, and his great fists hammered Stumpy unmercifully, so that, in self-defence, Stumpy had to hammer back!

The two men rolled over and over, pummelling each other, yelling and shouting for all they were worth!

It was pitch-black in the little cabin. Andy flashed his torch down just once, and grinned with delight to see the two rogues going for each other. Let them get on with it, by all means!

The boy slammed down the hatch, and bolted it. The noise startled the two men, and they stopped fighting.

It also startled the three hidden children and they jumped. "What was that?" whispered Jill. "I wish I could see what's happening!"

A cheerful voice came over to them through the darkness. "You all right, Tom and the girls?"

"Yes, Andy! But what was all the yelling and smashing, and that last big slam?" called back Tom, glad to hear

Andy's voice again. He had had no idea why Andy had left them, nor what he was doing.

"Oh, Bandy got down into the cabin, and I shoved Stumpy in to keep him company," said Andy, still more cheerfully. "I don't think Bandy welcomed Stumpy much, because they've been fighting like wild cats! The slam you heard was the hatch closing down. It's well and truly bolted too!"

There were squeals from the two girls and a loud shout from Tom.

"Andy! You've got them prisoner! Good work, Andy, good work!"

Soon the four were on the fishing-boat, and Andy told them proudly once more how he had made the two men prisoner. It seemed too good to be true! Bandy and Stumpy, who now knew they had been fighting each other, were doing their best to bang open the hatch.

"It's no good!" Andy yelled down to them gleefully. "It's too hefty to smash open, and you should see the bolts! Make as much noise as you like, though, so long as you can't get out."

"Are they really caught?" asked Mary, sitting down on the deck, feeling suddenly sick again. "Oh dear – all this has made me feel bad again!"

"You'll soon be all right, Mary," said Jill. "I feel quite better now. Golly, Andy, that was a good trick of yours! What are we going to do next?"

"Well, I don't somehow think anyone will be along this way tonight, so we can let those two fellows shout all they want to!" said Andy. "When dawn comes we'll set free the motor-boat, and somehow get her down the creek and out of the way of the *Andy*. Then we'll take the *Andy* and run for home."

"With Bandy and Stumpy?" asked Tom, his eyes wide with excitement.

"Well, they'll have to come too, whether they want to or not," said Andy, with a grin. "Two nice little prisoners, who will have to explain quite a lot of things to quite a lot of people very soon."

"I'll be awfully glad to get home safely," said Jill.

"So will we all," said Andy. "I vote we have a rest till dawn. We can't mess about with the motor-boat whilst it's dark."

"Oh, Andy—we've slept for ages!" said Jill. "Can't we talk? I want to know all about your adventures—and tell you what happened to us too."

"Well, fire away," said Andy. "Tom and I have had a good sleep today too. We'll all talk. Let's get back to the motor-boat and talk in the cabin there. It's cold here. Bandy and Stumpy have got all the rugs down in our little cabin!"

The four of them went to the motor-boat and curled themselves up in the two bunks there. They lighted the lamp too, and soon it looked quite cosy.

"Did anything much happen after we had gone?" asked Andy.

"Well, Mary and I didn't hear you leave the cave when you went to follow the trail of shells," said Jill. "We didn't wake up till morning. We remembered where you had gone, of course, and we hoped you wouldn't be too long. We had breakfast, and then we squeezed out of the cave to wait for you."

"You didn't come," said Mary. "So we thought we would follow the trail of shells ourselves, and see if we could find you! We followed them and came to where they stopped. . . ."

"I bet you didn't know where to go next!" interrupted Tom.

"We didn't," said Jill. "We couldn't imagine why the shells ended at a blank wall of rock. And then suddenly the rock opened!"

"Golly!" said Tom. "That must have scared you!"

"It did," said Jill. "It scared us terribly. We ran away — but that bandy-legged man tracked us back to our cave and yelled to us to come out."

"We had to come out in the end," said Mary, "because he threatened to smoke us out again. He thought you two boys were in there and he yelled and yelled to you to come out too. When you didn't, he crawled in — and found the cave empty!"

"What did he do then?" asked Andy, with great interest.

"He raved at us, and tried to make us say where you were," said Mary. "He was horrid. Then he hunted about all over the place and still couldn't find you. Then some other men came, and they had a sort of meeting. We couldn't hear what they said."

"They sent Bandy into our cave and he brought out everything," said Jill. "Then we were taken, blindfolded as before, back to that high-up cave in Smuggler's Rock — the one we were all put in before. We didn't have any food or drink for ages, and then Bandy came with some."

"And we think that what we drank must have had sleeping-medicine in it," said Mary, "because when we had drunk it, we simply couldn't keep our eyes open!"

"Yes. They must have given you sleeping-draughts," said Andy. "Beasts! Then they meant to bring you here and lock you into the *Andy*, keeping you as hostages in case Tom and I had escaped, and could report the whole affair to someone. What a bit of luck we happened to be here too!"

"Yes! Now tell us how *you* came to be here!" begged Jill. "Go on, Andy, tell every single thing."

So Andy and Tom told their tale too — and when they had finished, the dawn was coming up, and it was time to get to work again. With luck they should be home that day — and what a surprising lot of news they had for the grown-ups so anxiously looking for them!

CHAPTER XXV

RUNNING FOR HOME

AND now the four children began to be very busy indeed! The daylight filtered into the narrow, hidden creek and gave them just enough light to see by. The boys clambered on board the motor-boat, and tried once more to start up the engine. But for some reason or other again they could not get the boat to go.

"Let's untie her and give her a jolly good push!" said Andy. "She'll perhaps float away then, and give us room to get out the *Andy*."

So they untied the rope that held the motor-boat moored to a post-like rock. Then, all together, the children shoved and pushed.

The boat slid away from the ledge they stood on and floated away down the creek.

"She's going!" cried Jill. "She's going down to the sea all by herself!"

"Now she's stuck," said Andy, as the boat seemed to get herself wedged against a rock. "I'll get an oar from the *Andy*, and climb into the motor-boat, and push her along by the oar."

Tom fetched him an oar from the *Andy*. Andy ran down the ledge, jumped to a rock, and from there to the deck of the motor-boat. He shoved the oar against the rock and pushed the boat out of her corner. She bobbed there, not seeming to know which way to go. Andy shoved with the oar again.

"Mind you don't break it!" yelled Tom, seeing the oar-blade bending a little. "Oh—there she goes, down the creek. Come on out, Andy, or you'll go with her!"

But Andy did not get out of the motor-boat till she was

352

right out of the little channel. Then, when she was safely bobbing about in a patch of water outside, he clambered over the side, slithered down to a rock that was under water, and began to wade back to the rocky ledge that ran beside the creek. An enormous wave nearly sent him flying, but he managed to keep his balance.

He went back to the others, grinning. "Well, the motor-boat's out of our way all right!" he said. "That's good. Now to get the *Andy* out. We'll have to use the oars again. We'll put up the sail when we get the wind."

A great noise began again down in the cabin of the *Andy*. Bandy and Stumpy evidently knew that something was up! How they crashed and banged against the bolted hatch. But it was good and strong, and they couldn't make it budge.

"Make all the noise you like!" Andy called to the men cheerfully. "We don't mind! By the way, your motor-boat's been turned loose. I hope it won't smash to pieces on the rocks. There's a pretty good tide running, with this strong wind!"

All kinds of terrible threats came up from the cabin, but the children only laughed at them. They were feeling very happy now. They had the *Andy* back, they were all together again, they had two fine prisoners and a wonderful secret—and they were going to run home before the wind. Hurrah!

Tom, of course, wanted to finish the rest of the food in the tins that he and Andy had brought down the cliff. Andy looked at his watch, and decided they might have ten minutes for a meal. It was a very merry meal. Jill and Mary were hungry, for both girls felt perfectly all right again by now.

Then they set off. The boys worked away with the oars, getting the *Andy* carefully down the little creek of water. Big waves splashed up it now, but they managed very

353

cleverly. The boat gradually went down the little channel, and was at last bobbing on the open sea.

"We have to follow that sea-path there between the rocks," said Andy. "Then we round the point and find ourselves opposite the shallow bay where we anchored the *Andy* before. Then we turn into the channel of water between the two long ridges of rock and run for home!"

The boat bobbed violently on the surging water. The tide was running very high indeed. The wind whipped by them, sending their hair straight up.

"Tom, take the oars and keep her off the rocks there," said Andy. "I'll put up the sail. Jill, take the tiller for a minute. That's right. Keep her headed the way she is."

Andy was just about to put up the sail when he heard a cry from Mary. "Oh look – the motor-boat is going on the rocks! Look at her!"

The children looked. Mary was right. The motor-boat was indeed on the rocks! With no one to guide her or control her she was quite at the mercy of the waves, and they had taken her right on to the wicked rocks that dotted the sea just there.

There was a smashing, grinding noise. The children's faces grew grave and solemn. It wasn't nice to see a boat smashed to pieces like that.

"Don't let's watch any more," said Tom. "It's awful to see the waves smashing it up – poor thing, it's on its side now – and look at that great hole there! When next it's swept off the rocks, it will fill with water and sink."

"One less boat for the smugglers," said Andy, and put up the red sail deftly.

The wind filled it gleefully, and the sail flapped eagerly. Andy slid down to the seat by the tiller and took it from Jill. "Put the oars in, Tom," he said. "We're all right now. Off we go with the wind!"

It was glorious to feel the little boat leaping along. "If

she could sing, she would!" said Mary. "Even as it is I sometimes think her sail flaps out a kind of song!"

There came a noise from below. The children listened, trying to make out the voice against the sound of wind and waves.

"It's only Bandy saying that they feel sick down there and want some fresh air," said Tom, with a grin.

Jill put her mouth to the crack of the hatch and called down. "You made me and Mary feel sick with your horrid sleeping-medicine. It's your turn now! You won't come up here!"

"I should think not!" said Andy, and swung the tiller round as the boat entered the channel between the long, wicked rows of sharp black rocks. "Do they really think we'd let them come up here — to overpower us, and whisk us back to Smuggler's Rock? What a hope!"

Plainly Bandy and Stumpy didn't feel there was much hope for it, for they said no more. The children forgot about them as they raced along. They revelled in the speed of their boat, and loved the way she seemed to gallop over the white-topped waves.

Andy looked the picture of happiness as he sat at the tiller, his brown face glowing and his deep-blue eyes reflecting the sea.

"Dear old Andy!" thought Jill, looking at him. "He's got back his boat, and he's happy again. It's true that it's our boat too — but he's the real skipper!"

For a long time the boat swept on over the waves, and they made very good time indeed. "We'll be home about eleven, at this rate!" shouted Andy, the wind whipping his words away as he called them out.

They swept into their home-waters just after eleven, the red sail making a bright speck on the blue waters. The children eyed the shore eagerly. Would their mother be there? Would Andy's father be there? Of course not —

because they didn't know the children were coming home at that very moment!

But they *were* there, all the same! Someone had sighted the *Andy* as she turned into the harbour and the word was sent round at once. "The *Andy* is back! There she is! The *Andy* is home again! Let's hope the children are safe and sound!"

The children's mother was fetched at once and ran down to the jetty, her face bright with hope. She had been very unhappy the last few days. Andy's father stood there too, his blue eyes watching the incoming boat. Then a shout went up.

"They're all on board, the whole four of them. They're safe! Thank God for that!"

Andy's father turned to the children's mother. "They're safe, ma'am," he said, his eyes bright with joy. "I knew they'd be all right with my Andy. Look at them waving to us. They're all right, ma'am, they're all right!"

Many willing hands made the *Andy* safe as she stopped beside the jetty.

The children leapt off and ran to their mother. Andy got a big hug from his father, and then he pointed back to the boat.

"We've two prisoners there, Dad. Look out for them, they're pretty dangerous fellows. We've got them bolted down."

Everyone gaped. Andy's father rapped out a few questions and Andy answered breathlessly. Then three of the listening fishermen, stalwart, sturdy fellows, started grimly towards the *Andy*. They opened the hatch – and up came Bandy and Stumpy, looking very green indeed. They were grasped by rough, strong hands and jerked off the *Andy's* deck to the jetty.

"It's a case for the police, Dad," said Andy. "There's something very queer going on in the Cliff of Birds and

356

Smuggler's Rock. We found cases upon cases of guns and ammunition."

The fishermen whistled and looked at one another. One of them went off to fetch the local policeman. It was all very exciting indeed!

"I'm jolly hungry," said Tom. The girls laughed. It was so like Tom to say that, in the middle of all the excitement. His mother put her arm round them.

"Come along and have a good meal," she said. "I'm so happy to have you back. You've no idea how worried I've been. Andy's father and uncle, and many of the other fishermen all went out hunting for you — and there wasn't a trace of you to be found! I'm longing to hear every single thing."

Andy's father and Andy went with them. Bandy and Stumpy were left in charge of the fishermen until the policeman came. Tom wondered what his mother had got for their meal. He felt he really could enjoy one now that all worry and trouble were ended!

Whilst Andy and the others were sitting down to a noisy and exciting meal, many things were happening. The policeman decided that all these curious affairs that the children had reported were quite beyond him, and he had rung up the superintendent in the next big town.

The superintendent, listening carefully, had been filled with amazement. Yes, certainly this was a very big affair indeed. He telephoned in his turn to headquarters and soon dozens of telegraph wires were humming with news and instructions.

Bandy and Stumpy were safely in prison, and, fearful of their own skins, they gave away all the secrets of their Chief. The children knew nothing of this, but laughed and chattered as they told their mother that afternoon all that had happened. They had quite forgotten how afraid they had been, and how worried.

"When things end well, nothing seems to matter," said Tom. "I do wonder what will happen to all those smugglers, Mother!"

CHAPTER XXVI

THE END OF IT ALL

THAT evening, when the children had talked themselves out, and really thought they had nothing more to say, a very large and shining car drove up to the cottage.

Out of it stepped a neat and well-dressed little man, whose sharp clever eyes looked in turn at each of the four children.

"You don't know who I am," he said, "but I am someone in charge of very high-up affairs, and I want to ask you a few questions. My name is Colonel Knox. I've heard most of your story from Andy's father. Now, can you tell me this. Did any of you ever see the man that Bandy and Stumpy call the Chief?"

"Well—I did see a man once in the store-cave with Stumpy, a man wearing glasses, but dressed like a fisherman," said Tom. "I don't know if he was the Chief though."

"No. That wasn't the Chief," said the sharp-eyed man. "Stumpy has told us who that man was. We are hoping to get him tomorrow, with all the others."

"What are you going to do?" asked Tom, with great interest.

"We're going to round up all the smugglers and their boats," said Colonel Knox. "We're combing out all the passages and tunnels and caves. We're opening every case and box and crate. We shall cross-examine every man we get—and we shall set that great lamp burning you told us of, and watch for the ships that answer the signal. We shall get them too!"

"Why did they smuggle those guns and things in?" said Jill.

359

"There is a country that is not allowed to import fire-arms of any kind," said the Colonel. "Those arms you found were made in a distant land, and have been smuggled here to take across to this other country, where they are forbidden. As you can imagine, very high prices are paid for these forbidden fire-arms. Men in our country, I regret to say, have been acting as a go-between — that is, they smuggle the arms here, and, for a price, take them to the buyers. They make a very pretty fortune out of it."

"Oh," said the children, wide-eyed and astonished. Andy considered a moment.

"And the man you'd really like to get hold of is the one they call the Chief?" he said. Colonel Knox nodded.

"Yes. All the other fellows merely obey orders. He's the Big Brain behind it all. We've suspected this affair for a long time, but we couldn't find out how the forbidden goods were brought here, or where, nor did we know who the brain behind it was."

"And if you don't get him, he'll probably start off again somewhere else?" said Tom. "Well, I wish we could tell you who he is. Don't Bandy and Stumpy know?"

"No — all they know is that he is a tall fellow, who always wears a mask when visiting them," said Colonel Knox. "And they *think* he lives in the nearest big town, so that he can get to the Cliff of Birds without too great a loss of time, when he needs to. But as there are about fifty thousand people living in that town, it's like looking for a needle in a haystack!"

"Yes. I see," said Andy. "I do hope you get him, Colonel Knox. I say, wasn't it a bit of luck we stumbled on their haunt? It was quite an accident."

"A very happy accident for us!" said the Colonel. "We don't want our country mixed up in any affair of this sort. It was a clever idea — to have a hide-out of motor-boats in such a hidden cove — and a lamp to signal out to sea, from a place that no one else ever saw at night — and to use the tunnels and caves as store-houses."

"How did the Chief get the goods out of the Cliff of Birds and Smuggler's Rock?" asked Andy, puzzled.

"We're not quite sure yet," said Colonel Knox. "But we think there is another way out of the Cliff of Birds, leading to a flat piece of ground at the back — a good place for aeroplanes to land. It is likely that the Chief took off loads of fire-arms in his 'planes."

"My word!" said Tom. "What a dangerous plot we found! I wonder the men didn't guard us more carefully than they did!"

"Ah — they didn't know what wily birds you were!" said the Colonel, with a laugh. "But they quite meant to use the two girls as hostages, if you got home and reported their doings. That would have been very unpleasant for Jill and Mary — and I'm afraid we would have had to let the miscreants free rather than risk anything happening to the girls."

"It's a good thing we captured Bandy and Stumpy," said Andy.

"A very good thing," said Colonel Knox. "We got out of them a tremendous amount of valuable information. Enough to capture all the rest of the gang, and round up their hiding-places, and stop all their plans. It's just the Chief we can't seem to lay our hands on."

"It's a pity we never saw him," said Tom.

"A great pity," agreed Colonel Knox. "Well, I'm proud to have met you children — you're a fine brave adventurous four! I must go now — but I want you to come over to the big town where I live, and have lunch with me tomorrow for a treat. Will you do that?"

"Oh, *yes!*" cried the four.

"But how can we get there?" asked Jill. "There is only one train."

"I'll send my car for you," said Colonel Knox, and got up to go. The children took him to his sleek black car. They liked him very much.

"He's clever and kind and goes straight to the point in everything," said Tom. "I only wish we could tell him who was Chief of the smugglers is. But we can't."

The next day the car was sent to fetch the four children. They climbed into it proudly, and were soon whisked away to the nearest big town. They stopped at the grandest hotel in the place, and were met in style by Colonel Knox at the door.

They felt most important walking in with him—and when Tom read the menu for the lunch he looked at his host in awe.

"Can we have all these things?" he said. "Oh, it will be the best meal we've ever had. Look, it says 'Mixed ice-creams' at the bottom. Can we have vanilla, strawberry and chocolate all mixed?"

"Yes—and coffee ice-cream as well, I believe," said Colonel Knox, laughing. "Well, sit down. Now, who wants ginger-beer to drink, and who wants lemonade, or orange?"

Soon the children were in the middle of a most glorious meal. Tom looked blissfully happy. He thought this was a wonderful reward for all the adventures they had been through.

When he was in the middle of his mixed ice-cream, he looked up and saw a man seating himself at a nearby table. He was a tall, burly fellow, with deep-set eyes and black wavy hair. He nodded to Colonel Knox.

"Who's that?" asked Tom in a low voice. The Colonel looked surprised.

"Oh—just one of the inhabitants of this town," he said. "One of our very richest, though you wouldn't think it to look at him."

Tom was staring at the man curiously. He certainly didn't look rich, for he wore his clothes carelessly and the sleeve of his coat wanted mending. His red shirt was open at the neck, and lacked a button half-way down.

Tom suddenly went as red as a beetroot with excitement. He began to burrow deep into first one pocket and then another. "Whatever's the matter?" said Andy. "Why do you look like that, Tom?"

Tom brought something out from his pocket. He pushed it across to Colonel Knox, who looked at it in the greatest surprise, thinking that Tom had suddenly gone mad.

"Sir," said Tom in a whisper. "I found that red pearl button in a cave in the Cliff of Birds. It must have belonged to one of the men there, though I never saw one with a red shirt on. But look at that man over there. He's got on a red shirt—and it has red pearl buttons exactly like this —and one is missing!"

Colonel Knox's eyes flashed from Tom's button to the man's shirt. He slipped the button into his pocket.

"Say no more now," he commanded. "Don't even look at the fellow. Understand?"

There was something in those commanding tones that made the children feel a little frightened. They obeyed, eating their ices, and keeping their eyes carefully away from the man at the other table. Colonel Knox scribbled a note on a piece of paper, beckoned to a waiter and told him to deliver it somewhere. Then the Colonel became his own charming, joking self again, and apparently took no notice at all of the man in the red shirt nearby.

"I'll let you know if your button has solved our problem," he said to Tom, when the man got up and went. "It may have! It may have! He's the one man we never even suspected. Good for you, Tom! My word, this is a great affair, and no mistake!"

So it was! Before long the whole of the motor-boats in the cove had been taken, all the crews too, and every smuggler found in the caves. The smuggled goods had been confiscated, ships that helped in the smuggling were captured, and the whole plot exposed.

And the man in the red shirt was the leader, the Chief of the whole gang! It was too good to be true that Tom should have found the button that led to his capture. Colonel Knox was very pleased about it indeed.

"You shall certainly have a fine new camera for your help with the button!" he said to Tom. "Without you we should never have known who the Chief was — no one even suspected him! He ran the whole business very cleverly indeed, and not even the men themselves ever saw him face to face. He has made a fortune out of his smuggling — but he won't make any more money for many, many years to come!"

"What a lot has happened in a week or so!" said Jill, as they all sat on the jetty that night, waiting for the fishing-boat to come back with Andy and his father. "Look, there she goes! Leading all the rest of the boats as usual. Ahoy, Andy, ahoy! We're waiting for you!"

Their mother came up to see the fishing-boats come in. As Andy stepped off on to the jetty, Tom turned eagerly to his mother.

"Mother! Can we go out with Andy in his boat next week — when he has a day off? I know a lovely place I'd like to go to."

"Certainly *not!*" said his mother. "What, lose you again for days on end, and not know where you are! My dears, I shall never, never let you go out alone with Andy again!"

All the same, I expect she will. After all, they are the Adventurous Four, and there may be plenty more adventures waiting for them yet!

The Children of Willow Farm

CHAPTER I

GOODBYE TO LONDON!

ONE wild March day four excited children looked down from the windows of a tall London house, and watched three enormous vans draw slowly up in the square outside.

"There they are!" cried Rory. "They've come at last!"

"The moving has begun!" said Penny, jigging up and down beside the window-sill.

"Won't it be funny to see all our furniture going into those vans!" said Sheila.

"I shouldn't have thought that we would have needed *three* vans!" said Benjy, astonished.

"Oh, there are three more coming after these, too," said Sheila. "Oh goodness—isn't it lovely to think we are going down to Willow Farm! A farm of our own! A farm as nice as Cherry Tree Farm."

"Nicer," said Benjy. "Much nicer. It's got more streams. And it's built on a hill so that we get a marvellous view, not down in a hollow like Cherry Tree Farm."

The four children were very happy indeed. The year before they had all been ill and had been sent for some months to live on their uncle's farm. The life had suited them well at Cherry Tree Farm, and all the children had grown strong and red-cheeked.

Then, when the time had come for them to return to their London home, their father had found that his business was bringing him in very little money—and Uncle Tim had suggested that he should put his money into Willow Farm, five miles away, and take up farming for his living.

The children's father had been brought up on a farm, and knew how to run one. The children, of course, had been mad with delight at the idea — and here it was, really coming true at last! They were all going to move into Willow Farm that very week!

It had taken three months to buy the place and arrange everything. Rory and Benjy, the two boys, had been to boarding-school, and had just returned home in time to move down with the girls, Sheila and Penny. Their mother had been very busy packing, and everyone had helped. It was such fun!

"I like London if we just come up for a pantomime or a circus," said Rory. "But the country is best to live in!"

"I'm simply longing to see Tammylan again," said Penny. "Oh, won't he be pleased to see us!"

Tammylan was a great friend of theirs. He was a strange man, who lived in a hillside cave in the winter months, and in a tree-house made of willow branches in the summer. He was called the 'wild man' because he lived alone with animals and birds. Most people were afraid of him, but he was the children's greatest friend. He had taught them all about the birds and animals of the countryside, and now they knew more about all the big and small creatures than any other children in the kingdom. It would be marvellous to see Tammylan again.

Mother put her head in at the door. "It's time for you to put your things on," she said. "Daddy will soon be bringing the car round. Say goodbye to all the nooks and crannies here that you have known since you were babies — for you won't be seeing them again!"

The family were going down by car, and the vans were following. Mother wanted to be ready for them when they came. The children looked at one another.

"I'm glad to be leaving here," said Benjy. "But we've had some good times in this tall old London house!"

He ran out of the room.

"Benjy's gone to say goodbye to the plane trees he can see from his bedroom window!" said Rory. "He always loved those."

It was true. Benjy leaned out of his bedroom window and looked at the trees with their last year's balls hanging from bare boughs.

"Goodbye," he said. "I've known you for eleven years, and you are nice all the year round! I like you now, with

371

bare boughs. I like you when you are just leafing, with bright green leaves shining in the sun. I like you in the summer when you are thick and dark green. I like you in the autumn when you turn yellow and throw your leaves away. Goodbye, plane trees! I'm going where there are no plane trees, but willows, willows, willows all around, growing along the banks of silver streams!"

The plane trees rustled in the wind as if they were whispering back to Benjy. He drew in his head and suddenly felt a little sad. He would never forget those London trees — and he would always remember the little grey squirrels that sometimes ran up and down the branches.

Sheila went to say goodbye to every room in turn. "I don't want to forget anything," she said to Rory, who was with her. "I always want to remember our first home, though I am going to love our second home much much better. Goodbye, drawing-room — you look funny now with all the furniture just anyhow! Goodbye, study. I won't forget how often I've slipped down to you to take a book to read out of your bookcases! Goodbye, dining-room, I never liked you very much because you are so dark!"

Eight-year-old Penny stayed up in the nursery. That was the room she knew and loved the best. It was not called the nursery now, but was known as the schoolroom, because it was there that the two girls worked with their governess. Penny loved it.

She ran her fingers over the wallpaper, which showed a pattern of nursery rhymes. It had been repapered for Penny, four years before. She had chosen the paper herself. She knew every single person on it, every animal, every tree. How often she had looked at Jack and Jill always going up the hill, and how often she had wondered how there could possibly be room in the Old Woman's Shoe for all the children that were playing around it!

She opened the built-in toy cupboard and looked inside. It was empty now, for every toy had been packed in boxes. There were shelves there that had held trains and bricks and dolls.

"I wish you were coming with us, toy cupboard!" said Penny. "I've always loved you. It was always so exciting every morning to open your doors and see my toys looking at me again. And it has always been such fun to creep right inside you and shut the door and pretend I was a toy too!"

Penny was the baby of the family. Rory was a big boy now, fourteen years old, black-haired and brown-eyed. Sheila was thirteen, curly-haired and pretty. Benjy, dreamy old Benjy, who loved and understood all wild creatures so well, was two years younger — and then came Penny, three years behind him! She tried to be grown-up, so that the others would let her into their secrets and take her about with them, but it was sometimes rather difficult.

She looked round. She was quite alone. Rory and Sheila were saying goodbye to each room in turn. She could hear them in the spare-room now. Sheila was talking to Rory.

"Do you remember counting the cracks in the ceiling when we were both in here with measles? There's one crack over in that corner that looks exactly like a bear with horns — look, there it is."

Penny heard the two of them talking. She stared at the toy cupboard.

Should she just get inside the last time, and pretend she was a toy? Nobody would know.

She squashed herself in. It wasn't so easy now as it used to be, for Penny had grown. She shut the doors and peeped through the crack — and at once it seemed as if she was only three or four years old again!

"I'm a big doll, peeping through the crack in the door at the children playing in the nursery!" she said to herself. "What a funny feeling it is!"

Before she could get out again, Benjy came into the room. He looked round. Where were the others?

"Sheila! Rory!" he called. "Where are you? Penny!"

Penny didn't answer. She was too afraid of being called a baby to come out and show herself. She stayed as quiet as a mouse in the cupboard.

The other two came running in. They carried coats and hats for everyone. "Mother says we are to come at once," said Sheila. "Here are your things, Benjy. Where's Penny? Now wherever has she gone?"

Penny didn't move. She stared out through the crack. It was funny to see the others through the narrow chink. They looked different somehow.

The three children put on their coats. Mother came in. "Are you ready?" she said. "Where's Penny?"

Nobody knew. "Oh dear!" said Mother. "Wherever can she have got to?"

Penny was suddenly afraid that everyone would go without her. She pushed open the doors of the toy cupboard and looked out. Benjy almost jumped out of his skin with surprise.

"I'm here," said Penny, in a small voice.

Everyone burst into laughter. They all knew Penny's old trick of getting into the toy cupboard and pretending to be a doll. Sheila was just going to call her a baby when she saw Penny's red face and stopped.

"Come along," she said, holding out her hand. "Daddy's waiting for us. Hurry, Penny!"

Penny squeezed herself out and put on her coat in silence. All the children went downstairs, their feet clattering loudly on the bare stairs. The house seemed suddenly strange and unfriendly. It would soon belong to somebody else.

They crowded into the car. Daddy and Mummy looked up at the tall house, remembering many things. They had had happy times there. The children had grown up there. It was sad to leave — but how happy to be going to a lovely farmhouse set on a hill!

The engine of the car started up. They were off!

"Goodbye!" cried the children, waving to the old house. "We may perhaps call in and see you sometime in the future. Goodbye! We're off to Willow Farm, Willow Farm, Willow Farm!"

And off they went, purring through the London streets on their way to a new life down in the heart of the country.

CHAPTER II

WILLOW FARM

NOTHING is quite so exciting as moving house. Everything is strange and thrilling and upside-down. Stairs sound different. Meals are taken just anywhere, at all kinds of queer times. Furniture stands about in odd places. The windows are like staring eyes with no eye-brows, because the curtains are not yet up.

It was like that at Willow Farm when the family moved in. Penny thought it was too exciting for words. Everything was fun. It was fun rushing through the different counties to get to Willow Farm. It was fun to pass Cherry Tree Farm on the way and stop for a few minutes' chat with Uncle Tim and Auntie Bess.

"Wouldn't you like to get rid of the children for a few days and let them stay with us?" asked Aunt Bess. But for once the children did not smile at the idea of staying at their beloved Cherry Tree Farm.

They looked quite dismayed. Mother laughed. "Look at their faces!" she said. "No thank you, Bess dear — they are all looking forward so much to settling in at Willow Farm. It is true that they will get in the way and be under my feet all the time — but . . ."

"Oh Mummy, we won't!" cried Penny. Then she saw the twinkle in her mother's eye and laughed.

"Aunt Bess, we love Cherry Tree Farm, but we wouldn't miss arriving at Willow Farm, our own farm, today, for worlds!" said Benjy.

"Have you seen Tammylan lately?" asked Rory.

"The wild man?" said Aunt Bess. "Yes — let me see, we

saw him last week, didn't we? He wanted to know when you were coming, and said he would love to see you all again."

"Oh good," said Benjy, pleased. "He's got my pet squirrel for me. He's been keeping it for me while I was at school. I shall love to see Scamper again."

"Well, we mustn't stay longer," said their father. "Goodbye, Tim, goodbye, Bess. We'll come over sometime and let you know how things go."

Off they went through the lanes. The hedges were just beginning to leaf here and there. Celandine turned smiling, polished faces up to the sun. Primroses sat in rosettes of green leaves. Spring was really beginning!

The car turned a corner and came in sight of a rounded hill. Glowing in the afternoon sun was an old farmhouse built of warm red bricks. It had a thatched roof, as had Cherry Tree Farm, and this shone a deep golden-brown colour, for it had been re-thatched for the new owners.

"Willow Farm!" shouted Rory, and he stood up in the car. "Willow Farm! Our farm!"

Benjy went red with pleasure. Sheila stared in silence. Penny gave little squeaks, one after the other. All the children gazed with pride and delight on their new home.

It was a lovely old place, three hundred years old, long and rambling, with queer tall chimneys, and brown beams that showed in the walls.

The windows were leaded, and there were green shutters outside each. The old front door was made of heavy brown oak, and had a curious little thatched porch above it, in which stood an old bench. Not far from the front door was the old well, rather like a Jack and Jill well. The water was not used now, but in the olden days there had been a bucket to let up and down.

Little gabled windows jutted from the thatch. The children stared up at them, wondering which windows belonged to their bedrooms. How lovely to peep out from those little windows in the early morning, and see the green fields and distant woods and silver streams!

Many streams flowed in and about Willow Farm. Along the banks grew the many many willows that gave the farm its pretty name. In the spring-time the pussy willows broke into gold when the catkins became the lovely golden palm. Other kinds of willows grew there too, and the bees murmured in them all day long later on in the spring-time.

"Daddy! Hurry up!" cried Rory. "Oh, let's get to the farm quickly!"

The car ran down a winding lane, with high hedges each side — then up on to the hillside beside a gurgling stream. Then into a big gateway, whose great wooden gates always stood open.

And there they were at the farmhouse door! Behind the farmhouse were the farm-buildings — great barns with old old roofs, big sheds, stables and pens. The farmyard lay at the back too, and here the hens pecked about all day long.

The children tumbled out of the car in great excitement. They rushed to the door — but it was shut. Their father came to open it with a very large key. The children laughed to see it.

The door was thrown open and the children gazed into a large hall, with great beams in the rather low ceiling, and red, uneven tiles on the floor. Beyond lay open doors leading to the fine old kitchen and other rooms. How marvellous to explore them all while they were empty, and to arrange everything in them!

Everyone trooped in, chattering and exclaiming in

378

delight. The place was spotless, for two village-women had been in to rub and scrub the whole week. The windows shone. The floors shone. The old oak cupboards, built into the walls, glowed with polish and age.

"Mummy! This farmhouse has such a happy, friendly feeling!" said Benjy, slipping his arm through his mother's. "People have been happy here. I can feel it."

So could they all. It was lovely to stand there and feel the happiness of the old house around them. It seemed glad to have them, glad to welcome them.

"Some houses have a horrid feeling in them," said Sheila. "I remember once going to see somebody in an

379

old house down at the seaside, Mummy—and I was glad to come away. It made me feel unhappy. But other houses feel so content and friendly—like this one."

"Yes—I think people have loved Willow Farm very much, and have worked hard and been happy here," said their mother. "I hope we shall work hard too and be happy. It takes a lot of time and hard work to make a farm pay, you know, children. We must all do our bit."

"Of course!" said Rory. "I'm going to work like anything! I learnt quite a lot on Uncle's farm last year, I can tell you!"

"Let's go all over the house!" said Penny running to the stairs. They ran up to a wide landing. There were seven rooms upstairs, one fine big room that their mother and father were going to have, one big room for the children's own playroom, a small room for Rory, a tiny one for Benjy, a bigger one for the two girls, a spare-room for friends, and a room for Harriet, the cook, who was coming in the next day.

And over the bedrooms was a queer attic, right under the thatch itself. It was reached by a funny iron ladder that slid up and down. The children went up it in excitement.

"Oooh!" said Penny, when she saw the dark cobwebby loft. "It smells queer. Oh look—this is the thatch itself. Put your torch on, Rory—have you got it?"

Rory had. He took it out of his pocket and switched it on. The children gazed round the loft. They could only stand upright where the roof arched. They touched the thatch. It was made of straw. There was nothing between them and the sky but the thick straw—no plaster, no tiles—just the straw.

"The thatcher hasn't finished thatching the kitchen

end of the house," said Sheila. "I heard Daddy say so. We'll be able to see exactly how he does it. Isn't it fun to be going to live in a thatched house? We shall be lovely and warm in the winter-time!"

The children climbed down the loft ladder. Rory slid it back into place.

"I do like all these black beams," he said, looking round. "I think they look exciting. Daddy says they came from old wooden ships. When the ships were broken up, the beams were used in houses—so once upon a time all the wooden part of Willow Farm was sailing on the sea!"

"I like to think that," said Benjy, touching the black oak beam near him. "Funny old beam—once you knew the fishes in the sea, and you creaked as great waves splashed over you. Now you live in a house, and listen to people's feet going up and down the stairs."

The others laughed. "You do say odd things, Benjy," said Rory. "Come on—let's go down. I want to see the rooms below too."

Down they went. The big dark hall they had already seen. There was a large room that Mummy said would be a lounge or living-room. It had an enormous stone fireplace. Rory looked up it. He could stand on the hearth and look right up the chimney, and see the sky at the top. It was really enormous.

"I could climb up this chimney!" said Rory, in surprise.

"Little boys used to," said Daddy, with a laugh. "Yes—you may well stare. It's quite true. In the days when most houses had these big fire-places and chimneys, little boys used to be forced to go up them to sweep them."

"I do wish I could climb up and sweep it when it needs it," said Rory, longingly.

"You might want to do it for fun, but you wouldn't

want to do it every day of your life!" said his father.

The children went into the next room. It was a long dining-room, panelled with oak. "I wonder if there are any sliding panels!" said Benjy, at once. He loved reading stories of hidden treasure, and in the last one he had read there had been a most exciting sliding oak panel, behind which a safe had been hidden.

"The one over there by the door looks as if it might slide!" said his father. Benjy stared at it. Yes—it really didn't seem to fit quite as well as the others. It *might* slide back! In great excitement he tried it.

And it did slide back! Very silently, very neatly it slid back behind the next panel. Benjy gave a yell.

"Daddy! Look!"

And then everyone laughed—for behind the sliding panel were four electric light switches! The people who had lived at Willow Farm before had hidden their switches there, rather than spoil the look of the panelling by the door! So poor Benjy didn't find hidden treasure or anything exciting.

The kitchen was a very big room indeed, with plenty of leaded windows, opening on to the farmyard at the back. It had an enormous door that swung open with a creak. The sinking sun streamed through it.

"It's got the biggest fireplace of all!" said Sheila.

"Yes—many a fine meal has been cooked there!" said her father. "And look here—at the side is a funny bread-oven, going right into the thick wall. Harriet will be able to bake her bread there!"

"I like the uneven floor," said Penny, dancing about over it. "All these nice red tiles, higgledy-piggledy. And I like the great old beams across the ceiling. Just look at all the hooks and nails, Mummy!"

Everyone gazed up at the big beams, and saw the rows of hooks and nails there.

"That is where people have hung up hams and onions, herbs and spices," said Mummy. "It's a shame to see all the kitchen beams empty and bare—but never mind, soon Harriet will use them, and then our kitchen will look a most exciting place!"

Off the kitchen was a great cool room with stone shelves—the dairy. Here the milk was set for the cream to form, and the eggs were washed, graded and counted. The butter-churn was there too. All the children tried their hands at it.

"Oh Mummy! Won't it be fun to bring in the eggs and sort them, and to make the butter, and see the cream coming on the big bowls of milk!" cried Penny. She danced about again and fell over an uneven tile in the floor.

"Well, it's a good thing you weren't carrying eggs just at that moment!" said Sheila. "That would have been the end of them!"

There was just one more room downstairs — a tiny cubby-hole of a room, panelled in black oak — and Daddy said that was to be his study and nobody was to use it except himself.

"Here I shall keep my accounts and find out if Willow Farm is paying or not!" he said.

"Of *course* it will pay!" cried Rory.

"Farming isn't so easy as all that," said his father. "You wait and see!"

CHAPTER III

THE FIRST DAY

BENJY awoke first the next morning. The sun came in at his window, and when he opened his eyes he saw a golden pattern of sunlight on the wall. He remembered at once where he was, and sat up in delight.

"It's our first real day at Willow Farm!" he thought. "I shall see Tammylan today—and Scamper. I wonder if Rory is awake."

He slipped into Rory's room, but Rory was still fast asleep. So Benjy put on his clothes and went downstairs all by himself. He let himself out into the farmyard through the big kitchen door. The early morning sun was pale and had little warmth in it, but it was lovely to see it.

"I wish there were hens and ducks clucking and quacking," thought Benjy. "But there soon will be. My word, how the birds are singing!"

The early morning chorus sounded loudly about Benjy's ears as he wandered round the farm. The chaffinches carolled merrily — "chip-chip-chip-cherry-erry-erry, chippy-ooEEEar!" they sang madly. Benjy whistled the song after them.

Blackbirds were sitting at the tops of trees singing slowly and solemnly to themselves, listening to their own tunes. Thrushes sang joyfully, repeating their musical sentences over and over again.

"Ju-dee, Ju-dee, Ju-dee!" sang one thrush.

"Mind how you do it, mind how you do it!" called another, as Benjy jumped over a puddle and splashed himself. The boy laughed.

385

"Soon the swallows will be back," he thought. "I wonder if they'll build in the barn. It will be lovely if they do. After all, their real name is barn-swallow — and we have lots of barns. I must peep in and see if I can spy any old nests."

It was too dark in the barn to see if the remains of old swallows' nests were on the rafters high in the roof. But Benjy saw the old nests of house-martins against the walls of the farmhouse. Two or three were just below his own window!

"I say — how lovely if they come back next month and build again there," thought Benjy, gazing up at his little jutting-out window, tucked so cosily into the thatch. "I shall hear their pretty twittering, and see the baby martins peeping out of the mud-nests. I hope they come back soon."

Far in the distance the shepherd moved in the fields. He was doing something to one of the sheep. Nobody else seemed to be about at all. There were no animals or birds to see to, nothing to feed.

But wait — somebody *was* about! Benjy saw the end of a ladder suddenly appearing round the corner of the farmhouse. Who could be carrying it?

A man came round the corner, whistling softly. He saw Benjy and stopped.

"Good morning, young sir," he said.

"Good morning," said Benjy. "Who are you?"

"I'm Bill the thatcher," said the man. "I'm just thatching the house for you — and after that I'm going to take a hand on the farm to get you all going!"

"Oh, that's fine!" said Benjy, pleased, for he liked the look of the man very much. His face was burnt as brown as an oak-apple, and his eyes were like bits of blue china

386

in his brown face. They twinkled all the time.

Bill took the ladder to the kitchen end of the farmhouse. Lying on the ground nearby was a great heap of straw.

"I do wish I could thatch a roof," said Benjy. "You know, we learn all sorts of things at school, Bill — like what happened at the battle of Crecy and things like that — and yet nobody thinks of teaching us how to do really useful and exciting things like thatching a roof. Think how good it would be if I could say to my father — 'Let *me* thatch the roof, Daddy!' or 'Let *me* clean out the duck-pond!' Or, 'Let *me* sweep the chimney!'"

Bill laughed. "Well, you come and watch me do a bit of thatching," he said. "Then maybe next year when the old summer-house over there wants patching up with straw, you'll be able to do it yourself!"

Bill had a great many willow-sticks that he had cut on his way to Willow Farm that morning. He began to cut them into short strips and to sharpen the ends. Benjy watched him. "What do you want those for?" he asked.

"To peg down the straw thatch near the edge, young sir," said Bill. "Look and see the piece I've finished."

Benjy looked, and saw that the thatcher had made a very neat edging near the bottom of the thatched roof. "It looks rather like an embroidered pattern!" he said. "Do you put it there just to look pretty?"

"Oh no," said the thatcher. "The straw would work loose if it wasn't held towards the bottom like that — but the pattern is one used by many thatchers. My father used it, and his father before him. Look at the top of the roof too — see the pattern there? Ah, thatching isn't so easy as it looks — it's a job that goes in families and has to be learnt when you're a boy."

"Oh good," said Benjy, glad that he was still a boy and

could learn to thatch. "I say, do you think you could just wait till I call the others? They'd love to see you do the thatching."

"You go and get the others, but I'll not wait," said the thatcher, going up the ladder with a heavy load of straw on his shoulder. "A minute here and a minute there— that's no use when you've work to do. I don't wait about. I'll be at work all day and you'll have plenty of time to see me."

At that moment the other three came out. They saw Benjy and rushed at him. "Why didn't you wake us, you mean thing? You've been up ages, haven't you?"

"Ages," said Benjy. "Everything's lovely! Look—that's the thatcher. His name's Bill. See those willow-twigs he's been sharpening—they're for making that fine pattern to hold down the straw at the edges of the roof."

"You *have* been learning a lot!" said Rory, with a laugh. "Tell us how a roof is thatched, Benjy!"

"Well," said Benjy, making it all up quickly in his head, "the thatcher pulls off all the straw first—and then he . . ."

The thatcher gave a shout of laughter. Benjy stared at him. "What's the matter?" he asked.

"I'd just like to set you to work thatching!" he chuckled. "My, you'd give yourself a job! Now look what I do—I pull out about six or seven inches of this old rotten straw —see—and work in handfuls of the new—about twelve inches thick. That'll work down flatter when the rain comes. You don't need to pull off all the old straw—that would be a real waste. When a roof is re-thatched we just pull out what's no use and pack in the new."

"Do you mean to say then, that there is straw in our roof that may have been there for years and years and years?" asked Rory, in surprise.

"Maybe," said the thatcher, with a grin, as he swiftly pulled and pushed with his strong hands, working in the new straw deftly and surely. "Ah, and you'd be surprised the things I've found hidden in old thatch—boxes of old coins, bits of stolen jewellery, bags of rubbish—a thatched roof was a favourite hiding-place in the old days."

The children stared at him, open-mouthed. This was marvellous! "Did you find anything in *our* thatch?" asked Penny hopefully.

"Not a thing," said Bill. "It's the third time I've thatched and patched this roof—I don't reckon I'll find anything this time if I didn't find it the first time! Now look – isn't that somebody calling you?"

It was the children's father, looking for them to come to breakfast. They left the thatcher and hurried indoors, full of what Bill had said. Penny thought it must be the most exciting thing in the world to be somebody who might at any moment find treasure in a roof. She made up her mind to go up into the loft above her bedroom and poke about in the thatch there. She might find something that the thatcher had missed!

"You must get out of our way this morning," said their mother, as they finished up their breakfast with bread and marmalade. "The other vans are coming and we shall be very busy."

"Oh – can't we stay and help?" said Benjy, disappointed. "I do like seeing the furniture being carried up the stairs, Mummy."

"Well, the men don't feel quite so excited about that as you," said Mummy. "No – I shall make you up a picnic lunch – and you can go and find Tammylan!"

There were loud cheers then! Everyone wanted to see Tammylan.

"Good," said Benjy, pleased. "I'd like that better than anything. And it will be fun to come back and see all the rooms with their furniture in, looking so nice and homey."

"Oh, you won't find that yet!" said his mother, laughing. "It will be a week or two before we are straight. Now, what would you like for your picnic lunch, I wonder? I'll make you some potted meat sandwiches, and you can take some cake and a packet of biscuits. There is a big bottle of milk between you too, if you like."

Before they started off to find Tammylan the girls made the beds and the boys helped to wash up and to cut the sandwiches. Just as they were packing the things into two bags for the boys to carry, there came the rumbling of the big removal vans up the lane.

"Just in time," said their mother, running to the door. "Now we shall be able to get rid of you children for a while whilst the men unload!"

The children got their hats and coats and went outside the big front door. The first van drew up outside and the men jumped down. They opened the doors at the back and the children gazed inside and saw all the furniture they knew so well.

"There's the nursery table!" yelled Penny.

"And there's the old bookcase," said Rory. "I suppose Mummy has got to tell the men which room everything's to go into. I half wish we could stop and help."

"Go along now!" cried his mother. "Don't wait about there in the cold!"

The children set off, looking behind every now and again. They decided to go over the top of Willow Hill and across Christmas Common to Tammylan's cave. It was about two miles away. When they reached the top of the hill they looked down at Willow Farm. It stood firmly in the hillside, smoke curling up from the kitchen chimney. It looked alive now, with people running about and smoke coming from the chimney.

Then over the hill went the four children on their way to old Tammylan. They sang as they went, for they were happy. It was holiday time. The spring and summer were coming. They had a home in the country instead of in London. And Tammylan could be seen as often as they liked! They had missed him so much.

They rounded a small hill. Bracken and heather grew there, and birch trees waved lacy twigs in the wind. The

391

children made their way to a spot they knew well.

It was a cave in the hillside. In the summer-time tall fronds of green bracken hid the entrance, but now only the broken, russet-brown remains of last year's bracken showed. The new bracken had not even begun growing. Heather dropped its big tufts from the top edge of the cave.

The children stood outside and called. "Tammylan! Tammylan!"

"Let's go inside," said Rory. "I'm sure he's not there — but he *might* be fast asleep!"

"Don't be silly!" said Benjy, scornfully. "Why, old Tammylan wakes if a mouse sits up and washes his whiskers! He would have heard us coming round the hill long ago if he'd been here."

They went into the cave. It was exciting to be back there again. It opened out widely inside. The ceiling rose high, dark and rocky.

"Here's his bed," said Rory, sitting down on a rocky ledge, on which Tammylan had put layers of heather and bracken. "And look — he still keeps his tin plates and things on the same shelf."

The children looked at the little rocky shelf opposite the bed. On it, clean and neatly arranged, were Tammylan's few possessions.

"There is the stool that Rory and I made for Tammylan for Christmas!" said Benjy, in delight. "Look — see the squirrels I carved round the edge!"

"And here is the blanket that Sheila and I knitted for him," said Penny, patting a neatly folded blanket at the foot of the bed of heather and bracken. "I do hope he found it nice and warm this cold winter!"

"I wonder if the little spring that gives Tammylan his drinking-water still wells up at the back of the cave," said Rory. He went to see. He flashed his torch into the darkness there, and then gave a squeal.

"What's the matter?" asked Benjy, in surprise.

"Nothing much — except that one of Tammylan's friends is here!" said Rory, with a laugh. The others came quietly to see. Tammylan had taught them to move silently when they wanted to see animals or birds.

Lying by the tiny spring that welled up from the rocky floor, was a hare. Its enormous eyes looked up patiently at the children. It could not move.

"Look — his back legs have been broken," said Sheila, sadly. "Tammylan is trying to mend them. He has put them into splints. Poor hare — he must somehow have been caught in a trap."

The children gazed down at the patient hare. It dipped its nose into the springing water and lapped a little. Benjy felt sure that it was in pain.

Penny wanted to stroke it but Benjy wouldn't let her. "No hurt animal likes to be touched," he said. "Leave it alone, Penny."

"Listen!" said Sheila, suddenly. "I can hear Tammylan I think!"

They listened — and they all knew at once that it was dear old Tammylan. No one else had that sweet clear whistle, no one else in the world could flute like a blackbird, or whistle like a blackcap! The children all rushed to the cave entrance.

"Tammylan!" they shouted. "Tammylan! We're here!"

CHAPTER IV

GOOD OLD TAMMYLAN!

TAMMYLAN was coming along up the hillside, his arms full of green stuff and roots. He dropped it all when he saw the children, and a broad smile spread across his brown face. His bright eyes twinkled like the sparkles on a stream as the children flung themselves at him and hugged him.

"Well, well, well," he said, "What a storm of children breaking over me! Rory, how you've grown! Sheila, let me have a look at you! Benjy — dear old Benjy, I've thought of you so often. And my dear little Penny — not so very little now — quite grown-up!"

Chattering and laughing, the five of them sat down on a heathery bank. They were all delighted to see Tammylan again. He was a person they trusted absolutely. He would always do the right thing, never misunderstand them, always be their trusted friend. He was as natural as the animals he loved so much, as gay as the birds, as wise as the hills around. Oh, it was good to see Tammylan again!

"Tammylan, have you seen Willow Farm?" cried Penny. "Isn't it lovely?"

"It's a fine place," said Tammylan. "And a good farm too. With hard work and a bit of luck you should all do well there. The land's good. The fields are well-sheltered just where they need it, and it has always had a name for doing well with its stock. You'll all help, I suppose?"

"Of course!" said Rory. "We boys are doing lessons with the vicar again this term — and the girls are going to as well! So we shall have all our spare-time for the farm

394

and Saturdays and Sundays as well. Aren't we lucky, Tammylan?"

"Very," said their friend. "Well, if you need any help at any time, come to me. I can work as hard as anybody, you know—and I know many strange medicines to help sick creatures."

"Oh, Tammylan—we saw that poor hare in your cave," said Benjy, remembering. "Will it get better?"

"If it lives till tonight, it will mend," said Tammylan. "I have some roots here that I want to pound and mix with something else. If I can get the hare to take the mixture, it will deaden the pain and help it to live. An animal who is badly shocked, or who suffers great pain dies very easily. Poor little hare—it is a great friend of mine. You have seen him before, Benjy."

"Oh—is it the hare who came so often to your cave last year?" asked Benjy, sadly. "He was such a dear—so swift-running, and so gentle. I did love him. What happened to hurt him so badly, Tammylan?"

"I don't know," said the wild man. "It almost looks as if he had been hit hard with a stick, though I should not have thought anyone could have got near enough to him to do that. I don't know how he dragged himself here to me, poor thing. He only had his front legs to crawl with."

Penny was almost in tears. She watched the wild man pound up some roots with a heavy stone. He mixed the juice with a fine brown powder and stirred the two together. Then he went into his cave, followed by the children.

The hare gazed up at the wild man with big, pained eyes. Tammylan knelt down and took the soft head gently in his left hand. He opened the slack mouth and deftly thrust in a soft pellet of his curious mixture. He shut the

395

hare's mouth and held it. The creature struggled weakly and then swallowed.

Tammylan let go the hare's mouth, and ran his strong brown fingers down the back of the creature's head. "You'll feel better in a little while," he said in his soft voice.

They all went out into the open air again. Benjy asked a question that had been on the tip of his tongue for some time.

"Tammylan — where's Scamper?"

"Well, well — to think I hadn't mentioned your squirrel before!" said the wild man with a laugh. "Scamper is

396

doing exactly what his name says—scampering about the trees with all the other squirrels. He stayed with me in the cave in the cold weather, hardly stirring—but this last week it has been warm, and the little creature has often gone to play in the trees with his cousins."

"Oh," said Benjy, disappointed. "Isn't he tame any more then?"

"Of course!" said Tammylan. "You'll see him in a minute or two. I'll whistle him!"

Tammylan gave a curiously piercing whistle, loud and musical.

"It's a bit like an otter's whistle," said Benjy, remembering a night he had spent with Tammylan when he had heard otters whistling in the river to one another. "I hope Scamper hears you, Tammylan."

"He will hear me, no matter in what part of the woods he is!" said Tammylan. The wild man was right! In about half a minute Benjy gave a shout.

"Look! There comes Scamper up the hillside, look!" Sure enough they could all see the little brown squirrel bounding gracefully up the hill, his bushy tail streaming out behind him. He rushed straight up to the little group, gave a snicker of joy and leapt up to Benjy's shoulder!

"Oh you dear little thing, you've remembered me after three months!" said Benjy, joyfully. "I wondered if you would. Oh, Tammylan, isn't he lovely? He's grown—and his tail is magnificent!"

The squirrel made some funny little chattering noises, and gently bit Benjy's ear. He ran round and round the boy's neck, then up and down his back and then sat on the very top of his head! Everybody laughed.

"He is certainly delighted to see you, Benjy," said Tammylan. Scamper looked at the wild man, leapt to his shoulder and then back to Benjy again. It was almost as if he said "I'm pleased to see Benjy, but I'm very fond of you too, Tammylan!"

"Do you think he will come back to Willow Farm with me?" asked Benjy. "I do want him to."

"Oh yes," said the wild man. "But you mustn't mind if he goes off by himself at times, Benjy. He loves his own kind, you know. I will teach you the whistle I keep specially for him, and then he will always come to you when you want him."

"I'm jolly hungry," said Penny, suddenly. "We've brought a picnic lunch, Tammylan. You'll share it with us, won't you?"

"Of course," said Tammylan. "Come with me. I know a warm and sheltered spot out of this cold March wind. It will be April next week, and then the sun will really begin to feel hot!"

He took them to a spot above his cave. Here there was a kind of hollow in the hillside, quite out of the wind, where the sun poured down. Primroses grew there by the hundred, and later on the cowslips nodded there. The children sat down on some old bracken and basked like cats in the sun.

"Lovely!" said Benjy. "Hurry up with the food, Rory."

They ate a good dinner, and talked nineteen to the dozen all the time to Tammylan, telling him about school and London, and Willow Farm. Then Tammylan in his turn told them his news.

"It's not so exciting as yours," he said, "because I have lived quietly here in my cave since you left. I was very glad of your woolly blanket, Sheila and Penny, when that cold snap came—and as for your carved stool, Rory and Benjy, I really don't know what I should have done

398

without it! I have used it as a table, and as a stool every day!"

"Good," said the children, pleased. "Now, Tammylan, what animals have you had for company since we saw you last?"

"Well, as you know, a great many of them sleep the winter away," said Tammylan. "But the rabbits have been in to see me a great deal, and have skipped round my cave merrily. They soon disappeared when the weasel came though!"

"*Weasel!*" said Benjy, astonished. "Was a weasel tame enough to visit you?"

"Yes," said Tammylan. "I was pleased to see him too, for he was a fine little fellow. He smelt the smell of rabbits and that is how he first came into my cave. You'd have liked him, Benjy. He used to bound about like a little clown."

"Who else came to see you?" asked Penny, wishing that she had lived with Tammylan in his cave for the last three months!

"Plenty of birds," said Tammylan. "The moorhens often came. Thrushes, robins, blackbirds, chaffinches— they all hopped in at times, and for a whole month a robin slept here in the cave with me."

"Did the fox come again?" asked Rory, remembering the hunted fox to whom Tammylan had given shelter one winter's day when they had all been there.

"Yes," said Tammylan. "He comes often. He is a most beautiful creature. He always goes straight to the little water-spring at the back of the cave and laps two or three drops from it, almost as if he remembers each time how the waters helped him when he was so weary with being hunted!"

The children stayed talking in the warm hollow until almost tea-time. Then they got up and stretched their legs.

"We promised Mummy we would be back at tea-time," said Sheila. "We must go. Come and see us at Willow Farm, Tammylan, won't you? We'll be awfully busy soon, and may not have time to come and see you every day, though we'd love to. But you can come and see us whenever you like. Daddy and Mummy will love to see you — and we do want to show you everything at Willow Farm."

The children said goodbye to the wild man and left. Before they went they slipped softly into the cave to have a look at the hare.

Rory shone his torch down on to it.

"Oh, it looks better," he said, pleased. "Its eyes haven't got that hurt, glassy look. I believe it will mend. Poor hare — don't look so sad. One day soon you will be bounding over the fields again, as swiftly as the wind."

"I doubt that," said Tammylan. "He will never run fast again. I shall have to keep him as a pet. He will limp for the rest of his life. But he will be happy here with me if I can tame him."

The children ran home over Christmas Common, came to the top of Willow Hill and ran down it to their home. It was nice to come home to Willow Farm. The vans had gone. Bits of straw blew about in the yard. Smoke came from three chimneys now instead of one. Bill the thatcher was talking to their father in the yard. Somebody was singing in the kitchen.

"It really feels like home," said Sheila, running in at the kitchen door. She stopped when she saw somebody strange there.

A plump, red-cheeked woman smiled at her. "Come

along in," she said. "I'm Harriet. I've been wanting to see you children all day!"

The children all came in. They liked the look of Harriet. A young girl of about fifteen was busy laying a tea-tray. She glanced shyly at the children.

"That's Fanny, my niece," said Harriet. "She's coming in daily to help."

"I'm Sheila, and this is my sister Penny," said Sheila. "And that's Rory, the eldest, and this is Benjy. Is that our tea being got ready?"

"It is," said Harriet. "Your mother is upstairs putting things to rights, if you want her. She was wondering if you were back."

The children ran to find their mother. They peeped into each room downstairs. Oh, how different they looked now, with all the familiar chairs and tables in them!

The children went upstairs. They looked into their bedrooms. Not only were their beds there now but their own chests and chairs and bookcases! Penny's dolls' cot stood beside her own little bed. The big ship that Rory had once made stood proudly on his mantelpiece.

"Oh, it all looks lovely!" said the children. "Mummy! Where are you?"

"Here," said Mummy, from the playroom. The children rushed in. The playroom looked fine too with all their own chairs and the two old nursery tables. The old rocking chair was there too, the two dolls' houses, the fort, and a great pile of old toy animals belonging to Penny and Benjy.

"This is going to be a lovely room for us!" said Benjy, staring out of the window down the hill to where the silver streams gleamed in the dying sun. "Mummy, how quick you've been to get everything ready like this!"

"Well, it may look as if it's ready," said his mother, with a laugh. "But it isn't really. We must put the rugs down tomorrow—and the pictures up—and you must sort out your books and put them into your bookcases, and Penny must arrange her toys in the cupboard over there. There's a lot to do yet."

"Well, we shall love doing it!" said Rory, thinking with joy of arranging all his belongings in his new bedroom. "Everything's fun at Willow Farm!"

CHAPTER V

A SURPRISE FOR PENNY

THE next few days were great fun. The children arranged all their things to their liking. They made friends with Harriet and Fanny—though Fanny at first was too shy to say a word! Harriet was very jolly, and nearly always had some titbit ready for the children when they trooped into the kitchen.

Bill the thatcher finished the roof, and did not find anything exciting in the thatch at all, much to Penny's disappointment.

"I'm glad that job's finished," he said. "Now I can get on to the farm-work. There's a lot of sowing to be done—and I must get the garden ready for your mother. She wants to grow all kinds of things there!"

"Isn't there anything *we* can do?" asked Rory. "I want to WORK! I wish we could get in our hens and ducks and pigs and cows and things—then we could help to look after them."

The children asked their parents when the birds and animals of the farm were coming.

"Soon," said their father. "Your uncle Tim is bringing over the poultry tomorrow. The hen-houses are ready now. Which of you is going to take care of the hens?"

"I will," said Sheila at once. "I like hens—though I like ducks better. Let me take care of the hens, Daddy."

"Well, Sheila, if you do, you must really learn about them properly," said her father. "It was all very well at Cherry Tree Farm for you and others to throw corn to the hens when you felt like it, and go and find nice warm

403

eggs to carry in to your Aunt Bess—but if you are really and truly going to see to the hens and make them your special care, you will have to know quite a lot."

"I see, Daddy," said Sheila. "Well—have you got a book about them?"

"I've two or three," said Daddy. "I'll get them for you."

"Sheila, could I help with the hens too?" asked Penny. "I want to do something. The boys say they are going to do the pigs and milk the cows when they come."

Sheila badly wanted to manage the hens entirely by herself, but when she saw Penny's small, earnest face her heart melted.

"Well," she said, "yes, you can. You can read the books too."

Penny was overjoyed. She felt tremendously important. She was going to read books about poultry-keeping! She longed to tell somebody that. She would tell Tammylan as soon as ever she saw him.

Daddy fetched them the books. They looked very grown-up and rather dull. But Sheila and Penny didn't mind. Now they would know all about hens! Sheila handed Penny the one that looked the easiest. It had pictures of hens inside.

"Daddy, you'll let us see to the pigs when they come, won't you?" asked Benjy. "And milk the cows too. We can clean out the sheds quite well. I did it once or twice at Cherry Tree Farm."

"You can try," said Daddy. "Soon the farm will be working properly—cows in the fields, pigs in the sty, horses in the stable, hens and ducks running about, butter being made, sheep being dipped—my word, what a busy life we shall lead! And we shall all have breakfast at seven o'clock in the morning!"

"Goodness!" said Sheila, who was a lie-abed. "That means getting up at half-past six!"

"Yes—and going to bed early too," said her father. "Farmers have to be up and about soon after dawn—and they can't be up early if they go to bed late!"

None of the children liked the idea of going to bed early. But still, if they were going to be farmers, they must do as farmers did!

Sheila and Penny went up to the playroom with the hen books. Penny struggled hard with the reading. She could read very well indeed—but oh dear, what long words there were—and what a lot of chapters about things called incubators and brooders. She soon gave it up.

"Sheila," she said, in a small voice. "I really can't understand this book. Is yours any easier?"

Sheila was finding her book dreadfully difficult too. It seemed to be written for people who had kept hens for years, not for anybody just beginning. She felt that she wouldn't know how to feed them properly—she wouldn't know when a hen wanted to sit on eggs, she wouldn't know how to tell if they were ill.

But she wasn't going to tell that to Penny! So she looked up and smiled. "Oh, Penny dear," she said, "what a baby you are! *I'll* read the books, if you can't, and I'll tell you what they say. I can tell you in words that you'll understand."

Penny went red. "All right," she said. "You will just have to tell me."

The little girl was quite ashamed because she couldn't understand the books. She left the playroom and went downstairs. She thought she would go and talk to the old shepherd up on the hill. So off she went.

The sheep were peacefully grazing on the hillside.

Little lambs skipped about, and Penny laughed to see them. She wished and wished that she could have one of her own. She had fed some at Cherry Tree Farm from a baby's bottle, and how she had loved that!

"Really, I think lambs are much nicer than hens," said Penny to herself. "I know Sheila likes hens—but I do think they are a bit dull. They all seem exactly alike, somehow. Now, lambs are like people—all different."

She stood and watched the lambs skipping about. Then she looked at the sheep.

"It's a great pity that lambs grow into sheep," she thought. "Sheep are like hens—all exactly the same. I suppose the shepherd can tell one from the other—but I certainly couldn't!"

She looked to see where the shepherd was. He was at the top of the hill, where a rough fold had been made of wattle hurdles. Penny ran to it.

"Hallo," she said, when she came to the shepherd. "I've come to see you."

"Well, little missy," said the shepherd, leaning on his staff and looking at the little girl with eyes as grey as his hair. "And what's your name?"

"Penny," said Penny. "What's yours?"

"Davey," said the shepherd. "That's a funny name you've got. When you were small, I suppose they called you Ha'penny? Now you're Penny. When will you be Tuppence?"

Penny laughed. She liked Davey. "No, I didn't have those names," she said. "My real name is Penelope, but I'm called Penny for short."

"Well, I shall call you Tuppenny," said the shepherd. "A penny is too cheap!"

They both laughed. A big collie-dog came running up to them and licked Penny's hand. She patted him.

"That's my best dog, Rascal," said Davey. "He's a wonder with the sheep!"

"Is he really? What does he do to them, then?" asked Penny.

"Oh, you come along one day when I'm moving the sheep from one hill to another," said Davey. "Then you'll see what old Rascal does. Do you know, if I were ill and wanted my sheep taken from here to the top of the next hill, I've only got to tell Rascal—and before two hours had gone by, those sheep would all be safely down this hill and up the next!"

407

"Goodness!" said Penny. "I'd love to see him do that. Davey, there's another dog over there. What is his name?"

"That's Nancy," said Davey. "She's good too, but not so obedient as Rascal. And look, over there is Tinker. He's not a sheep-dog, but he's almost as good as the others."

"Rascal, Nancy and Tinker," said Penny, thinking what nice names they were. "Davey, is it easy to keep sheep?"

"Yes, if you know how," said Davey. "I've been doing it all my life, little Tuppenny, and I've made all the mistakes there are to be made—but there's not much I don't know about sheep now!"

"Do you know, I used to feed lambs out of a bottle at Cherry Tree Farm?" said Penny. "I did love it. I do wish I was like the Mary in the nursery rhyme who had a lamb of her own. I do so love lambs."

"Well, you come and have a look at this poor little lambie," said Davey, taking Penny's hand. "Now, if you'd been here six weeks ago I'd have asked you to take it and care for it, for in the lambing season I've no time for sickly lambs. Still, I've tried to do my best for this one."

He took Penny to a small fold in which lay one lamb. It was some weeks old, but was tiny, and very weakly.

"It's mother had three lambs," said the shepherd. "She liked two of them but she just wouldn't have anything to do with this one. So I took it away and gave it to another ewe whose lamb had died. But I had to skin the dead lamb first and cover this one with the hide."

"But what a funny thing to do!" cried Penny. "Why did you do that?"

"Because the mother would only take a lamb that smelt like hers," said Davey. "Well, she sniffed at this one,

408

covered with the skin of her dead lamb, and she took to it and mothered it."

"Oh, I'm glad," said Penny.

"Ah, but wait a bit," said Davey. "She mothered it for a week. Then she took a dislike to it and butted it away with her head every time it came near, poor thing. It was half-starved, and I had to bring it away and try to feed it by hand out of a bottle."

"Did it wear the skin of the dead lamb all the two weeks?" asked Penny.

"Oh no—as soon as the mother sheep took the lamb, I stripped off the skin," said Davey. "But there must be something about this wee thing that the ewes dislike. No one will feed it."

"Davey, I suppose I couldn't possibly have it for my own, could I?" asked Penny, her eyes sparkling. "I could get a baby's milk-bottle—and Harriet would let me have milk. Oh, do let me!"

"Well, I'll speak to your father," said the shepherd. "It would help me if you took it and cared for it. I've not much time now—and the lamb will die if it doesn't begin to grow a bit soon!"

Penny looked at the long-legged lamb in the fold. It had a little black face, a long wriggly tail, a thin little body, and legs just like her toy lamb at home.

"It's not a very pretty lamb," she said. "It looks sort of miserable. Lambs are always so full of spring and leap and frisk, aren't they—but this one isn't."

"That's because it isn't well," said Davey. "I'll talk to your father about it, Tuppenny. Ah—there he is. I'll have a word with him now. See—is that somebody calling you down there?"

It was Penny's mother. Penny rushed down the hill to

see what she wanted. "Mummy, Mummy!" she yelled, as soon as she got near, "Davey the shepherd says perhaps I may have a lamb of my own to feed. Oh, Mummy, do you suppose I can? Davey is going to talk to Daddy about it. He says the lamb will die if somebody doesn't take care of it properly."

Sheila overheard what Penny said. "I thought you were going to help with the hens," she said.

"So I will," said Penny. "But I do feel I shall understand one lamb better than a whole lot of hens, Sheila. Anyway, it won't take long to feed each day."

Penny's mother had called her in to make her bed. She had forgotten to do it. It was the rule that each of the children should make their own beds and tidy their own rooms.

Penny made her bed quickly and dusted and tidied her room. She looked out of the window to see if Daddy and the shepherd were still talking. No—daddy had left Davey and was now walking down to the farm.

Penny put her head out of the window. "Daddy!" she yelled. "Can I have the lamb?"

"Yes, if you'll really care for it properly," said her father. The little girl gave an enormous yell and rushed downstairs, nearly knocking over poor Fanny as she went. "I'm going to have a lamb!" she yelled to Fanny.

She tore up the hill as if a hundred dogs were after her. She meant to get that lamb before anybody changed their minds about it!

"What a whirlwind!" said Davey, as Penny raced up to him. "Well, you're to have the lamb. Mind you bring it up to me sometimes so that I can see how well it is growing."

"Oh, I will, I will," said Penny. "I'm going to buy it a feeding-bottle out of my own money."

"You needn't do that," said Davey. "You can have this one." He held out a feeding-bottle to Penny. It had a big teat through which the lamb could suck the milk just as a baby sucks from a bottle. "I've fed him this morning. Give him another bottle of milk at dinner-time, and another at tea-time. Just give him as much as Harriet can spare."

Penny took the bottle. Then Davey undid one of the hurdles of the fold and took up the lamb. He tied a rope loosely round its neck.

"He won't follow you till he knows you," he said. "Take him gently down to the farm. Ask your mother if you can keep him in the little orchard till he knows you. Then he'll keep by you and not wander, as you go about the farmyard."

Penny was most excited and joyful. She had always wanted a lamb of her very own. She wondered what she would call the little creature.

"I'll call it Skippetty," she said. "It isn't very skippetty now—but perhaps it soon will be."

She took hold of the rope and tried to lead the lamb down the hill. At first it held back and tugged at the rope as if it wanted a tug-of-war with Penny. But soon it followed her peacefully enough and once it even ran in front of her.

When she got down to the farm, the other three children came to stare in astonishment.

"What are you doing with that lamb?" asked Benjy. "What a dear little black-faced creature!"

"It's mine," said Penny, proudly. "Its name is Skippetty."

"Yours!" said Rory, in amazement. "Who gave it to you!"

"Davey the shepherd," said Penny. "He's awfully nice. He's got three dogs, Rascal, Nancy and Tinker—and he says when he moves the sheep, we are to go and watch how well his dogs work for him. He gave me this lamb for my own to look after because it is such a poor little thing and he hasn't got time for it."

"You *are* lucky!" said Benjy. "I like it almost as much as I like Scamper."

Scamper was on his shoulder. The squirrel had not left Benjy once since he had brought it back to the farm. It even slept with Benjy at night!

"I'm going to show Skippetty to Mummy," said Penny,

and off she went. She took the lamb into the lounge and Mummy cried out in surprise.

"Oh no, Penny dear—you really can't bring the lamb into the house! Keep it in the orchard."

Well, it was all very well for Mummy to say that Penny wasn't to bring Skippetty into the house! The lamb lived in the orchard for a day or two and then Penny set it free to see if it would follow her, like Mary's little lamb. And it did!

It followed her everywhere! It followed her to the barn. It followed her into the kitchen. It even went up the stairs after her to the playroom! It just wouldn't be left without Penny.

The little girl loved it. She fed it as often as Harriet would spare her the milk. It was such fun. Harriet emptied the milk into the bottle and then Penny would take it to the lamb. It ran to her at once, and sometimes even put its funny long legs up on to her waist to get at the milk more quickly. It emptied the bottle in a trice, sucking noisily at the teat.

It grew even in three days! It became frisky and skippetty, and Penny loved it.

The others sang the nursery rhyme whenever they saw Penny coming with her lamb trotting behind her.

> "*Penny had a little lamb,*
> *Its fleece was white as snow,*
> *And everywhere that Penny went,*
> *The lamb was sure to go!*"

Mother grew used to the lamb trotting in and out of the house—but she scolded Penny for letting it go into the bathroom when Penny bathed at night.

"Oh, Penny darling, I really can't have that!" she cried. "You'll be bathing it in the bath next!"

Penny went red. She had secretly thought that it *would* be great fun to bath the lamb, especially one evening when it had rolled in some mud and got dirty.

"All right, I won't take it into the bathroom again," she said.

Harriet joined in the conversation. "*Nor* in the larder, *nor* in the dairy, *nor* in the broom-cupboard!" she said, her eyes twinkling.

"I'll make my lamb be good," promised Penny, laughing. "I'll make it just as good as I am!"

"Good gracious!" said Harriet, smiling, "what a monkey of a lamb it will be!"

414

CHAPTER VI

SHEILA FINDS A FRIEND

PENNY's lamb had been a great excitement—and something else was too! The hens came. This may not sound a very exciting thing, but to the four children at Willow Farm, it was very thrilling. Hens of their own! Hens that would lay eggs and make money—this was a real bit of farm-life to the children.

Sheila had studied the three books and had learnt very little from them. She hadn't liked to own up that the books were too difficult—but she had found help most unexpectedly.

It came from Fanny, the girl who came in daily to help Harriet. She had come in to clean the playroom when Sheila had been sitting there trying to puzzle out what the poultry books meant.

"Oh, Fanny!" sighed Sheila. "I wish I knew a lot more about hens. I'm going to look after them, you know, and I really must learn about them, or they won't lay eggs, and won't do well at all. And I do want to help my mother and father to make our farm pay."

"Well, Miss Sheila, what do you want to know?" asked Fanny, shyly. "My mother keeps hens, and I've looked after them since I was a tiny thing. You don't need to worry about your hens, surely—you've got a fine hen-house—and plenty of coops—and Harriet will cook the scraps for you—and there's corn in the bins."

"Fanny, tell me about hens," begged Sheila. "From the very beginning. I don't want to make any mistakes."

Fanny laughed. "Oh, you learn by making mistakes,"

she said. "First of all, what hens are you going to have? There are a good many kinds you know. Are you going to keep yours for egg-laying or for meat—you know, eating?"

"Oh, egg-laying," said Sheila. "I want lots and lots of eggs. Uncle Tim is bringing the hens over tomorrow. They are to be Buff Orpingtons."

"Oh, those nice fat brown, comfortable-looking hens!" said Fanny, pleased. "They are like ours. They lay a fine lot of eggs. You know, Miss Sheila, they're the best hens to have in the winter-time anyway, because they'll lay when other kinds won't."

"Well, that's good," said Sheila. "But will they sit on eggs well too?"

"Oh yes," said Fanny. "Ours do, anyway. Oh, Miss Sheila, it will be fun to set some eggs, won't it, and see the chicks come out?"

"Goodness, yes!" said Sheila. "Fancy, Fanny, I don't even know how many eggs to put under a sitting hen!"

"Oh, I can tell you things like that," said Fanny. "You put thirteen good fresh eggs. And you'll have to see the hen doesn't leave her eggs for more than twenty minutes!"

"Why, would they get cold?" asked Sheila.

"Freezing cold," said Fanny. "Then they wouldn't hatch out. That's why we put a sitting hen into a coop, Miss. So that she can't get out and leave her eggs."

"But how does she get food and water?" asked Sheila.

Fanny laughed. "That's easy enough!" she said. "You just let her out for a feed of corn and a drink and a stretch of her legs each day."

"What would happen if I forgot to do that?" asked Sheila.

"Well, the poor thing would sit till she got so hungry she'd peck her own eggs and eat them," said Fanny. "It's

416

just common sense, Miss, that's all. Did you know that a hen turns her eggs over now and then, to warm them evenly? I've often watched our sitting hens do that. You wouldn't think they were clever enough to do that, would you?"

"How long does the hen sit on her eggs?" asked Sheila. "Ages and ages, I suppose."

"Oh no—only for three weeks," said Fanny. "Oh, Miss Sheila, it's fun when the eggs hatch and the baby chicks come out! You'll love that."

"Yes, I shall," said Sheila, thinking with delight of dozens of tiny cheeping chicks running about the farm-yard. "Oh, Fanny, I've learnt more about hens from you in five minutes than I've learnt from all these difficult books!"

"If I've got time, I'll come and see the hen-house with you this afternoon," said Fanny. "You'll want some peat-moss for the floor, you know. That's the best stuff to have —you only need to change it once or twice a year."

"Oh, Fanny, hurry up with your work then, and we'll go and plan for the hens!" said Sheila. "I'll tell Daddy we want some peat-moss."

Fanny was just as pleased as Sheila to make plans for the hens. She had been used to keeping them all her life, but only in a tiny back-yard with a very small hen-house. Now they would be kept properly, with plenty of room for coops and chicks too. What fun! She flew over her work that morning and her Aunt Harriet was very pleased with her.

"You've earned your time off this afternoon, Fanny," she said. "You've been a good girl this morning. You scrubbed my kitchen floor well for me, and that stove shines like glass!"

"I'm going to help Miss Sheila get ready for her hens," said Fanny. "Goodness, Aunt Harriet, you wait and see what a lot of eggs and chicks we get!"

"Don't you count your chickens before they are hatched!" said Harriet.

Sheila and Fanny and Penny spent a very happy afternoon indeed. The three of them cleaned out the hen-house. It was not very dirty, and had already been white-washed inside. Fanny got some peat-moss from the village in a small sack and brought it back to the farm. It was lovely stuff, dark brown and velvety. The three girls let it run through their fingers joyfully.

"I should love to tread on this and scratch about in it if

418

I was a hen," said Penny. "Do we scatter it over the floor?"

"Yes, like this," said Fanny. Soon the hen-house floor was strewn with the dark brown peat-moss and looked very nice indeed.

"Do we put it into the nesting-boxes as well?" asked Penny, looking into the row of neat, empty nesting-boxes.

"No. We'll get some straw for those," said Fanny, happily. She was enjoying herself. She was a real country-girl, liking anything to do with farm-life. The three girls found some straw in a shed and took enough back for the nesting-boxes. They patted it down flat, and tried to make it comfortable for the hens.

"I wish I was small enough to get right into one of the nesting-boxes, and sit down on the straw to see how it felt," said Penny.

The others laughed. "You're funny, Penny," said Sheila. "You hate to be treated as if you were little—and yet you are always wanting to be smaller than you are—a toy in a cupboard, or a hen in a nesting-box!"

The hen-house had a hen-run, with wire netting around. It was overgrown with grass.

"That won't matter," said Fanny. "The hens will soon peck that up! Anyway, you'll let them free to wander over the yard, won't you, Miss Sheila?"

"Oh yes," said Sheila. "But I hope they won't lay their eggs away anywhere—you know, under a hedge or something. It would be a pity."

"Well, we'll just have to watch out for that," said Fanny. "Now, what about food? Look—there is corn in this big bin. We'll give them some of that each day! Corn helps them to lay often, and we shall get bigger eggs if we give them plenty."

419

"What else do we give them?" asked Penny.

"Well, my Aunt Harriet will cook up all the household scraps," said Fanny. "You know—potato peel, milk-pudding scrapings, crusts of bread—anything we have over. It will all go into the hen-food. Then we will mix it with mash—and give them a good helping early in the morning, and after tea. We'll let them have the corn at midday. They'll like that."

"It does sound exciting," said Penny. "What about water? They want plenty of that, don't they?"

"Yes—a big dishful," said Fanny. "Look—that trough will do. We'll fill it full each day. They must have fresh water. And I'll get my aunt to give us all the cabbage stalks and things like that. The hens will love to peck them."

"We'll clean the house each day," said Sheila. "I'll scrape the dropping-board with this little hoe. Oh, I *do* hope my hens do well!"

"They should do," said Fanny. "The thing is not to make too much fuss of them; but to be sure to give them a clean house, good food, fresh water and plenty of space to run. Well, they'll have all that. Oh—I've quite forgotten something important! We must give them grit to help them to digest their food—and lime or oyster-shell broken up as well," said Fanny.

"Broken oyster-shell! Whatever for?" said Penny in surprise. "Hens won't like sea-shell, will they?"

Fanny laughed. "They don't like it as food," she said, "but they need it to help them to make the shells for their eggs. If they don't get it the eggs will be soft-shelled and no use."

"I saw some stuff in a bag where we saw the corn," said Sheila. "I think it must have been broken oyster shell—and there was some grit there too. Let's get it. We can put it into this wooden box inside the house—then the rain won't spoil it."

By tea-time there was nothing else to be done to prepare for the hens. The boys came in and the girls showed them everything. Scamper leapt down from Benjy's shoulder to examine the hen-house. He went into one of the nesting-boxes and peeped out of it cheekily.

"Are you going to lay a squirrel-egg, Scamper?" laughed Benjy. "Funny little thing, aren't you?"

"Uncle Tim is bringing the hens tomorrow afternoon," said Sheila. "Oh, Rory—won't it be fun if we have some baby chicks? I should so love that."

"Well, maybe one or two of your hens will go broody and want to sit all day long," said Benjy. "Then you can give her some eggs, and she'll hatch them out for you."

"We can get out the coops then," said Sheila. "You know, Benjy, Fanny's been awfully helpful. I couldn't understand a thing in those books—but she's told me everything."

"Good," said Benjy. "Hie, Penny, where are you going? It's tea-time." Penny was tearing off to the little orchard. She climbed over the gate. "I'm going to fetch Skippetty!" she shouted. "It's his tea-time too. Fanny, ask Harriet if she can let me have another bottle of milk for him. He looks so hungry, poor lamb!"

The lamb came tearing up to Penny. She took it to the farmyard. Benjy was there with Scamper. Scamper leapt from his shoulder and sat on the lamb's back. "He wants a ride!" laughed Penny. "Oh, how I wish I could take a picture of them both!"

"Aren't you two ever coming?" called Sheila. "There are hot scones and honey for tea—and I can tell you there won't be any left if you don't come AT ONCE!"

CHAPTER VII

THE COMING OF THE HENS

NEXT day the hens came. Uncle Tim brought them over in a great big box. Aunt Bess was with him. It was the first time they had visited Willow Farm since the family had settled in. They jumped down from the wagon they had come in, and everyone ran to greet them.

"Uncle Tim! Aunt Bess! Look at my own pet lamb!" yelled Penny.

"Uncle Tim—I've got Scamper again!" cried Benjy.

"Hallo, Tim, hallo, Bess!" cried the children's parents. "Welcome to Willow Farm! We are getting straight at last! Come along in and have something to eat and drink."

Everyone went indoors, talking and laughing. After a while Sheila and Penny slipped out. They went to the kitchen. Harriet was there, cleaning the silver and Fanny was helping her.

"Harriet! Could you spare Fanny just a few minutes?" begged Sheila. "The hens have come! I thought it would be such fun to put them into the hen-house ourselves! I do want to see how they like it."

Harriet laughed. "Yes—Fanny can come. Go along, Fanny—but see you finish that silver when you come back!"

"Oh yes, aunt!" said Fanny. She ran out into the drive with the two children. The hens were still in the big box, strapped on to the back of the wagon.

They were clucking loudly. "Oh, there's a fine cock too!" cried Sheila, pleased. "See his beautiful tail-feathers sticking out of the crack in the crate! Fanny, how are we to get the hens to the house?"

"We'll carry them," said Fanny. "I'll show you how."

The three of them undid the rope round the crate, and Fanny forced up the top. She put in her arm and got a hen. It squawked loudly and struggled wildly.

But Fanny knew how to calm it and carry it. She showed the others how to take the hens by the top part of their legs, very firmly, and hold down the wings at the same time. "Put the bird under your left arm, so," she said. "That's right. Now you've got your other hand to hold the legs. We'll take them one at a time."

The three enjoyed carrying the squawking hens. One by one they were all taken to the big hen-house. There were twenty Buff Orpingtons, and one fine cock.

"Aren't they lovely hens?" said Sheila joyfully. "They look so brown and shiny, so fat and comfortable. I do like them. Look how straight up their combs are."

"They are nice young hens," said Fanny, pleased. "They should lay well. Twenty is just about the right number for the house and yard. If you have too many and they are overcrowded, they don't keep healthy. My word, your uncle has picked you out some beauties — they look as healthy as can be. It's always best to start with the finest hens you can possibly get."

The hens clucked about the house. Then they found the opening that led down the ladder-plank to the run. Down it they went, stepping carefully, their heads bobbing as they walked. "Cluck-cluck!" they said as they each entered the run. "Cluck-luck, what-luck!"

"Did you hear that!" said Penny. "They think they are lucky to come here!"

"Cluck-luck, what-luck!" said the hens again, and they

423

pecked at some cabbage stalks that Fanny had brought from the kitchen.

"We'll give them some corn to scratch for," said Fanny. The three went to the corn-bin and each got a handful. They scattered the corn in the run. The hens ran to it, clucking and scratching eagerly.

Sheila counted them. "One cock—and only nineteen hens," she said. "Where's the other?"

It was in one of the nesting-boxes, laying an egg. Penny gave a shout of delight.

"It *must* feel at home to do that already! Sheila—let's see if they laid any in the crate on the way over."

The girls went to look—and sure enough there were two nice big brown eggs on the floor of the crate! How pleased they were!

"I'm going to keep a proper egg-book," said Sheila. "I shall put down in it every egg that is laid! Then I shall be able to find out how much money my hens make for me, because I shall know the market-price of eggs each week, and reckon it up. Oh—it will be fun!"

Just then everyone else came out from the farm-house. Uncle Tim had said that he really must take the hens out of their crate—and lo and behold the crate was empty!

"Oh! The girls have done it all themselves, the mean things!" cried Rory, with a laugh. "No wonder they slipped out so quietly! Oh, look at all the hens in the run, Uncle. Don't they look fine?"

Everyone went to look at the brown hens. They seemed quite at home already, pecking about for the corn.

"One of them is laying an egg," said Sheila proudly. "I shall enter it in my egg-book."

"Sheila is going to manage the hens for us," said her father. "We shall just see how well she can do it!"

"Does she understand everything she has to do?" said Aunt Bess. "You know, the children only just gave the hens corn at times, and took the eggs in, when they were with us—they didn't really know much about the keeping of them."

"Have you got grit and oyster-shell, Sheila?" asked Uncle Tim. "Fresh water? Corn? Mash? Ah—I see you have studied some books!"

"Well," said Sheila, "I did try to study the books Daddy gave me—but actually Fanny told me most of what I had to do. Uncle Tim, I shall make my hens do even better than yours. You just see!"

"I hope you do," said her uncle. "Then I will come and take a few lessons from you on poultry-farming!"

It really was fun having hens to look after. Sheila said that she knew which was which after a few days, though the others could never tell more than one or two from the rest, and they secretly thought that Sheila couldn't either.

It was lovely to go and look in the nesting-boxes for the eggs. One day Sheila actually got twenty eggs! She was so delighted that she could hardly write it down in her egg-book! She and Penny used to go to the nesting-boxes morning and evening and take the eggs in. If they were to be sold, the children wiped them clean and sorted them into sizes.

"I do like eating the eggs that my own hens lay," said Sheila, each morning. "And I must say that the brown eggs always *seem* to taste nicer, though I can't think why they should."

The hens were soon let loose in the farmyard. Then they were very happy indeed. They scratched about everywhere, and the place was full of their contented clucking. The cock was a fine fellow. He stretched his neck and crowed loudly, and his tail-feathers were really magnificent. They were purple and green and blue.

"He's a real gentleman, you know, Penny," said Sheila. "He never helps himself first to anything but always waits till his hens have eaten. And look—when he finds a grain of corn, he doesn't eat it himself. Watch—he's found one—and he's calling to his favourite hen to come and have it. Really, he has most beautiful manners!"

The two girls found that they were quite busy with the hens. The house was cleaned of droppings each day. Fresh water was put into the trough in the run, and into the dish in the house too. The box was kept full of oyster-shell. Harriet cooked the scraps, and gave them to Sheila before breakfast. Then the two girls mixed the smelly stuff with the mash out of the bin and gave a good share to

426

the hungry hens. In the middle of the day they gave them corn, and a helping of mash again in the evening.

At night either Sheila or Penny shut the hens into their house. They liked seeing the big brown birds perching so solemnly there. They always counted them to make quite sure that every hen was in for the night.

Their parents were pleased with the way they looked after the poultry. "We'll have ducks later on!" they said. "Perhaps you will be able to manage those as well!"

The boys were anxious to do their share too. They were glad to hear that the cows were coming at once, and that their father had bought a sow and ten little piglets.

"The farm will really be a farm then!" said Rory. "How are the cows coming, Daddy? By train?"

"No—they are walking," said his father. "It is not far from the market where I have bought them, and they are coming along by the roads and the lanes."

The cows were to be short-horns. Uncle Tim said that they were excellent milkers, and made good beef.

"What colour will they be?" asked Rory.

"Oh, mostly red and white, I expect," said his mother. "I must say it will be nice to look from the window and see cows standing in the pasture. I always like cows standing about the countryside!"

"I'm looking forward to milking them," said Benjy. "It's quite easy!"

"I suppose they will feed on the grass?" asked Penny. "They won't cost much!"

"Oh, the grass won't be good enough yet for them to feed on that alone," said her father. "We must give them swedes or mangold-wurzels. The boys can cart them each day to the fields and throw them out on the grass."

The cow-sheds were all clean, and prepared for the

cows. They were to be milked there. The pails were scoured and shining, everything was ready.

"Once we have the cows to give us milk we shall be able to have our own milk, take our own cream, and make our own butter!" said Mother. "I am looking forward to that."

"When will the cows come?" asked Benjy. "I want to watch for them."

"Sometime tomorrow afternoon, I expect," said his father. "It's a good thing we have so many streams on our farm. We shan't have to cart water to the field-troughs — the cows can water themselves at the stream."

"I wish tomorrow would come!" sighed Penny. "I want to see our cows. Do you think they'll have names already, Rory? Or can we give them names? I'd like to name them all. I know such pretty cow-names."

"What names do you know?" said Rory smiling at Penny's earnest face.

"Oh, Daisy and Buttercup and Pimpernel and Kitty and Bluebell," began Penny.

"Why, those are the names of the cows at Cherry Tree Farm!" said Rory. "I'd think of a few new ones if I were you."

So Penny thought of some more. "Honeysuckle, Rhododendron, Columbine, Snapdragon," she began, but the others squealed with laughter.

"Fancy standing at the field-gate and shouting 'Rhododendron, Rhododendron!'" said Sheila. "Everybody would think you had gone mad."

"Well, anyway, I shall name *some* of the cows," said Penny, firmly. "I do so want to do that. I shall wait for them tomorrow, and see which looks like one of my names!"

CHAPTER VIII

SIXTEEN COWS FOR WILLOW FARM

THE cows arrived the next day, just before tea. Rory saw them first. He was swinging on the gate, waiting to welcome the cows to their new home. The others had gone to watch Skippetty frisking among the hens in the farmyard. The lamb was now much bigger, and was as springy and as frisky as any other lamb on the farm.

Everyone loved him, for he was a most friendly and affectionate creature. He had even gone into Penny's father's study one morning and pushed his little black face into the farmer's elbow!

"Hie! The cows are coming, the cows are coming!" yelled Rory, almost falling off the gate in his excitement. "Hurry up, you others — the cows are coming. They're MARVELLOUS!"

Sheila, Benjy and Penny tore to the gate. They saw the cows rounding the corner of the lane. They came slowly, swaying a little from side to side as they walked.

"They're red, and red-and-white!" shouted Rory. "Just the kind I like. Oh, aren't they nice and fat?"

They certainly looked good cows. They gazed at the children as they went through the field-gate, and whisked their tails. They smelt nice.

They were glad to get into the field and pull at the grass. "They twist their tongues round the grass when they pick it!" said Penny. "Oh look — there's Tammylan at the back with the herdsman!"

Sure enough it was Old Tammylan, come to see how the farm was getting on! He smiled at the children.

"So you've got your cows now!" he said. "And your hens too. And does this lamb belong to *you*, Penny? It seems to follow you close!"

"Yes, Skippetty is mine," said Penny, giving Tammylan a hug and then a hug to the lamb. "Tammylan, aren't our cows beautiful?"

"Yes — they look fine creatures," said Tammylan. "Have you plenty of names for them, Penny?"

"Oh, don't ask her that!" said Rory. "She keeps on and on thinking of names! I say, Tammylan, won't it be fun to milk the cows each day?"

"Rather!" said Tammylan. "Look at them all — how pleased they are to be able to stand and graze, after their long walk. They will soon get all their four stomachs into working order now!"

"*Four* stomachs! Whatever do you mean, Tammylan?" asked Sheila, astonished. "Has a cow got *four* stomachs!"

"Well — perhaps it would be truer to say that she has four compartments in her stomach!" said Tammylan, with a laugh. "Watch a cow eating, Sheila. She only bites the grass now and swallows it — she doesn't chew it. Watch one and see."

The children watched the cows. They saw that each one curled her tongue around the blades of grass, pulled them into her mouth, and then swallowed straightaway.

"And yet I've seen a cow chewing and chewing and chewing!" said Benjy. "It's called chewing the cud, isn't it, Tammylan?"

"Yes," said Tammylan. "What happens is that when she swallows the grass straightaway it goes down into the first part of her stomach. Then, when she is in her byre, or lying down resting, the swallowed grass comes up again into her mouth in balls all ready for chewing. Then

430

she has a fine time chewing for a while. She enjoys that. You wait and see how she loves it, chewing with half-shut eyes, thinking of the golden sunshine and the fields she loves!"

"Does it go back to the first part of her tummy again?" asked Penny, wishing that she had four stomachs too. "I'd love to swallow a sweet and then have it back to chew whenever I felt like it."

Tammylan laughed. "I expect you would!" he said. "No—when the cow has finished chewing the cud, the food goes down to the next part of her stomach, and then on to the third and the fourth. Have you ever seen a cow's upper teeth, Penny?"

"No—what are they like?" asked Penny, surprised. The wild man went to a cow and took its nose gently into his hand. He opened her mouth and pushed back the upper lip. "Tell me what her upper teeth are like!" he said, with a smile.

"Gracious! The cow hasn't any!" said Sheila.

"No—just a sort of bare pad of flesh," said Rory.

"How funny!" said Penny. "But a horse has upper teeth. I know, because I once saw a horse put back its lips and it had big teeth at the bottom and at the top too."

"Yes, a horse is different," said Tammylan. "It only has one stomach. And its hooves are different too. Look at this cow's hoof!"

He lifted up the front foot of the surprised cow. The children saw that it was split in two.

"Why is that?" asked Rory, astonished. "A horse only has one round bit of hoof—the cow's is split in two."

"She so often walks on soft, wet ground," said Tammylan. "Her split hoof helps her to do that without sticking to it."

431

"I like the way cows whisk their tails about," said Penny. "This one whisked hers round so far that it hit me. I do wish I had a tail like a cow."

"So that you could go round whisking people, I suppose?" said Tammylan. "Now, Penny, I will set you a little problem. I would like to know if a cow and a horse get up from the ground in the same way. Will you please watch and tell me next time you see me?"

"I should have thought they would both have got up exactly the same way!" said the little girl, surprised.

"Well, they don't," said Tammylan. "You just see!"

"We've got sixteen cows," said Rory, who had been

counting. "They are all fat and red and nice. I do think they look funny from behind – sort of wooden."

"Let's go and ask the herdsman when they have to be milked," said Sheila. "I'm just longing to do that!"

The herdsman was talking to their father. He was a tiny little fellow, with very broad shoulders and long arms. Although he was small he was tremendously strong. The children's father was keeping him on the farm, for he was a useful man with cows, and good at many other jobs too. His name was Jim.

"Can we help to milk the cows?" cried Benjy. "When is it time?"

"Oh, not till well after tea," said the man, smiling. "Are you sure you know how to? Milking isn't as easy as it looks, you know!"

"Of *course* I know how to!" said Benjy, scornfully. "And I get a jolly good froth on top of my pail too!"

"Ah, that's fine," said Jim. "A good milker always gets a froth. Well – you shall help if you like. I can do with one or two good milkers! Are you going to be up at five o'clock in the morning to help me, young sir?"

That made Benjy look a little blue. Five o'clock in the morning!

"Well – if I do, shall I have to go to bed very, very early?" he asked his mother.

"I'm afraid so, Benjy," she said. "An hour earlier."

"Oh. Then I'm very sorry, Jim, but I think I'll only help you in the evenings," said Benjy, who simply couldn't bear the idea of going to bed an hour sooner than the others.

"That's all right," said Jim. "I can get someone else, I daresay, to give me a hand in the morning!"

The children were all pleased when milking-time

came. They took the cows down to the cow-sheds, and got the shining pails and the little milking-stools.

Penny hadn't milked before. All the others had. Benjy was a fine milker. His hands were strong, yet gentle. Sheila was quite a good milker too, but Rory was poor. He could *not* make a froth come on the top of the milk in his pail as the others could. It was most annoying!

"I only get plain milk!" he said, "and I don't get my pail full nearly as quickly as you others! Look at Jim—he has milked three cows already and I haven't even done one!"

"You've got rather an awkward cow," said Jim. "She doesn't like to give her milk to a stranger. I'll finish her for you. The last milk from a cow is always the richest, you know, so we must be sure to get it. Try the next cow—Daisy, she's called. She's an easy one to milk."

"I love this warm milk," said Penny, putting her hand against the warm sides of a pailful of milk. "Jim, can I try to milk an easy cow?"

"You come over by me and watch me," said Jim. "Then you can try." So Penny stood by Jim and watched. She soon felt sure she could do what he did—but her little fingers were not nearly strong enough for milking and she gave it up. "Can I have a little milk for my lamb?" she asked. "It's time for his supper."

"No—you go and get some of the old milk from the kitchen," said Jim. "And keep your lamb by you—look at him nosing into that pail over there! My goodness, we don't want him emptying the pails as fast as we fill them!"

So off went Penny to the kitchen. "You know, Skippetty," she said, "I like lambs much better than cows! But please don't grow up too soon, will you? You won't be nearly so sweet when you are a sheep!"

CHAPTER IX

FUN IN THE DAIRY

THE days were very busy at Willow Farm now. There was always something to do! The hens had to be fed and looked after, the eggs taken and counted, the cows had to be milked, and swedes had to be carted to and from their field. The milk had to be set in the dairy for cream — and butter had to be made!

The dairy was a lovely place, big, airy and cold. The floor was of stone, the walls and ceiling were white-washed, and all the shelves were of stone too. It was very cold in there when the wind was in the east or the north. In the summer it would be a lovely cool place — the coolest place on the farm!

The children's mother loved the dairy. She was glad when the cows came because now she would be able to make her own butter. The children longed to see exactly how butter was made.

"What is going to be done with all the milk from our cows?" asked Rory. "There will be gallons each day!"

"Well, some is to be sold, in big churns," said his father. "Some we shall keep for ourselves. Some we shall skim for cream, and sell the cream. The skim-milk will be given to the pigs, or the calves when we have any — and the rest we shall make into butter."

"It all sounds lovely," said Sheila. "Do we empty the warm milk straight into the milk-churns, Daddy?"

"Good gracious no!" said her father. "We can't send warm milk out — it would soon turn sour. It has to be cooled."

"How can we cool it?" asked Benjy. "There are all kinds of funny things in the dairy, Daddy—does one of them cool the milk?"

"Come and see, next time the milk is taken to the dairy," said his father. So all the children trooped into the cool white room to see what happened that evening.

"Do you see that box-like thing fixed to the wall over there?" said their mother. "That is a kind of refrigerator —a machine for making things cold. See this pipe running to it—it brings cold water to the refrigerator, which has many pipes to carry the ice-cold water."

Mother poured some milk into a big pan on the top of the machine. The milk ran over the cold pipes and then fell into the big milk-churn standing below. It was quite cool by then!

"That's clever," said Rory, pleased. "Now I suppose the cool milk in the churn is ready to be taken to the town to be sold, Mummy?"

"Yes, it is," said his mother. "And what we are going to use ourselves has been taken to Harriet in the kitchen."

"What's going to be done with these big pails full of creamy milk?" asked Penny.

"That milk is going to be made into butter. But alas— our separator hasn't arrived yet—so we must separate our milk and cream in the old-fashioned way, and wait until our separator comes when we can then do it much more quickly," said her mother.

Mother put the creamy milk into big shallow pans, which were set on the cold stone shelves.

"What will the milk do now?" asked Benjy. "I suppose the cream will all come up to the top, as it did on our bottles at home."

"Yes," said his mother. "You know that light liquids

always rise to the top of heavier ones – and as cream is lighter than milk, it will rise to the surface, if we leave it to do so."

"How long will it be before the cream has all risen to the top?" asked Penny. "Ten minutes? I want to make some butter from it!"

Everybody laughed. Penny was always so impatient and expected things to be done at once.

"Penny! Don't be silly!" said Mother. "It will take twenty-four hours!"

"Gracious! I can't wait and see it come all that time!" said Penny. "Can't we make the butter today then?"

"Oh no, Penny," said Rory. "We've got to get enough cream first, silly. There won't be enough cream from one lot of milk, will there, Mummy? We'll have to store it a bit and wait till we have enough to churn into butter."

So Penny had to be patient and wait until the next day to see the cream being skimmed and stored for the making of butter. The children loved seeing the rich yellow cream lying smoothly on the top of the pans. Penny dipped her finger in and wrinkled the cream – it was almost as stiff as treacle!

"Don't, Penny!" said Sheila. "Do keep your fingers out of things!"

Mother skimmed the lovely cream off very carefully. She put it into a big cool crock. It did look fine. Mother put a little into a jug too.

"What's that for?" asked Penny.

"For your porridge tomorrow morning!" said Mother. "Take it in to Harriet when you go."

"What's going to be done with the blue-looking milk that's left," said Sheila.

"That can go to the pigs when they come tomorrow,"

said Mother. "Calves love it too—but we haven't any yet. It is called skim-milk, because we have skimmed the cream off."

Just then there was a great commotion outside, and Jim appeared, carrying something that looked extremely heavy over his broad shoulder. It was well packed up.

"Goodness! It's our separator!" cried Mother in delight. "Come and help to unpack it, everybody."

"Now we shan't have to wait ages for the cream to separate itself from the milk!" said Rory, pleased. "We can separate it in a few minutes."

Everyone wanted to see how the separator worked. It

looked a queer machine when it was unpacked. The main body of it was painted a bright clean red. On the top was a round pan. A big handle stood out from the side. Two pipes came out from the middle part. It really looked a most business-like machine.

Jim ran some water through the machine to clean it. "I reckon you can start it straightaway," he said. "It's a new machine, quite ready to use."

"Pour some fresh milk into the pan at the top, Rory," said Mother. So Rory poured some in, filling the pan full.

Then Sheila was allowed to turn the handle. "I feel as if I'm turning the handle of a barrel-organ!" she said. "I wouldn't be surprised if the separator played a tune!"

"Well, I would!" said her mother, with a laugh. "Go on turning, Sheila. Now children, watch these two pipes that come out at the front."

Everybody watched—and lo and behold, from the top pipe came out good thick yellow cream—and from the bottom pipe flowed the separated milk, free from any cream!

"Goodness—isn't that clever?" said Rory. "I see now why this machine is called a separator—it really does separate the milk from the cream. I suppose as the cream is the lighter of the two liquids, it always comes out of the higher pipe, and the milk comes out of the lower one because it is heavier."

"Yes," said Mother. "This clever little machine does in a few minutes what it takes us quite a long time to do by hand!"

Rory swung open the front of the machine when all the milk was separated. It was very neat inside. The children loved to see how things worked, and they tried to follow out what happened. It wasn't very difficult.

"Well now," said Mother, "that is another lot of cream for us! Pour in some more milk, Rory. Penny, you can have a turn at playing the barrel-organ this time!"

It was lovely to watch the milk and the cream spurting out from the two pipes. The children begged to be allowed to take it in turns to do the separating each day, and their mother said yes, they could.

"It is all part of the work of the farm," she said. "So you may certainly do your share. But don't come to me and say you are tired of using the separator in a week's time, because I certainly shan't listen to you!"

The children couldn't imagine being tired of playing about with the separator. They were simply longing to use the butter-churn too, and see the butter being made.

Harriet was to make the butter, with Mother to help her. Harriet had been a dairy-maid before, and she was good at butter-making.

"You know, butter comes well with some folks and it doesn't come at all with others," she said, solemnly, to the children. "Now I'm going to make butter on Tuesdays and Saturdays so if anyone wants to help, they can come along to the dairy then."

"We'll all come!" said the children at once. "We're not going to miss doing a single thing at Willow Farm!"

CHAPTER X

BUTTER – AND PIGS

ON the following Saturday Harriet bustled into the cool dairy. The sun poured down outside, for it was now mid-April, and spring was well on the way. But the dairy was as cool as ever.

In the big cold crock there was a great deal of cream. Harriet was going to turn it into golden butter. Penny peeped into the dairy with Skippetty behind her.

"Are you going to begin, Harriet?" she asked. "Shall I tell the others?"

"Yes," said Harriet, turning up her sleeves. "But just you leave that lamb of yours behind, please, Miss Penny. I never knew such a creature for poking its nose into things! It would gobble up all my precious cream as soon as look at it! You keep it out of the dairy. Do you know that it went into my larder this morning and nibbled the cheese?"

Penny giggled. Skippetty was a marvellous lamb, always doing the most unexpected things. She went to fetch the others. They came crowding into the dairy.

The butter-churn was in the middle. It was a funny-looking thing. "It's just a strong barrel mounted on a framework of wood to hold it," said Rory. "And there's a handle to turn the barrel over and over and over."

"All hand-churns are like this," said Harriet. "This one's made of beech. The last one I had was made of oak — but I always say butter comes fastest in beech!"

Harriet poured the thick, yellow cream into the barrel-shaped churn. She fixed on the lid firmly. Then she took the handle and turned it strongly and regularly. The barrel at once turned over and over and over, swinging easily as it went.

"What a lovely noise the cream makes, splashing about inside!" said Sheila. They all listened. They could hear the cream being dashed about inside the churn.

"Why do you have to turn the churn over and over like that?" asked Benjy. "Is that the way to make the cream into butter? I know I once helped our cook to whip some cream for the top of a jelly, and after I had whipped it with a fork for a while it went all solid."

"Yes—cream goes solid when it is whipped," said Harriet, still turning the churn by the handle. Her face was red, and she looked hot.

"Let me have a turn," begged Sheila. "I could do it just as easily as you, Harriet."

All the children had a turn, though Penny found the churn heavy for her small arms. Harriet took the handle again, and soon she nodded her head.

"The butter's coming," she said. "I can feel it. The churn is heavier to turn."

"It's taken about twenty minutes," said Rory, looking at his watch. "I call that quick. Harriet—please take off the lid and let's look inside. I can't hear so much splashing now!"

So Harriet stopped churning and took off the lid. The children all peered inside. There was no thick cream to be seen! Instead there were lumps of yellow butter floating in some milky-looking liquid.

"That's the buttermilk that the butter is swimming about in," said Harriet. "Now a few more turns and I'll get out the butter!"

It was really exciting to see the butter forming like that

442

from the cream. It seemed like magic to Penny. The children watched closely as Harriet poured away the buttermilk and then washed the lumps of butter till it was quite free from the milk.

She took up two flat wooden butter-handles and picked up the butter. She placed it all on a wooden tray, and then took the wooden butter-roller. With clever hands she pressed and rolled the butter till it was quite free of all moisture, and was firm and hard. Then neatly and deftly she made it into pound and half-pound pieces.

"There!" she said, wiping her hands on her apron. "Good rich butter, yellow and firm! Some to sell, some to eat. You shall have some for breakfast tomorrow morning!"

"Daddy is going to have paper wrapping printed to wrap our butter in when it's sold," said Sheila. "It is going to have 'Willow Farm Butter' printed on it. Oh dear—I shall feel so grand when I see that. Harriet, can we wrap the butter up when the new wrappings come?"

"If your hands are clean and you can wrap the butter neatly," said Harriet. "I'll show you how later on."

"Now we know how to separate cream from milk, and how to make butter from cream," said Penny, patting the wooden churn with her hand.

"I do think we are lucky," said Benjy, as they all left the cool dairy. "Our own eggs for breakfast—our own milk to drink—our own cream for porridge—and our own butter for our bread!"

"And I expect we shall have our own cheese too," said Rory. "Harriet says she can make cheese. She says she can make it from milk. She puts rennet into the milk and that separates the curds and the whey in the milk. Then she presses the curds, and they make cheese!"

443

"Gracious! It all sounds very easy," said Penny. "I shall help her when she does it."

The children were very happy. The weather was kind, the sun shone down warmly, and work on the farm went smoothly. The hens laid well, the cows gave splendid milk, and twice a week butter was made in the dairy.

The piglets were the next excitement. They arrived in a cart, squealing loudly! How they squealed! The children could not imagine what the noise was when they heard the cart coming slowly up the lane.

"Oh! It's the piglets!" yelled Benjy, and gave Scamper such a fright that the little squirrel shot up into a tree and would not come down for a long time. The children, with Skippetty the lamb behind them, rushed up the lane to meet the cart.

"The old mother-pig is there too," said Rory, in delight. "Gracious, what a giant she is! Oh, look at the piglets — aren't they sweet?"

All the children crowded round the pig-sty when the pig-family were put into it. The old sow grunted and lay down. The piglets scampered about busily.

"I simply *must* catch one and feel what it's like!" said Rory and he jumped down into the sty. He bent down to pick up a piglet — but it slipped away from him. He bent to get another — but that slipped away too. No matter how he tried he could *not* get hold of a piglet.

"They're all soft and silky and slippery!" he called to the others. "I can't possibly catch hold of one — they all slip off like eels!"

The others went into the sty to see if they could catch a piglet too, but to their surprise they found that it was just as Rory had said — the tiny creatures were far too slippery to hold!

444

They all went out of the sty a good deal more quickly than they went in! The sow didn't like to see them trying to catch her piglets, and she rose up in anger. She rushed at Rory and he only just got out of the way in time!

"Goodness! I didn't think she would be so fierce!" said Rory, rubbing his legs. "Isn't she ugly? But I like her all the same. Good old sow!"

"What's a father-pig called?" asked Penny.

"A boar," said Rory. "We haven't got a boar. But do you remember there was one at Cherry Tree Farm? He had a ring through his nose."

"Yes, why did he?" asked Penny. "I always meant to ask Uncle Tim and I never did."

"It's because pigs root about so," said Rory. "They try to root up the grass to get at any grubs or insects underneath, you know—and Uncle Tim didn't want his grass spoilt so he put a ring through the boar's nose."

"Well, I don't see how that stopped him from rooting about," said Penny.

"Well—would *you* like to go rooting up grass if Daddy put a ring through your nose?" asked Rory. "Wouldn't it hurt you every time you tried to nose up the grass?"

"Oh, I see," said Penny. "Yes, of course it would. Well, what about bulls? They have a ring through their noses too because I've seen them. And they don't go rooting up grass, do they?"

"No, they don't," said Rory. "But their ring isn't because of that, silly! It's so that they can be led by their nose, and not run away or get fierce, because if they try to pull away, their nose will be dreadfully hurt!"

The little pigs were really sweet. All the children loved them and begged to feed them each day. The big sow fed them herself for a while, but soon they grew big enough

to want other food than her milk. Then the big trough was filled with food for them. How they loved it!

"Hie, little piglets, here is the butter-milk for you from our butter-making!" cried Rory. "And here is some whey from our cheese-making! And here is some separated milk from our cream-making!"

"And here are kitchen scraps!" cried Sheila, putting them into the trough. The little pigs squealed with excitement and rushed to the long wooden trough. There was plenty of room for them all, but they couldn't see that. They tried to push each other away to get at the food and made such a noise that the children laughed with glee.

"Oh look — three of them have got right into the trough itself!" cried Penny. "Oh you naughty little piglets! Get out of your dinner! Oh, how I would hate to eat dinner I was treading on!"

The pig-wash in the trough soon disappeared. The piglets loved it. They grew fat and round and big. The sow ate well too. She loved little potatoes and the children often brought her a meal of these, or of potato parings.

"I really believe the old sow would eat anything!" said Rory, as he watched her gobble up enormous mouthfuls. "I don't wonder we have a saying 'As greedy as a pig'!"

"What about the saying 'As dirty as a pig'," said Sheila. "People always seem to think that pigs are dirty animals. But our sow is beautifully clean — and so are her dear little piglets."

"It depends on how they are kept," said Jim, who was passing by with the cows. "If pig-sties aren't regularly cleaned out of course the pigs will be dirty. How can they help it, poor creatures? Now, your sty has a good run, and it is cleaned out well — so your pigs are clean and healthy. Maybe you'll let them run on grass a bit later on. They'll love that."

Jim was right. The piglets and the sow had the run of the orchard, and they were very happy.

Skippetty often went to join them, and once he jumped on the side of the old sow when she was lying down basking in the sun.

447

But he didn't do it again! The old sow was very angry, and she ran all round the orchard after Skippetty till he was quite frightened!

"Skippetty, you must behave yourself!" said Penny. "Come with me, and don't worry the sow any more! Keep out of mischief for an hour or two!"

But the lamb couldn't be good for long. He went into the hen-house and began to nibble at the box of broken oyster-shell there! How Penny laughed!

"Look, Benjy! Look, Rory!" she called. "Skippetty wants to lay eggs with hard shells. He's nibbling the broken oyster-shell in the hen-house! Whatever will he do next!"

Nobody knew — but nobody minded, for who could help loving a black-faced, skippetty lamb?

CHAPTER XI

A LITTLE EXCITEMENT FOR SHEILA

THE weeks went by, and the four children were sad when their holidays came to an end. Then they all went walking across the fields to the rectory, and there, with three other children, they had lessons. But always they looked longingly out of the window, wondering what their hens were doing, what Scamper was doing, if Skippetty was in mischief, and whether the three dogs were helping Davey with the sheep.

How they raced home after school! Saturdays and Sundays were whole holidays, and if they had worked hard they were allowed Wednesday afternoon off as well. So they could still help a good deal, and Sheila could manage her hens very well.

Skippetty hated to see Penny going off each morning without him. He bleated after her most piteously, and the little girl begged to be allowed to take him. But Mother always said no, most firmly.

But Skippetty was determined to be like the lamb in the nursery rhyme, and one day he managed to squeeze through a gap in the hedge and trot after Penny to school. The children were quite a good way off, but Skippetty could hear their voices far ahead and he followed them eagerly.

Just as the children got to the Rectory they turned and saw Skippetty!

> *"Oh! Penny had a little lamb*
> *That followed her to school!"*

shouted the children in delight. The rector came to the door and laughed.

"Well, like Mary's lamb, I'm afraid it's against the rule," he smiled. "Penny, take the lamb to the apple orchard and shut it in."

But Penny couldn't have shut the gate properly because the lamb got out and went to the schoolroom door. The children saw the door open just a little—and then they saw Skippetty's black, blunt nose appearing round the edge!

They squealed with laughter, and Skippetty was frightened and ran back to the orchard. This time Rory was sent to see that he was safe, and the lamb was seen no more in school that morning.

Scamper *was* allowed to come, because he was quite content to wait for Benjy in the trees outside. Scamper was a little restless now that spring had really come. He sometimes went off for a day or two to the woods, and Benjy missed him terribly then. But he always came back. Once he came back in the middle of the night, and jumped in at Benjy's little window under the thatch. Benjy got a shock when Scamper landed on his middle and ran up to his face!

Fanny was a great help with the hens. She always did them if Sheila was kept late at school, and she and Sheila kept the egg-book with enormous pride.

"Fancy—over four hundred eggs already!" said Fanny, proudly, counting them up in the book. "Miss Sheila, a hen is supposed to lay about two hundred and twenty eggs a year, if it is a good layer—but it looks as if ours will each lay far more than that."

Then there came a week when there were not so many eggs—and one night when Sheila went to shut up her

hens she found that there was one missing!

"Fanny!" she called. "There are only nineteen hens and one cock. What's happened to the other hen?"

"I can't think," said Fanny. "She must be somewhere about. Oh, I do hope she's not wandered away too far and been stolen. There have been gypsies in that field over there this week — maybe they've taken her."

The girls called Benjy, Rory and Penny, and they all began to hunt for the lost hen. It was Penny who found her!

The little girl had hunted all round the orchard and in the hedges of the fields. As a last hope she went into the farm-garden. There was a big clump of rhododendron

451

bushes there, and Penny pushed her way into the middle of them.

And there, sitting quietly down by herself, was the lost brown hen! She looked up at Penny when the little girl came near, and gave a quiet cluck as if to say "Hallo! Don't disturb me. I'm all right!"

"Oh, Sheila, I've found the hen, I've found her!" yelled Penny. "Shall I bring her? She's here under the rhododendron bush!"

"No, I'll come and get her, don't you touch her!" shouted back Sheila, who hated anyone to touch her precious hens. She ran into the garden and went to the clump of rhododendrons. She pushed them aside and looked at the hen.

"Oh you naughty Fluffy!" she said. "Why didn't you come to bed when I shut up all the rest tonight?"

She lifted up the hen — and then she and Penny gave a yell. "She's sitting on eggs! Look, she's sitting on eggs!"

Sure enough, in a neat cluster, were eleven nice brown eggs! The hen clucked and struggled as Sheila lifted her off the eggs.

"Oh! No wonder the eggs have been short the last week or so!" said Sheila. "And I do believe you must have stayed away for three or four nights out here, you bad hen! I haven't been counting you all as I should, because I felt sure you came when you were called. Well, well — what shall we do with you?"

Fanny was pleased and excited. "We'll put her and her eggs into a coop," she said. "We'll give her two more. We'll have our own chicks now, Miss Sheila. Oh, that *will* be fun!"

So the clucking hen was given a nice coop for herself, and her eggs were put neatly under her — thirteen now —

452

and she settled on them happily, near the hen-house. Everyone went to see her every day. She looked out at them from the coop, and gave little clucks.

Each morning Sheila lifted her off the eggs, and gave her a good meal of corn and fresh water.

"Don't let her be off too long," said Fanny. "If the eggs get cold they won't hatch and we won't have our chicks."

So Sheila timed the hen each day, and gave her exactly twenty minutes off her eggs and no more. She felt the eggs just before the hen went back, and they were quite warm.

"Twenty-one days she's got to sit," said Fanny. "But of course we don't exactly know when she began."

"Do you know, Fanny, there's a hen that sits all day in one of the nesting-boxes, and never lays an egg!" said Sheila, a few days later. "It is most annoying of her. I. keep shooing her out, but she always goes back."

"Well, that means she wants to sit on a nest of eggs and hatch out chickens just as old Fluffy is doing," said Fanny. "Oh, Miss Sheila — my uncle has a clutch of duck's eggs. I wonder if your father would like to buy them, and let the hen sit on them! Then we'd have ducklings!"

"But do hens sit on duck's eggs?" asked Penny, who was listening. "Won't the hen know they are not hen's eggs?"

"Of course she won't know!" said Sheila. "How could she? Oh, Fanny, that would be fun! I'll ask Daddy straight-away."

Sheila's father gave her the money to buy the duck's eggs. She and Fanny went to get them. Sheila liked them very much.

"What a pretty greeny colour they are!" she said. "They are bigger than hen's eggs too. Fanny, don't ducks sit on their own eggs? Why must we give them to a hen to sit on?"

"Well, ducks aren't very good mothers," said Fanny. "They leave their eggs too long — and sometimes they get tired of sitting and desert them. But a hen is a good mother and nearly always hatches out her eggs."

The thirteen duck's eggs were put into a coop, and the broody hen was put over them. She got up and down a few times, and then settled on them quite happily. All the children watched with interest while she made up her mind.

"Goodness! We'll have twenty-six new birds soon!" said Benjy, pleased.

"Oh no!" said Fanny. "You hardly ever get thirteen chicks from thirteen eggs! Maybe one or two are bad, you know, and won't hatch. We'll be lucky if we get twelve out of the thirteen."

"Will they hatch out at the same time?" asked Penny.

"No," said Fanny. "Duck's eggs take twenty-eight days to hatch, you know — a week more than a hen's. I love little ducklings. They waddle so — and my word, when they first go into the water, you should see how upset the hen is! She thinks they are her own chicks, not somebody else's ducklings, you see! And she knows that water's not good for chicks, so she gets into an awful state when they waddle off to the pond!"

"Oh, I shall like to see that!" said Penny.

The two hens were very contented and happy sitting on their eggs. Each day they were lifted off and given a good meal and fresh water. Penny told the others that she had seen the hens turning their eggs over so that they were warmed evenly on both sides. She thought that was very clever of them.

Then there came the exciting day when the first chicks hatched out! Penny heard the hen clucking and she ran across to the coop. She saw a bit of broken egg-shell — and then she saw a yellow chick peeping out from beneath the mother hen. She ran squealing to the house in excitement.

"Come quickly! The chicks are hatching out!"

The others ran to see. But only one chick had hatched out so far. The hen kept putting her head on one side as if she could hear more chicks getting ready to break their shell. The children were so thrilled.

One more chick hatched out before they had to go off to school. That was a yellow one too. They begged to be allowed to stay and see all the eggs hatching out but their mother shook her head.

"No," she said. "The eggs were not all set at the same time, because the hen laid them herself. It may be to-morrow or the next day when they all hatch out."

So the children had to wait in patience — but at last all but two of the egg-shells were empty, and eleven little chicks scampered about the coop.

"These two won't hatch," said Fanny, picking up the last two eggs. "They are addled. Well — eleven isn't bad — and good healthy chicks they look!"

The chicks were given nothing at all to eat for the first twenty-four hours — then Fanny showed Sheila what to give them — a scattering of bread and oatmeal crumbs, and a tiny saucer of water. They soon pecked up the food and cheeped in little high voices for more.

Everybody loved them. Some were all yellow, as bright as buttercups. Some were yellow and black, and one was all black. The mother-hen took them about the yard and showed them how to scratch for food.

When she found a titbit she called loudly to her chicks and they all came running at once. She shared it with them, which the children thought was very nice of her.

"She's a real proper mother," said Penny. "Just like ours!"

When one of the stable cats came into the yard the hen called to her chicks in quite a different voice. They heard the warning in her clucks and ran to her at once. If she was in the coop they got under her wings and breast-feathers, and not one could be seen! Then, when the danger was past and the cat had gone, first one little yellow head, then another and another would poke up from the hen's feathers and look out with bright beady eyes.

That made the children laugh.

The duck's eggs hatched out some time later. The children were glad because it was a Saturday and they could watch everything from beginning to end.

The little ducks uncurled themselves from the egg-shells and stood on unsteady feet. They fluffed themselves out and the children looked at them in amazement.

"How *could* those ducks ever have got into the eggs?" cried Sheila. "They look twice as big already!"

The children liked the ducks even better than the chicks. They were so funny as they waddled about the yard. They were not so obedient as the chicks, and the mother hen had a lot of trouble with them.

Then the day came when they all wanted to go to the duck-pond! They had wandered quite near the edge of it, and suddenly one little duck felt that it simply MUST splash in that lovely water! So it waddled off, while the mother hen clucked for it to come back.

But to her annoyance the other ducklings also ran off to join the first one – and then, with little splashes and cheeps of delight every duckling slid or fell into the water and sailed off in excitement on the pond!

The mother hen went nearly mad with worry. She rushed about beside the pond, clucking and calling, while the other hen with her chicks stood looking on in horror. The ducklings had a wonderful time on the water and took no notice at all of their mother hen's scolding when they came out.

"Cheep, cheep," they said to one another. "That was fine! We'll do it again! Cheep, cheep!"

"Don't you worry so much, old mother-hen," said Sheila, sorry for the fluffy brown bird. "Your chicks are not chicks—they are ducklings! Can't you see the difference?" But the hen couldn't! She worried herself dreadfully every time that the ducklings took to the water —and then she grew tired of them and left them to themselves. She joined the hens in the yard, and scratched about contentedly, laying eggs again, and forgetting all about the naughty family of chicks that had so unexpectedly turned into ducklings!

The other mother-hen taught her chicks all that they should know, and then she too left them to themselves. They were quite content to run about together, scratching in the ground, and pecking at the cabbage stalks with the bigger hens. But the children did not like them nearly so much as they grew.

"They're leggy and skinny!" said Benjy. "They're not so pretty. I like hens to be either hens or chicks. I don't like them in-between!" But Sheila and Fanny were proud of their young chickens, and entered them in the egg-book. "Eleven chicks, twelve ducklings." That was a real feather in their caps, to have twenty-three birds more than they had started with!

CHAPTER XII

THE WONDERFUL SHEEP-DOGS

PENNY often went to see Davey the shepherd. She took Skippetty with her and the lamb was very funny with the other sheep. It seemed to turn up its little black nose at them, and to think itself much too grand to frisk about with the lambs!

"It nibbles the grass now, Davey," said Penny. "It doesn't want nearly so much milk. And oh, it does eat such a lot of things it shouldn't!"

"It's like its mistress then!" said Davey, with a laugh, for he knew that Penny loved picking off the unripe gooseberries, and liked sucking the tubes out of the clover heads. "Now, Tuppenny, you've come at the right moment this afternoon! I'm going to take the sheep from this hill to the next—and you can see Rascal, Nancy and Tinker at work if you like!"

"Oh, I *would* like!" cried Penny in delight. "May I go and tell the others? They'd so like to watch too."

"Well, hurry then," said Davey. "I'll give you ten minutes—then I must set the dogs to work."

It was Wednesday afternoon, and the four children had a half-holiday. Sheila had meant to give the hen-house a good clean. Rory had said he would work in the fields and Benjy had meant to help his mother in her farm-garden, where lettuces and onions, carrots and beans were all coming up well.

But when they heard that the sheep-dogs were to be set to work to help the shepherd, they all of them changed their minds at once!

"Golly! We *must* go and see that," said Rory, and he rushed to tell Jim that he would finish his work in the fields after tea. In ten minutes' time all four children were up on the hill with Davey.

He smiled at them, his grey eyes twinkling. "It's marvellous how quick children can be when they want to do anything!" he said, "and wonderful how slow they are when they have to do something they don't like. Now look—I want my sheep taken to the sheltered slope you can see on the next hill. They've got to cross over three of your streams, two of which only have narrow plank bridges—but my dogs will take them all safely without any help from me!"

"But Davey—aren't you going with them?" asked Penny, in surprise.

"No, little Tuppenny, I'm not!" said Davey. "I just want you to see how clever my dogs can be. Ah, you should see old Rascal at the sheep-dog trials! My word, he's a wonder! He can round up strange sheep and take them anywhere quicker than any other dog. I tell you, he's worth his weight in gold, that dog!"

The four children stood on the sunny hillside, eager to see what was going to happen. Davey whistled to his dogs. They came running up, two of them beautiful collies, the third a mongrel.

"Round them up, boys," said Davey, and he waved his arms towards the sheep grazing peacefully on the hillside. "Take them yonder!" He waved his arms towards the next hill.

The dogs stared at him with wagging tails. Then they bounded off swiftly. They ran to the sheep and made them leave their grazing. The sheep, half-frightened, closed in together. One or two took no notice of the

459

dogs, but Rascal ran so close to their heels that they too had to join the others.

"Sheep always flock when anything troubles them," said Davey. "Now watch those silly little lambs!"

Some of the lambs, instead of joining the sheep, had run away down the hillside. Tinker went after them, and very cleverly headed them back. As soon as a lamb seemed to be running away again, Tinker was there, close beside it, and it found that it had to go with the others!

"Goodness! I wish I was a sheep-dog!" said Penny. "I'd like to make the sheep do what I told them!"

Soon the sheep were in a bunch together, with the three dogs running round them. Davey waved his arms. That was the signal for the dogs to begin guiding the sheep to the next hill.

In a trice the sheep were set running downhill. Rascal ran round and round the flock, keeping it together. He didn't bark once. Nancy helped him. Tinker kept in front, making the leading sheep go the right way. It was marvellous to see how he made them keep to the path he wanted.

They came to a stream, too broad for the sheep to jump and too deep to wade. A narrow plank bridge ran from side to side. The leading sheep did not want to cross it. They ran along the bank, bleating.

It took Rascal half a minute to get them back to the bridge. But still they wouldn't cross.

"He can't make them!" cried Benjy, excited. "The sheep are too stupid!"

"Oh, the stupider they are, the easier," said Davey. "It's the ones that try to think for themselves that are the most difficult to manage. The ones that don't think, but just blindly follow the others, are very easy indeed. But watch Rascal—he can't be beaten by a few silly sheep! There—look—he's got one on to the bridge!''

How Rascal had got the first sheep there nobody quite knew. The dog seemed to go in and out and round about the sheep till it found itself on the bridge! It couldn't go backwards, because Rascal was just behind it—so it had to go forward!

Once one sheep had crossed the others felt they must follow! Rascal leapt off the bridge and stood close beside it. Tinker stood the other side. Nancy kept the sheep together behind, forcing them forwards to the bridge.

It was marvellous to watch. The dogs worked together

461

beautifully, never letting a sheep get away, and making them all go over the bridge as quickly as possible.

The sheep were sure-footed, and trotted easily over the narrow plank. Penny was afraid that one of the lambs might fall in, but of course not one lost its footing.

"Sheep are really mountain animals," said Davey. "I used to keep them in Wales on the mountainside. Some of the hills there were so rocky and steep that I couldn't get near the sheep—but they leapt from rock to rock and didn't slip once. So a narrow bridge like that means nothing to them!"

All the sheep passed over the bridge. Rascal leapt ahead of the flock and turned them to the left instead of to the right. Nancy brought up the stragglers. Tinker ran round the flock. They all went on to the next stream, where a little stone bridge was built across.

The sheep went over without any difficulty. "They know by now that the dogs are taking them somewhere," said Davey. "They don't like leaving the hill where they have been for many weeks, but they will soon get used to new grazing."

Just then the dogs paused and looked back to the hillside they had left. They had come to a forking of the hill-paths, and were not sure which one to take—to the east or to the west.

Davey knew what they wanted. He waved his arm and gave a shrill whistle. "That means I want the sheep taken to the west side of the hill," he told the children. "Watch how the dogs understand me!"

The dogs had hardly seen Davey wave and heard his whistle before they headed the sheep towards the West! The children were amazed.

"Why, it's as if they were men," said Rory. "Though

men couldn't run around the sheep as quickly as the dogs. But they understand just as we do. Oh Davey, you couldn't do without your dogs, could you?"

"No shepherd could," said Davey. "We depend on our dogs more than on anything else. Why, once when I was ill for two days, those dogs of mine looked after the sheep for me just as if I was out on the hills with them. Sharp as needles they are, and think for themselves just as much as you do!"

"Are they born as clever as all that?" asked Rory.

"Oh, sheep-dogs are always clever," said Davey, "but they have to be trained. I train them a little, but the other dogs teach a pup much more than I can by just letting him run around with them and see what they do. Some sheep-dogs are more clever than others, just as some children are sharp and others are not. I can tell in a few months if a pup is going to be a good sheep-dog or not."

The sheep were made to cross another stream and then they were allowed to scatter on the western side of the hill. The dogs lay down, panting and tired. They had run many miles, because they had had to tear round and round the flock so many times! The sheep dropped their heads and began pulling at the short grass with enjoyment. It was good to be out there on the hillside in the sun, with new grass to eat!

"The dogs will stay with them till I come," said Davey. "Well—what do you think of them? Pretty sharp, aren't they?"

The shepherd was very proud of his dogs, and the children were too. "I think they're marvellous," said Rory. "I wish I had a flock of sheep and dogs like that!"

"Do you know, one winter's day two sheep got lost in a snowstorm," said Davey. "I reckoned I'd never get them again—but old Rascal there, he went out in the snow—and he brought back those sheep six hours later!"

"Did he really?" said Benjy, astonished. "But how could he find them in the snow? Was it deep?"

"Yes," said the shepherd. "I counted the sheep and told Rascal that two were gone—and off he went. He must have hunted all up the hills and down before he found them. He was so tired when he got here that he couldn't even eat his supper! He just lay down with his head on my foot and fell fast asleep! Ah, he's a good dog that!"

"Well, thank you Davey, for letting us watch what your dogs can do," said Sheila. "Please tell us when they do anything else exciting!"

"You must come and watch the sheep-shearing in a fortnight's time," said Davey. "And when we dip the sheep you'll like to see that too. I'll let you know when to come!"

The children ran off down the hill. "Aren't there exciting things to do on a farm!" cried Penny, as she skipped along just like Skippetty the lamb. "Oh, how glad I am that we've left London and come to Willow Farm, Willow Farm, Willow Farm!"

CHAPTER XIII

THE SHEARERS ARRIVE

ONE day three strange men appeared at the farm. The children looked at them in surprise, for they met them just as they were going off to school.

"Is your father about?" asked one of the men. "Well, tell him we're the shearers, will you?"

"I say! The sheep are going to be sheared!" cried Rory. "Oh golly—if only we could stay home today and watch!"

"You'll see plenty, young sir," said the shearer, with a smile. "We'll be at work all day long, till night falls. We don't stop—once we're on the job!"

Rory flew off to tell his father. The four children watched the men being taken to one of the big open sheds.

"So that's where the sheep are to be sheared!" said Benjy. "I saw the shed being cleared yesterday, and I wondered why. I shall simply *tear* home from school today to watch."

"Do the shearers cut off all the poor sheep's wool?" asked Penny, feeling quite sad for the sheep. "Poor things—they *will* be cold!"

"Well, they're jolly hot now, in this sunny weather!" said Rory. "How would you like to wear a heavy woolly coat to go to school in this morning, Penny? I guess you'd be begging and begging us to let you take it off!"

Penny looked down at her short cotton frock. "Well, I'm hot even in this," she said, "and I'm sure I should *melt* if I wore a woolly coat like the sheep. I expect they will be glad, after all."

"Of course they will!" said Sheila. "But they *will* look funny afterwards! I expect they feel funny too—all sort of undressed."

When the children came back from school they found the air full of the noise of bleating! The mother sheep had been separated from their lambs, and each was bleating for the other! What a noise it was!

"Look—they have driven the sheep into hurdles in the field near the shearing-shed," said Rory. "Last year's lambs are with them—but not this year's babies. So Skippetty won't lose his nice little woolly coat, Penny!"

"I'm glad," said Penny. "I don't want him all shaven and shorn! He's sweet as he is."

The dogs had had a busy morning bringing in the sheep for the shearers. They had had to collect them from the hills, and bring them all back to the farm. They had worked hard and well, and Davey was pleased with them.

The shearers sat in the open shed. The sheep that had already been sheared had been set free and stood in a small flock, with Tinker on guard. He was to take them to the hills to graze as soon as another dozen or so sheep were ready.

The children ran to see exactly what happened. The farm felt busy that day—men hurried here and there with sheep, and the children's father gave loud orders. It was fun!

Rory watched the first shearer. A big sheep was taken up to him. Very deftly the sheep's legs were tied together so that it could not move. It might hurt itself if it struggled and got cut by the clippers.

Then the shearer got to work with his clippers. The children thought he was marvellous. He clipped the sheep's wool so that it came off like a big coat! Snip,

snip, snip, went the clippers, and the wool was sheared off swiftly and cleanly. How queer the sheep began to look as its wool fell away from its skin!

The shearer looked up and smiled at the watching children.

"Are you my next customers?" he asked. "I've done nineteen sheep already today. One of you going to be the twentieth?"

"We're not sheep!" said Penny, indignantly.

"Dear me, so you're not!" said the shearer. He twisted the sheep he was doing so that he could shear the wool from its back. The wool fell away neatly.

"The wool's dirty," said Rory. "And it smells!"

"Well, these sheep haven't been made to swim through water," said the shearer. "If they are sent swimming a week or two before they are sheared, their fleeces are cleaner. Washed wool is worth more money. On the other hand, it doesn't weigh so much as unwashed, so there's not much in it!"

"What's the biggest number of sheep you have sheared in a day?" asked Benjy, who was longing to try his hand at clipping too.

"Sixty-eight," said the shearer. "But they were small ones. The bigger the sheep the longer it takes to shear it. I like shearing fat sheep the best — they are easiest of all to shear."

"Why?" asked Rory, surprised. "I should have thought it would have been difficult to get round them!"

"Well, you see," said the shearer, "a fat sheep's wool rises up well from the skin and makes it easier to shear. It's skin is oilier than a lean sheep's, and the oil makes the wool rise nicely. Wait till the shepherd brings along a really fat sheep and you'll see what I mean."

The shearer nearby was shearing the year-old lambs. They hated the shearing and bleated piteously.

"Are they being hurt?" asked Penny, anxiously.

"Not a bit!" said the shearer. "Sheep hate two things —one is being sheared, and the other is being dipped."

"*Dipped!*" said Rory. "What do you mean, dipped?"

"Oh, you'll see soon enough," said the man. "Davey here will show you one day soon!" He finished his lamb and sent it away with a smack. "These shearlings are quick to do," he said. "Their coats are not so thick as the big sheep's."

"Is a shearling a yearling?" asked Benjy.

"That's right," said the man, and took another shearling to clip. It was wonderful to see how quickly he clipped away the wool.

As each sheep was finished, and stood up, bare and frightened, Jim daubed its back with tar, and then sent it off to Tinker.

"What are you doing that for?" asked Benjy.

"Marking the sheep with your father's mark," said Jim. "Then if the sheep happen to wander, the mark is known and the sheep are sent back."

The children looked at the mark. It was a big crooked letter W. "W for Willow Farm," said Penny. "Oh—now we shall always know our own sheep!"

Jim rolled each fleece up tightly and tied it together. He threw it into a corner of the shed.

"They will all be packed into sacks and sold," he said. "It looks as if your father will do well this year with his wool. It's good wool, and weighs very heavy."

"Oh, I'm glad," said Rory. "I know he wants to buy some new farm-machinery, and he said if the sheep did well he would be able to. We've had lots of lambs, and not one of them has died. Skippetty was the only weakly one, and as soon as Penny took him for a pet, he began to grow big and fat."

"I notice he doesn't come into the shearing shed!" said Jim, with a grin. "I reckon he's afraid he will lose his nice little coat if he does!"

Skippetty was keeping well out of the way. He didn't like all the noise of bleating and crying. When the clipped sheep came out from the shed Skippetty looked at them in amazement. What were these curious-looking creatures? He didn't like them at all!

The sheep certainly did look queer when they ran back to the fields, shaven and shorn. They looked so small without their thick woolly coats. They felt cold too, but the month was warm, and they would take no harm. The

shearing was never done when the winds were cold — only when it seemed as if the weather was going to hold fine and sunny and warm.

"Another day's work and we'll be finished," said the first shearer, busy with a fat sheep. He showed the children how easily he could clip the wool. "Your father hasn't a very big flock. If he had, he wouldn't get *us* to do his shearing!"

"Why not?" asked Rory.

"Well, he'd buy a clipping-machine," said the man. "You should see one at work — it's marvellous! Clips the sheep in no time. And it's better than hand-shearing too, in some ways; a machine can clip a sheep more closely than our hands can, so the fleece weighs more heavily, and brings in more money."

"Perhaps we shall have a clipping-machine next year!" said Rory. "I'd love to work one."

"How much does a fleece weigh?" asked Sheila, looking at the grey fleeces thrown at the back of the shed.

"These fleeces are good," said the shearer. "I reckon they weigh about nine pounds apiece. The shearlings don't weigh so much of course. That shepherd of yours knows how to look after his sheep. These are fine and healthy!"

The shearers did not stop their work till dusk. Then, tired and thirsty they went to the farm kitchen for food and drink. Harriet made them wash under the pump before they came in.

"You smell like sheep yourselves!" she said. "And my, you're covered with fluff!"

"That was fun!" said Rory, as he and the others went indoors. "Next year we'll get a clipping-machine, and *I* shall work it! My word, I *shall* enjoy that!"

CHAPTER XIV

A BAD DAY FOR THE SHEEP

DAVEY had wanted to dip the sheep a week or two back, because he said the flies were getting at them and laying eggs in the wool. But things kept happening to prevent the dipping, and then Davey found that one or two of the sheep were really in a bad way.

"If we don't dip the sheep as soon as possible, we'll be sorry," he told the children's father.

The children went to look at the dipping-trough. "It looks like a funny kind of bath, sunk into the ground," said Penny. "Isn't it deep—the sheep will have to swim through it, won't they, Rory?"

"Yes, I should think so," said Rory. "It's about eighteen or twenty feet long—goodness, by the time they've swum through that, their wool will be soaked! That's just what we want, of course."

"What's put into the bath?" asked Sheila.

"A very strong disinfectant!" said Rory, proud that he knew so much about it. "The men are going to dip the sheep tomorrow. We'll see all that happens then. How the sheep will hate it, poor things!"

Rory was right! The sheep hated the dipping even more than they hated their shearing. Jim and Bill got the bath ready. They filled it full of water, into which they emptied a big tin of something.

"Pooh, it smells!" said Penny, and she went away a little. She always hated smells. The men stirred up the bath with sticks. It became cloudy.

Rascal, Tinker and Nancy had got the sheep in from the

hills that morning. The flock were in a fold nearby. They bleated, for they knew that something unpleasant was about to happen to them!

"There's Tammylan!" said Rory, pleased. "He said he'd come. Hallo, Tammylan — you're just in time!"

Davey was pleased to see Tammylan. The wild man was so good with animals, and he would be a help in dipping the sheep, who were always very difficult when being dipped in the trough.

"Hallo, children," said Tammylan. "I'm glad your sheep are being dipped today. I reckon it's only just in time to save some of them from illness, Davey."

"How would they be ill?" asked Sheila.

"Well, in this hot weather the flies' eggs hatch out in a few hours in their wool," said Tammylan. "The maggots eat away hungrily and do the sheep a lot of harm. There's a few in your flock that are in a bad way."

"Look!" said Rory. "The first sheep is being driven down the passage-way to the trough!"

Hurdles made a narrow passage from the fold to the swimming-trough. The sheep was made to run down the passage-way and came to the dipping-trough. It stood there, not at all wanting to go in. A farm-hand seized it — and into the bath it went! It bleated piteously as it found itself in the water and struck out with all its legs.

"It's swimming!" cried Penny. "I've never seen a sheep swim before! Look — it's going quite fast!"

The sheep swam through the trough. It seemed a very long way to the panting animal. It was afraid of the water, and afraid of the men who shouted at it. It only wanted to get out and run away!

"Why does the poor sheep have to swim such a long way?" asked Penny, indignantly. "It's a shame! Why

472

couldn't they make the bath much shorter?"

"Well, Penny, the disinfectant *must* soak in to every single part of the sheep's wool and skin," said Tammylan. "If the bath were very short, then the sheep might not be thoroughly soaked, and the eggs and maggots might still be alive to work their harm. By making the sheep swim a long way, we make sure that it is soaked to the skin!"

The sheep at last reached the other end of the bath. It went up a slope and stood still in a little enclosed place, shaking itself now and again.

"That place is called the 'dripper'," said Tammylan. "The sheep stand there and let the disinfectant drip off them. See it falling in drops and rivulets off that sheep, Penny? Look how it runs back into the bath, so that very little is wasted!"

The children saw that the disinfectant dripping off the sheep ran back into the trough. They felt sorry for the dripping sheep and hoped that it would soon be allowed to go back to the field.

"Can it soon go back to eat grass on the hills?" asked Penny. "I wish it would."

"Not till it is dry," said Tammylan. "You see, if the liquid drips from the sheep on to the grass, it taints the grass, Penny—and then, if the sheep eat it, they might become ill. So they have to wait a little, and get dry before Davey lets the dogs take them back to the hills to graze."

"Another sheep is going into the dipping-trough!" cried Rory. A second sheep was being driven down—and then a third and a fourth—and soon the air was full of frightened bleatings as the sheep struggled in the water, and swam pantingly to the other end.

The cries of the sheep in the trough made the waiting

473

sheep feel afraid. They ran round the fold and bleated too. Davey looked at Tammylan.

"Can you say a few words to them?" said the old shepherd with a smile.

Tammylan went into the fold. He spoke to the sheep in the deep low voice he kept for animals, and the sheep stood still and listened. It was curious to see Tammylan with animals or birds. They *had* to listen to him. They had to be still. His voice always quietened any animal at once, even if it was in great pain. He had a wonderful way with him.

Benjy watched him. The sheep crowded round the wild man, comforted. They were no longer frightened by the wild bleatings of the sheep being dipped in the trough.

"How I wish I could handle animals as Tammylan does," thought Benjy. "My goodness, if I could, I'd try to tame animals like lions and tigers, bears and elephants! What fun that would be!"

One by one all the sheep had to go down the slope into the trough. They did not make such a fuss now. The men were pleased, because the job was over more quickly when the sheep were docile. It was always a messy job, and they were glad when it was over.

Each sheep stood for a while in the dripper. When half of them were done the water was very dirty indeed. The men emptied it and put in fresh water.

"That's good," said Tammylan, pleased. "That gives the rest of the sheep a good chance to be thoroughly disinfected now. It's a mistake to use the water too much before changing it."

As soon as the sheep left the dripper they went into a big fold and there they had to stay until they were dry and there was no fear of drippings spoiling their grass.

Rascal, Tinker and Nancy lay down, patiently waiting

until the sheep were ready. Then they would take them off
to the hills again, at a wave of the hand from old Davey.
They kept well away from the trough! They had no wish
to be bathed there too!

Penny suddenly missed Skippetty. Where could he be?
Had he been frightened by the bleatings and gone running
away by himself somewhere? The little girl called him.

"Skippetty! Skippetty! Where are you? Come here,
Skippetty!"

A pitiful bleating answered her — and to Penny's horror
she saw Skippetty running down into the dipping-trough

475

with some other sheep! He had got into the fold and had to take his turn.

"Oh, stop Skippetty, stop him!" cried Penny. "Oh, he'll be drowned! Davey, save him!"

But it was too late to stop the lamb from going into the trough. In he went with the others, and scrambled through, bleating at the top of his loud voice. He climbed out, with everyone laughing at him.

Penny rushed to get him. "No, Tuppenny, no!" cried Davey. "Don't you touch him while he's fresh from the bath. You'll get yourself all messed. Let him stand in the dripper with the others. That lamb of yours is always up to something!"

So poor Skippetty had to stand in the dripper with the others, and then he went into the fold to dry. Penny was dreadfully upset, but the others laughed loudly.

"You *are* horrid to laugh at poor Skippetty!" said Penny, almost in tears. "What would you feel like if your squirrel went into that horrid dipping-trough, Benjy?"

"Oh, he wouldn't be so silly," said Benjy, putting his hand up to caress Scamper, who, as usual, was on his shoulder. "You must teach Skippetty a little common sense, Penny—though you could do with some yourself sometimes!"

Penny said that Skippetty smelt, after he had dried himself. She wanted to pet the lamb and comfort him after his horrid bath—and yet she could not bear to have her hands smell horrid. So she went and put on her old gloves, which made everyone laugh still more loudly!

"Don't you worry, Tuppenny!" cried Davey. "Your lamb hasn't come to any harm. It has probably done him good. You watch and see how much better my sheep are, after their bath!"

476

So they were. They were much livelier and happier, and Davey was pleased with them. "You see, all the eggs and grubs are gone now," he said. "If I can keep my sheep healthy and fit, the flies are not so likely to go to them, and I shan't have to keep dipping them. One year I had to dip sheep so many times that they almost got used to it!"

"Was there ever a year when you didn't dip them at all?" asked Penny.

"Well, there's a law that says we *must* dip our sheep so many times each year," said Davey. "It's a good law. It stops disease from spreading among the flocks. One careless farmer can do a lot of harm to others, you know. We should take as much care of our animals as we do of ourselves."

"I never knew there were so many things to be done on a farm," said Rory, seriously. "As I mean to be a farmer when I grow up I'm glad I'm learning now. Farming's fine, isn't it, Davey?"

"It's a man's job!" said Davey. "Ay, young sir, it's a man's job!"

CHAPTER XV

A VISIT TO TAMMYLAN – AND A STORM

In June the hay-fields at Willow Farm were a lovely sight. The grass waved in them, and all kinds of flowers peeped here and there. The children loved to walk beside the hedges that ran round the fields. They were not allowed to wander in the grass, of course, for fear of spoiling the hay – and Skippetty had to be kept out too.

"The hay crop is good this year," said the children's father, pleased. "That means that we shall have plenty of hay for the cattle in the winter – good feeding for them. Well – when hay-making time comes I am going to get you four children a holiday, because we shall want your help!"

"Oh good!" cried everyone, delighted at the idea of an unexpected holiday.

"We'll work jolly hard," said Rory. "Feel the muscles in my arm, Daddy – aren't they getting hard?"

His father felt them. "My word, they are!" he said, surprised. He looked at Rory closely. "Who would have thought you were the same boy as the ill-grown, pale, weedy Rory of last year!" he said. "Well, we work hard – but it's worth it when I look at you all, and see how bonny and rosy you are. Now about this hay-making – we shall begin on Monday, because the weather is beautiful at present."

"Can we only make hay properly when the weather is nice, then?" asked Penny.

"Well, you surely know the old saying 'Make hay while the sun shines!'" said her father. "Yes – we have to cut and cart the hay while the weather is dry and warm. Wet hay isn't much good, and needs a lot more labour."

"It has to be cut, and turned, carted away and stacked, hasn't it?" said Rory, remembering what had happened at Cherry Tree Farm the year before. "Daddy, what happens if hay is stacked before it is quite dry?"

"It becomes very hot," said his father. "So hot that the hay actually gets blackened by the heat — and it may even get on fire. I remember one summer helping your Uncle Tim with his hay, and it was such wet weather that it was impossible to get it really dry."

"What did you do, then?" asked Rory.

"We had to put thick layers of straw into the hay-stack as we built it," said his father. "That prevented the hay from becoming too hot because the straw sucked up the moisture. The straw made splendid fodder for the winter, I remember."

"I do like hearing all these things," said Rory. "I shall remember them when I have a farm of my own."

The children went to find Tammylan on Sunday, to tell him that hay-making would begin the next day. Tammylan was not in his cave, so they guessed that he must be in his tree-house by the river. They went to see.

Tammylan's tree-house was a lovely place. It was built of willows which, although cut from the trees, still grew green leaves — so that it looked almost as if Tammylan lived in a growing house! The children loved it. The wild man had a bed of heather and bracken. It was there in the house, but Tammylan was nowhere to be seen.

"I wonder where he is," said Benjy, looking all round. "Oh look — there's the hare! It's come to the tree-house with Tammylan!"

The hare was crouching in a corner, half-afraid of the

479

children. But when Benjy went towards it, it did not run away. It knew he was a friend and heard in the boy's voice the same gentle, friendly tones that it knew in Tammylan's. It allowed Benjy to stroke it, and then, with a few swift bounds it fled out of the tree-house into the woods.

"It does limp a bit," said Benjy, watching. "But it's wonderful the way its poor leg's mended. How can we find Tammylan, I wonder?"

"Send Scamper to look for him!" said Penny.

"Good idea!" said Benjy. "Where *is* Scamper?"

The squirrel was bounding about the tree-house, sniffing for his friend, Tammylan. Benjy spoke to him. "Scamper—find Tammylan, find him!"

Scamper was very sharp. He understood what Benjy meant, because he himself wanted to find the wild man too! So off he went into the tree, keeping a sharp look-out for Tammylan from the branches.

And before very long the four children saw their friend coming from the river-bank with Scamper on his shoulder!

"Hallo, Tammylan!" they shouted. "So Scamper found you!"

"Yes, he made me jump!" said the wild man. "I was lying down on the bank, watching a kingfisher catching fish, when suddenly this rascal landed right in the middle of my back! I knew that you must be somewhere about so I came to see."

The children went with the wild man to watch the brilliant kingfisher fishing. It was marvellous to see how he sat on a low branch, watching for fish in the water below.

"There he goes!" cried Penny, as the blue and green bird flashed down to the water. He was back again in a

second, with a small fish in his mouth. He banged it against the bough and killed it. Then he flew off with it.

"Isn't he going to eat it?" asked Penny.

"He would have liked to!" said Tammylan. "But he has a nest at the end of a tunnel in a bank nearby—and no doubt his wife is sitting on a nest of fish-bones, warming her white eggs, hoping that her mate will soon bring her something to eat. Well—she will have fish for dinner!"

"Tammylan, we came to tell you something," said Benjy, lying on his back and looking up into the brilliant blue sky. "I say—isn't it gorgeous weather!"

"Is that what you came to tell me?" asked Tammylan, looking astonished.

"No, of course not!" said Benjy, laughing. "We came to tell you that we are having a holiday for a few days—so will you come and see us?"

"But why the holiday?" asked Tammylan. "Have you been specially good at your lessons lately? I can't believe it!"

The children laughed. "No," said Rory, "but we are going to begin hay-making tomorrow. Won't that be fun, Tammylan?"

But Tammylan did not smile. He looked worried.

"What's the matter, Tammylan?" asked Penny.

"I hope you *won't* begin hay-making tomorrow," said Tammylan. "There will be a great thunderstorm tomorrow night—with a good deal of rain. It would be best to put off your hay-making until the end of the week, although I know the hay is ready now."

"Tammylan! How can you possibly know that a thunderstorm is coming?" said Benjy, sitting up. "Why, it feels simply lovely today—not a bit thundery."

"To you, perhaps," said Tammylan, "but you must remember that I live out of doors all the time, and I know the weather as well as you know your tables! You can't live as I do, looking at the sky and the hills day and night, feeling the wind on my cheek, seeing how the trees blow, without knowing exactly what the weather is going to be. And I am quite sure that there will be a storm tomorrow night, and your hay will be spoilt if it is cut tomorrow. The weather will clear again on Tuesday, the wind will be fresh, the days warm, and the hay will be perfect for cutting by Thursday or Friday."

"We must tell Daddy," said Rory, at once. "Oh, Tammylan, I hope he believes what you say! Bother! We shan't have a holiday tomorrow!"

"Well, that doesn't matter, surely, if you save your hay-crop, does it?" said Tammylan.

"Of course not," said Rory. "Well, we'd better get

482

back and tell Daddy at once, or he will be making all kinds of arrangements for the hay-making."

The children said goodbye and went quickly home. They ran to find their father. He was in the fields, looking at the cattle. They ran to him.

"Daddy! Don't cut the hay tomorrow! There will be a storm and heaps of rain tomorrow night!" cried Benjy. "Tammylan says so."

"Oh, Tammylan says so, does he?" said his father, looking thoughtful. "Well, well—I don't know what to do. I've made all arrangements to start tomorrow—but Tammylan has a strange way of foretelling the weather. Look, there's old Davey the shepherd. Call him here and we'll see if he thinks there will be a storm too."

The children yelled to Davey. He came up with Tinker close at his heels. The other dogs were guarding the sheep.

"Davey, what do you think about the hay-making tomorrow?" asked the children's father.

"The grass is in fine fettle," said the old shepherd. "And the weather's right. But I doubt you'll get caught by a storm tomorrow."

"That's just what Tammylan said!" cried Penny.

Davey's grey eyes twinkled at her. "Did he, Tuppenny?" he said. "Well now, that's not surprising, seeing that he and I spend our days watching the things that make the weather! The clouds tell us many things, the way the trees turn to the wind, the feel of the air, the look of the far-away hills. And I say there's thunder coming, and a mighty storm. So, sir, if I were you, I'd put off the hay-making tomorrow, and wait for a day or two till the rain's dried out, and you can cut in safety. 'Twould be a pity to spoil a fine crop like yours!"

"Thanks, Davey," said the farmer, and the old shepherd went on his way, his dog at his heels. The four children looked at their father.

"Well, hay-making is off!" he said. "We'll see if the storm comes. If it does, we'll be glad the hay wasn't cut — if it doesn't, there's no harm done. We can cut the next day!"

So the children went to school after all on Monday. They looked up at the sky. It was brilliant blue, without a single cloud to be seen.

"Perfect for cutting hay," said Rory. "Oh goodness — I wonder if that storm will come tonight."

When the children went to bed that night the sky was still clear. But Mother said she had a thunder-headache, and Harriet said that some of the milk had gone sour.

"There's a storm coming," she said. And sure enough there was! The children awoke at two o'clock in the morning to the sound of an enormous crash of thunder! Then the lightning flashed vividly and lighted up the room. The children leapt out of bed and ran to their windows. They all loved a good thunderstorm.

The wind blew through the trees with a curious swishing noise. Then the rain came down. It fell first in a few big drops, and then it pelted down savagely, slashing at the trees and the flowers, the corn and the grass as if it wanted to lay them to the ground.

Crash after crash of thunder came and rolled around the sky. The lightning lit up the whole of the countryside and the children were quite silent, marvelling at the magnificent sight. Fanny crept into their room, trembling.

"Oh please, Miss Sheila, can I come in here with you?" she asked, in a quivering voice. "I can't wake Aunt Harriet, and I'm so frightened."

"*Frightened!*" said Sheila and Penny together, in astonishment. "What are you frightened of?"

"The storm!" said poor Fanny.

"But why?" asked Penny. "It won't hurt you! It's grand and beautiful. Come and watch it!"

"Oh no, thank you," said Fanny, crouching behind the wardrobe. "I can't think how you dare to stand at the window."

"Have you ever been hurt by a storm?" asked Sheila. "You haven't? Well, then, why are you frightened, Fanny?"

"Oh, my mother always used to hide under a bed when there was a storm," said Fanny. "And that used to frighten me terribly. So I always knew there was something dreadful about a storm!"

"How funny you are!" said Sheila, going to Fanny. "You're not frightened of the storm itself—but only because your mother showed you *she* was frightened. Don't be silly! Come and watch."

So Fanny went to watch—and when she saw how marvellous the countryside looked when it was lit up so vividly by the lightning, she forgot her fear and marvelled at it just as the others did.

"My word, it's a good thing we didn't cut the hay today!" she said. "That would have been out in the field, lying cut—and the rain would have soaked it so much that we'd have had to turn it time and time again! Now if we get sunny weather and a fresh wind tomorrow, it will dry standing and be quite all right in a day or two."

"Tammylan was quite right," said Rory. "He always is! I *am* glad we took his advice. Good old Tammylan!"

CHAPTER XVI

MAKING HAY WHILE THE SUN SHINES

THE weather cleared up again on Tuesday, and the sky shone brilliant blue.

"I can't see a single cloud," said Sheila to Fanny, when she went to feed the hens. "Not one! But look at the puddles everywhere underfoot! We must have had torrents of rain last night."

"We did," said Fanny. "The duck-pond is almost overflowing this morning—and the ducks are as pleased as can be to find puddles everywhere. Wouldn't it be nice to have webbed feet and to go splashing through every puddle we came to!"

Sheila laughed. "That's the sort of thing Penny would say!" she said. "Look—there she is, taking the calves to their field. Penny! Penny! Isn't everywhere wet this morning?"

"Yes," shouted back Penny. "The grass is soaking my shoes. They're as wet as can be. What a good thing we didn't cut the hay yesterday—it would be terribly wet today."

By the end of the day the hot sun had dried the grass well. A fresh wind sprang up that night and finished the drying, so that the children's father felt sure that it would be safe to cut the hay on Thursday.

"We've got a holiday till Monday!" cried Rory, joyfully, when he heard the news. "Isn't that marvellous! Daddy says we've to be up at dawn tomorrow to start the hay-making. Everyone's going to help this week, even Mother and Harriet."

Two cart-horses, Darling and Blossom, pulled the machine that cut the grass. It fell in swathes, and soon the hay-fields looked as shaven and shorn as the sheep had looked after their shearing. In a very short while the cut hay turned to a grey-green colour, and a sweet smell rose in the summer air.

"I love the smell of the hay!" said Sheila, sniffing it. "No wonder the cattle like to have it to eat in the winter. I feel as if I wouldn't mind it myself!"

The new-mown hay did smell lovely, especially in the evening. It was so beautifully dry that the farmer said it need only be turned once.

The hay lay in long rows. The children played about in it to their heart's content, flinging handfuls at one another, and burying themselves under the delicious-smelling hay.

"It doesn't matter us messing about in the hay-fields like this, does it?" said Penny.

"Not a bit," said her father. "The more the hay is flung about the better I shall like it! You are helping to dry it. Tomorrow it must be properly turned."

"How was hay cut before machines were invented?" asked Rory. "Was it cut by hand?"

"Yes," said his father. "And a long job it must have been too! The big hay-fields were all cut down by men using scythes — sharp curved blades, set in a large handle — and it took them days to mow it. Our modern machines help us a great deal. I wish I had more of them — but when the farm begins to pay I shall buy what I can, and you shall learn how to use the machines on Willow Farm."

"Good," said Rory, pleased.

The next day everyone worked hard in the hay-fields, turning the hay over with hand-rakes, so that the moist bits underneath could be exposed to the sun and well-dried. The hay was in fine condition and the farmer was pleased. He looked up at the sky.

"This hot dry weather is just right for the hay," he said. "I'm glad we took Tammylan's advice and waited a few days."

Tammylan was helping to make hay too. He and the children had great fun together, especially when they found Penny and Skippetty fast asleep in a corner, and buried them both very carefully under a pile of the sweet-smelling hay. Penny couldn't *think* where she was when she awoke, and found the hay all on top of her!

"We must get the hay into windrows," said the farmer. "Big long rows all down the field."

"Oh," said Sheila, in dismay. "What a lot of hard work that will mean!"

"Not for you!" said her father. "We will let Captain do that work for us! He will pull the horse-rake that rakes the hay into windrows."

Rory helped Jim to get out the big horse-rake. It was twelve or fourteen feet wide, and had two strong wheels and a number of hinged steel teeth. Captain was harnessed to it and was soon set to work. The big horse was guided up and down the hayfields by Rory.

Penny went to watch, running along beside the machine. "Rory, it's clever!" she cried. "The big steel teeth slide along under the hay and collect it all."

"Yes," said Rory, proudly. "Now watch what happens. The rake is full of hay—so I pull this handle—and that lifts up the row of steel teeth—and the big load of hay is dropped in a long row on the field. That's more clever still, isn't it, Penny?"

The horse-rake did the work of six or seven men. Jim and Rory worked it by turns, and soon the hay-fields were beautiful with long windrows of turned hay.

The next thing was to build it up into hay-cocks—small stacks of hay down the field. The children helped with this, and when they left the field one evening, tired out but happy, they thought that the hay-cocks looked simply lovely, standing so peacefully in the fields as if they were dreaming about the sun and wind and rain that had helped them to grow when they were grass.

"What else has to be done to the hay?" asked Penny.

"It's got to be built into hay-stacks," said Tammylan, picking up the tired little girl and carrying her on his shoulder. "You'll find that Bill is the best man at that! He knows how to thatch, and can build the best hay-stack for miles around."

"I shouldn't have thought that it was very difficult to build a hay-stack," said Penny, sleepily. "Just piling the hay higher and higher."

Tammylan laughed at her. "You wait till you see one being built," he said. "Then you won't think it is quite such an easy job!"

The hay was carted to the rick-yard on the old hay-wagon. The children liked that. They climbed on the top of every wagon-load and rode there, while Darling went clip-clop, clip-clop down the lanes that smelt of honey-suckle. The hedges reached out greedy fingers and clutched at the hay as it passed.

"You can see the way we go by the bits of hay on the hedges!" said Sheila. "Oh, isn't it fun to lie here on the top of the hay-wagon, with the soft hay under us, and the blue summer sky above. I hope Darling doesn't mind our extra weight!"

Darling certainly didn't. It made no difference at all to her whether she had four, six or twelve children on the hay-wagon. She plodded down the lanes to the rick-yard, strong, slow and patient.

Some of the hay was stored in a shed, but the farmer hadn't enough room for it all, so most of it was to be built into stacks. Bill took command at once.

The first stack was begun. The children watched with great interest. It was a big stack, and was to be oblong. When it was fairly high, Bill and two other men stood up on the top.

"We've got to press the hay down as much as we can," he told the children. "Ah, here comes another wagon-load."

The hay-wagon was pulled up close to the stack. Rory was allowed to climb up on top of the hay and use a pitch-fork. He had to toss the hay from the wagon to where Bill stood waiting for it on the half-built stack.

"You watch your pitch-fork well, the first few times you use it," Jim warned Rory. "It's a dangerous thing till you're well used to it."

Rory was very careful indeed. He turned away from the man helping him, so that his fork would not jab him at all, and threw the hay quite cleverly from the wagon to the stack. The men there worked hard and well, tramping down the hay and stacking it firmly and neatly. The stack rose higher and higher.

Benjy was told to go round the stack with a rake. "Rake out the loose bits of hay," said Jim. "You can keep the stack for us and make the sides neat. Is your father down there? Good. He'll tell us if the stack gets a bit lop-sided and will prop it up till we put it right."

"I'll get an elevator next year if I can," said the farmer. "That sends the hay up by machinery and saves a lot of labour."

490

Rory thought that an elevator would be a very good thing, for he was tired out by the time that the stack was finished! His arms ached with throwing the hay!

Bill thatched the stack beautifully to keep the rain out. He had made the centre of the top of the thatch higher than the surrounding sides, so that the rain could run down and drop off the eaves, just as it runs down the roof of a house.

"And now to give the finishing touch!" said the thatcher. The children watched him. He twisted up some hay together and began to make something at the very top of the stack in the middle. The children saw that it was a crown!

"There!" said Bill. "Now anyone coming this way will know that I've built and thatched this stack, for the crown at the top is my mark."

"It does look fine," said Penny, admiringly. "It's such a big fat stack, and smells so nice. How the animals will love to eat the hay from it, when it is cut in the winter from the big stack!"

Hay-making time was over when the last stack was built and finished. Three fine stacks then stood in the rick-yard and the farmer and his men were pleased. They liked to think that there was such good fodder for their animals in the winter. The children liked the stacks too, and often remembered the waving grass, so beautiful in the wind, that had gone to make the sturdy stacks on the farm.

"I'm sorry hay-making time is over," said Penny. "That's really been most exciting. I'm sure there won't be anything *quite* so exciting on Willow Farm this year."

"Wait till harvest-time!" said Rory. "That's the big event of the year! You wait till then, Penny!"

CHAPTER XVII

HARVEST HOME

THE summer was very fine and warm that year. The four children grew browner and browner, and Penny grew so plump that Rory said he was sure he would one day mistake her for one of the fat piglets!

Everything grew, just as the children did! The wheat and the clover were strong and sturdy, the potato fields were a sight to see, and the other crops looked healthy and well-grown.

"Well, it may be beginner's luck," said Uncle Tim, one day when he came over, "but your farm is certainly flourishing this year! It's doing a good deal better than mine. I've got four cows ill of some mysterious disease, and my wheat is very poor."

"Well, the children have been a great help to me, bless them," said the farmer. "Sheila really manages wonderfully with the poultry, and helps in the dairy too, and little Penny has looked after the calves just as well as Jim or Bill might have. As for my two boys, I don't know what I should do without them—they see to the horses for me, and work as hard in the fields as anyone."

"Well, you'll need all the help you can get at harvest-time," said Uncle Tim. "You've a fine grain crop, no doubt about that! My word, you'll make some money this year—and be able to buy all the machinery I've been longing for myself for years! Lucky man!"

When the summer was full, the farmer went to look at his wheat fields with the children. They looked lovely.

"The corn is such a beautiful golden colour!" said

493

Sheila, "and I do love to see it bend and make waves of itself when the wind blows."

"I like the whispering noise it makes," said Penny.

"It always seems to me as if every stalk of wheat is whispering a secret to the next one — and the next one is listening with its ear!"

Everybody laughed. "An ear of corn can't hear, silly!" said Rory.

"Well, the ears always bend to one another as if they *are* listening," said Penny.

"First the corn was like a green mist over the brown field," said Sheila. "Then it grew thicker and greener and taller. Then it was tall enough to wave itself about, and looked rather like the sea. Then it grew taller still and turned this lovely golden colour. Is it ripe, yet, Daddy?"

"Yes," said her father, picking an ear of corn and rubbing it between his hands. "Beautifully ripe. Just ready for reaping."

"How are we going to reap it?" asked Rory. "With sickles or scythes? I've always wanted to use one — swish, swish, swish — and down goes the corn!"

"I've no doubt that this is the way the corn in this field was cut many years ago," said his father. "And it still is cut that way on some very small farms. But not on this one! I'm going to borrow your uncle's reaping-machine. It's a very old-fashioned one but it will reap our fields all right! Then next year maybe I can buy a really modern machine — one called a tractor-binder — a really marvellous machine."

"When are you going to begin the reaping?" asked Penny, eagerly. "We've got our summer holidays now and we can help."

"We'll begin it this week," said her father. "I'll telephone to Uncle Tim tonight and see if he can lend us his machine. He won't be reaping just yet because his crops are rather later than ours this year."

The next excitement was the arrival of the reaping-machine. It came clanking up the lane to Willow Farm drawn by two horses. They were Boy and Beauty, two of Uncle Tim's strongest horses. Rory unharnessed them, and the carter who had come with the machine led back the two horses to Cherry Tree Farm.

The children looked at the reaping-machine. Jim explained it to them. "See this long bar that rides a few inches from the ground?" he said. "That's the cutter bar. Look at its steel fingers. And now see this bar—it's the knife bar—look at the sharp knives it is fitted with. Now when the reaper goes along, the knives pass between the teeth of the cutter bar—and the corn is cut just as if big scissors were snipping it down!"

"Oh, isn't that clever!" said Rory. "What happens to the corn when it is cut like that? Does it fall to the ground?"

"It falls on to this little platform," said Jim. "It has to be raked off by hand by the man who sits on the seat here. Then the cut corn is gathered up by the people following behind—we call them lifters, because they lift up the corn —and they bind it into sheaves."

"I'm longing to see the reaper at work," said Benjy. "Is it starting today, Jim?"

"Right now," said Jim. "I'm just going to get Darling and Blossom to pull it. You get them for me, Rory, will you, then I can have a word with your father about which field he wants reaping first."

Rory and Benjy went proudly off to get the two big horses, who were in the nearby field, waiting to be set to

495

work. The boys led them back to the reaper and harnessed the patient animals to it.

The reaper was taken to the glowing field of yellow corn. The children gathered round, watching. Bill took the reins to guide the horses. Jim sat on the reaping-machine with a wooden rake. The machine was started, and the two horses pulled with all their might.

How the corn fell! It was cut as neatly and as quickly as if somebody with an enormous pair of scissors had snipped off great patches of it! Jim pushed off the cut corn as it fell on the little platform or tilting-board as he called it, and it tumbled to the ground.

Behind the reaper worked the other men of the farm — and Mother, Harriet and Fanny as well! Yes, everyone had to help at harvest-time, and how they loved it, although it was not easy. But it was so lovely out there in the golden sunshine, working together, laughing and chattering in the corn.

The children watched to see what the 'lifters' did. They gathered up a bundle of the cut corn, and tied each one round with wisps of straw.

"I've made a sheaf!" said Penny, suddenly. The others looked. Sure enough, the little girl had managed to tie up a bundle of corn very neatly with some stalks, and there was her sheaf — a bit smaller than the sheaves that the other lifters had made, it was true — but still, a very neat and presentable one!

"You others can try your hands at making the sheaves!" called Mother. "It's just a knack. The more we do, the better for the corn. Once it is in sheaves, we can stand it up in shocks."

So all the children tried their hand at being lifters too. Very soon they had become quite good at gathering and binding the corn into sheaves—though Penny was rather slower than the others. Soon they had made enough sheaves to build up into a nice shock.

"Sixteen sheaves to a shock!" called out Jim, as he went by with the reaper. "Set up the sheaves in pairs—lean them against one another—that's right, Rory. See how many shocks you children can make!"

Penny got tired of gathering up the corn and binding it, so the others let her stand up the sheaves and make shocks for them. She liked doing that. "Don't the shocks look fine?" she said, as she finished a very neat one. "This is as good as building castles on the sea-shore!"

The reaping and binding went on all day long. The farmer was pleased with the way the work went.

"Next year, when I buy a self-binder," he said, "you will not have nearly so much work to do!"

"Why?" asked Sheila. "Does it do even more work than our reaper does?"

"Oh yes!" said her father. "It not only cuts the corn, but it gathers it into sheaves, ties each one neatly round with strong string, and then throws each sheaf out on to the ground! It's like magic! It goes through the field of waving corn leaving rows of sheaves behind it. So all you will have to do next year is to pick up the sheaves and place them in shocks, ready to be carted away!"

When all the corn-fields were reaped, and lay quiet and still with rows of shocks in the evening sun, everyone was glad.

Tammylan came down to see the fields and nodded his head as he saw the fine shocks. "It's a good crop," he said to the farmer. "You've had luck this year. It won't be long before you can cart the corn to the rick-yard, for it's already as dry as can be."

The wild man slipped his brown hand into the middle of a nearby sheaf. He felt about and then withdrew his hand. "The corn's in rattling order!" he said. Penny laughed.

"Why do you say that?" she asked. "Does it rattle?"

"Put your hand into the middle of the sheaf," said Tammylan. "Then you will feel how crisp and light and dry it is — and if you move your hand about you will hear a whispery, rattly noise. Yes — the corn's in rattling order!"

Tammylan and the farmer, followed by the four children, moved to other sheaves here and there in the field and felt to see if the corn was ready to be carted.

"We'll cart it tomorrow," said the farmer. "It is lovely weather—my word what a summer we've had!"

So the next day the wagons were sent into the cornfields to cart the corn away. Jim and Bill took their pitchforks and threw the sheaves deftly into the wagons. It was good to watch them, for they worked easily and well. A sheaf was picked up by a fork, lifted and thrown into the wagon—then down it went again for another sheaf. Another man stood in the wagon to arrange the sheaves properly inside. If they were not stacked well there, the whole thing might topple over, once the cart began moving.

It was easy work as long as there was not much corn in the wagon—but as it got full, and the sheaves were built up higher and higher in the cart, Jim and Bill had to throw more strongly, right above their heads. Soon the wagon was groaning with the weight of the corn, which had been built up neatly in the cart, and was not likely to topple out.

"Come along, Benjy!" shouted Jim. "The wagon's ready. You can take it to the rick-yard."

Benjy and Rory ran to the horses harnessed to the loaded wagon. Sheila and Penny climbed up on to the load. It was not so soft as the hay had been, but was very pleasant to sit on as the creaking wagon rumbled slowly down the lanes.

The corn was pitched out of the wagon into the rick-yard, ready for the building of corn-stacks—then back to the cornfield went the two horses with the empty wagon. By that time the second wagon had been filled with corn-sheaves by the men, and Rory and Benjy had to unharness the two horses and take the second wagon to the yard, leaving the first one in the field to be filled again.

It was glorious fun. Each time the girls rode home on the corn, high up in the air. Their mother saw them and smiled.

"Harvest home!" she said, when the last load was safely in. "Harvest home! Come along in — and you shall have a very special harvest-home supper, for I'm sure you are all hungry and thoroughly deserve it!"

So in they went — and the farm-hands went too, tired but happy because the harvest was in safely. What a lot they ate and drank, for they were all hungry and thirsty and tired!

The children fell asleep as soon as their heads touched their pillows that night. "It was the nicest day of the year," said Sheila to Penny, as she closed her eyes. "Harvest home! The very nicest day of all the year!"

CHAPTER XVIII

GOOD LUCK FOR WILLOW FARM!

THE year went on. September came and lessons began again. All the crops had been gathered in and stored. The potatoes had been harvested, and the farmer was pleased with them. The mangold wurzels had not done so well, because so many of the seeds had not come up. But the farmer said that was quite usual with mangolds.

"We must get them in before the frosts come," he said, when the autumn came. So the big mangold wurzels were gathered and stored in pits, covered with earth and straw.

"The sheep and cattle will be glad of these in the winter," said Bill, as he stored the big roots in their pits. "The turnips will give them good eating too. I've stored them in a pit in the field. We've plenty for all the animals."

When the early days of December came a large machine arrived at Willow Farm. It was drawn by a traction engine which made an enormous noise coming up the narrow lanes. "Whatever is it?" asked Rory.

"Oh good—it's the threshing-machine coming," said the farmer, pleased. "I hired it for the beginning of December, and here it is! It has come to thresh our corn and get the wheat for us!"

"Why didn't you borrow it from Uncle Tim?" asked Sheila.

"He hasn't got one," said her father. "Farmers don't usually own threshing-machines—it is easier and cheaper to hire them when we want them. They go from farm to farm. Now it is our turn to have it."

"But why do we want it?" asked Penny. "We've got our corn in!"

"Ah, but the grain has to be beaten from the ears!" said her father. "We can't eat it straight from the corn-stack, Penny—or would you like to try it?"

"No, thank you," said Penny. "But we don't eat corn either, Daddy, do we? The hens do that."

"Well, we shall sell our corn to the miller," said her father. "He will grind it into flour—and we shall buy it to bake our bread and to make our cakes and puddings."

Soon the air was full of a deep, booming sound. "That's the thresher at work," said the farmer. "You can go and see it when you come back from school."

The children raced home from their lessons. They went to the rick-yard, where the corn-stacks stood, and there they saw the big threshing-machine. Nearby stood the traction-engine that had brought it, and that set it to work.

When Scamper heard the noise nearby he leapt from Benjy's shoulder and bounded into the bare trees. He was really frightened of it. Penny felt a little bit scared too, but she soon became brave enough to go near and see what was happening.

It was very interesting. Bill was up on a stack, forking out the sheaves that he had so carefully arranged there. He threw them to Jim, who quickly cut the bands that bound the sheaves together. Then he put the loose cornstalks into the mill just below him—and they fell into a swiftly revolving drum in which were six long arms or 'beaters' that struck the corn and beat out the grain from the ears.

The grain fell through into another kind of machine called a winnowing machine, where the chaff was blown away from the grain. Then the wheat fell out into sacks held ready by the farmer himself. He was pleased to see such yellow grain filling his sacks! As soon as one sack was full he heaved it away and put another empty one to be filled. Rory and Benjy helped him. It was great fun.

The straw tumbled out loose, and was stacked in a shed. "It will make fine bedding for the cattle in the winter," said Rory.

"Yes, and we'll chop it up and put it into their food too," said Jim. "There's not much wasted from the corn!"

"What about the chaff?" asked Sheila, as she watched the light chaff being put into sacks too.

"Ah, my wife will be along for some of that," said Bill. "Our mattresses are filled with chaff, you know — and we like good new chaff each year. We shall have fine bedding now!"

"Goodness!" said Benjy, "what a lot of good the corn is! Wheat for making flour — straw for animal bedding and for thatching — and chaff for mattresses!"

All that day and the next the threshing-mill boomed on the farm, as it worked in the rick-yard. Soon all the farmer's corn was turned into grain, straw and chaff, and the farmer and his men looked with pride at their full sacks.

"It's a good harvest," said the farmer, as he dipped his fingers into a full sack and let the grain trickle through them. "Our fields have done well this year."

When the threshing-mill had rumbled away again down the lanes, pulled by the heavy traction-engine, the weather changed from cold and sunny, to damp and grey. Rain-mists hid the countryside and the children could no longer go over the fields to their lessons. Instead they had to go down the lanes and along the main road. This was very much farther, and they had to start out earlier and get back later.

Penny was tired. She didn't like trudging so far in bad weather, and was very glad when the Christmas holidays came and she had no longer to get up early and walk three miles to school.

"Do you think we had better send the children to boarding-school?" said their father one day. "They can't walk all that way all the winter through. Penny looks quite tired out. It's impossible to spare a horse and wagon four times a day. I almost think they had better go away to school."

But when the children heard this idea they were really horrified. "What!" cried Rory, "leave Willow Farm for nine months every year, just when things are beginning to be exciting! Oh Daddy, how can you think of such a thing!"

The four children were so worried about this idea that they went to tell Tammylan. It was five days before Christmas. They set out over the damp fields, and came to his cave. He had left his tree-house, of course, and was now living cosily in the cave. His friend the hare was, as usual, beside him.

"Hallo!" called the children, and ran to meet their friend. "How are you, Tammylan? We haven't seen you for ages."

Tammylan told them his news, and then he asked for theirs.

"Tammylan, we've bad news," said Rory. "Do you know, Mummy and Daddy are actually thinking of sending us all away to boarding-school, because we have such a long way to walk to our lessons now that the winter has come and we can't go across the wet fields!"

"Oh, that would be dreadful!" said the wild man. "I should miss you all terribly."

"Tammylan, go and talk to Daddy and Mummy about it," said Penny, slipping her hand into Tammylan's. She thought that the wild man could do anything. She could not bear the thought of leaving Willow Farm to go to school. What, leave the calves and Skippetty—and not be able to have new lambs to feed in the spring—and not see the new chicks and ducklings! It was too dreadful to think of!

"Well, I'm going over to Willow Farm tomorrow to take your father something," said Tammylan. "I'll have a word with him—but I don't think that anything I can say will make any difference! After all, it *is* a long way for you all to walk, especially little Penny."

The children were out Christmas shopping when Tammylan went over to the farm the next day, so they did not see him or hear if he had said anything to their parents. Indeed, they were so excited over their shopping that they even forgot to worry about going to school after the Christmas holidays!

"Can Tammylan come for Christmas Day?" asked Penny. "Do ask him, Mummy!"

"Oh, he's coming," said her mother. "He'll be along after breakfast."

Christmas Day dawned cold and sunny and bright. The children woke early and found their stockings full of exciting things. Even Rory and Sheila had stockings, for that was the one day of the year when they felt as childish as Penny and begged for stockings too!

Mummy had given them a watch each. Rory and Sheila had had watches before, but Rory had lost his and Sheila had broken hers. Now each child had a neat silver watch and they were overjoyed. They all strapped them proudly on their wrists.

They went down to the kitchen and gave presents to Harriet and Fanny. Fanny was delighted to have so many presents. Her face beamed with joy as she opened her parcels and found a smart pencil from Rory, a book from Sheila, a thimble from Benjy and some sweets from Penny.

"And thank you, Fanny, for being such a help with the hens," said Sheila. "Won't it be fun to have chicks again in the spring!"

The children left the kitchen and then Rory said something that had been in everyone's mind.

"How funny! Everyone has given us a present, except Daddy!"

Their father overheard him. He smiled.

"My present is coming along soon," he said. "I couldn't find room in your stockings for it! Watch out of the window and you'll see it arriving soon!"

The children squealed with joy and ran to the window. They simply could not imagine what their father was giving them.

But they soon found out! Tammylan appeared—but he was not alone! With him were four grey donkeys, plump and lively. The children could hardly believe their eyes.

"Daddy! Are the donkeys your present?" shouted Rory. "One for each of us?"

"Yes—one for each of you!" said his father with a smile. "Tammylan came along the other day and begged so hard for you to stay on at Willow Farm instead of going to school—and he suggested giving you a donkey each to ride over the fields, so that you might still stay on here. Your mother and I thought it would be a splendid idea; and Tammylan said he would go to the market and buy the donkeys in time for Christmas. He knew someone who

was selling six. So he chose four and here they are!"

The children tore out of the door and rushed to Tammylan! They were so pleased and excited that they could hardly wish him a happy Christmas!

"Which is my donkey?" cried Rory. "Oh, aren't they beauties!"

Tammylan gave each child a donkey. The two biggest went to the boys, and the other two to the girls. Each child mounted at once and galloped off round the farm. They were so happy that they sang as they went.

"Now we shan't have to leave Willow Farm, Willow

Farm, Willow Farm!" they all sang. "Gee-up, donkeys, gee-up! Oh, what a fine life you'll have here!"

The children's parents watched with Tammylan, laughing as they saw the happy children galloping all over the place.

When they came back at last, their father spoke to them. "You have all worked so well this year," he said. "You have been such a help. You haven't grumbled or complained, you have been cheerful and happy, and you have helped to make our farm a great success. So it is only fair that you should share in that success, and that is why I have spent part of the farm's money on each of you. What are you going to call your donkeys?"

"Mine shall be Neddy?" said Rory.

"Mine's Bray!" said Benjy.

"Mine's Canter!" said Sheila.

"And mine's Hee-Haw!" said Penny. And just as she said that her donkey threw up his head and brayed loudly. "Hee-haw! Hee-haw! Hee-haw!"

"There! He's saying his name to me!" said Penny, with a laugh. "Oh Daddy—what a lovely present! And to think we don't need to go away to school now! How lovely! Oh, what fun it will be to ride to lessons on four grey donkeys every morning and afternoon!"

And there we will leave them all, galloping in delight over the fields of Willow Farm. "Our dear, dear farm!" said Penny. "Oh, I wonder what will happen next year— there's always something exciting on a farm. I'm sure next year will be greater fun than ever!"

But that, of course, is another story.